ANGRON
THE RED ANGEL

WARHAMMER 40,000

ANGRON
THE RED ANGEL

DAVID GUYMER

BLACK LIBRARY

A BLACK LIBRARY PUBLICATION

First published in 2023.
This edition published in Great Britain in 2023 by
Black Library, Games Workshop Ltd., Willow Road,
Nottingham, NG7 2WS, UK.

Represented by: Games Workshop Limited – Irish branch,
Unit 3, Lower Liffey Street, Dublin 1,
D01 K199, Ireland.

10 9 8 7 6 5 4 3 2

Produced by Games Workshop in Nottingham.
Cover illustration by Halil Ural.

A CIP record for this book is available from the British Library.

ISBN 13: 978 1 80407 305 6

See Black Library on the internet at

blacklibrary.com

Find out more about Games Workshop
and the worlds of Warhammer at

games-workshop.com

Printed and bound in the UK.

For more than a hundred centuries the Emperor has sat immobile on the Golden Throne of Earth. He is the Master of Mankind. By the might of His inexhaustible armies a million worlds stand against the dark.

Yet, He is a rotting carcass, the Carrion Lord of the Imperium held in life by marvels from the Dark Age of Technology and the thousand souls sacrificed each day so that His may continue to burn.

To be a man in such times is to be one amongst untold billions. It is to live in the cruellest and most bloody regime imaginable. It is to suffer an eternity of carnage and slaughter. It is to have cries of anguish and sorrow drowned by the thirsting laughter of dark gods.

This is a dark and terrible era where you will find little comfort or hope. Forget the power of technology and science. Forget the promise of progress and advancement. Forget any notion of common humanity or compassion.

There is no peace amongst the stars, for in the grim darkness of the far future,
there is only war.

ACT ONE

A BROKEN LEGION

CHAPTER ONE

It was raining over Mount Anarch. Drops of liquid ethane spotted the towering glassteel panes. In under one-fifth of standard g, the rain was not falling so much as gliding, parading towards the desolate surface of Titan as though time had already surrendered to its legions.

Graucis Telomane stared out through the cold grey eyes of his own reflection. He could not remember the last time he had looked so young, so naïve, but then it had been half a millennium since he last returned to Titan to set foot in this hall.

'No,' he whispered softly. 'Not here.'

'You are not ready, Telomane. Not for this. Grand Master Taremar is wrong to beg it of me and I refuse to permit it.'

In his memories, Justicar Aelos was a giant that he had never quite been in reality. Experience had painted the warrior's hair grey, as it had decorated his oath plate with records of valour. In many ways, Graucis had outgrown his former mentor, but he had never seen him again after this, and so he remained the colossus of a newly initiated line brother's remembrance.

'I am ready,' he said.

'That you believe yourself to be so only proves how unready you are.'

'The Grand Master of the Third Brotherhood believes I am.'

A shake of that head, never greyer. 'There is a reason the Grey Knights do not temper their youngest brothers in battle. Do you know why?'

'No,' he said, frowning. 'Not here.'

It was raining over Mount Anarch. Drops of liquid ethane spotted the towering glassteel panes. Graucis Telomane stood at an empty table in the midst of an empty hall. The Saturnalium was deserted, silent but for the patter of the hydrocarbon rain and the slow mechanical grinding of the great orrery that made up the cathedral-like ceiling. Dark but for the stain left by several thousand candles. Illumination was not their purpose. Candles had been lit to bridge the two sides of the veil since humanity's first tentative dabblings with witchcraft. They were grey: the colour of wisdom, learning and defence against malefic forces.

The orrery continued to whir through its orbits.

Graucis looked up.

His fellow novitiates had called it the Deimos Clock. According to legend, it had been assembled and first set to motion by the forge moon's Fabricator General to commemorate its removal from Mars' orbit. Saturn rotated at its centre, a silver orb the size of a Rhino chassis held in a web of arcane suspension fields, its rings represented by concentric bands of crystal less than a nanometre thick. Titan itself was the size of a bolt-shell. Its orbit took it along a track of frictionless glass wire a hundred yards and more in radius, which it completed every three hundred and eighty-two hours. So flawlessly was the whole system rendered that, according to Justicar Aelos, a Grey Knight of sufficient acuity, patience and learning could deduce the exact time and Imperial Calendar year from the relative positions of Saturn and its eighty-two natural satellites alone.

And for eight and a half thousand years, it had been keeping perfect time.

It was 444.M41.

'No,' he said, becoming angry now. 'Not here.'

It was still raining. A crimson deluge splattered and sizzled against the consecrated silver and gold of his war plate. Before him it had been worn by Eygon of the Fourth Brotherhood, and by the legendary Paladin Phox before him. Graucis still had the suit, but this was the first time he would wear it in battle. The memory was bittersweet.

Justicar Aelos had been right, of course, but of the one hundred and nine Grey Knights who had teleported down to the floodplains of the Styx River that day, which of them had done so fully prepared to face the Cruor Praetoria and the Lord of the XII Legion?

Not the ninety-six who had gone and not returned.

Not the thirteen who did.

Graucis was the least of those on the field that day. Why he had survived while the likes of Dymus, Galeo and Taremar the Golden had been allowed to fall, he did not know, except perhaps as proof the laws of the tempus materium were grounded in unreason.

'No!' he yelled, into the twisted red-meat mask of hatred worn by the Emperor's son. 'Not here!'

* * *

Drops of liquid ethane spotted the towering glassteel panes. He was in the Saturnalium, in the Citadel of Titan, but seated now where before he had been standing. He kneaded the muscle of his thigh with the heel of his palm as though it ached, although of course it did not. Not here.

'Why do I keep on returning myself to this place?'

Nyramar, sitting across the table on the other side of a set regicide board, shrugged.

The other Grey Knight was one year Graucis' senior, but though they had been friends, it was a gulf he had always felt in more than just time. All that Graucis had accomplished in his years on Titan, Nyramar had achieved sooner. When he had passed through the final tiers of the Chamber of Trials to be inducted into the line brotherhoods of the Grey Knights, it had been Nyramar who welcomed him there in a warrior's armour. He looked none the worse here for his death. It would happen five weeks after this game had been played.

'These are your memories,' Nyramar said. 'What do you expect to find here that you do not already know? Or that you could fully trust?'

'To name a thing is to know it,' Graucis countered, reciting the words from the five hundred and eighteenth canticle of the *Liber Daemonica*. 'To know the daemon is to command its nature. I know the limitations of my own mind, brother, and the sanctity of my soul.'

Nyramar nodded, looking at the table between them as though planning his next move on the regicide board. 'Then look, brother. The answer you scry for is in front of you. You only have to see.'

Graucis studied the board, as directed. In the psychic realm, even the most inconspicuous of details could convey meaning.

The board was circular and made of wood, evenly divided

into black and white squares. He was playing as black. Nyramar, white. The game was already several moves old, the white peons arranged in the opening positions of the Praetorian's Gambit. Nyramar had always been an adroit, if uninspired player. Graucis' own peons had advanced more aggressively, as was his way, opening up the board's left hemisphere for his ecclesiarch to go on the offensive. The stratagem had many common names but to Graucis, and those of his dwindling generation, it would always be known as the Armageddon Manoeuvre, involving as it did the wholesale sacrifice of one's middle-ranking pieces to surround and capture the opponent's emperor.

He almost smiled, in spite of himself. 'I remember this move.'

'Of course.'

'We never finished the game.'

'Of course.'

His finger perched over the black ivory figurine of his primarch. The piece had no particular features to identify it as any single one from the twenty. Rather, it was an idealist's impression of a *primarch* as a gestalt plurality. It had the feathered wings of a Sanguinius, the laurel wreath and lorica of a Guilliman, but some effect of candlelight and suggestion made it snarl. Graucis' primary heart gave a jolt, and he let the piece go, withdrawing his hand to his lap. 'But this is the past. I am here to see the future.'

'Is time so straight a line, brother? Or does it bend? Is it, in fact' – Nyramar gestured to the board with a slight tilt of the head – 'a circle?'

Graucis nodded to himself.

The circularity of history and the repetition of one's forbears' mistakes was a common enough motif in the mythologies of Old Earth and represented no special insight on his subconscious' part.

'Angron's shadow lengthens across the galaxy once more. I have seen the signs, read the portents, heard his voice as he rages across the thinness of the veil. I have felt the screams of the lesser choirs that herald his coming. They all point towards a purpose that the Great Beast has not shown since Armageddon, but where is that shadow doomed to fall? If not here, where I wait for him, then where?'

'Be careful what you wish for, brother.'

'The oldest admonition in sorcery.'

'And yet one the hero so rarely heeds.'

Graucis' lip curled into a smile. 'I am no hero.'

'So the hero always believes.'

'I have spent the six hundred years since Armageddon in preparation. I have gathered my allies. I have honed my skills. I am ready for whatever comes.'

'That you believe yourself to be so only proves how unready you are.'

Graucis frowned to hear that familiar, paternal criticism in his old friend's voice. He felt the smile on his face freeze, contorting in apparent slow motion into a grimace as pain swelled unexpectedly in the muscle of his thigh. His hands went to it. Blood soaked up through the pale grey cloth of his robe.

'No,' he murmured, pressing down on the never-healed wound. 'Not here.'

It was raining over Mount Anarch. Still. Drops of liquid ethane spotted the towering glassteel panes. The striated hydrogen monster of Saturn loomed massive over the ice-blistered vista, the yellow-brown eye of a cosmic giant peering down on a dead and frozen world. As a neophyte, Graucis Telomane had stood under these windows to meditate. Justicar Aelos would often challenge any of his wards to look into the eye of that awesome world, to feel its gravity, the Newtonian precision by which it ordered its army of little worlds, and not feel the pre-eminence of physical law over a chaotic universe.

He had never been wrong. Except in this.

'Why do I–'

He turned from the window, leaving his question unasked, drawn by the subtle twitching of the empyreal curtain much as those worlds above him were drawn to Saturn's mass. The candles, mounted on the walls in marble sconces, and in silver candelabra on the tables, were no longer grey. They were red, burning with a brimstone odour and spitting like fat over a thermic element. Graucis felt the prickling sense of danger inching up his spine as, one by one, the candle flames bent until every last one of them was flickering at an unnatural right angle to their wicks.

They were pointing at him.

No, he realised, not at him.

He turned, slowly, lifted his gaze and looked out through the huge glassteel clerestory. The world hanging over him was no longer Saturn. Nor, as he had long suspected and fervently hoped, was it Armageddon.

Graucis had never seen it before, but he committed every detail of its visible hemisphere to his genetically perfect memory. It was small and rocky, roughly Terran-sized, but swathed entirely in sand. He bade his focus to shift, his view drifting back to see a dry, brownish orb as it turned slowly around the barycentre of two smouldering red suns. The Imperium of Man encompassed a million human worlds. If this was one of them then Graucis would find it.

Above him, the Saturnalium continued to whirl, converting angular momentum into neat parcels of linear time as it had since the inception of the Imperium.

'Be careful what you wish for,' said the voice behind him, and at the sound of an ivory piece scraping across a wooden board, Graucis turned. He looked towards his old table, where the white primarch, making an entirely impossible move, had just forced through its own peons and Graucis' to stand before the black emperor.

Nyramar grinned up at him, his head hanging on a snapped neck, his face cracking over the scaffold of bone that lay beneath. Graucis told himself it was not Nyramar. None of this existed outside of his mind.

'Check, brother,' the dead man said. 'Your move.'

Young Pious MMXIV emitted a concerned tone. The cyber-cherub hovered over him, reeking of formaldehyde preservatives, and of the aloe-gels it applied to his burnt skin. Epistolary Graucis Telomane stared glassily through it, his dilated pupils still focused on some *other* place, but there was a comforting familiarity to the hum of the cherub's archaic anti-gravitics and the stiff-velum creak of its imitation wings. Even the touch of its foetal-stage mind and its thin but unspoiled soul helped to ground him.

He was in his meditation chamber aboard the Grey Knights strike cruiser *Sword of Dione*. The ship was in high orbit over Armageddon.

He blinked his eyes. It felt like polishing a piece of sandstone. He wondered how long he had spent sitting there, staring into the warp.

Young Pious MMXIV issued another tinny parp from the vedigrised flute sunk between its mummified cheeks and retreated to allow for Graucis to straighten on his own.

He gripped the silver-inlaid armrests of his chair, his armour clicking and humming as it roused itself from dormancy and directed new strength towards his grip.

He groaned stiffly as the myriad aches and niggling injuries that his mind had left behind returned like blood to a necrotised limb. Three-quarters of his skin, much of it hidden by armour, was covered in welts and burns. They were psychic burns, and tended to break out afresh whenever he probed the warp too deeply. The Apothecaries on Titan had warned him the injuries might never heal, and they never had. He had learned to ignore them. It was only pain. There were other hurts too, diffuse and variable and arising mostly from being five hundred years past what most of his brothers would consider his prime, but none came close to that of his leg.

He rubbed at his aching thigh through the thick ceramite plate.

It had been the hero, Hyperion, the one the Wolves had dubbed *Bladebreaker*, who had shattered Angron's sword into a thousand unholy pieces on Armageddon, but it was Graucis who that corrupted shrapnel had struck. A single piece of tainted bronze was still in there. He was aware of it always. Sometimes it made the limb feel hot. At others, agonisingly numb. There were days when it drove him to pain-fuelled rages, or into quiet despair at the unfairness with which the cosmos distributed its tests and its glories. When he sought it out it shifted under his fingers like a lipoma, but the moment it went under a bio-scanner, or an Apothecary cut into the surrounding tissue with a knife, it became inexplicably psychosomatic.

In his darker moments, and in over six hundred years on this quest such times had been plentiful, he had considered cutting off the entire leg himself and ridding himself of Angron's taint, but he had always pulled back at the last.

It felt too much like a concession. Or worse, a surrender.

The injury had been his trial, yes, but it was also his gift.

It was his bond to Angron.

He rolled his head stiffly to one side, staring bleary-eyed towards the windows. The cold light of Armageddon's star, Tisra, shafted in through the hardened glass.

The *Sword of Dione* sailed under the heraldry of the Chapter Librarius, and of the Titan fleet, but over centuries of increasingly esoteric pursuits it had become Graucis' personal flagship in all but name. It knew his purpose. It responded to his will. The warship had been part of a purgation operation in the Beta-Thyracuse Sector when the first tentative portents of bloodshed on a galactic scale had started to seep through the empyreal veil and into the tempus materium. Such was Graucis' authority within the Chapter that Grand Master Cromm of the Fourth Brotherhood had not even sought an explanation as the *Sword of Dione* withdrew from the sector for an early return to the warp.

Graucis' psychic powers were at their strongest here. His ability to perceive his nemesis was at its keenest.

'No,' he murmured, his voice a hoarser and harsher thing than that belonging to the younger man his psychic self preferred to remember. 'Not here.'

But if Angron was not returning to conquer Armageddon, as Graucis had predicted that he would, then where was he?

He leant forwards in his chair and pinched his tired eyes. An image of the planet he had pulled from the warp flashed again across them: a desert world orbiting binary red giants. The *Sword of Dione* had navigational archives going back thousands of years, but Graucis did not believe this description alone would be enough to expedite any search. The Milky Way was an old and stagnant galaxy. Three-quarters of its stars were slowly fading reds, and half of those were binaries. It was also vast, too irredeemably huge even for a vessel as storied as the *Sword of Dione* to have visited a full one per cent of its worlds.

There was work to do.

He raised his hand, feeling the wobble of the Nemesis force staff from across the room where it lay in the moment before it took flight and snapped into his waiting grip. He rose from his chair, the staff arriving at the precise moment to take his weight. 'Raise the Navis Imperialis station at St Jowen's Dock on a vermilion frequency and requisition an astropathic chorus,' he commanded Young Pious MMXIV.

Word from Titan had become infrequent, and increasingly difficult to interpret of late. He knew that the Grey Knights had stood alongside the Adeptus Custodes in the defence of the Imperial Palace, and been greatly diminished in Imperium Sanctus as a result. Their brotherhood had always been thinly spread, and never more so than now. Even with only half a galaxy left to defend.

If Angron was to be pre-empted and his plans thwarted, then it rested on Graucis to ensure that it was done.

The cyber-cherub replayed its short hymn and flapped its facsimile wings, anti-gravitics sputtering as it drifted away across the echoing chamber.

Graucis watched it go.

It was time to summon the others.

CHAPTER TWO

Kossolax's finger tapped on the engraved arm of his osseous throne, as though pulling repeatedly on the trigger-stud of a chainaxe that had been inexplicably removed from his reach. It was a tic, and one that always manifested itself when someone other than Kossolax the Foresworn was doing the killing. He forced himself to remain seated, massively gauntleted hands grinding the armrests of his throne to fine powder. Self-denial was a neglected virtue. If one was not pitted in opposition to temptation, then one inevitably became its slave. And Kossolax had been a slave. To the Emperor. To Angron. To the Legion. He would never be one again. He was *better* than those men had been. With the throne crumbling in his grip, he eyed the void battle playing out in the sanguilith.

The sanguilith was a large brass font situated in the middle of the *Conqueror*'s command deck. Eight witches branded with the rune of Khorne had been hanged from the ceiling above it, bleeding into a bowl that was forever on the brink of overflowing but never full. Gathered around the basin, a cabal of stunted incubi with needle-teeth and stub-wings muttered and cursed to one another in the unspeakable dialect of the Dark Gods, adding to the tri-D rendering of the battlesphere in the air with every stroke of their blood-dipped claws.

Every droplet of scattered blood became a cloud of fighters, frigates, corvettes, cruisers and capital ships of various classes running into long, jagged smears.

Kossolax directly commanded dozens of those scarlet needles. Twice as many again belonged to the flotsam of traitors and renegades that had been drawn to his flag, rather than the Despoiler's, since Cadia's fall. Stiletto cruisers in the midnight blue of the Night Lords prowled the battlesphere's outer edges in search of weakened prey. Death Guard battleships floundered towards the orbital defence grids, drawing ordnance the way sickened whales drew gulls and yet somehow never quite managing to die.

They had followed Kossolax into Nihilus rather than join in Abaddon's push for Terra because Kossolax consistently rewarded their loyalty with blood.

The world of Kalkin's Tribune was arguably more heavily defended now than it had been prior to the opening of the Great Rift. Formerly an Ecclesiarchal garrison world, home to eighteen preceptories of the Adepta Sororitas and upwards of three billion frateris militia, it was now the spiritual capital of a small interplanetary fiefdom here in Nihilus.

The challenges of travel and communication on this side of the galaxy had turned whole swathes of the Emperor's former realm dark. Worlds like Kalkin's Tribune, with the resource base and the facilities to look to their own fleets, had done so, while those without sank quietly, unseen, unheard and unmissed into the oblivion of humanity's New Night. The Imperium was fragmenting before his eyes, collapsing into smaller and smaller fiefs navigable by short jumps or near-light drives. Realspace travel between the nearest of stellar neighbours was an undertaking of years or even decades, but in these desperate times Kossolax had seen it attempted, the last human link holding creaking post-Imperial commonwealths in unity.

Shorn of the domineering hand of the Imperial ministries, individuals of rare charisma and martial brilliance were free to rise up while the weak and the unready floundered or knelt before their betters.

The Age of Despair had made hypocrites of them all, and Kossolax would have their skulls. He would break open these bastions of hope one by one, and let the scavengers feast on the burning protectorates left behind in his wake.

'Hail the Wrath of Kamedon and the Void Razer,' a tattered crone dressed in ethereal scraps hissed, pitching her voice to be heard over the background commotion, apparently oblivious to the fact she was addressing a horned skeleton crucified across a faded banner depicting Angron at the Ullanor Triumph. 'They are getting carried away. Order the shipmasters to hold formation until the rest of the fleet is in position.' The wraith drifted to another station, unhurried, wisp hands clasped behind her back and trailing bloody mist. She passed an empty look over their screens. Her face was the reflection of smoke in glass, featureless, but with eerie patterns that occasionally suggested at thought and mood, and those creatures caught under her gaze cringed from it but could not say why. 'A squadron has broken through the starboard cordon. Four Cobra-class vessels inbound. Where in the primarch's name are my escorts?'

With his throne crumbling under the weight of his grip, Kossolax watched her stalk the command deck.

He did not know her name. He did not know where she came

from. Only that she had been a part of the *Conqueror* since Kossolax had first laid claim to it after the defeat on Armageddon and presumably long before that. He called her the Mistress, but though she spoke, she never answered, and though he saw and heard her, it had soon become apparent that he was the only one who did.

Where the Mistress drew close, mortal slaves shuddered and fled to pursue other duties elsewhere. Even those daemons, beast-headed and cloven-hooved, who would breach the deck every so often to seize a screaming menial and feed them to some thirsting piece of equipment, shied from her path until she passed.

The Mistress drifted towards a sputtering console sheened in blood. '*Order the* Rage Incarnate *to port. They need to address our flank.*'

'You know that they do not even know you are there,' said Kossolax, but the Mistress gave no sign of having heard him and continued on her restless tour of the deck. With a growl, he turned from her and barked his orders to the crew. 'Bring the *Wrath of Kamedon* and the *Void Razer* to heel.' The *Conqueror* was a place of brimstone and ash. There were no defined stations as an Imperial shipmaster would recognise them. Kossolax did not know how it was crewed, how it was armed, or how it was fuelled. Its functions responded to fealty and sacrifice. But somehow, so long as he was seated in the command throne, orders were heeded and actions performed. 'We deploy to the surface when I order it and not before. And as for the *Rage Incarnate*...' He glanced towards the Mistress with the beginnings of a smile. Kalkin's Tribune and the Imperium Veritas were not the only foes he meant to crush in this battle. His trigger finger *tap-tap-tapped* on the arm of the throne. 'Have them hold to their current course. Let the Imperial destroyers through.'

The Mistress turned slowly, throwing a disgusted look towards the dais, as though noticing for the first time that there was a giant seated in her throne.

As though he had not attempted every means of killing her, binding her or banishing her before this.

'The ship resists the order,' said the Warpsmith, Mohgrivar, with a bleeding hiss of scrap code.

'Good,' said Kossolax, tightening his grip on the armrests while resisting the urge to rise from his seat and pace. 'Track it. Find me the source of the *Conqueror*'s resistance.'

'Yes, lord regent.'

There were few World Eaters still at large aboard the *Conqueror*. Most, by now, would have been crammed onto gunships and its complement of Dreadclaw assault pods, waiting impatiently for the ground assault. Kossolax was under no delusions that he commanded them so much as pointed them towards the battles of his choosing.

Those who remained were called the Four. Together, they represented the World Eaters' best, drawn from warzones across the galaxy's breadth to serve, not always willingly, at his side. Mohgrivar stabbed belligerently at a dripping console. Shalok the Skulltaker obsessively sharpened his axe blade, pouting, smiling, whispering from the corner of his lips to the heat-cured heads that dangled from the shoulder of the axe. Lorekhai, renowned throughout Imperium Nihilus as the most prolific Butcher-Surgeon since Ghenna, when the primarch had ordered the wholesale implantation of the Legion with the Butcher's Nails, knelt on the deck as though in meditation, determined to play no part and take no joy in this battle. The significant numeral was completed by Vigious Khovain, the Dark Apostle, who was roundly loathed and avoided by the others for the grating influence of his gifts on the Butcher's Nails, as well as his tendency to blurt prophecy in the words of the gods.

Mohgrivar continued with his arcane rite.

Kossolax was sufficiently ancient to recall a time when technology had been a tool to be employed rather than a daemonic force to be entreated. When a little temperamentality in the machine had been a source of wry amusement rather than a lethal challenge. The *Conqueror* was a case in point. It was not so much a ship he commanded any more as a god he had chained. It defied his hand. The Mistress was the voice and shape of that defiance.

Kossolax admired their belligerence and even respected it. But enough was enough. He had spent the millennia since the breaking of the Legion at Skalathrax rebuilding that which the Betrayer had destroyed. Angron's flagship was to be the jewel in his crown.

It was time for the *Conqueror* to yield to its true master.

'Damn it,' the daemon figure hissed, billowing towards a clattering difference engine tended by an abhumanly massive serf clad in riveted brass. *'The Cobras have launched torpedoes. Impact in seven minutes. What has happened to my escorts?'*

Kossolax made to laugh, then grunted.

A dull throb of pain built inside his head.

The Butcher's Nails.

If Angron had actively *tried* to leave a more painful legacy to the sons he had despised in life, he could not have succeeded. Kossolax knew only a little more about their origins than most, only that they were relics of the Dark Age of Technology, developed and then all but abandoned before the rise of the Imperium of Man. On the primarch's foundling birthworld of Nuceria their use had persisted in the gladiatorial slave pits. When implanted, the device fused inseparably with the victim's brain, co-opting their neural chemistry to reward violence and to punish every thought or sensation that was not directly geared towards achieving that end. Every brain was subtly different in its wiring, no two surgeons equally skilled, and no one still alive knew exactly how the Butcher's Nails had been originally intended to work, and so every warrior suffered their implants differently.

Kossolax had come to appreciate the pain.

As he saw it, it was just another battle to be won.

Shalok gurgled, drool running down his chin, as the sub-psychic resonance of Kossolax's Nails triggered his own. Khovain glared hungrily at the crew slaves bustling around them. Kossolax raised his twitching hand and pulled it firmly into a fist until the urge to lash out had passed.

'Kill the shields,' he said, ignoring Khovain's sudden snarl and turning to Mohgrivar. 'All of them. Let the torpedoes hit us.'

'Resistance!' the Warpsmith barked.

'Where?'

A growl of frustrated static resonated from the depths of Mohgrivar's sealed helm. 'The ship's sentience is buried too deep.'

'The voids are still lit,' said Khovain, looking up towards the ceiling where stalactites of congealed blood stretched towards the deck plates and the crew hunched beneath them. He jerked once, his eyes rolling back into his head. '*Alfaitha haxtata y gadhab.*'

Kossolax again resisted the urge to strike him. He despised the prophet's gift, but unlike many in the Foresworn and its subjugated warbands, he saw its purpose. Khovain shuddered, withdrawing into himself with a grinding whir of blood-caked armour.

'You should have given the task to me, lord regent. I would have found where the Mistress' daemonic essence lairs.'

'I will find her,' Mohgrivar insisted.

Satisfied that the Four were suitably motivated, Kossolax gave his attention back to the void battle being played out in the sanguilith. 'The *Void Razer* has not yet returned to formation.'

'It is accelerating to attack speed,' Mohgrivar confirmed, looking up from his console and briefly comparing its read-outs to the sanguilith's tri-D display. 'And launching boarding torpedoes on the main orbital fortress.'

A taut smile traced itself around Kossolax's mask of self-discipline as he weighed his options.

Ending the *Conqueror*'s resistance to his rule meant drawing the Mistress out and terminating her spirit once and for all. That meant locating the real Mistress. Not the wraith that stalked the command deck, issuing orders in her stead.

And if he meant to do that, then he was going to have to *make* her come out.

'Open fire on the *Void Razer*.'

From her place on the deck, the Mistress shot him a glare. The ghastly swirl that was her face became a look of confusion as the reality of the World Eater in her chair finally forced its way through to her dissociated consciousness, then became only more horrific from there. Her smooth appearance ran like molten glass, pale skin sloughing away until Kossolax could see the waxy ridges of bone underneath. A mouth slit across the lengthening bulb of her head, filled with row upon row of shiny, fishlike teeth.

Kossolax was unmoved.

A wraith with the power to stupefy the mortal thralls he commanded held no power at all.

'You want to fire on your own ship?' said Mohgrivar.

They were all betrayers, to greater or lesser degrees, although none perhaps so great as Kossolax, who had fought and slaughtered his own brothers in battles that had since become legendary or forgotten altogether. They were blood-soaked beyond mortal comprehension and still thirsted after more regardless of where it came from, but even to a corrupted, half-machine abomination like Mohgrivar the cold-blooded destruction of one's own ships in the midst of a battle reeked of insanity.

'The *Conqueror* will be mine and mine alone. I refuse to share her. Give her to me, Warpsmith, or I will allow Khovain to do it in your place.'

Mohgrivar dipped his head and snarled. 'Lord regent.'

With the Nails beginning to pinch on the pain centres of his brain, Kossolax thumped the armrest of his throne and snarled. 'Kill that ship, Warpsmith.'

The *Void Razer* was a Hades-class heavy cruiser. It was five miles in length, its scarred profile deviating considerably from its Martian template over six thousand years of strife and periodic retrofitting in the shipyards of Medrengard. It had a complement of seventy thousand, bore ninety World Eaters warriors, and had shed blood across the Imperium and countless alien domains over its unnatural life.

Its death lasted less than a minute.

Kossolax watched its sanguilith icon disintegrate under the *Conqueror*'s vastly superior guns. One of the psychic wretches, hanging from a loop of barbed wire above the basin, jerked at the end of her noose. 'Ship death,' she whispered, tears welling up in her faraway eyes. 'Ship death. Ship death. Ship death.'

With a shriek that blew out the frontis glass on instruments in a fifty-yard radius around her, the Mistress flew at the command dais. The menials did not even see her. Those in her path simply collapsed, wide-eyed, white-haired and with violently stopped hearts, to the deck as she swept through them. She raced up the dais like a tattered cloud pushed ahead of a wind.

Kossolax did not get up.

With a scream that sent shivers through the Butcher's Nails, she lunged, hitting his armour like fog hitting a wall. Kossolax felt nothing, except perhaps a faint chill, as the Mistress broke across him, dispersing into the air scrubbers and the general cacophony of the deck as though she had never been there at all.

Kossolax loosened a crick from his neck.

'Lord regent.' Mohgrivar looked up. His helmet lenses glittered with triumph. 'I have her location.'

Only *then* did Kossolax consent to rise.

With a grunt, he clenched his fists around the armrests of his throne and pushed himself up out of his seat. His ancient Cataphractii-pattern suit was white, as the armour of the World Eaters had once been, although in truth Kossolax had lost count of the centuries since his free will had extended so far as the colour of his wargear. The gods knew well the hearts of those they claimed. For all their ghoulish inconstancy, the champions transformed into degenerate spawn, the heroes driven mad by the weight of their gifts, they knew how to torment a warrior with his innermost desires. And so, when Kossolax the Foresworn led his broken Legion into battle, he did so wearing the white of the XII before its ruination at a monster's hands. Exposure to the warp and the corruptions of the *Conqueror* had transformed the Terminator suit into one of living, self-healing bone. The broad slab of his chest plastron was a sharklike skull.

Every step a minor ship-quake, his living suit otherwise uncannily silent, he descended the steps from the dais, drawing the Four along behind him like dogs.

The *Conqueror* had suffered for years under Angron's leash.

Now, finally, it would wear his.

Once the Mistress was dead.

CHAPTER THREE

From what little Ortan Leidis had seen of this moon – before that fool Corvo, in his eagerness to engage the Imperial light cruiser that had been anchored in low orbit for resupply, had driven their ship into its atmosphere – it was ice-locked from pole to pole. They had been lucky, or as Arkhor the Redbound had seen it, blessed, that their crash had put them on the same continent as the moon's small vox-relay station and its precious fleet of Arvus lighters.

Taking cover behind a frost-dusted impact barrier, he peered out and towards the row of enormous sheds that bulged out of the snow on the other side of the take-off strip.

Corvo should have been off to the right amongst the promethium drums, covering the strip with his heavy bolter. Verroth was somewhere behind him, finishing off the Imperial defenders in the funicular terminus. Warleader Arkhor and the rest of the warband, meanwhile, would be making their way across the permacrete apron from the compound at the far end of the strip.

The fireball that was currently devouring the auspex tower and vox-dish there, both barely visible through the snow, was evidence enough that the warleader's work was done.

The sound of the explosion came to Leidis on a two-second delay, a rumble, as though something, somewhere, perhaps on the next mountain over, was being flattened from orbit. Bits of foamstone and ferrocrete turned the snow a dirty grey, banging like hailstones on the corrugated roofs of the transorbital sheds.

Of Corvo, however, never mind his blasted heavy bolter, there was precious little sign. Leidis had the sense that the bloodthirsty howls arising from a quarter of a mile to the east of where Corvo was meant to be were the work of the Techmarine and his supposed covering fire.

It looked as though Leidis was on his own.

He cursed loudly as a snow truck, front-tracked and with its side armour painted with camouflage splotches of white and grey, roared through the half-open doors of one of the nearest sheds. He swore again as no fewer than four full squads of mortal Guardsmen surged out behind it. Their uniform was a lorica segmentata of white flak plate worn over ankle-length coats, with fully enclosed helms fringed with short-range auspex gear and rebreathers.

The humans took up defensive positions around the truck.

They were good.

The Gremulid System had seen heavy fighting over recent years, ork pirates spilling out of the Minos Cloud in search of new worlds to attack, and war was good for nothing if not breeding better soldiers. Arkhor's warband had been in the system for months now, for want of a warp-capable vessel to take them anywhere better, raiding Imperial bases and ork pirates without discrimination.

The local constellations had become hateful with familiarity.

In the truck's open back, the pintle gunner bashed ice from the barrel of a multi-laser, snapped on the leads from a pair of brick-like charge packs, and pivoted the humming barrels towards Leidis.

The irony was that before his itinerant wanderings had stranded him at Gremulid, he would have charged that multi-laser down without a moment's doubt. He would have trusted his armour to take its fire, broken the Guardsman before him with sheer transhuman might and presence, and then pulled the snow truck to pieces with his bare hands. That instinct was, in part, why he had left his home world of Eden in the first place. His arming serf, Ginevah, did her best to keep his wargear in working order, but there was a limit to the maintenance rites that could be performed without a ready supply of replacement parts or a proper shrine.

He was fortunate that Kraytn had died in the crash. He would not be wearing a nearly complete suit of battleplate otherwise, nor have a full magazine for his bolter.

A frustrated yell ripped through his helm's voxmitter grille as he sprinted across the open snow towards the next block of hard cover. The turret multi-laser hounded him every step of the way, the stab and hiss of las-bolts hitting snow turning into an angry hammering on rad-shielded lead as he slammed in behind a stack of supply crates bound for the Dauntless-class warship waiting for them in orbit. He tuned it out, his genetically perfect hearing allowing him to cancel the distraction entirely and focus instead on the truck gunner's rasping curses, followed by the roar of the vehicle's engines and the heavy clattering of its tracks.

It was leaving its infantry behind. Flanking him on his left.

Leidis calculated the relative positions. Lips moving soundlessly, he drew himself a map in his mind. Every supply stack, fuel barrel and mound of snow large enough to shelter a man or stop a las-bolt. The huge transorbital sheds. The hazard-striped plastek fencing dividing the permacrete apron into orderly quadrants. He plotted the positions of Arkhor and the others, estimated how long it would take for them to gun their way through the Imperial positions there and cross one and a quarter miles of open ground.

He considered Corvo and his heavy bolter, then shook his head and immediately discounted both.

Verroth slammed into cover alongside him.

His fellow renegade's armour was a pitted jumble of yellow and green plates, the edges blended to brown with blood, rust and the dirt of several dozen Kuiper-belt objects and minor moons. He had originally hailed from a Chapter known as the Emerald Snakes. Their nomadic fleets had operated across the galactic north-west and the Halo Stars, before the loss of the Astronomican had cut their ships adrift and led ultimately to their extinction. Like Leidis himself, he wore no helmet, having cannibalised its materials and circuitry to keep the rest of his suit vaguely functional, and his face never failed to startle with its lack of monstrosity. He had no horns. His skin was unscaled. His eyes did not flicker with balefire. But he had a way of staring, as though the warrior before him were no more nor less a person than the snow they stood on.

'Any grenades, brother?' Leidis had expended his own clearing the funicular terminus. He held out a hand.

Without a word, Verroth unfastened a pair of frag grenades that had been secured to his breastplate by mag-lock and handed them over.

'Go right,' Leidis said.

'When did Arkhor die and name you warleader?' Verroth hissed. His lips were thin and bloodless. His tongue was forked.

'Now.'

Leidis pulled the pin from his borrowed grenade, the metal pin twinkling away, and tossed it blind over his shoulder.

The Guardsmen never saw it for the snow.

The fuse fizzled down with the grenade still falling, the belated cries of alarm cut off mid-syllable by the muted *crump* of an airburst.

The explosion rocked the hollow crate that Leidis was sheltering behind. The las-hail hitting it dropped away to a desultory shower, but Leidis was already moving. From crouch, to walk, to run, he accelerated. Verroth's bolt pistol roared like a dragon, shivering in the cold, but well behind and receding further into the snow with every stride.

The snow truck was exactly where Leidis had known it would be.

It was circling the supply crates and snow-banked auto-loaders he had been sheltering behind in order to flank him, its multi-laser traversing to keep overwatch on the infantry supposedly pinning him down. No sooner was Leidis pounding out of the snow towards it than the pintle gunner pulled reflexively on the trigger.

Thousands of collimated beams seared the snowy ground around his boots. Most missed. Of those that didn't, most refracted harmlessly off his armour. A multi-laser was primarily an anti-infantry support weapon, highly effective against ork pirates, but a renegade Space Marine was a tank. Its threat in this instance lay in its monstrous rate of fire, the general disrepair of Leidis' wargear, and the fact that out of the hundred or so beams it had spun out over the last few seconds, only one of them needed to be lucky.

Leidis roared as he gathered speed. His body fizzed with hyperdrenaline. His twin hearts thumped with anticipation and rage.

This was what he lived for.

Even before the light from distant Terra had dimmed and madness had overrun the galaxy, he had *lived for this*.

The gunner yelled a warning as Leidis charged under the multi-laser's fire arc. The driver gave a belated cry of panic, struggling to pull a sidearm and escape out of the far-side door, just as Leidis shoulder-barged the passenger-side door and buckled it.

The light reconnaissance vehicle was far too heavy even for a Space Marine to lift, but momentum was a gift that gave freely.

The nearside tracks flapped wildly, gritting salts and powdered snow scattering off Leidis' plastron plate, as they came up off the rockcrete. Those on the driver's side bit in deeper instead, causing the entire vehicle to skid into a sudden pivot around its middle axis. The pintle gunner screamed as centrifugal forces hurled him from the back of the truck while the half-open door on the driver's side was sheared off its hinges with a shriek of roughly sawed metal and buried itself in a shed wall fifty yards away. The spinning trackbed crashed into Leidis' face with two tons of armoured truck behind it.

The impact cracked against his jaw and hurled him back with both arms flailing.

The truck spun once more before the driver was able to pull his foot off the accelerator pad. It heaved over onto its back and lay still.

Leidis spat out a loosened tooth and pushed his weight over onto his front. He grinned, drawing his stone-dry tongue across the bloodied gums.

The Thirst was maddening, but he was determined to enjoy this.

Perhaps, after he had slain as many men for his own gratification as he had in the glorification of a distant Emperor, he would reassess whether or not this made him a monster. There was a beauty in death and an artistry in bloodshed that he had always appreciated. He had long suspected there was more to the universe than a rote repeating cycle of empty slaughter and solemn penance.

There needed to be a purpose to all this death.

Shouts rang out through the tumbling snow as, with impressive discipline, the line officers got their Guardsmen up and stabbing fire towards Leidis' last position by the upturned truck and Verroth's las-scorched barricade. His renegade brother had already drawn back into cover and was keeping his head down. Las-fire painted the snow truck's armour black, drawing desperate shouts from the driver pinned inside, but the collision had clearly thrown Leidis further than they realised as all but the most poorly placed shots zipped clear over his head.

Keeping himself low, he reached under and pulled out his bolter. He set it on the ground, rested his chin on the buttstock. His bruised jaw reported a flare of pain. He ignored it and took aim. When one half-empty magazine was all he had, every shot became as precious as the blood it was intended to spill.

He squeezed the trigger. Single shot.

The bolt punched a Guardsman through his central mass, cracked his ice-camouflage flak vest like underbaked clay, and showered his squad mates with the contents of his erupted torso. Leidis laughed, licking the snow off his lips as though he could taste the blood on them, and then put a second bolt through the helmet of another. He lifted his chin from the bolter's stock, mouth falling open, awed in that moment by the sheer aesthetics of blood, bone and brain matter spraying across virgin snow and the glossy white armour of the dead Guardsman's erstwhile comrades.

He wished his former brothers on Eden could have been here to see this.

Maybe then they would understand.

Distracted, as no true Space Marine was supposed to be, Leidis failed to notice the unit sergeant gesticulating wildly towards him before going to ground. The remaining Guardsmen shortened their aim, and las-bolts fell across his prone form like a creeping barrage finding its range.

He lay flat, covering his head in the armoured crook of his elbow, and lay his bolter across the wrist to fire blind. Before he could pull the trigger, however, there was a wet *bang* and one of his assailants erupted in a welter of gore.

The sound became a roar.

Men and snow alike burst from the permacrete surface of the apron like hidden geysers. Heavy shells carved through the crippled snow truck, its helpless driver no longer screaming, shredded Verroth's barricade while the renegade cursed and hit the ground, and punched fist-sized holes through three of the closest sheds.

Leidis felt a hot stab of anger.

Corvo and his damned heavy bolter.

He refused to be stranded on this moon, murdering stray Guard units until the local Imperial presence either collapsed under the weight of greenskin attacks altogether or removed their orbital supply station to some better defended rock.

Leidis wanted more.

It had been Corvo who had been responsible for their crash-landing here in the first place, and if he was careless enough to put a bolter shell through their best chance at escape then Leidis would kill the Techmarine himself.

He rolled onto his back, hard rounds whistling across his body, and brought up his bolter. He picked Corvo out from the snow.

The Techmarine's insanely modified armour steamed in the cold. He gripped the heavy bolter in both hands, its recoil kicking back against his breastplate like a maltreated animal. In spite, or maybe because, of the clear intent of the weapon's spirit to do its wielder harm, Corvo roared with laughter throughout, a coal-furnace glow flickering from behind his helmet's malformed grille.

'Cease fire,' Leidis voxed.

Corvo did not answer. He continued to unload his heavy weapon into the shed.

With a snarl, Leidis took careful aim. It would not be the first time he had murdered a brother. Nor for the least of reasons.

With extreme reluctance, he forced his aim two feet up and to the left, and fired.

The bolt-round blew out one of the antenna bundles protruding from the Techmarine's backpack.

Corvo stumbled back with an enraged roar echoing from his helmet, too massive and inured to pain to do anything so climactic as fall. The storm of rocket-propelled explosive rounds, however, did cease, and the handful of demoralised Guardsmen broke for the sanctuary of the shuttle hangars.

Verroth stuck his head out of cover and smiled thinly. 'I thought about shooting Corvo once,' he said, before turning to take potshots at the soldiers' backs as they ran.

Leidis sat up as Corvo stomped towards him.

Leaving his heavy bolter to hang from its shoulder strap, the Techmarine turned his head to look up over his pauldron at the ruined antennae. It looked as though they had been smashed with a hammer. 'You shot at me,' he growled.

'A warning shot,' said Leidis. 'If I find you have damaged any of the Arvus shuttles inside then the next one won't miss.'

Corvo lowered his hand. The lenses of his helm steamed. 'I demand the first use of your armourer slave once we are airborne.'

Leidis made to correct him. Ginevah had followed him from Eden of her own free will. He stopped himself from doing so when he realised he did not care what Corvo believed.

Of them all, it was only Arkhor himself whose opinion he valued. Strykid was a traumatised wreck. Lestraad was an animal. Verroth had a cold-blooded charm but would need no reason at all to slit all their throats while they slept. Arkhor was no renegade like the rest of them. He was a true World Eater. He alone had the answers Leidis craved.

'Consider her at your disposal, brother.'

'I will,' Corvo snarled, and stomped past him into the reddened snow.

With a whine of misaligned servos and a shudder of protesting armour joints, Leidis stood up and turned towards the nearest shed. The doors were ajar from where the snow truck had pushed through, the sounds of human infantrymen being clubbed to death with a heavy bolter ringing out from inside.

He prayed for a shuttle. He prayed that the Dauntless-class light cruiser was still in orbit to take him away from this system. With five Space Marines and the advantage of surprise, they could take her easily.

He prayed *to the gods*.

He had fled the Chapter because he had known, in some intangible way, that he had outgrown them. Their morbid obsession with inherited guilt. Their denial of the appetites that defined them.

The promise of half a trillion stars, all of them ripe with blood and battle and hidden beauty had drawn him to Gremulid, a homing sense he could neither name nor describe pulling him into this company of renegades. And it had not released him yet. He felt the same uncanny sense of *pull* that he had felt on Eden. A throbbing in his skull. As though the blood rushing through his ears could say it in plainer terms if he could only understand. He looked up, snowflakes melting as they touched the unnatural warmth of his upturned face, and his eyes, perfect though they had been engineered to be, drifted out of focus.

A grey sky filled with snow wobbled and blurred.

The tumbling flakes began to drift. As though drawing him a map.

Pulling his tongue over his dry lips, Leidis shook his head and blinked. The snowfall, he noted, resumed its usual unhurried pattern, but the sense of summons it had briefly awoken remained strong.

Giving his head another shake, he hoisted up his bolter and crossed towards the shed to join Verroth and Corvo.

Leidis was done with the Gremulid System.

There was a galaxy out there, and he wanted to be a part of it.

CHAPTER FOUR

The *Conqueror* had tried to kill Kossolax numerous times.

He had lost count of the occasions where the deck he happened to be crossing had explosively decompressed, lost all power or had its centre of gravity mysteriously inverted. Terminals had a tendency to spontaneously combust when he was nearby, and his presence in any given section led to marked increases in the occurrence of plasma leaks, furnace overpressures and suicides amongst the underclasses.

The *Conqueror* was a beast, forever turning to try and gnaw at the leash around its neck. Every day brought another uprising from the bilge quarters, another daemon goading the crew tribes that dwelled there to crusade into the populated areas in pursuit of blood, war and salvation.

Mutant wretches, three hundred generations removed from the ancient warship's original complement and only residually human, eyed the Traitor Marines from ducts and crawl spaces as they stomped past, but did not quite muster the will to attack.

In addition to the Four, Kossolax had summoned a pair of Mutilators from their drop-ships, as well as ten warriors of what he nostalgically thought of as a Tactical Squad. The two Mutilators gurgled inanely to one another where they trudged ponderously after the rear. Kossolax did not pay too much heed to what they said. The Obliterator technovirus that had infested their systems and left their bodies sticky with pluripotent flesh had also rendered both warriors insane.

If the *Conqueror* tried to kill him today, then it would find him well prepared.

'We are close,' Mohgrivar announced, splitting his attention between a hand-held data-slate and a portable auspex unit.

They had been walking for several hours.

It had brought them to an abandoned section, one of the many void spaces that existed within the bowels of the ship and had never quite aligned with the mag-lift shafts and corridors that bent around them. The gravity was weak. There was no atmosphere. His warriors had all affixed helmets.

The long corridor flexed ahead of them like a capillary. Fresh blood covered everything. It glazed the bulkhead walls, oozing around the rivets in tune to some hidden pulse, dripping towards the deck plates in spite of the deep cold and gravity's lack of urgency. Those interface panels and doors that Kossolax could still make out were little more than unhealed wounds in the metal, scabbed over and partially hidden.

The occasional murmur from a passing munitions train trembled through. The distant vibration of the *Conqueror's* batteries.

The war for Kalkin's Tribune had not been paused while the Foresworn stepped away from his bridge. If anything, it would have accelerated now that the shipmasters and warlords under his command were no longer feeling his hand on their chains.

'*Sergeant Solax.*'

The voice shivered through the crude metal stent of the Butcher's Nails and directly into his auditory cortex. He had not been called by that name in a thousand years, and he had killed the warrior who had done so. He had been a mere line warrior of the Third Assault Company at the time of the purging on Isstvan. Over the ensuing years of war, the rate of attrition amongst the officer ranks and the dearth of lucid candidates for promotion had elevated him to the rank of sergeant, but no higher.

He looked down. The Mistress floated before him in her misted uniform. She had no eyes, no face, but somehow he knew that she was looking up at him.

Did the daemon know him? Did he know her?

Or did she, in the manner of the gods, simply see through him to that part of his past that could still hurt him the most?

'You're not authorised for the command deck. If you've a problem with those orders then you're welcome to take it up with Khârn.'

Kossolax snorted. She deigned to speak now. That could only mean he was getting close to something she did not want him to reach.

'Or perhaps we could simply summon Angron.'

Kossolax laughed, earning himself puzzled looks from those who could neither see nor hear the daemon with whom he spoke. She spoke of dead men and madmen, as ghosts nearly always did.

'We go on,' Kossolax growled.

'You'll regret this insubordination, sergeant.'

Ignoring her, Kossolax gestured for his warriors to follow.

He was not Solax any more.

Times had moved on, and he had played a greater part than most in moving them. It was Kossolax who had claimed the *Conqueror* at Armageddon, Kossolax who had marshalled the greatest strength of the World Eaters for the assault on Cadia, and even held them together long enough afterwards to smash through the iron cordon of the Astartes Praeses and press a wedge through to the Segmentum Solar. He did not fear Khârn. He certainly did not fear Angron.

And he was not Solax any more.

Were Kossolax the Foresworn to confront his father today, then perhaps his defeat would not be quite so certain as it would once have been.

There could be only one Lord of the XII.

'You force me to take measures, sergeant.'

A bark of bolter fire, unheard except via the strident vibrations it put through the deck plates, gave weight to the daemon's threat. The bloodied surfaces glistened under the World Eaters' cracked shoulder lamps as a pair of gun-servitors lurched unsteadily into the light.

They looked like cadavers that had just fumbled their way out of a mortuarium cryo-drawer and picked up weapons. The surface-exposed organic components of arms and faces were pinched by hard vacuum, blotched by anoxia and the flowery bruise pattern of burst capillaries. One of the pair bore an anti-quated rotor cannon on a shoulder-mounted rig. The other had a volkite caliver welded to the stump of its wrist.

The entire section was a time capsule from the Great Crusade. As if this part of the ship had been swallowed up by the *Conqueror*, sealed off from the World Eaters and their descent into madness since the rout from Terra, or even before.

The corridor the servitors were marching from contracted and then suddenly dilated, the walls fluttering as though communicating to him in some kind of code.

Spots appeared in his vision, turning into stretched and leering faces that beckoned to him from someplace past the corridor's end. Calling to him.

Pulling him.

He grunted, shaking it off, as the Butcher's Nails responded to the subtle sorcery with a cleansing stab of pain, though not all of his warriors endured it with his equanimity. Shalok and Lorekhai both howled, spraying the narrow corridor with automatic fire and splattering the bulkhead walls with pulp from the ruined servitors.

The Mistress, Kossolax noted, had already disappeared.

'With me.' He advanced, crushing a bolt-riddled carpet of meat under his colossal tread. 'Today the *Conqueror*. Tomorrow, the Legion.'

A second pair of servitors were already marching with a brain-dead ambivalence towards their imminent demise. Bullets sprayed from shoulder cannons to tear into the spongy layer that covered the bulkheads and spray the World Eaters with blood.

A sustained burst from a rotor cannon could cut through rockcrete, but the heavy shells pinged off his altered Terminator plate, cloaking him in bone dust and sending ricochets rattling through the Four.

They took cover behind his greater bulk and thicker armour, and returned fire. A blast of heat from Mohgrivar's melta reduced a gun-servitor to a steaming heap of dribbling flesh and slag metal. The other continued to advance, hammering the bulkheads with shot until a hail of bolts from the Chaos Space Marines blew it apart.

The corridor branched. The rip in the scab layer quivered like a heart valve. Mohgrivar consulted his slate and announced that the Mistress' lair lay ahead, and so they passed it by and strode on.

Two more heavily armed gun-servitors trudged from the overlooked corridor and shadowed them from behind. Two others closed from ahead. They were like ants roused in defence of their nest, but with enough numbers and weaponry even ants could prove deadly.

With a harsh blurt of scrap code, Mohgrivar dropped back, switching out his armament from the meltagun to a flamer, and hosed the corridor behind them with balefire. The two Mutilators, one of them partially aflame, raged at being denied the chance to rend the constructs themselves as competing bursts from Shalok, Lorekhai, Khovain and the Tactical Squad accounted for the two in front.

The corridor branched twice more. Kossolax suspected the *Conqueror* was opening new passages on purpose.

Six heavy servitors trudged purposefully towards them. Two more marched to replace the two that Mohgrivar had burned. The Mutilators gurgled aggressively and stomped towards them, weird fleshmetal fusions of claws, axes and saws already sprouting from their sticky fists.

Kossolax had spent decades trying to chart the labyrinth of ducts, corridors and crawl spaces that made up the *Conqueror*'s grisly and ever-changing innards. Such knowledge of one's own flagship had once been routine, after all. It was not madness, he had told himself, to seek to understand his own vessel. Survey teams, armed like combat patrols and in platoon strength, had ventured into the *Conqueror* and never returned. They resurfaced from time to time, even centuries later, their entrails marking the boundaries of tribal territories, or walking the halls as spirits as the Mistress did, still caught in the purgatorial task of mapping the *Conqueror*'s corridors with no respite even in death.

The *Conqueror* was a ship of death, and it did not lightly let go of those it claimed.

Kossolax had never seen this section on any map.

A close-assault servitor, its chest broadened to Astartes stature with muscle grafts and welded with armaplas shields, soaked up

the Chaos Space Marines' firepower, even as lighter units alongside it burst like overripe gourds. Shalok the Skulltaker mumbled
an oath to the Lord of Skulls as he stepped ahead of Kossolax.

A sudden shift in local gravity threw him sideways, right at the
moment of his swing, and slammed him into the bulkhead wall.

Unaffected, the servitor thudded past.

Kossolax snarled. With every weapon at its disposal, the
Conqueror opposed him. Had it lured him here? he wondered.
Did the Mistress even haunt this section at all, or had she only
ever been just another spirit lost in its halls, an anthropomor-
phised figment for Kossolax to rage against when the *Conqueror*
itself was his true foe?

The servitor came on. It had been fitted with a power claw
in each hand.

It threw a right hook for Kossolax's chest.

He raised a gauntlet to block. The power claw beat against his
wrist with enough force to punch through an aegis defence barrier.
Bits of bone shaken loose from his vambrace spat across Kossolax's
head. He barely felt it. The return punch from his left gauntlet
crumpled the servitor's head beneath his fist. The servitor whirred,
resisting death even with its crushed head hanging by a limp scrag
of neck, and threw a lazy uppercut towards Kossolax's chin.

He opened his left gauntlet and caught it.

A slight squeeze crushed the power claw in his grip.

Sparks drizzled from between his fingers as he wrenched the
weapon attachment from the servitor's truncated wrist, and then,
hoisting the whining unit clear of the deck, hurled it back down
the corridor like a wrecking ball.

Preoccupied with the planning of the Kalkin's Tribune campaign, Kossolax had not killed something in days and the rush
it triggered from the Butcher's Nails was so fierce he roared at
the ceiling like an ambull.

With a grin stapled to his broad, transhuman features, he drew the flickering red power axe from the clasp bolted into his thigh. The weapon snapped and hummed as his thumb hit the activation rune, cutting into the thick, coppery vacuum as it came free.

He lengthened his stride.

A warrior in conventional Terminator plate could not run, but Kossolax's corrupted harness presented no such inhibition.

A gun-servitor blarted a warning in distorted binharic and doused him in flame. Kossolax ignored it, chopping through the unit's weapon arm at the elbow and sending the servitor blundering into the wall. He backhanded the next, striking it so hard that its jaw and every bone connected to it shattered, dislocated bionics spraying out from the ruin of its face and riddling the units coming up behind with shrapnel. Kossolax shouldered it aside.

A brass pylon framed a set of adamantine blast doors at the end of the corridor. They looked like exact replicas of those on the command deck, only considerably older and criss-crossed by strings of bleeding meat. From serried rows of sconces in the bulkheads to either side, defence servitors continued to unplug. They stepped down from their alcoves and turned in lockstep, two by two, to address the threat Kossolax and his warriors presented to whatever, whoever, lay beyond that door. There were dozens of them now. Ahead and behind. Reaper auto-cannon turrets, nested in ceiling-mounted cupolas above the doors, pulled against the scabs preventing them from rotating fully and opened fire.

Kossolax bared his teeth and bore it, his living armour already healing, even as two of his Chaos Space Marines went down under the torrent of shells.

'Armsmen,' the Mistress hissed, suddenly behind him. *'Escort these legionaries from my bridge and confine them to barracks.'*

Kossolax felt a chill, deeper than the cold of the void, prickle its way down the nape of his neck.

He turned.

Shalok unloaded his bolt pistol into a servitor point-blank, entirely oblivious to the wraith taking shape beside him. She appeared to be dressed in a starched white jacket with blood-red trim, more solid here than she had ever been on the command deck and yet at the same time *stretched,* her midriff smoky and distended, making her inhumanly thin and yet almost equal to the executioner in height.

'Do you not see her?' Kossolax growled, less interested in warning his Master of Executions than proving his own sanity.

Shalok tilted his helm towards Kossolax, just as the Mistress slashed her talons across his throat.

Blood squirted through the ripped gorget seals into the depressurised corridor, the hypercoagulants in his plasma singularly failing, in that moment, to do the one thing they had been engineered to do. The warrior slumped against the bulkhead, hand slippery around his throat, as Chaos Space Marines blazed wildly at something they could neither see nor hit. Lorekhai dropped into a crouch beside him, rattling a spray canister, and sprayed the executioner's torn throat with bubbling liquid ceramite sealant.

Without any discernible transition, the Mistress shrank back to human scale. She clasped her blood-drenched hands behind her back. *'I don't care who you are. I won't tolerate disrespect on my bridge.'*

The daemon was insane.

Whoever she had been in life, assuming she was not simply a symptom of the *Conqueror*'s own corruption, she had no clear grip on the reality of her surroundings.

Taking up Shalok's bolt pistol in his massive gauntlet, he fired a savage burst through the spirit's chest. The shells punched through her as if through a fog, triggering their mass-reactive cores in the bulkhead behind and showering the marching servitors with steel shavings and lumps of scab.

'Khovain!'

There was a reason he kept the priest to hand. The Dark Apostle began to chant.

The Mistress reared in response until her head was bent against the ceiling, swelling, devouring mass until she filled the width of the corridor.

Still, none of his warriors reacted to her presence.

Shalok continued to bleed out against the bulkhead. Lorekhai wrestled with him whilst firing one-handed into the closing servitors. Mohgrivar just about kept them both alive, switching out weapons faster than they could be reloaded to maintain a punishing rate of fire. The Chaos Space Marines drowned them all in mass-reactive explosions while the two Mutilators, still at the rear, furiously tore servitors apart.

'The primarch will hear of this...' The Mistress flexed her claws, her outline roiling as though some tiny flicker of uncertainty had made her hesitate. 'The primarch will... The primarch...'

With a snarl, Kossolax sent another salvo through the wraith's lengthened chest, targeting not the Mistress herself this time but the combat servitors still dutifully trudging through her and into melee range.

Until, all of a sudden, they stopped.

The servitors lurched to a standstill. Their weapons powered down. Even the autocannon turrets spun down, hanging limp in their cradles and turning dark as power bled from the corridor.

Mohgrivar looked left and right, static panting from his baroque helmet grille. Shalok squirmed and growled, struggling against Lorekhai's grip on his throat, both of them shrouded in a fog of aerosolised ceramite that hung in the vacuum like a choking cloud. The Mistress was gone. As though she had never existed.

Kossolax felt the ache of the Butcher's Nails return.

It was worse than before.

Gritting his teeth, determined to defeat it as he had defeated everything else, he lowered Shalok's borrowed pistol and took a step towards the doors. A servitor stood in his way. He pushed it over. It fell against the bulkhead like a mannequin of meat and metal and made no attempt to stand back up.

He felt drawn now, *pulled*, as though whatever lay beyond the Mistress' doors wanted him as badly as he wanted it.

'Come,' he ordered, and strode towards them.

The *Conqueror* would be his.

CHAPTER FIVE

Shâhka stared into the window.

There was a war going on out there. A small one, but he wanted it. Wanted it badly. He could feel the thoughts flitting around his head, mosquito things buzzing inside his skull, and only blood made them go away. He groaned, scratching furiously at the back of his hand with broken fingernails, but the window was smashed. Nothing to see there but snowflake patterns in the shatterproof glass.

Tilting his head from side to side, he caught the dull reflection of a face looking back at him.

It was a luckless face. Pale as a week-hung corpse, hollow pits for eyes, a wreckage of misplaced ears and lips and a mouth that looked like a crater filled with broken teeth. He grimaced at it.

It grimaced right back.

The Butcher's Nails throbbed in his brain.

'What do you want from me?'

The words slipped wetly around his tongue. Getting them

out in a coherent order took more concentration than he was used to giving.

The face in the broken window twisted with hatred.

The pain in his head worsened.

'What?' he yelled, and mashed his head against the glass.

The shatterproof fragments ground themselves into smaller bits around his forehead. Pain sliced across his face, but nothing compared to the torture of the Nails. Something wet trickled into his eye. He blinked it away, but it was nothing, already gone, just a trick of the reflection and he headbutted the pane a second time. Then a third. A fourth.

A fifth.

He lost count, the splinter-pattern in the glass taking on a new shape each time until his vision swirled and dizziness took him–

He blinked as he came back.

The face was still there in the window. A flap of torn skin hung from its forehead, blood dribbling over the eyebrow and running down its cheek. Shâhka felt his nerveless lips draw up into the crooked 'U' shape of an inhuman grin.

Hesitantly, uncertain why, he touched fingers to his forehead.

He pulled them away and looked at them. They were scarred and dirty, half of them missing fingernails, but there was no blood on them anywhere. He prodded again at the site of the pain, scratching, watching the face in the glass frenziedly doing the same and sending blood running down its face.

He spread his hands in front of him and stared at them again.

Shâhka Bloodless – that was what they called him.

He lowered his head until it was against the broken window. It shivered. Shatterproof crystals ground together like bits of bone in a fractured knee. He didn't even care that it hurt. His long life was one of pain. What was a little more?

There was a war going on out there.

He wanted it.

Somewhere, buried deep inside his head, he felt he knew what was being fought over and why, but his memory was a drum filled with broken glass. It was impossible to know what was in there. Not without ripping his fingers.

Whatever it was, it wasn't worth it.

Better not to know.

By instinct alone, he translated the vibrations as they ran through the glass and into his skull. Atmospheric fighters duelling overhead. Siege artillery, pounding something far away. Super-heavy armour, trundling right beneath his window towards some battlefield he could not see.

Shâhka stared into the window.

The face looked back at him.

It was a luckless face. Pale as a week-hung corpse, hollow pits for eyes, a wreckage of misplaced ears and lips and a mouth that looked like a crater filled with broken teeth.

He grimaced at it.

'Hnnng-nnng-nnng–'

The attack passed.

It had been a mild one. Like dunking his head in acid. Forcing a flamer up his nose and pulling on the trigger as he inhaled. He smacked his head, slowly but increasingly firmly, with the heel of his palm, and blinked his eyes until the world crunched itself back into some kind of sense.

He was at the window still, but facing the opposite way from it, sitting on the floor with his back to the glass and watching the three great lords of the World Eaters argue back and forth around a table.

Their names were Goreth, Drak the Unchained, and Tōrn.

He remembered now.

The table had belonged to the Astra Militarum force command on Tourmalin until about an hour ago. Drak stood with one massively armoured boot on it while Tōrn paced up and down and Goreth stood with bare, brawny arms folded across his breastplate and frowned. The chairs had been broken up and used to crucify the force command personnel, or scattered to the corners for the warriors' acolytes and retainers to gnaw on or play with.

On a strange whim, Shâhka looked up from the floor.

Two warriors, their red armour chequered with white diamonds, looked down at him. Their eyes were lensed, but Shâhka could smell their terror.

He had the sense they belonged to him.

He shrugged and looked away.

'The corpse-worms are as good as beaten,' Drak declared, stamping his heel on the table's surface as though announcing the rebirth of a champion to the Realm of Blood and Brass. His power armour was of an ancient mark, and wrapped in chains as though he were about to be thrown into the sea.

The World Eaters had used to fight that way, Shâhka remembered, long ago, chained together like the slave-gladiators of their gene-father's abusive childhood.

He gave his head a vigorous shake.

No, no. Better not to remember.

'The first skulls are claimed but the greater feat of bloodletting is still at hand,' Drak went on.

Goreth pursed his lips, eyes wild, and shook his head.

If he was capable of speech, then Shâhka did not know it. He communicated with grunts and pointed glares. He was clad in a piecemeal harness of power armour and leather straps, made vicious with spikes. Blood ran down his body and leaked through the joints in a continuous trickle. Not all the spikes were on the outside.

The third lord, Tōrn, looked more like a courtier than a warlord. A black cloak draped his crimson war plate and a golden circlet sat on his bare head. 'Why such haste?' he said. 'A short delay before the final slaughter will give us the time to sacrifice the last of the captives.'

Goreth growled again and ground his teeth.

Tōrn smiled at him. 'The smallest cut bleeds the longest.'

'Finish this world now,' growled Drak, 'and we can still join the Foresworn at Kalkin's Tribune.'

'If Kossolax is still there,' said Tōrn.

Shâhka felt he knew that name. It made him want to scratch his face off and forget all over again. He did not want the glorious and the familiar. He wanted to haunt unfamiliar places, surrounded by nothing names. That was why he had screamed at his crew, murdering them until the decks were red, until they had turned his ship towards Tourmalin, for no better reason than it lay in the opposite direction to Kalkin's Tribune.

He growled to himself, and Tōrn the Courtier went on.

'The murder savants on my ship sensed the passage of his warp wake days ago.'

Drak leant forwards. His weight sent cracks splintering through the table's surface as though through thin, black ice. 'I missed the fighting at Cadia and was late to the destruction of Agripinaa. I will not miss the summons again.'

Goreth made a contemplative chewing sound. Tightened the grip of his arms around his huge chest.

'Indeed,' Tōrn agreed. 'He praises the Foresworn as a latter-day Despoiler.'

Drak spat on the table. 'The Eye squeezed Abaddon out

thirteen times over, only to see him crawl back inside.' He thumped his breastplate. '*We* have never stopped fighting.'

'This time is different,' said Tōrn, softly. 'He had split the galaxy asunder, and let Khorne himself through to strike at Terra.'

'And lose,' said Drak. 'Shave that long hair to a topknot and join the Black Legion if you are in such thrall to the Despoiler's brilliance. Leave the spilling of blood and the taking of skulls to real warriors.'

Tōrn spread his arms, black cloak tumbling from the shiny crimson of his armour, but said nothing.

'We attack now,' Drak growled, seemingly recalling that they were waging a different argument now to the one they had begun, and with his boot on the table for leverage, pushed himself up straight. 'The Imperials on Tourmalin are beaten. Broken. My hounds tell me they pull their warriors from raising defences and send them instead to the cathedrals to pray.'

'Then I would ask what honour there is in slaughtering those who have already vanquished themselves?'

'Stay behind then, and it will be all *my* honour.'

Shâhka bowed his head, pinching the bridge of his nose, and growled through the pain emanating from his skull.

Arguing? About fighting? With words? Spitting great names like *Foresworn* and *Despoiler* and *Khorne* as though they were Bearers of the Word calling on the Powers. And none of *them* cared who bled, or who died, or whose fire burned so very briefly the brightest for their pleasure. None of the Powers cared if the fight to come was fair. Was it fair that Shâhka had become this... this *thing*? Had he chosen it? Had he *asked* for any of–

'Hnnng.' A line of spittle lapped over the corner of his mouth and ran down his chin. He spat it out and shuddered in pain.

What was war but sweet oblivion for its loser and the crushed hopes of its supposed victor? There was no honour in it. No glory. Only blood.

And the promise of an end.

With the short-circuiting of the Nails linking brain functions that would never ordinarily communicate, he suffered through something of an epiphany.

Drak the Unchained genuinely wanted to end this conflict today and join what he saw as the greater war being waged elsewhere. But he was loath to commit the warriors and the machines that Tōrn would not match and risk leaving himself weakened. While Goreth… Goreth, he thought, was a simpleton, greatly favoured by the gods.

He smacked the side of his head. Smacked it harder. Thoughts were like flies. Even with all the windows ajar they struggled to flit out alone.

They were all of them pathetic.

And none more so than Shâhka Bloodless.

He looked up. His latest bout with the Nails had drawn attention. Tōrn was looking across the table, proud chin raised, lips pursed as though in mockery or perhaps simply in appraisal. Drak the Unchained snarled like a beastman with blood on its chin. Goreth chewed on something only he knew of and glared.

'We could argue all day,' said Tōrn. 'It's high time we heard what Shâhka Bloodless thinks–'

What did Shâhka Bloodless think?

That was a question.

Did they think Shâhka Bloodless knew? How could he?

It changed depending on the day. On the mood of the gods. And when the Nails bit *hard* and his Space Marine powers of healing put his brain back together as best they could, then the Shâhka who awoke was not always the same as the

Shâhka who had just died frothing up blood and screaming for it all to end.

What did this Shâhka Bloodless think?

Kill them, raged the voice that was clearly his own, given that it came from inside his head. *Kill them kill them kill them kill them.*

Preening Tõrn.

Oafish Goreth.

Drak, who liked to count himself so high in the esteem of the mighty.

Kill them all.

Shâhka thought how he would tear the chain from the warlord's armour and throttle him with it until his gorget seals came apart and his windpipe collapsed. His thoughts rang to the sudden *snap* of cartilage and the pain against his skull eased just a little. The Nails tingled like a dose of a familiar drug. A pleasant dullness radiated outwards from stunted reward centres, and for a few priceless moments he knew relief. Tõrn then, he thought, as the balm faded and the agony returned. Tõrn. So devout. Shâhka would behead him with the serrated edge of his own crown. The pleasing ache of a saw-action throbbed through his knuckles, all the way to his shoulders. Goreth he'd save until last. He'd break apart the barbarian's rib plate with his bare hands, peel him open and eat his main heart while the secondary kept him alive to rage against it for a few seconds more. Because in this galaxy all gave praise to Khorne. Whether they wished to or not.

Shâhka licked his lips. Meat caught between his teeth. Something sticky and wet on his tongue.

What did Shâhka Bloodless think?

What did Shâhka Bloodless think–

* * *

'Hnnng-nnng-nnng.'

Shâhka bent double, hands on the crusted armour of his knees, and vomited up a welter of undigested meat.

He was standing now. Didn't remember getting up. In the wood and plastek debris of a table he had no memory of destroying.

He blinked, and looked around.

There had been twenty World Eaters in the room with him.

Now there were none.

At some point between their presence and their disappearance, the walls had been painted red. The floor was a crimson flood. Had he been barefoot like Goreth it would have been glooping between his toes. Even the ceiling, thirteen feet up, had been coated, the occasional messily torn limb or loop of entrail swaying from a cornice or garlanding a gargoyle's neck.

He spotted Drak the Unchained's darkly ornamented armour, lying half-buried under what was left of the desk. Red pulp leaked out through the armour's joints and congealed, sticking it to the floor like a glue.

As though the champion had been roasted alive inside his armour and bubbled out through the joins.

'What…?'

Shâhka looked at his hands.

One of them was gripping tight around a blood-smeared gold crown large enough to fit a transhuman head. Otherwise, his hands and armour were pristine.

He looked down.

Even when he lifted his boot from the mire, the blood slopped off the chipped ceramite like rainwater off an oiled sheet.

There was no honour in it. No glory. Only blood.

But not for him.

And the promise of an end.

But not for him.

Scratching furiously at the backs of his bare hands, trying in vain to make them bleed, he turned back towards the window. The two warriors that appeared to have been with him had not been spared. Their armour had been torn open as if by an ursid, limbs scattered and left to lie like the pretty wrappings of a gift left out for a child playing host to a daemon of Khorne. The broken window was red now. No view of the warzone. No taunting face.

Only blood.

His lips pricked up at that, and he scratched harder at his face as though trying to start a fire. Being cursed was tolerable. Amongst the ranks of the World Eaters, being broken was practically the norm. He could abide a great deal, so long as there was blood.

'Bleed...' he muttered, cocking his head to one side as he pushed a finger into his mouth and bit down. It hurt a little, but not so much. It tasted of nothing. He gnawed on it, working through gristle and crunching into the bone, but it did not bleed.

Something at the corner of his perceptions growled.

Shâhka glanced up, bloodless finger in his mouth like a ghoul chewing on a worm, and saw an Angel looking back at him over the shattered table.

He knew its face.

It was a face he had forgotten more times than any other, a face he loved and despised, the face of the one who had shunned him, and that he had spent ten millennia trying to escape. A broken Angel, but no less of an Angel for that.

It was his own face. Or it might well have been.

The Angel bared its rusted-sword teeth. Its eyes were cratered wounds all the way down to a volcanic soul. A mane of darkened, electrically writhing dreadlocks spat from its long, beast-like brow. It growled at him, and nodded, and smote the air between its lips with a word.

'Follow…'

Shâhka saw nothing in this that was unusual.

A hesitant-sounding snarl of augmitter static sounded from the door.

Shâhka looked aside and found a pair of World Eaters now standing over him. The outer door was open, blood draining slowly out and lapping down the stairs. The two warriors looked over the carnage, saying nothing, completely failing to notice the Angel who breathed its hatred of them from the middle of the floor.

In this, too, Shâhka saw nothing worthy of comment.

'Fight', it said.

'Lord Shâhka?' one of the warriors said.

Shâhka wondered which warband they had belonged to. To which of the four warlords they'd pledged their souls.

He supposed it didn't matter any more.

They were done arguing now.

He drew his limp mouth wide, pulled out his sawed finger and bared his broken teeth in a bloodless smile. The Nails were throbbing again, pain returning to his head in pulses, but he knew how to make it go away.

If only for a little while.

'Follow,' he said, and behind him, his Angel snarled in satisfaction.

CHAPTER SIX

Armageddon was one of the great worlds of the Imperium of Man, and it was not a safe place for any ship to be. Ork marauders warped in from the embattled neighbour worlds of Granica, Ruis and Golgotha to launch hit-and-run attacks on a daily basis, drawing the Naval patrols from the sector HQ at St Jowen's Dock into running void battles across the plane of the system. The world's orbital bands were littered with debris from half a millennium of invasion and counter-invasion. Wrecked ships. Defunct defence platforms. Even the rocky, moonlike chunks of obliterated ork roks, many of which had since been hollowed out into bases from which ork freebooters and Navy deserters raided greenskin and Imperial shipping alike. The entire region was an auspex blind spot, a barely navigable astrogation hazard seared into the tempus materium by six centuries of violent ship death and mega-weapon fallout.

This much had been true before the Cicatrix Maledictum. The

Imperium's grip on its hyper-industrialised grey jewel had only become more parlous in the decades since.

The empyreal fault known as the Red Angel's Gate had been a wandering eyesore over the planet's tropics since Angron's defeat there six hundred years ago. As had been the fate of secondary warp anomalies throughout the galaxy, the splitting of the Eye of Terror had torn it wide. It had become a roiling crimson sun, wreathed in strings of blood and streamers of effervescent plasma, baking the entire hemisphere of the world below into the virulent crust of a daemon world, and bringing insanity to the minds of man and ork who fought each other over it still.

It was there that the *Sword of Dione* was bound.

Graucis Telomane strode onto the command deck, the silver-engraved blast doors sliding silently closed behind him. Dozens of capped heads turned from glowing consoles as he passed, every crew-serf eager for a glimpse of the Grey Knight who had commanded them and their vessel for longer than many of them could know. The majority of the mortal crew would have been born to the vessel, where tales of Graucis and his deeds had taken on the substance of a foundational myth. He had commanded the *Sword of Dione* for fifteen generations, and the rare occasions when he emerged from his meditations to appear directly before them invariably presaged dark and glorious times ahead.

The grey-uniformed serfs were seated in long banks, workstations arranged into chevrons either side of a central aisle and angled towards the primary visual display.

The vast multiplexed screens were crimsoned by the fierce un-light cast by the Red Angel's Gate. The frequent static-like flicker of things-that-should-not-be meeting violent ends on the *Sword of Dione*'s point guns as they poured out of the anomaly's event horizon and into realspace broke the swirling red uniformity. Graucis ignored the peripheral distractions, the open sore of the Gate drawing his eyes like a vortex. He stared, the psyk-reactive circuitry of his psychic hood radiating a furious cold as it channelled the energies passing between himself and the hungry singularity at the heart of the Gate. Graucis felt a stabbing pain in his thigh. He muttered a banishment from the pages of the *Corpus Exspiratum* and ignored it, force staff clacking on the smooth metal flooring as he continued on down the central aisle.

Six Grey Knights stood under the main screen.

'Brother Telomane,' said Geromidas, breaking from the conferring group and smiling broadly, the skull helm of the Chaplaincy held under the crook of one arm as he grasped Graucis' wrist in his other hand. 'We came as soon as we received your signal.'

'Four days' warp travel from Monglor is exceptional time.'

'The warp currents were behind us all the way. It is as though something or someone drove us here.'

'Or pulled.'

The Chaplain's smile faded by stages. He was grey-haired and hugely broad, bulky transhuman muscle turning very, very slowly to dough as though, were he to live to a thousand and know some peace, he might yet run to fat. He was almost half Graucis' age. 'Do you believe that...?'

Graucis closed his eyes. 'Yes, brother. There is no doubt that the Lord of the Twelfth Legion has returned.'

'It is good to see you, regardless.' The Chaplain drew Graucis into a rigid embrace.

Graucis clapped the Chaplain brusquely on the back. The Grey Knights were a closed order, but psychic ties and the shared trials of being insulated from the greater Imperium forged a brotherhood that was stronger than most. It had been painful for Graucis to be apart from that brotherhood for as long as he had, but the galaxy was vast and like-minded warriors like Geromidas, whom he had commanded down the centuries, were so few.

'Our missions across the galaxy have separated us for too long.'

Graucis drew himself from the Chaplain's embrace. 'You were successful?'

Geromidas nodded, indicating the various trinkets and curios that adorned his silver armour. Every one was the relic of a Grey Knight who had fought and died on Armageddon. A similar array of artefacts bedecked the armour of the five warriors gathered behind him. Graucis alone bore the tokens of the thirteen who had lived. They had taken centuries to track down and acquire. A fallen Space Marine left little behind.

With Angron having subverted expectation and returned somewhere other than Armageddon, where Graucis' ability to contain him would have been at its greatest, such symbols of potency had become ever more necessary.

'And how is the old injury?' Geromidas' cold blue eyes became suddenly hard, those of a Chaplain, studying Graucis' face for lies as his mind did likewise in his thoughts.

Graucis rebuffed both with a skill the Chaplain could not rival. 'I endure it, brother. As I always will.'

+Where is the Beast if not here? And what has become of the other six members of our brotherhood?+

Liminon leant into the long haft of his Omnissian power axe and peered at them both through the sleek silver discs of his augmetic eyes.

After Graucis himself, the Techmarine was by some distance the most potent psyker in their company, and Graucis felt the probing touch of his mind as it ventured into his own. The Techmarine was older than Graucis' six hundred years too, in pure sidereal terms, but had spent the greater part of the 41st millennium engaged in combat with the greater Neverborn known to the pages of the *Liber Daemonica* as the Artful Sublime. By his own reckoning, the duel had lasted mere hours, but it had been centuries later by the time Graucis, Geromidas and a number of others, including Brothers Epicrane and Lokar, who were also with them now, had come to his aid and banished the Sublime. The experience had cost him his eyes and, though there was no obvious physical cause, he had never spoken again.

Of his life before, however, the records were old and scant and Graucis knew little.

'Of Angron, I do not yet know,' Graucis answered, speaking aloud for the benefit of all. 'But Dvorik and Gallead are where I sent them, and beyond the powers of any astropath to reach.'

He looked up, his face painted red by the roiling maelstrom that was now filling the towering main screen.

'Prepare yourselves, brothers, and gird yourselves in the verses of the *Cabulous Luminar*. We are heading into the Red Angel's Gate.'

The glowing fog of teleportation faded from Graucis' eyes. The consecrated air he had carried with him from the *Sword of Dione*'s teleportarium dispersed into the hellish atmosphere of the Red Angel's Gate with a long, slow hiss. Akin to that of holy water trickling into semi-molten rock.

Liminon and Geromidas were silvered presences to either side of him. Acid-etched verses from the *Canticles of Absolution*, the *Cabulous Luminar* and the daemon-lore of the *Liber Daemonica* burned white from their armour against the cloying profanity of the red fog. The hallowed pages of the *Liber Daemonica*, which every Grey Knight wore inset upon his breastplate, fluttered violently like predatory birds denied flight. Geromidas gripped his crozius, while Liminon sought out the ground ahead of him beneath the fog with the butt of his Omnissian axe, his eyes scanning the daemonscape all the while.

The Strike Brothers, Anchrum, Lokar, Baris and Epicrane, spread out into a half-circle around them and took up guard positions, wielding swords that had been worked with oils thrice blessed by the Chamber of Purifiers. Bladed weapons were often more effective than conventional arms against the choirs of the immaterial realms. The Neverborn were naught but malign reflections of the human psyche. Their unholy resilience to the common weaponry of the Imperium was but another manifestation of human fears.

Blade, fire and witchcraft: these were the instruments the Neverborn feared.

'We shall delve into the dark shadows,' Graucis intoned.

'We shall seek out the tainted, and pursue the vilest evil,' the six Grey Knights concluded together.

Geromidas gave the tightest of smiles.

Liminon peered out. Whatever he had lost to the knives of the Artful Sublime, it had not blunted his focus.

They had teleported into the Red Angel's Gate. The Grey Knights stood on the very threshold of the Sanguinary Unholiness' infernal domain. Physical law and mental reason no longer applied. The 'sky' had an unnatural curvature that extended far beyond the natural point where a horizon should have intersected it. It was jagged, faceted, often bleeding – a broken mirror holding up a million fractured images of Armageddon's warped surface. 'Ground' was a term of orientation rather than of substance. It was what lay beneath them rather than above, and appeared no more substantial for all that it bore their weight.

The unnatural geographies rang with the screeches of things that had no lungs and felt no pain. Lithe, red-skinned Neverborn raced across ground and sky and the space between as though they were one and the same. As though it were raining nightmares. Some were winged and armed with spears. Others rode on thundering monstrosities of brass, loped after by fearsome scaly hounds in spiked collars that bled the very essence of pain. The insane topography would have shattered a mortal's mind into more pieces than the sky above. Even a Space Marine, venturing into such a realm unprepared, would have found himself crippled by an existential nausea his gene-perfect physiology was ill-equipped to abide.

But this was the battlefield for which the 666th Chapter of the Adeptus Astartes had been founded.

'It is we who stand guard,' Graucis continued, his voice building in strength, exploiting the cadence of the canticle, and its deep familiarity, to thread his thoughts through those of his brothers, linking his psychic aegis to theirs.

To be a part of a Grey Knights squad was to be of one mind, to harmonise one's very existence with others. Some of these warriors had never fought together, or even met in person before today, but Graucis had led them all at one time or another. Some, like Liminon and Geromidas, had quested alongside him for centuries at a time. Graucis was the lynchpin that held them, made them greater than the sum of their already potent parts.

'Our eternal watch shall not fail.'

The Emperor's Gift, the genetic inheritance wrought by the Master of Mankind Himself, made the Grey Knights anathema to the Neverborn. Graucis had seen waves of lesser Neverborn simply disintegrate in his presence. He had heard of even daemons of the greater choirs recoiling from the sheer divinity of a Grey Knight's genetic sequence.

'We are the *brethren incorruptis*.'

At the conclusion of the verse, a psychic kine-shield burst to life about the six-man squad.

'Follow me.' Gripping his Nemesis staff tightly in one hand, Graucis waded into the fray. 'Our brothers cannot be far.'

No two Grey Knights manifested their abilities in the exact same way.

Pyrokinesis was common. The power of fire to drive back the shadows was so deeply ingrained into the human psyche it often persisted even after the mind-wiping rituals that all neophytes underwent, but Graucis' gifts had always manifested as fulmination. Lightning arced from the headpiece of his force staff, incinerating screeching Neverborn, while inviolate sheets of energy crackled around his brotherhood's collective aegis as though around the bars of a psychic Faraday cage. Of the billions swarming through the threshold of the Red Angel's Gate, however, most paid Graucis and his warriors little heed.

To the Sanguinary Unholiness all battles were created equal and it was the greater conflict on Armageddon that drew their ire. The incursion of seven Grey Knights into their lord's domain paled beyond insignificance in comparison.

Graucis saw his objective ahead.

The Stormraven gunship was a bright splinter in the brutal hellscape. Its silver hull bore the stamp of the Grey Knights Fourth Brotherhood and the *Sword of Dione*. Five Brotherhood Terminators in shining armour had withdrawn into a defensive ring around the gunship's rear hatch, up to their thick greaves in red fog and with storm bolters blazing. Ripples of mental fire coruscated about their circle, a single Grey Knight every so often taking a portion of the collective aegis into himself and expelling it as a gout of mindflame or a fireball, immolating swathes of the Neverborn into the un-matter from which they arose.

A sixth Grey Knight fought on outside of the Terminators' defensive bulwark.

He was ornately armoured, replete with back banner, relics

and a great helm adorned with silver wings. His tilt shield bore the heraldry of the Hall of Champions, a diagonal sword across a red bar, as well as a dozen vertical blades signifying feats of martial excellence, three skulls denoting the greater Neverborn he had personally vanquished and a fourth that was wreathed in flame. That last heraldic charge had been worn by only thirteen Grey Knights in the ten-thousand-year history of their Chapter. Graucis was one of them. It marked them as members of that elite order who had faced Angron on Armageddon and lived.

'Reinforce Justicar Gallead and his brothers,' Graucis called to the others, drawing psychic energy into his Nemesis staff until the metals of his psychic hood prickled against the back of his neck like a bed of pins. 'I will aid Paladin Dvorik.'

'As you command, brother,' said Geromidas, the null shells in the Grey Knights' storm bolters screaming against the hostility in the air as they peeled off towards the gunship.

Lightning blazed from the headpiece of his staff as Graucis charged ahead towards his embattled brother. The electrical spray smoked off the bronze armour of a daemonic creature two and a half times his size, thrown across too great a distance to do serious harm, but stinging the brute enough to draw its attention.

It turned from the Paladin and snarled.

Curling horns erupted from the sides of a gargoyle-like head. Leathery black wings were unfurled behind it, claws erupting across their span only adding to its imposing size. Its breath was smoke. Its eyes were a diabolic yellow. Its entire body was wreathed in a halo of pinkish steam, its own blood mingling with consecrated silver where it defied the psychic aegis of thirteen Grey Knights with its presence.

Graucis knew this creature.

Stovrwrath the Brazen Eighth.

Not a true Neverborn at all, but something far worse – a perverse union of mortal flesh, emotion and ambition with daemonic power.

A daemon prince.

Its nostrils flared with an unnatural fury, muscles bulging to the size of rockcrete-filled sandbags as it brought a gigantic flanged mace thrashing around towards the side of Graucis' helmet. Graucis caught the blow across his Nemesis staff. In-built refractor fields flared with countervailing energies, psychic lightning creeping up the daemon prince's wrists as its weapon was pushed aside. Stovrwrath bellowed in rage, fingers tightening around the weapon's grip as it prepared for a reverse swing, only to arch back, sink to its knees, and roar in pain as the silver point of Dvorik's Nemesis force sword burst through its chest from behind. Graucis stepped up before the daemon prince could recover, raising his left hand to Stovrwrath's back-tilted forehead and uttering a short passage from the *Liber Daemonica*.

The daemon prince howled as though in mortal agony, thick plumes of meat smoke billowing from underneath Graucis' touch.

He withdrew his hand.

The black symbol of the Sigillite that was acid-etched into the silver of his gauntlets' palms, and tattooed into the corresponding position on his flesh, now burned from Stovrwrath's crimson brow.

Graucis stepped back, resetting his two-handed grip on his staff, watching in satisfaction as the daemon prince struggled and failed to move.

For as long as the mark of the Sigillite held, the daemon prince would rage helplessly.

'*I see you,*' Stovrwrath snarled, in spite of its paralysis. '*The rage inside that you seek to quell. Telomane the wrathful. Telomane the wasted. You are in Khorne's realm now, brother. End me. This is no place for a fool's restraint.'*

The sliver of daemon metal buried in Graucis' thigh pulsed like a buried mine.

Graucis could not say he was not tempted, but temptation had become his burden and after six hundred years he was well practised in the skill of denial.

He grunted and ignored it.

'Why have you followed me here?' Dvorik asked, speaking over the daemon prince's frustrated bellows and the roar of Grey Knights storm bolters. 'The hunt for this abomination was my quest.'

'Brother, I dispatched you months ago.'

'Months?'

Graucis shook his head. Even across the physical fabric of the tempus materium, time did not flow as evenly as most Imperial citizens assumed. It could be bent, accelerated or slowed by warp anomalies or the emanations of the Cicatrix Maledictum, even by the densities of different stellar regions. In liminal realms such as this one, it barely flowed at all, moving instead by the random and ever-changing whim of whichever greater power was presently pre-eminent. All the more reason then to move swiftly, lest he escape the Red Angel's Gate only to discover that centuries had passed in his absence and that he was already too late.

'There is no time for me to explain, brother. Angron has returned to the galaxy and every moment that remains to us now is precious.'

Dvorik signed the aquila across the tattered copy of the *Liber Daemonica* bound to his breastplate, causing Stovrwrath to writhe in fresh pain.

The Paladin had been a veteran line brother at the time of the

First War for Armageddon, twenty-five years Graucis' senior, but the grinding movement of centuries had narrowed the chasm of experience that had once lain between them. Dvorik, for all his honours, had never desired the burden of leadership, and in this matter deferred wholly to Graucis' foresight.

'We have collected the one hundred and nine relics of our brothers,' Graucis continued. 'This is the last step we must take if we are to face him again.' He turned back to Stovrwrath.

As a vessel for the infinite wrath of the Sanguinary Unholiness, the daemon prince was immensely powerful, immeasurably superior to Graucis in every sense, but he had no fear of it. He had faced the Lord of the XII Legion on the battlefield and would never afterwards be intimidated by the Blood God's lesser subjects.

'Captain Stover of the World Eaters Eighth Company,' he said, and the daemon prince hissed as though stung by its mortal name. The twisted XII Legion icon on its bronzed pauldron reshaped itself into a literal maw, wet meat and acidic saliva stringing between its ceramite teeth as it strained to gnash at Graucis' hand.

According to Graucis' readings – and as a senior Librarian of the Grey Knights, he had access to texts that would condemn whole star systems to Exterminatus if the Ordo Malleus were to learn of their presence there – Stover and his Eighth Company had fought under Angron on a world called Nuceria.

It was a world about which the written record had little to say. The planet had either been resettled under a different name in the aftermath of the Horus Heresy and the records lost, or it had been destroyed in the anarchy of the time. However, intriguing excerpts from contemporaneous documents in the Citadel of Titan named Nuceria as the site of the very battle in which Angron had finally committed his soul to the powers of the warp.

And now, courtesy of those same powers, Graucis had found a witness.

'Alas, we have no time to be subtle.' He returned his hand to Stovrwrath's upturned forehead, drawing out another hiss of steam and a snarl of pain. His helmet lenses blazed with the power of the Emperor's Gift. 'Show me the hour of Angron's downfall. Give me the True Name of the Beast.'

Stovrwrath's expression melted into one of agony, as Graucis drove his thoughts into the insubstantial meat of the daemon prince's mind...

The sky is bleeding, weeping, the heavens themselves protesting the defilement that his presence brings. The words of a chant thread themselves through their agonies, binding them, their very anguish a conduit for the names of the Neverborn. The air is breathless, as if with the anticipation he feels too. Power enough to break a world. Enough to remake a god.

The heavens finally break under the strain, bursting before a scream-ing lance of light too straight and true to be mistaken for lightning. It strikes the reddened, bone-flecked earth with a thunderclap of pure rage, the peals rolling out through the devastated ruin of a once human city. In a mute, numb, sightless moment, the fighting stops, shadows bearing no resemblance at all to the warriors that cast them flaring and clawing across the shattered ground.

It is an epiphany.

And there in the heart of the fading light, his shadow the most majestic and monstrous of them all, is Angron. With a gigantic, broken chainsword he hacks at the cobalt-blue-and-gold gauntlet raised up in defence of its owner's bleeding face.

And yet, somehow more arresting and powerful than the sight of one primarch brutalising another, the chant goes on.

It was all.

It described all, revealed all, foretold all; to comprehend those baleful, dulcet words was to know the True Names of the gods themselves. Flesh, bone, body and mind begin to vibrate to the rhythms of the Sea of Souls and, with a howl of fury, Angron begins to change...

Graucis pulled his mind from Stovrwrath's with a cry. He clutched his staff as though it were the only genuine physical presence in the universe, its psyk-reactive circuitry responding to his flailing thoughts with random, jerky flares of lightning and spontaneous activations of the embedded refractor fields. The roar of storm bolters sounded all around him, like the after-effects of some tempestuous dream.

The touch of Dvorik's heavy silver gauntlet on his shoulder finally snapped him fully from the daemon prince's memories.

With an effort, he brought his breathing back under control, and swallowed, moistening his dried-out lips. 'Thank you, brother.'

'Tell me you saw what you came here for.'

Graucis shivered, his pure genetics reacting to the corruption into which he had been submerged, then gave a nod.

Yes.

He still had the taste of Nuceria's dust on his tongue. It was rust and bone and broken dreams. He could almost feel the raw emotion of a primarch at the instant of his damnation. It burned under his skin, and Graucis wished he could be certain that the anger would abate in time. Angron was deserving of no pity, but he had not been the architect of his own fate, and nor had he accepted it willingly. Through the agony of the transformation, Graucis had felt the primarch's rage. Here was a being who should have been perfect, one who *felt* on a level far beyond the baseline human range, but who had been so thoroughly abused, left so broken, that there was nothing left to fill his heart but hate. For all the cruelty of the Nucerians to which he had been subject, more barbarous by far was his treatment by the one being in the galaxy who should have known better.

The Emperor had allowed His son to remain broken. He had bestowed upon him a Legion to remind him of the comrades he had lost, brothers to exemplify how far from the ideal he had fallen, and how greatly he had been wronged.

It would have been better for all, surely, if He had simply disposed of his damaged XII as He had engineered the elimination of the II and XI.

Angron himself would have likely welcomed it.

But Graucis had no pity for him. Only contempt. The Emperor had given him every chance to become the Angel he was meant to be and he had squandered them.

Graucis let out a deep breath, willing his hearts to slow, and eased his grip on his staff. This was an unexpected revelation. Angron had come into great power on Nuceria, but at the cost of making himself beholden to the same rules that governed all power flowing from the warp.

To name a thing is to know it. To know the daemon is to command its nature.

He would need time to properly meditate on what he had seen, and it was true that Angron, like Stovrwrath the Brazen Eighth, was not wholly Neverborn. The same rules could not be unilaterally applied. A part of his True Name and nature would forever remain a secret known only to the Emperor. Graucis had spent decades with the inscrutable writings of the Sigillite, the founder of the Grey Knights Chapter and right hand to the Master of Mankind, for any hint of his given name and found no answers there.

But even a partial name held power.

'Yes,' he managed to gasp. 'Yes, I believe I did.'

'Everyone aboard the Stormraven,' Dvorik yelled, ripping his greatsword from Stovrwrath's back and turning towards the others. 'We have no time to tarry.'

One by one, the Grey Knights broke off and withdrew. Justicar Gallead and his Brotherhood Terminators were the last to back up the Stormraven's ramp, single-mindedly holding the lesser choirs of the Sanguinary Unholiness at bay with their flame-wreathed aegis.

Thirteen Grey Knights.

A small number, but an auspicious one. The same as that which had walked away from the Lord of the XII once before.

Only this time, Graucis was prepared. This time, he would wield his True Name and the strength of the fallen against him.

'The gods do not forget an insult against their own,' Stovrwrath growled, cursing Graucis from his knees. *'Your soul will be forever forfeit until it is repaid in blood.'*

With a two-handed swing of his Nemesis staff and a grunt of aggression that shamed him for all that it was short-lived, he staved in the side of Stovrwrath's skull and sent the paralysed daemon prince crashing to the heaving, fog-wreathed ground of the Red Angel's Gate.

'Brother,' Dvorik called out to him, already halfway up the Stormraven's ramp and withdrawing under the cover of the Terminators' guns.

Graucis nodded.

This time, he swore, he would not settle for simply banishing Angron to the abyss his infernal patrons called home. He would not make it so that another like him would be forced to fight the beast all over again in another six hundred years' time.

No.

He would bind the daemon primarch's screaming essence to

the earth of Armageddon that he had befouled, and consign him to the Chamber of Purity for all time.

CHAPTER SEVEN

Mohgrivar cut through the magnetic seal on the blast door with his meltagun while Lorekhai and Shalok, the latter's throat still blistered like flash-cooled lava, hauled them apart on their respective tracks. Kossolax strode through, hissing axe in hand, Khovain reluctantly close behind, the balefire leaking from his tainted crozius struggling to throw back the gloom.

The chamber was a mirror of his own command deck. It was a perfect likeness, except that there was genuine, if long-disused, equipment here, and one could almost define stations from their placement. Over there was auspectoria, and there, vox, plastek hardlines draped over its forgotten parapets like vines. The armoured bunker of the strategium stood off to his right, encircled by black screens. No brass fonts, no strangled witches, no half-daemon savants painting the exterior scene for their lord in blood.

With an ache in his breast, Kossolax took it in.

He had almost forgotten what the command deck of a Gloriana was supposed to look like.

'What is this place?' said Lorekhai.

'It...' Khovain paused, as though assuring himself of the language in which he spoke. 'It looks like the command deck.'

'It *is* the command deck,' said Kossolax.

He did not know how that could be true, or why, only that it was. He had served aboard the *Conqueror*, albeit very briefly, at the height of the Great Crusade. It would be millennia before he did so again, and that was time in which every aspect of its layout had been altered in some way. The *Conqueror* could have swallowed the entire section like a tumour at any point between the great limp from Terra and the catastrophe of the First War for Armageddon and Kossolax would never have been the wiser.

With a shuddering of magnetised boots on the steel decking, Mohgrivar, Lorekhai and Shalok moved up from the door, the Warpsmith taking up a position to his left, the executioner to his right. The Apothecary, he bade remain at the rear with Khovain. The Apostle's attention was fixed forward.

There was a command throne there, raised above the deck on a steel dais. It faced away from them, back turned, immersed in the pervading gloom as though cloaked and hooded and hunched in conference with its semicircle of moribund screens. Unlike the huge bone chair that Kossolax had claimed, this was all darkened steel and brushed chrome, studded with bronze decals and with plug-in ports for direct nervous control. Kossolax looked up, hunting for a glimpse of a figure in that chair or a reflection amongst the hanging screens that surrounded it.

There was none. But no matter.

Kossolax knew exactly what he was going to find there.

Leaving the ten Chaos Space Marines and the two Mutilators to guard the open door, he drew the Four along behind him.

'Come with me.'

Six long, but ponderous steps and he was at the foot of the dais.

He felt his primary heartbeat quicken, the secondary sputtering into life as though in response to a fear he had undergone too many corrective genetic surgeries to properly feel. Untroubled, even as his hearts raced on and his biscopea dosed his bloodstream with hyperdrenaline, he noted how the darkness slunk through the abandoned command posts. Flanking them. Cutting off their retreat. Even in the non-existent air there was a bitter smell to the shadows. It was rust, and sulphur, and struck sparks. The Butcher's Nails began to ache in his skull. As they always did in the presence of potent sorcery. He ground his teeth and turned to Khovain, but the Dark Apostle was seizing, droplets of blood squeezing out from the angles of his helmet lenses and blebbing off in the feeble gravity like tears shed upside down. Lorekhai was the only thing holding him upright.

'We are World Eaters,' said Kossolax, ignoring the slur in his own voice. He raised a finger and wiped the slow bleed from his nose. 'That used to mean something.' Firming his grip on the bolt pistol he had taken from Shalok, he pressed on. 'Whatever sorcery is at work, fight it.'

He began to climb.

There were eight steps, just as there were eight steps from the deck to the foot of Kossolax's throne. He had made doubly sure and counted them, and Kossolax did not make mistakes, and yet eight steps later he was still climbing, no nearer to the summit of a dais that had risen above him to become mountainous. The blackness roiled beneath them like the tops of clouds. Kossolax shook his head to dispel the illusion, but the mountain did not shrink. His thighs ached with the effort of the climb. His chest burned. The Butcher's Nails buzzed urgently in his thoughts.

After counting his steps to eight times eight times eight, many times more than there rightfully should have been, he finally set foot on the top of the dais.

A part of him wanted to beat his chest and roar of his triumph, and it took all his self-discipline to fight the urging down.

The darkness from that vantage was deep and thick. Something ancient roiled there in its shadows, brooding and angry. His third lung burned from breathing it. His hearts pounded so fast he could no longer separate the beats.

He forced himself to ignore it, closing his gauntlet over the command throne's steel back and leaning over the top to look down.

The cadaverous hag slumped back in its seat was a scarecrow in a dirty white uniform, a Red Hand in ancient blood flaking from the crumbling hollow of its breast. There, even the most superficial resemblance to the wraith that had haunted Kossolax's ship gave up any attempt at conjuring a likeness and went no further. It was a skeleton cloaked in too small a coverage of greying skin. Or it was leftover flesh, pinned together with birdlike bones that had not been made to fit. Either way, it drew the eye, and held it, like a spectacularly brutalised corpse or a lurid disease. There was a wrench of gristle, and its carrion head turned towards him. Nictitating membranes flitted across its dry, lidless eyes. Membranous nostrils quivered like a small animal in fear. She twitched away from him, but was wholly fused to her throne. Only her head and one hand retained some mobility, and of the latter only one bony finger, tapping on the armrests with the urgency of a dismembered spider, remained free.

Kossolax could have laughed, but something, some terror in the air, prevented him.

After all he had fought through to get here, *this* was his enemy. 'Mistress,' he said.

'Lord,' it croaked, with a voice as badly mistreated as its bones.

There was another cartilaginous snap and the creature looked away from him again. 'The *Conqueror* is yours.'

Kossolax's grip on the throne's back tightened.

At last. The *Conqueror* was fully his. The great task of rebuilding the XII Legion could begin. The World Eaters did not prostrate themselves before the symbols of their gods or their past as others might, but the killing potential and sheer firepower of the *Conqueror* was a symbol they would bow to or be annihilated by. Those champions of the Long War who dismissed him, or who still thought of the World Eaters as bolter fodder for their wars, would soon remember the force that the XII Legion had once been. Under Kossolax the Foresworn, the galaxy would burn again. He would achieve what the Eightfold Legions of the Cruor Praetoria had singly failed to do and break the Golden Throne of the Emperor under his axe.

'I have been waiting for you to return,' the Mistress went on, and it finally dawned on Kossolax that she had not been addressing him.

He looked up.

The darkness surrounding them growled.

Kossolax swung up the Skulltaker's pistol, resisting as he did so the white heat of agony that simultaneously drove Mohgrivar, Lorekhai, Shalok and Khovain howling to their knees. Like a shredded curtain, the darkness before him gave way and became flame. Infernal heat, hotter and dryer than the hydrogen furnace at the heart of a sun, reached up from the floor and towards the throne, hazing and infinitely multiplying the daemons that came loping in its wake. They were red-skinned and brutal-looking, hunched bodies topped with doglike heads and cruel nests of black horns. Each one clutched a serrated black sword as long as a human man was tall and sharp enough to make metal bleed. The pain that their intolerable existence drove through the

Butcher's Nails was crippling, but Kossolax refused to follow the Four's lead and kneel.

His bolt pistol spoke his refusal.

Immaterial bodies burst open, spraying the deck plate with hissing ichor as Kossolax mowed them down. They were unarmoured and effectively numberless. Kossolax could not even miss. Their only defence was their daemonic natures and that Kossolax denied with every fibre of his will and every pull on his bolt pistol's trigger.

'The *Conqueror* is mine!' He felt the warriors of the Four rousing themselves, his defiance an aura that was not limited to one mind alone, taking up cardinal positions around the dais and laying down fire of their own.

The Mistress produced a wizened hike of laughter as the first daemons scrabbled through the torrent of bolter fire and onto the foot of the dais. They were without number. It did not matter how many of them Kossolax slew.

He tightened his grip on his axe.

'Khovain!'

The Dark Apostle lowered his pistol, extended a hand and hissed a curse, a cone-shaped wedge of daemons spontaneously erupting into sizzling ichor.

It made no difference.

With a growl, Kossolax abandoned the Sisyphean task of holding endless hordes at bay and brought his axe to the Mistress. Its humming field-edge coloured her papery skin red. 'End this. Before I end you.'

The Mistress' eyes flicked from the bloodless massacre to him, and then back again. 'And what then, Kossolax Foresworn? Who will keep this ship's crew fed, its population in balance? Who will ensure its guns are loaded and its furnaces hot? The World Eaters?' She produced another dry, retching laugh. It left her face in the rictus shape of a smile. 'Do you even know when and where the *Conqueror* last took on fuel? Or from whom?'

Kossolax snarled. 'I will not share glory.'

The Mistress fell quiet. She did not answer.

'End this!'

'What makes you think that it is mine to end?'

There was another growl, similar to that which had sounded before but louder now, closer, its breathing like a furnace causing the bulkheads to creak in its heat. With footsteps like hissing solder, it emerged from the flame. It was element and emotion, brass and fire and fury, and impossible for the mind to accept in less abstract terms. It was a volcano, a walking eruption of hate. The very air combusted in its vicinity as though agitated to such a state of fury as could be expelled in no other way.

There should have been a hundred different emotions tearing through Kossolax's hearts in that moment. Despair at the rendering of half a millennium of ambition to ash would have been expected. Terror, even for a Space Marine and the Foresworn of Chaos, would have been accepted. Love, even for the creature he despised more than any other, could have been excused. But under the gaze of that monstrous avatar, he felt only rage.

Why here? he thought. Why now?

Why him?

'My lord Angron,' the Mistress rasped, skeletal body twitching as though attempting to rise from her long seat before suffering instead for a bow of the head as low as its fusion to the chair back could allow it. 'You have the bridge.' The lesser daemons shrieked, redoubling their efforts to run ahead of the primarch's wrath and onto the guns of the Four.

'No,' Kossolax snarled, gripping his axe tight and raising his bolt pistol over the horde, towards the deep crimson aureole of the monster's face.

He should withdraw.

This was unanticipated. No one could have anticipated it.

The wiser move would be to retire to take stock, to plan. He had not risen to the prominence and favour he now enjoyed by being a slave to the Butcher's Nails, but he could no longer think for his fury.

There was nothing he could think to do except stand there in the path of the eruption, gun in hand, and scream: 'No!'

He fired.

Time slowed, as though pure hatred had the mass to warp its flow around it. He heard the explosion of every shell as it cleared the barrel, and then the second as rocket propellant flared and sped it towards its target. A third round of explosions detonated through the daemon primarch's mouth and failed to slow it at all. Because no one had ever felled a god with a bolter. Not even a bolter wielded with hate.

And Angron roared, and raged at his son's impotence. And killed.

The Apothecary, Lorekhai, screamed as he unloaded his pistol into his father's chest. He screamed as a sword of black bronze smote him in two. The runes stamped across the blade ignited like bonfires in the darkness as immortal Lorekhai's soul was pulled in and incinerated. Too berserk to have noticed the Apothecary's fate, Mohgrivar sent a jet from his flamer attachment spurting across the primarch's shoulder. A valedictory burst of static tore from his helmet grille as the primarch, his shoulders on fire, struck his legs from his torso. Shalok the Skulltaker swung his enormous executioner's axe. As fast as a shadow ahead of the flame, Angron parried. Shalok's axe broke against the colossal chainaxe wielded in the primarch's right hand, explosions travelling the length of the haft until they arrived at his hands. The violence behind the parry shattered every bone in both the warrior's arms and kicked him back, snapping his neck instantly. Vigious Khovain did not even try to fight. His father butchered him just the same.

Angron. The name whirled through Kossolax's head as the best and brightest he had gathered to him over the centuries burnt up around him like flies in a fire trap. *Angron Angron Angron.*

'No, no, no!'

He held the bolt pistol's trigger down until there were no more explosions, only aware that he had been backing away when his foot disappeared over the edge of the dais and he fell.

The descent was far shorter than his tortuous climb.

He hit the command deck like a barrel that had been kicked off the edge of a cliff.

The Four were dead.

With a sound like a city collapsing into flame, Angron spread his wings and bellowed. Rivets popped from the bulkheads. Glass terminals shattered. Metal squealed and bent, melting, running, pockets of thin air igniting as reality tasted the ascension of a primarch. The Chaos Space Marines and Mutilators that Kossolax had left stationed by the door charged in as though unable to resist his pull, the former unloading their bolters into their monstrous father's breastplate while the latter manifested ever larger and larger weapons as they closed the distance.

Kossolax did not stop to watch them die.

He was no longer thinking at all. The Butcher's Nails had finally taken that ability from him. Instead, he did the one thing he knew he should have the moment he saw that furious colossus striding from the fire.

He spun around, gauntleted fingers scrabbling for purchase on the deck as the last of his warriors were slaughtered behind him, dragging up his axe from where it had fallen, and ran.

ACT TWO

IN THE BLOOD

CHAPTER EIGHT

Leidis and his brothers crowded around the broad, trapezoidal canopy of their shuttle and looked out onto the unusually congested void. The Dauntless-class light cruiser that had brought them this far, the *Oath of Saint Gremulus*, had refused to bear them any further and so they had abandoned it in favour of the shuttle. Its simpler machine spirit had crumbled more readily under Corvo's hexamathic tortures, while its smaller size had given Leidis and the others ample time to obliterate the Imperial iconography from its hull and have Ginevah repaint it in World Eaters red.

While the others looked ahead, Leidis craned his neck back.

The *Oath* was half a million miles behind them but still massive, two and a half miles and twenty million tons of Imperial ship of the line, dark green and gold armour as effective as camouflage against the blackness of the void. Its gunnery glinted as it crossed the incident angle of the local star and into daylight, dawn rising across the giant aquila stamped upon its steepled hull.

He smiled to himself as he watched her die.

There was something artful about death in the void. The way pockets of trapped atmosphere burnt off in stages, radiation rippling the blazes into abstract shapes before the airlessness of the surrounding void smothered them back. Like a trapped animal, struggling against the constraints of a transparent bag.

The light cruiser came apart under the sustained broadsides and prow lances of the World Eaters warships that had been lying in wait around the Mandeville point majoris. Leidis counted no fewer than five of them. They had been waiting for any excuse to unshackle their guns and the *Oath*, defiantly broadcasting Imperial transponder codes to the last, had provided. Even if Leidis and his brothers had left her with a living shipmaster and a command crew, she would never have stood a chance.

The *Oath* had been a good ship, but she had done what was required of her, and so now she could die.

The flames perished in the vacuum, the last glowing pieces of the *Oath of Saint Gremulus* spinning off to find new homes amongst the gases and debris left over from the system's creation to baffle future historitors, and Leidis turned away, joining his brothers in staring wordlessly forwards.

Leidis was younger than many of his new brothers, but he was no stranger to total war.

He had participated in wars that had sprawled across star systems. He had engaged in sector-wide campaigns drawing their millions-strong forces from every arm of the Imperial war machine he could name. He had been privileged to be waging war on Silens Anchorage when the Crusade of Extermination had broken warp for resupply there: five hundred warships of the Imperial Navy and a dozen Chapters of the Adeptus Astartes, carrying between them a billion men and machines, all bound out beyond the plane of the galactic disc for the Mu-4 globular cluster and the alien power that claimed those ancient stars.

But he had never seen a muster on the scale of that currently taking place around Kalkin's Tribune.

'There must be a thousand ships out there,' Via Ginevah murmured.

The human armswoman, alone amongst the transhuman giants, was strapped into her seat. It belonged to a short row of seating at the rear of the cockpit, with stowage webbing hanging from the seat backs and equipment lockers built into the aft bulkhead. She was half Leidis' chronological age of sixty Terran-sidereal years, but looked older. Age had dimmed her, but only somewhat, favourable genetics and the training regimen available to an Eden armswoman keeping her fitter than most women her age could expect to be.

'Two thousand,' Corvo growled back from the pilot primaris' couch. 'And likely more.'

'And where...?'

Leidis licked his lips. They were drier even than usual.

As a Space Marine he felt no fear, but in the presence of something so appallingly beyond his own existence as he was from common humanity, he knew awe. The unfiltered chatter of two thousand warships and more hissed out of the shuttle's basic vox set-up, and with the perfection of Space Marine hearing, he heard what they spoke of. Why so many like them had come.

He knew what was waiting for them over Kalkin's Tribune.

Angron.

'Where is the primarch?' he murmured.

No one answered. Aside from the snarl of the vox and the occasional proximity alert bleep from the shuttle control board, the cockpit was silent.

Arkhor the Redbound pressed his face to the viewing shield, bionic eye clicking loudly as he gazed hungrily into the busy void. The warleader reeked of stale sweat, unwashed armour and broken-down battle hormones. The skin around his temples fluttered, the Butcher's Nails, pulsing directly into the warleader's brain. The right side of his black-skinned face was lifeless and slack, brutalised by debilitating strokes, the corresponding limbs whirring with jury-rigged bionics, but Leidis envied him his tangible connection to his demigod father.

All Leidis had of his own gene-sire were crippling nightmares and the Thirst.

'There,' said Arkhor, pressing a bionic finger to the armaglass canopy. 'Our father.'

The World Eaters armada was neither orderly nor static. Battleships jostled for prime orbits around the wreck of Kalkin's Tribune like predators vying for the warmth and status of the pack. Debris shorn off in glancing collisions, both accidental and wholly deliberate, cluttered the world's orbits like a nascent ring system. Firefights twinkled in the darkness of the planet's shadow as warships the size of cities dumped continent-destroying firepower into their rivals' shields.

Leidis held his breath, feeling something akin to mortal dread, as their shuttle passed under the firing solutions of dedicated warships a thousand times their tonnage. The shuttle's butchered transponder shrieked its corrupted identifiers into the void and Leidis practically felt the monsters' breath on his neck as they sniffed its binharic scent.

One by one the great ships of the World Eaters armada gave way, sliding aside above and below, until Leidis saw what Arkhor had been pointing towards.

The battleship hung in a dense clutter of orbital wreckage, like a mountain surrounded by the remnants of another. A flotilla of dependent craft was anchored around it in an escort formation. At first glance he took them to be frigates and ship tenders, and it was only with the shuttle's blurted auspex returns that Leidis looked again and saw that they were grand cruisers in their own right, made to look tiny by the unimaginably colossal scale of their parent vessel.

Leidis had seen star forts, hollowed-out asteroid bases and orbital dockyards that were objectively more massive, and yet for something clearly laid out to be *a ship* there was nothing in his experience that came close. It was a gladiator of the void, twelve and a half miles of bronzed hull and scavenged armour riven across its great length by deep, deep scars. It wore them as proudly as any killer would.

'What is that?'

'The flagship of the old Legion,' said Arkhor. There was a melancholy in his voice that Leidis had never heard before, but he was too awestruck by that mighty vessel to wonder at it. 'The *Conqueror*.'

Excitement tingled through Leidis' armour.

'*Conqueror*.'

He breathed the syllables out.

A name from myth, a word befitting a legend.

Hearing it, thinking it in the silence of his own head, was not enough to make it real. There was a primarch aboard that ship. Not a fable. Not a parable to be repeated ad nauseum to warn of the hubris inherited by lesser souls from the Emperor's perfect sons and the perils of giving into the Red Thirst and the Black Rage, but an actual, living primarch.

Who else but a primarch, after all, could howl into the warp with such fury that even the Navigators aboard the *Oath of Saint Gremulus* had seen it, unable to turn away even as their faces melted and their warp eyes bled?

Leidis felt it still. Drawing him in. Challenging him to step aboard.

'It is not too late to turn back,' Ginevah murmured.

Arkhor glanced over his shoulder, drool trickling over his lifeless lip and down the synthetic plates of his chin. For a moment, he looked almost sympathetic. No sooner had the thought occurred, however, than the expression altered again. Arkhor's forehead sank, blood vessels popping across both eyes and turning them red. Metal squealed overhead as an abrupt surge of strength tightened his fingers on the ceiling grip-bars, and Ginevah shrank fearfully into her crash couch.

'It was too late before we even came,' he hissed, visibly forcing himself to leave her be and turn back to the forward view.

Leidis thought back to the day he had fled Eden and the fortress-monastery of the Angels of the Grail. He had not explicitly commanded her to leave with him, but neither had he exactly allowed her a decision about whether or not to do so. He had left and so she had followed. The serfs of Eden were exceptional in many ways, but if Ginevah and those like her had one deficiency then it was in their capacity for free will.

Such qualities were rarely held in high regard.

'Be silent,' Leidis growled at her.

As his brothers liked to remind him, they valued Ginevah more than they did him – she kept their armour functioning and their guns firing – but all it would take was for one of them to snap and the woman would die.

She bowed her head, and swiftly averted her eyes.

'You serve me well, Via,' he rumbled. 'You have always served me well.'

'You are too fond of her,' said Verroth.

Leidis grunted, refusing to be drawn.

'Entering broadcast range,' Corvo snapped.

With the fingers of his mechanical hand, Arkhor wiped spittle from his chin, the oily flicker of the *Conqueror*'s broadside running lights picking out the metals scaffolding his left side. His expression was characteristically unreadable, but his bloodshot eyes were full of rage. 'Open vox...'

'Signal,' the abhuman at the vox drawled. He was in a bronze fort, hunched over a semicircle of red-lit screens and communications handsets, attended by a number of similarly immense brutes wearing the shreds of officers' uniforms.

It had been many weeks since Angron's return, but daemonic incursions from below decks had become hourly occurrences since then, and the rate of adaptation amongst the crew had been necessarily swift. Crude fortifications of bone, thermoplas and brass had risen to encircle the most critical infrastructure, muscular brutes with bronze spears and battered autorifles glaring balefully from their rudimentary ramparts.

'*Store the frequency code and transponder coordinates and queue it in the system bank for a response,*' the Mistress whispered, and though the hulking Master of Vox gave no sign of acknowledging her presence, he stored the frequency code and transponder coordinates just the same. '*Port thrusters to full power,*' she continued, passing through the vox-bastion's walls and drifting across the deck. '*Main drive at one-eighth.*' As though triggered by her passage, lead shutters clattered down over the viewing portals in her wake. Live feeds from the outer hull went dark. Power was tithed from astrogation and main drive, triggering several skirmishes amongst their degenerate crews that were swiftly and brutally quelled. The disquieting hum of Geller generators building to charge grated through Kossolax's Nails, as though the spirit of Vigious Khovain were at his shoulder, whispering warp coordinates in his ear. '*Pull us out of orbit and into a full burn towards the nearest safe translation point at L-two. Lock down all systems for warp transit.'*

Too angry to sit, Kossolax surrendered to the impulse to push himself up out of his throne and pace. He loathed himself for the weakness, but did not force himself to stop, making and unmaking fists with the *crack* of as-yet-unhealed bone armour.

Pausing in front of the skull throne, he stabbed the vox activation rune worked in brass into the panel on the arm.

'How long until the *Conqueror* is fully ready to breach realspace?'

The voice at the far end of the link was lagged by the miles of interior bulkheads and containment fields it was forced to cross in order to reach him. A conventional Space Marine barge could rely on hardlines, but this was no conventional barge. *'The furnaces will arrive at temperature in an hour, lord regent. I estimate another two to three hours to achieve translation coordinates.'* Kossolax did not recognise the voice. From its depth and tenor, it was one of the human serfs whose gene-lines he had been weeding for obedience traits and mutational purity since before his rediscovery of the *Conqueror.*

'That is not enough time to draw all my warriors back from Kalkin's Tribune. Delay it.'

'Lord regent, I have tried. The ship overrules every command I give.'

Kossolax listened in on the background static for a moment before answering. 'Cull the furnacemen. The plasma fires cannot reach temperature without bodies to feed them.'

'Lord regent, I have only two men with me here and there are thou–'

'You have your orders.'

With that, Kossolax withdrew his finger from the vox-rune in the throne's arm, killing the link before he could hear any more excuses.

He cursed his father.

He needed Mohgrivar for this. Even Khovain might have done more to affect a delay than these mortal technicians.

The past weeks should have provided him with ample time to find replacements from the warbands, but Angron had stuck his boot into Kossolax's plans as only Angron could. Kossolax had tried locking down the primarch's deck, sealing every potential route in or out with force fields, flooded it with flesh-eating gases, stationed guards, but Kossolax could no more contain Angron than he could his own hatred for him.

The primarch had descended onto Kalkin's Tribune to join the slaughter there, and turned Kossolax's long-prepared conquest into a debacle.

World Eaters had abandoned their landing zones wholesale in order to flock to Angron's side. For many, this was their first encounter with their father's undiluted rage. It was a transformative experience, Kossolax knew, and little wonder it had broken what little sanity his warriors still possessed. Angron, with the World Eaters in tow, had spent the last weeks crushing city after city, suffering a level of attrition that might easily have been prevented had they struck at every city simultaneously, as Kossolax had intended.

Meanwhile, the Night Lords, the Death Guard and the more mercenary renegade commanders under his sway had quietly returned to their ships and slunk away in the anarchy.

Kossolax felt a stab of rage that, for once, was entirely of his own making.

He had worked for millennia towards the restoration of his Legion.

What had Angron *ever* done to earn the might he possessed?

All that he had ever been had been gifted to him, all that he had gone on to achieve had been pushed onto him by others.

And now he returned, as though he could just take it all back. The Legion. The flagship.

Kossolax bared his teeth and scowled.

There could not have been two beings less alike in this universe than Kossolax the Foresworn and his father. Kossolax refused to drift, to rise or be wrecked as the tides of the warp dictated his fate. He would turn this outrage to his advantage.

He would make Angron's return work in the service of *his* ambitions.

'Signal,' the Master of Vox drawled again.

It was the fiftieth hail that half hour.

His allies might have cut their losses, but over the weeks since Angron's return the system's Mandeville points had never been free of incoming World Eaters ships. Some once-in-a-millennium conjunction of Angron, the *Conqueror* and the slaughter they would enact together had lit a beacon in the warp that every World Eater on this side of the Rift could see. Kossolax's fleet had already grown by a factor of twelve and more were still coming, the *Conqueror*'s belligerent vox-equipment overflowing with the demands of system warlords and pirate kings to speak with their primarch, hear his voice and bask in the aura of his infernal presence.

As if Angron would have cared.

Even when Angron had shared in his sons' mortality, Kossolax could have counted on one hand the World Eaters he had tolerated in his presence. Ten thousand years on from that insult, the careless scorn of his father still stung like a slap across the jaw.

'What do you want with my ship?' he muttered to himself.

He was no restless berzerker, nor a fool like the thousands now piling into the system, desperate to throw themselves into whatever crusade their doomed demigod of a father might lead them to.

He was Kossolax, the Foresworn of Chaos, and he would rule.

'Master of Vox,' he growled.

The abhuman in ripped officer's whites produced an irked look, as though pestered by a voice he could not quite place, and lifted his head.

With a single shot from his bolter, Kossolax calmly blew it off, spraying his disrespect messily across the two-hundred-and-seventy-degree array of communication read-outs.

'Vox,' he said again.

A second bulky officer stood more firmly to attention. 'Lord regent?'

Kossolax lowered the bolter to his lap.

The buzzing in his head eased.

This was better.

'Call up the last hail and put me through.'

The little box suspended above him buzzed and crackled, as though there was an insect inside it, angrily tearing paper. Shâhka watched it, too curious to be confused as to what he was doing inside a one-man torpedo or why, as the box's black mesh front vibrated in time to the noise, like a gag over a man's mouth. Screens carrying hypnotically soothing static filled his field of vision. Thick cushioning restricted his movement to the occasional twitch in response to the random misfiring of the Nails.

The little box trembled again.

'This is Kossolax Foresworn of the Conqueror. *Respond. To whom do I speak?'*

Shâhka growled, shuddering as the Nails sent pain spiking through the scarified grey meat of his brain. Kossolax. He knew that name. Knew it and hated it. He tossed his head to make the voice go away, but the crash padding of the boarding torpedo limited his movements. His followers preferred to keep him isolated, and restrained.

He did not know why.

'Because you are the monster that monsters made, said his Angel. *They fear you and they are right to.'*

Shâhka nodded to himself. There was truth in that. Somewhere. He let the thought go before the Nails could punish him for harbouring something so profound.

Thinking of Kossolax made him want to turn and flee, though he did not know why. Nor had he, yet. As badly as he wanted to, he did not believe that he could. The pull of the Angel was too strong.

'And what will you do when you find me?'

Shâhka felt the sour-meat stench of his father's scorn from somewhere behind his shoulder, and smiled.

To fight with Angron one more time?

Or, perhaps, just to fight him and kill him, as a part of him had always craved?

He stretched his jaw, working his tongue around his broken teeth and reminding himself how to speak. 'I haven't... decided... yet.'

'What was that?'

Shâhka stared at the quivering little box in confusion.

'Hear him', mocked the Angel. *'Chasing dreams I made sure were dead thousands of years ago.'*

'The Conqueror *and its fleet will be breaking system in the next few hours. I invite you all to come aboard, and pledge your fealty to the primarch.'*

Shâhka turned his head, as far as the tight quarters of the torpedo would allow, and glanced over his shoulder. In defiance of all probability, because there was clearly no room for it to be there, his Angel snarled back at him. Blood and strings of meat drooled from the rusted iron of its teeth, its eyes smouldering like coals in a red pit.

He turned back to the box. 'He knows I come for him.'

The box was silent a moment. *'You will not be invited again,'* it said, after a handful of seconds had elapsed, and then cut out.

The torpedo fell to quiet. The wall of static continued to hiss and buzz and spit above his eyes, but it no longer had the calming effect it had had before.

Kossolax.

He knew that name.

'Kill him, and forget,' said the Angel.

Shâhka thought about it some more. 'Yes…'

The looted shuttle crossed a coherence field of unusually stiff surface tension, and glided onto a hangar deck that would have been large enough to receive the entirety of the *Oath of Saint Gremulus* side-on.

Hundreds of gunships, lighters and other light craft of unconventional design had already put down ahead of them, apparently wherever their pilots pleased, spilling red-armoured blobs into the gargantuan hangar as though their bellies had been cut. Nor were Arkhor's warriors the last to arrive, and the coherence envelope seething across the hangar's vast open wall continued to bulge and pop, a sea of liquid rock spitting out void craft. A coherence field was a thermodynamic barrier porous enough to allow large objects, like a shuttle, to pass unmolested, but there was something wilfully perverse about the *Conqueror's* envelope. It lapped over the bodywork, dragging, pooling between armour segments like a viscous fluid and visibly boiling off the paintwork before submitting to let a vessel pass.

As Leidis watched, an explosion lit up the shuttle's overhead canopy, a red-and-black Thunderhawk gunship that had been halfway through the field vomiting its flaming innards over the deck.

Leidis felt cold inside. It felt as though that could just as easily have been them.

'The *Conqueror* finds our craft worthy,' said Corvo. He was alone at the controls now, Arkhor and the others having retired to the aft compartments to make ready. 'You may express gratitude at your convenience.'

As they flew further in, descending relative to the plane of the deck, individual blobs within the crowd came into better view. Those who were not simply pouring out of their landing craft and fighting seemed to be gravitating towards the far end of the hangar. Leidis saw a large, raised platform there. It was probably a berth for some heavy class of transport that the Imperium had long since lost the knowledge or the facilities to build and which stood empty now, encircled by a jagged revetment of wrecked landers, shot down for the sin of attempting to land in that particular open space. A quartet of large individuals in shiny, almost liquescent red armour stood guard over the corners. Judging by their size and profile they could have been Terminators, but there was something ever so slightly off in their armament and outline that Leidis had not seen before and could not name.

His sense of nervous anticipation grew.

'There,' he said, rising from his seat and pointing down. 'I see an opening. It is narrow, but–'

With a small grimace, Corvo fired up the magna-meltas underslung from the shuttle's blunt nose and blasted the narrow space wider. Deploying landing gear, he set them down in the molten slurry leaking across the deck from the now-gutted Stormraven berthed alongside. That had not been strictly necessary, but Corvo had been itching for the chance to fire the shuttle's guns and so he had fired the guns. In spite of the doubts he could feel wriggling in his insides, Leidis could not deny that there was something *permissive* in the air that excited him.

There was a jolt as the shuttle's landing stage clawed into the hangar deck plate, followed by a sigh as it settled into its berth and locked.

Leidis felt a faint churn in his guts as the craft slaved itself to the *Conqueror*'s more bellicose gravity.

While Corvo powered down the engines and spat a prayer to the shuttle's tortured spirit, Leidis picked up his bolter and held it like a talisman.

They had just set down on the *Conqueror*. A Gloriana. Built to dominate the void at a time when the Emperor of Mankind had still walked.

He found himself wondering how different things might be had He been amongst them still. If He had not fallen in the defence of Terra. Would the galaxy have plotted the same path into decay as Leidis had witnessed? Would the fundamentalism of his brothers have forced him onto the same road? He had never thought to wonder, until then, if the Imperium had been a flawed project from its outset or if the Emperor had been failed by the lesser character of His successors.

Leidis was not a true son of Angron, after all. He had not inherited heresy, but he had chosen it. It was surely right of him to ask these questions although, as Arkhor had reminded his armswoman, it was somewhat late in the day for them.

He gave his head a violent shake as though to cast them out.

The worst breed of doubt, he had always found, was that which had no answer.

It had all been so much simpler when he had just swallowed the Chapter's doctrine without thinking about it at all. Human life was beautiful and precious, or so the Chaplains of Eden had taught, the seed that the Emperor had scattered over a dark and hostile cosmos. Taking a life, even one that had allowed itself to waste for want of His light, was a sin that needed to be atoned for.

One lash for a life taken. A full lunar cycle in the Tower of Purgatory, alone with the Thirst, for the greater evil of enjoying it.

Leidis had spent more time in the Tower than he had with his own brothers. His back was more scar tissue than skin. It had given him a great deal of time to nurse his Thirst, and to ponder all that was wrong in the Imperium of Man.

'Are we ready?' Arkhor the Redbound appeared in the cabin door.

In the time it had taken the shuttle to intercept the *Conqueror*'s heading and dock, the warleader had made himself magnificent. The brass edging of his armour shone again as it had not in months. His red cloak had been pressed flat and worked over with a steel brush, drawing out jagged-edged symbols that Leidis had never even noticed it carried. Parchment scraps bearing written characters in a language Leidis could not read had been stapled to his armour. Old bloodstains had, apparently, been reapplied. He had also donned a helmet. Leidis had only seen him wear it once. In his right hand, the warleader bore a heavy-bladed axe. In his left was a plasma pistol of byzantine design, florid with radiators and fans that accounted for half the weapon's prodigious bulk.

He looked every inch an Eater of Worlds.

Verroth, Strykid and Lestraad gathered behind him.

Their worn, muddy and mismatched plate had been buffed to the point that Leidis could almost see the varied hues of the paint under the grime. Leidis scanned their unhelmed faces, expecting to see the growing sense of excitement he felt mirrored there. Strykid was broken. Lestraad was mad. Verroth was a snake. Arkhor's visor, of course, betrayed nothing but the glitter of his lenses.

'I am ready,' said Leidis.

'Ready,' Ginevah echoed.

The armswoman had changed into the blood-red bodysleeve and cream carapace top layer of a Chapter-serf. She drew a hand-sculpted autopistol fitted with a tracking scope from its holster, testing the ease of the draw, and checked the load and the cleanliness of the engraved barrel before reholstering it. The weapon was a cherished heirloom, the etched figures of angels putting the sword to the witch, the alien and the heretic around its filigreed grip. At the opposite hip, she wore a sword with an angel-winged crosspiece and a garnet pommel.

Leidis grunted.

'Get on with it,' Corvo growled.

With his good hand, Arkhor pulled a panel away from the wall and punched in a short command sequence. The deployment ramp began to descend, the sound and fury of the *Conqueror*'s main assault deck taking the opening to seize the shuttle's rear compartment.

'It is time to meet your brothers,' he said.

CHAPTER NINE

Leidis had seen the crowds on entry and been prepared for them, but the din from the assault deck still took him aback. It was the whine of corrupted voxmitters, the whine of failing power armour. The air was hazy with rust. It was close and tasted stale, leaving a greasy feeling on the lips from the accumulation of weapon oils and the chemical breakdown products of Space Marine battle hormones. It curdled on the tongue, tingling against the neuroglottis, spicy with the fissile heat of more World Eaters Space Marines than Leidis would have believed existed in the galaxy. There must have been ten thousand in this hangar alone, and who knew how many elsewhere, crewing the ship and aboard their own vessels.

He ducked his head on instinct as a bolter barked from somewhere across the hangar. An answering rattle sounded from elsewhere, like wolves snarling at one another over an echoing battlefield.

A Space Marine stumbled into him as he descended the ramp,

fed up to them by the crush. His lenses burned as though the openings had been punched into his helmet with a hellgun, aggression rasping from his bent grille as Leidis shoved him back into the crowd.

The World Eaters pressed in close, most of them as motley in their appearance as Arkhor's band and, in a few cases, even more so. In ones and twos, they staggered out of gunships that an ork would have been privileged to fly, as though drunk on the hostility in the air. These comprised the majority of the Space Marines in the hangar, renegades and pirates, lone warriors with cracked helms or wild, lost looks, as if uncertain who they were or what was happening around them.

Then there were those that Leidis, in his secret heart, had been hoping to find, for if not here, on the *Conqueror*, then where?

The true World Eaters.

They stood out like the brass knuckles on a bloody fist, recognisable even amongst the riot of paint schemes and armour marks, gathered in company strength or greater around purring gunships and clad in huge suits of matching plate. Hooded machine-priests scuttled around them, tending to the rumbling war machines while bloodstained battle standards and trophy poles wafted in the hot breath of their engine fans.

'Out of my way,' Arkhor snarled, laying into the crush with the flat of his axe.

Corvo deployed his heavy bolter sideways-on, like an enforcer with their riot shield, while Lestraad stared about him, wild-eyed, and Strykid merely held one hand out as though feeling for the walls of the shuttle and wondering why they weren't there. Verroth smiled, plotting a painful death with every sanguine nod to a World Eater snarling in his face.

Leidis held his bolter close, uncertain whether to fire into the crowd or not. This was turning into something more like a boarding action than the reception he had had in mind. 'Stay between us,' he told Ginevah, holding his bolter one-handed while he shoved the armswoman roughly after Verroth and the others.

In hindsight, they would have been better leaving her behind to watch over the shuttle. It would be too easy for a mortal to get herself killed out here.

Leidis looked over the mad, frothing sea of bestial helms and scarred faces, as though appearances alone could tell him which of these warriors bore the Butcher's Nails and which did not. Arkhor had been unwilling or unable to tell him much about what the implants did, how they functioned, or how they were to be obtained. But now he was here, and with every World Eater still at large in the galaxy, or so it seemed, clamouring around him.

They were all so *free*.

Here, he would have all the answers that he craved.

'Where is Angron?' Leidis roared, suddenly overwhelmed by frustration at their slow passage across the hangar.

With a whine of overexerted hydraulics, he turned his bolter onto the crowd and opened fire, mowing down half a dozen warriors closest to him. Answering volleys rattled off nearby. One of the downed warriors gurgled as he sat back up, a string of mass-reactive wounds cratering his chest.

Leidis lowered his bolter and hissed.

'Where is he?'

'He was on the – *hnnng!* – the planet,' said Arkhor, his own belligerence triggering the Butcher's Nails as he pushed on into the space that Leidis had created. Blood flecked the bars of his helmet grille as he stoved in a World Eater's face with the back of his axe. 'He butchers the corpse-worshippers of Kalkin's Tribune to the last skull and drop of blood.'

'Then why are we here and not there?' Leidis snarled back.

Corvo spat on the deck. 'To make blood oaths to the Foresworn, of course.'

'Kossolax is master of this ship,' said Arkhor. 'I knew him once and he has grown mighty since. He commands the strongest warriors, and is held in the highest favour by the gods. Kneel to him, and perhaps he will lift us high too. The primarch will not.'

Leidis grunted, fighting to keep a hold of Ginevah only to find himself drawn into a tussle with a large warrior in spiked armour messily adorned with white diamond patterns. More warriors in a similar livery, fifty of them at least, were spilling out of the jumble of fallen plasteel girders and cooling metal slurry that was partially burying a small flotilla of crumple-nosed boarding torpedoes.

His boots squealed across the deck as the larger, heavier warrior pushed him back. He mag-locked them, his whole body tilting backwards as the World Eater battled to extricate his hands from Leidis' and get his fingers in under his helm.

Leidis could taste the burnt brain matter on the breath blasting out through the warrior's grille. The massive hormone cascade triggered by the Butcher's Nails had a chemical odour that Leidis had come to recognise, and provided the other warrior with a surge of strength that he struggled to match.

Warning tones blurted from his armour systems as his joints bent into positions that Mark VIII power armour had not been articulated to assume.

He ignored them.

'*Hnnng!*' the warrior snarled, digging his gauntleted fingers into the soft fibre bundles located around Leidis' throat as though his intent was to rip his head clean off.

Verroth, he saw, had been similarly engaged. The number of warriors piling out of their boarding torpedoes had driven a wedge between the pair of them and the rest of the warband. Ginevah, closer to Verroth now than to Leidis, ripped her artificer pistol from its holster and threw a look at Leidis.

'Shoot. The. Bastard,' he hissed around the gauntlet crushing his windpipe.

She opened fire, auto-rounds rattling harmlessly off the World Eater's armour.

His foe simply snarled at him.

From the corner of his eye, he caught a flash of movement and heard a crunch of ceramite. He risked a look away and saw that Verroth was no longer where Leidis had last seen him. He was on the ground ten yards further back with a gouge from some kind of horn in his buckled plastron.

An ogre of red meat and bleeding ceramite pawed at the deck in his place.

Leidis gawped.

His grip on his own opponent slackened as his strength turned to water.

The thing was a Space Marine, or once had been. Whatever had happened to it since then was beyond Leidis' power to imagine. At half again Leidis' height, it towered over the spreading melee. Only the gunships were bulkier, and even then, not always. Its armour was ropey and thick, individual plates straining against one another like muscle. Its head was slightly larger than a normal Space Marine's, but the two mountains of ceramite that made up its shoulders made it look tiny. The fusion of face and helmet had left its features a livid pink, its skull ridged and bald. Its teeth were crooked bronze pegs, its eyes a harsh radioactive green. A pair of heavy, reptilian wings hung from its back like a pair of gibbeted skeletons.

Ginevah turned her autopistol as it snorted and rampaged towards her. A flurry of auto-rounds went buzzing towards it, but the thing was so implausibly fast that she missed completely. Fortunately for her it ignored her, trampling over Strykid instead as though the Space Marine were constructed of straw bales, and reached Lestraad. The renegade warrior had an axe in either hand, but the monster had ripped his head from his shoulders before he had even seen what was coming, and a near-immortal Space Marine lay slain, as though the act had been no effort at all. Blood jetted from Lestraad's torn neck and bent before it could hit the World Eater's armour, whipping around its huge frame like a serpent repelled by the touch of ceramite.

'Lord!' Ginevah yelled, hastily correcting her aim as the monster bulled straight through Corvo and squared up to Arkhor.

Ginevah's expression was one of sheer terror.

The warleader squeezed off a white-hot blast from his plasma pistol that glanced off his attacker's armour before the monster had him by the throat and heaved him nine feet from the deck.

Leidis felt the hot, brazen touch of greatness shiver down his neck. Here before him now was a true champion of the World Eaters.

Leidis felt torn.

Was this not what he sought here?

But, in spite of everything he had sacrificed to come this far, he was still a Space Marine – the fraternal bonds of brotherhood still meant something.

Meanwhile, the World Eater in the diamond-pattern wargear had taken advantage of the distraction, shoving Leidis to the ground and pulling a bronze knife from a pocket of flesh that appeared to be a part of the warrior's plackart plate.

Leidis, however, was still holding his bolter.

With space between them and his arm now free, he put two shots in the warrior's plastron and one more in the plackart, cratering the ceramite and staggering him, if not slaying him outright, before turning his aim onto the champion.

Leidis had always excelled in marksmanship.

Sergeant Alkaios of the Tenth Company had once commended him for his keen eye, for his ability to draw blood at any range.

From supine, he fired off a burst that sent shots ricocheting from the champion's impenetrable skull and exploding amongst the crowd.

It turned from the thrashing Arkhor, then jerked its head as though experiencing a sudden stab of pain from within. 'I'm not...' it growled, in a voice like that of a Predator column rolling across a road laid with armoured corpses. 'I'm not... *hnnng!*'

Leidis sprayed another burst across the beast's body, which it ignored as surely as it had the one to its head, eyes focusing on the thin air between Leidis and where Verroth was picking himself up.

'No!' it roared, hurling Arkhor aside, and flailing at the empty space with which it appeared to have been speaking.

Leidis resisted the urge to shoot it again.

It would do him no good.

He lowered the bolter to his chest as the champion transformed before his eyes, shrinking to a scale more in keeping with the size of its head, reabsorbing its wings, livid features softening and blanching to leave a figure gaunt, pale and hideously ugly, and screaming something about his 'Angel'.

The World Eaters that Leidis and Verroth had been wrestling with drew back, snapping and twitching like rabid dogs at the end of a long chain, desperate to fight and kill but drawn instead to gather up their struggling champion and drag him back towards the crash site left by their torpedoes.

Elsewhere, the fight carried on without them, every renegade band and lone killer eager to shed the blood of their brothers in this most symbolic of places.

This, it occurred to Leidis to think, was freedom.

Verroth raised his bolt pistol towards the retreating World Eaters, unwilling to let them go so lightly. 'Everyone here is insane,' he opined, but before he could squeeze on the trigger a blizzard of heavy weapons fire sounded off from the central platform like a vox-horn. Several dozen World Eaters closest to the dais went down, silenced by sheer firepower, as Leidis, Verroth and Ginevah, mirroring the actions of thousands of others, lowered their weapons and turned as one towards the platform.

Kossolax the Foresworn had come.

The brass-plated Land Raider rolled back from the platform's edge with a growl of its daemonically charged engines. Its twin autocannons delivered another warning blast, Foresworn Terminators and hulking Helbrutes positioned throughout the hangar gratuitously relaying the message. As the echoes rang out, the discordant bray of a Mutilator squad's corrupted vox-horns announced Kossolax the Foresworn to the platform.

The gantry had been engineered to accommodate Angron's brutally up-armed Stormbird gunship and had borne his Land Raider without complaint, but under the weight of Kossolax's armoured tread it visibly shuddered. The air did something similar. It was oily and thick, vibrating with the howling of a hundred idling gunships and landers, with the nuclear *thrum* of thousands upon thousands of armoured Space Marines.

Kossolax allowed himself a moment to absorb it all.

A Legion.

The Butcher's Nails tingled at what Angron had unwittingly dumped in his lap.

Any world beyond Terra herself would be within his powers

to destroy, and not since the days of Terra had the World Eaters gathered together in such strength.

It did not concern him that it was Angron, and not he, who had called them, or that their roars of acclamation now were not for him.

Angron was a storm.

Where he howled, the World Eaters drew armoured shutters and tacked their sails, riding headlong with the wind at the risk of being capsized and dashed on the empyrean's rocks. He was functionally a god, but he was elemental, a deity who would suffer no worship, tolerate no offerings and answer no prayers except those that could be rewarded in blood. The force that bound father to sons was deep, however, and the mutable laws of distance and time. Kossolax did not have to understand or like it. Angron and the World Eaters were bound by shared blood and mutual hate.

When he called, the World Eaters could not help themselves but answer.

Kossolax approached the rostrum at the platform edge. The Mutilators were being kept busy holding back the crowd. The Terminator-sized brutes punched down into the throng, their weapons buzzing, sawing, snapping, whining as they extruded increasingly deadly variants from their fists between blows.

The hangar heaved with a force of tens of thousands, and hundreds of individual melees. Most were World Eaters in name only. Their armour came in every variant known to the Imperium of Man and the gods of Chaos. The void craft that had ferried them to the *Conqueror* from their own ships were equally brutish and hard-wearing. But the primarch had summoned them all the same, just as he had those armoured in red and brass and gathered under the tattered remnants of the old Legion's banners.

All who shed blood praise Khorne. Whether they wish it or not.

Someone had said those words once. Khârn's wearisome Word Bearer pet, perhaps. He had not understood them then, but he knew more now than any one soul could ever unlearn.

Regardless of heritage and blood, these warriors were all World Eaters in spirit.

Towering over the raucous horde from the platform's edge, Kossolax found himself torn between the conflicting impulses to address them as he had intended, and having the command deck disengage the coherence field and blast the unruly lot of them into the void.

Beginning anew from first principles and pure gene-seed was a tempting thought.

The Butcher's Nails responded with an approving tingle, but he resisted the all-too-brief surge of pleasure.

The *Conqueror* would not have allowed it in any case.

The ship had never been particularly protective about the short-lived microbiome that had colonised its halls, but when Kossolax's commands stood between it and battle, or when he actively threatened it with harm, it always found the means to deny him.

In light of Angron's return, he could not shake the conviction that the *Conqueror* was sparing his warriors for a purpose.

Angron's purpose.

'I am Kossolax the Foresworn,' he yelled, pitching his voice deep and loud, routing it through the Mutilator squad's vox-horns and through the satellite augmitters his enginseers had rigged throughout the hangar so that a hundred versions of him growled in almost-unison over every pocket of mayhem. 'I am the lord regent of the Twelfth,' he went on, even as his opening pronouncement was still ringing over the deck's more distant quarters. 'I slew my brothers on Ghenna. I betrayed humanity on Isstvan. I stood with our father as he put Nuceria to flame, and I watered the ground of Terra with the blood of billions who had once hailed us as saviours. The primarch returns to wage war again.'

The World Eaters responded to his pronouncement with a bloodthirsty howl, beating chainaxes on breastplates and firing bolt pistols into the air. The coherence field wobbled, as though it might fail of its own accord after all, its instability causing the star fields that could be seen through it to bleed.

'Angron sees no one, but me. He speaks to no one, except through me. My word is his,' he roared, shouting the warriors down. 'Within the hour, the *Conqueror* will cross this system's Mandeville point and enter the warp.'

Never mind that he was ignorant of their destination. The *Conqueror* plainly knew Angron's mind and that would have to suffice him for now. Angron went nowhere if there was not to be a slaughter of epochal scale at the journey's end.

'There is no time now for you to return to your ships, so you will remain here for the duration of our transit.'

He spread his arms wide, basking in the adulation of the Legion.

His Legion.

'And then, my brothers, I will give you blood.'

CHAPTER TEN

The *Conqueror* and its pursuing fleet sailed for the great twilight between stars. To the outboard observer it was already glowing brighter, its shields haloed by a spectrum of unnameable colours. Drawing on its straining enginarium, fed by the blood, sweat, tears and souls of the thousands toiling within, it burned a hole into the fabric of realspace.

The flames of the unreal spilled through the ragged tear. Gibbering screams and the echoing pleas of the damned rang through the airless void until the hulls of the approaching ships trembled in sympathy. Claws from the other side tested the integrity of the boundary. Blinking eyes that would have swallowed worlds in their orbits blinked open and peered out, only to recoil as the *Conqueror* drove its spiked prow through the gash.

Ensconced in her hidden throne, in an abattoir of meat and brass, the daemonic entity that had become the Mistress peered into the maelstrom of emotion and insanity that constituted the warp.

She did so unafraid.

The *Conqueror* was as much a ship of the warp now as it was one of the void, much as she had in turn become its creature, leaving behind the human thing that parts of herself occasionally believed she still was. They had evolved beyond the need for anything so limiting as a Navigator. Through lidless eyes she could see the eldritch flows of the warp, plot its eddies and currents and swells, identify its dangerous shallows and foresee its brewing storms.

Those same senses allowed her to perceive the beacon that shone from far across the formless, directionless ocean.

It was not the Astronomican, the blazing lighthouse that oriented all travel in the galaxy to Terra as all roads had once been said to lead to the Romanii capitolis of Old Earth. By the guile of the Despoiler had that light been veiled from Imperium Nihilus, but the light of this beacon, though different, burned with the same unbearable flame. It was the light of the Emperor, the Anathema, and to a creature such as her, facing it was akin to performing a naked-eye survey of the surface of a sun.

And yet it was Angron's destination, and where the *Conqueror* demanded she go.

'Yes, lord,' she chittered to herself through needle-fine teeth.

The world was called Malakbael. This much she could intuit from the patterns in the warp. She did not know what awaited the World Eaters there, but if the Emperor, in ancient times, had sited one of His great works there then that was surely reason enough for Angron to wish to see it burn.

And that, as it must always be, was reason enough for her.

Shâhka Bloodless tossed in the hard alloy of his cot. The cell was empty. The door was barred on both sides. His own warriors feared him, even when he slept. He had no memory at all of how he had come to be there.

His warriors, meanwhile, had withdrawn to adjacent corridors and barricaded themselves in, drawing lots to decide who would remain on hand to subdue him in the event that he woke before the ship's journey was over. But he did not wake, not yet, even as he muttered in his sleep and rolled over, averting eyes that were already half-closed from dreams that few still living could ever have believed were true.

'No,' he mumbled, reaching up with his hands to grapple with something that could not be touched. 'No... I won't... Don't let it... No...'

Fifteen hundred feet of adamantine and steel and a single dream-thin bubble of reality shielding separated him from the horrors of his past, but the warp in Nihilus was restless, and there was something about this ship.

His past had never felt so close.

Kossolax's eyes snapped open.

His ancient flesh was too disciplined, even with the mind still half-unconscious, to wake up screaming, but the panicked cries he heard ringing inside his skull were all his own. Blinking like a revived corpse, he looked around. The suite of rooms he had occupied breathed around him like a dreaming animal, their bladed furnishings murmuring with the *Conqueror*'s rough passage through the warp.

A warp transit was fertile ground for bad dreams.

These chambers had originally been set aside for the primarch, when he had been mortal and at least notionally required such comforts, although even then Angron had seldom used them.

Over the years leading up to the primarch's ascension to daemonhood, the space had come to be used as a depositary for the numerous gifts and offerings of tribute he had accrued over the Great Crusade and into the Heresy. Within these rooms might have been discovered a hand-crafted treasure from the anvils of Nocturne, a gift that Magnus of Prospero had spent decades in selecting just for his brother, the crown jewel of a lost xenos empire or another unrecorded victim of compliance. Once objects entered Angron's keeping, all were treated with equal disdain. He had never cared for material possessions and had barely acknowledged the artefacts' existence, rarely even touching them himself before throwing them away. But they had been *his* possessions and any artefact associated with the primarch held power to those who would wear his crown.

Wooden dummies three times the height of a man wore scraps of armour. Blunted weapons gleamed dully from display racks. Others hung from walls alongside campaign trophies and standards ripped from enemy banner poles. There were no stasis fields, no conscious efforts at preservation, and yet the sound of blood spattering to the floor from naked blades continued unabated as it had for ten thousand years. Metals that should have crumbled to dust millennia ago somehow conspired to shine, as sharp as the day they had been interred, under the red-glazed lumens.

At a hurried glance, the chamber might have passed as the quarters of any Imperial admiral or loyalist Chapter Master, if not for the keepsakes' uncanny habit of rearranging themselves when no one was looking.

When Kossolax was more than usually enraged, weapons would position themselves closer as though jostling for his grasp. When he was frustrated, or in despair at how far his former Legion had fallen since the betrayal at Skalathrax, the standards to old glories and half-remembered triumphs invariably found themselves in line to catch his eye.

There were few other furnishings. Angron disdained comfort and despised those who required it. Kossolax could not recall ever seeing him seated, and never still, though it would be a lie to say he had known the primarch well. Angron had infamously never slept. On the rare occasions that sheer exhaustion overcame even a primarch's vigour, the Butcher's Nails would allow him no more than a few seconds before jolting him awake in a sleep-addled rage.

Little wonder that Angron had been thoroughly insane by the end. Everything about the primarchs had been engineered to be extraordinary. When they broke, they broke in ways mere mortals could not conceive.

Kossolax did sleep, but he did so upright, surrounded by the Legion's relics. It was no longer feasible for him to extricate himself from his armour, and the mass of it made retiring to his old cot impractical.

He had learned to tolerate it, as he had learned to adapt his expectations to the new challenges of the age.

Alerted to his awakening, the palatial doors at the far end of the chamber creaked ajar and a small cohort of thrall labourers shuffled warily inside. They wore beige robes, sandalled feet scraping on the worn carpet. The first to reach him bore compacted ladders that telescoped and interlocked into a scaffold around him. These, they installed while others approached bearing brass salvers and clean towels. Kossolax remained still throughout, suffering their attention as shrieking hand tools ground down the cancerous regrowth of his armour, soapy water, rags and scented oils erasing the evidence of a restless night's slumber from his face.

Kossolax had not always been mighty.

Even before Angron's return to his ship, he had been acutely aware of the transiency of power and never once taken it for granted. Angron, the Nucerian slave made unwitting galactic warlord, had undoubtedly known this just as well. Being powerful meant projecting the image of power.

While the menials laboured at their ritual, Kossolax felt himself drifting back to the memory that had shaken him from sleep.

He had never come closer to death than he had then.

The Emperor's vengeful angels had harried Kossolax's ship for months, picking off the wounded, the floundering and the weak from its escorts until there was nothing left. The *Conqueror* had left him to die that day. Captain Shâhka, his commander at the time, the last time he had ever recognised one, had finally taken leave of his ruined mind and fled, leaving Kossolax and the broken remnants of his assault company to fend for themselves. Kossolax had fought dutifully throughout the Horus Heresy, but *that* had been the day he had sworn vengeance on an unjust and uncaring universe, and taken his first unguided steps to becoming a champion of the Dark Gods.

He had vowed that day never to put his fate in another's hands and to never ever bow to another's rule.

A frustrated shudder broke through his self-control.

'I will not be a passenger on my own ship,' he muttered to himself.

For as long as the *Conqueror* remained in the warp, there was little to do but wait. This was one thing that the World Eaters did exceptionally poorly. Their sleep was never restful, and their sporadic attempts at training were rarely halted by bloodshed. They lacked the patience, or the mental stability, to distract themselves over a long voyage with duties unrelated to violence.

This had already been a longer transit than Kossolax would have attempted on a World Eaters ship, and he was mentally resigned to losing a tenth of his new warriors to battle, accident or self-harm by the time he finally learned of their destination.

Reluctantly, he came to the conclusion that there was only one creature aboard, besides Angron himself, who might have that information.

The Mistress.

While he pondered the unpalatable notion of making peace with the spirit who claimed control of his ship, an armsman wearing a red surcoat over heavy bronze armour marched in through the partially opened doors. The thrall bulged with muscle grafts and bulky augmetics, bringing him as close to a Space Marine stature as it was possible for a post-adolescent human male to attain. Kossolax preferred the service of such wretches in securing his personal quarters. World Eaters were unreliable, and wildly unpredictable. The saner ones had a habit of becoming ambitious.

At the foot of the busy scaffold, the warrior-thrall dropped to one knee and prostrated himself on the carpet. 'Forgive the intrusion, lord regent,' he growled, the extent of his surgical remodelling deepening his voice beyond any normal human register. 'I would not have come if it were not urgent.'

'Have you found me a suitable Warpsmith to replace Mohgri-var?'

The armsman shook his head. 'It is not that, lord.'

'Speak then.'

'It is the champion calling himself the Bloodless.' The warrior swallowed, never once lifting his face from the floor. 'He is loose.'

CHAPTER ELEVEN

Leidis, Corvo and Verroth took turns holding Arkhor down, lest he injure himself or kill one of them in attempting to do so. The proximity of the warp's powers, be it the attacks of a greenskin psyker or straightforward empyreal travel, had always worsened the warleader's regular mental seizures. Even for him, however, this journey had been painful.

Corvo had found a restraint chair in the emergency storage cache below the cargo deck and installed it in the engine block where it could siphon power directly from the shuttle's small furnace. Leidis' best guess was that this shuttle had been used to transport high-value prisoners as well as crew or, if nothing else, had been fully outfitted to do so. Electrical restraints plugged directly into the subject's nervous system, which struck Leidis as an elegant solution, but not one that had been calibrated to something of Arkhor's enormous size or vigour.

Whatever the Butcher's Nails were doing to Arkhor's brain,

they were more than equal to the chair's ability to impede them, and Leidis wore the busted servos and bruises to prove it.

When it was his brothers' shift, Leidis took to pacing the troop decks, boots ringing from the empty berths, consumed by thoughts of Arkhor and the Butcher's Nails.

What did he need to prove, and to whom, to win that kind of strength for himself? He recalled the strength in the World Eater's hands as the Bloodless' warrior had throttled him. It was strength that he wanted to possess.

That the Nails came with drawbacks, and quite clearly they came with drawbacks, left him unaffected.

He wanted them.

On the rare occasion that both Verroth and Corvo left the cockpit unoccupied, he would sit in the pilot secundis' chair and look hungrily over the World Eaters ships scattered over the hangar like scrap from an upended metal recycler. He yearned to be out there, taking what he sought for himself, but even he had to concede that this was not the best of times to be wandering the *Conqueror* alone. Every lowly human could tell stories of ships and their crews lost to the madness of the warp, and every Imperial soldier knew those stories were true. Leidis had seen such happenings for himself but never on a Space Marine vessel, or any ship this size, and certainly not to the extent that he was witnessing from the cockpit viewing shield of the shuttle. Whatever malignant effect the transit was having on Arkhor, it was being borne out a thousand times over amongst the World Eaters out there.

Leidis bitterly wondered, and not for the first time, if he was the only warrior aboard the *Conqueror* to be denied the Butcher's Nails; if Corvo, Verroth and even Strykid were mocking him behind his back. He ached from the need to punish something.

It only made him want them more.

Strykid was the only member of the warband who took no shift with Arkhor. He was too unreliable to be trustworthy.

Leidis wondered if *warband* was even the right word for what they now were. With Kraytn dead on Gremulid, Lestraad slain by the Bloodless and Arkhor incapacitated, even if only for the duration of their voyage, they were little more than a gang. Corvo had already started openly considering his options in a more powerful crew and, in spite of the obvious risks, had taken to spending ever greater periods of time amongst the World Eaters elsewhere on the deck.

When Strykid sat himself mutely in the pilot primaris' couch to stare out the nearest viewing portal, Leidis understood that he had been sent by Verroth to fetch him.

It was Leidis' turn in the engine block.

'He has been restive these last few hours,' Verroth smirked, wrestling their raging warleader back into the restraint chair as Leidis walked in to relieve him.

'The warp is...' Ginevah broke into a yawn, shaking her head as she leant forward to apply a cold press to Arkhor's brow and dab blood from his chin. 'Disturbed,' she finished. She looked as though the days in transit had aged her. Her face was creased with tiredness. If she had ever harboured the notion that the duties of a Chapter-serf were onerous, then being beholden to a renegade crew was a harsh awakening. She was the only one amongst them who had not slept, because no one had allowed her to do so.

It was a miracle of some sort that she remained loyal. He wondered if that was an admirable trait, or whether it betrayed a lack of imagination on her part. Treachery took on a different hue, he supposed, when it was closer to home.

'If I did not know better, I would think that... that...' She was still reluctant to say the name aloud. 'That *Angron* agitates it somehow.'

With a clap on the back that left Leidis cold, Verroth rose and left, leaving him and his exhausted armswoman alone.

'I. Went. Seeking. *Conqueror*. Once Before.' Alternating jolts of current from the chair's neural plugs made Arkhor jibber, words frothing from his lips without any kind of rhythm or cadence. Leidis stood behind the chair, arms around the high back and holding the warleader's shoulders down. 'Long. Ago. But. Angron. Was. Already. Gone. I. Never... Never...' He started to jerk, tears beading in his wild eyes, losing coherence as the Butcher's Nails throbbed underneath his temples. 'Never. Saw. My. Father.'

Ginevah muttered a short homily as she backed away. Whether out of ignorance, habit or some lingering hope that her master might yet return to reason, she persisted in reciting the exact same prayers to the Emperor and the Great Angel that she had been taught on Eden.

It amused Leidis too much for him to correct her.

She sat down wearily at one of the workbenches.

'Where?' Arkhor started to flail. Leidis turned his face away to spare it the warleader's blows and leant harder into his shoulders. 'Where. Is. Angron?'

Verroth had not been lying.

'Why do they do this to themselves?' Ginevah asked quietly, as though thinking aloud rather than posing a genuine question.

Arkhor slumped back into the chair as its primitive machine-mind overcompensated for his aggression with a jolt powerful enough to overload his nervous system.

He would be peaceful for a minute or two.

Leidis released his hold around the warleader's neck and took the brief respite to loosen his muscles. Even delirious and semi-conscious, Arkhor was so much stronger than Leidis could dream of becoming without the Butcher's Nails.

'They do it for the strength,' he said.

'At the cost of this?' Her eyes drifted to Arkhor, slumped in his chair and growling in the half-sleep of shock. 'The degradation of the body. The destruction of the mind.'

In his chair, Arkhor was beginning to sweat, the Butcher's Nails stoking his metabolism to a fury his unconscious body was unable to burn off.

Leidis turned to Ginevah. 'Do you know what Arkhor taught me?'

'You would often complain that he taught you nothing.'

He smothered a laugh. 'That is fair, it is possible that he did not. But he showed me that I was right. That I still had brothers. Why do you think I left Eden? Were you never curious?'

'They say that curiosity is the child born of indolence, lord.'

'Indeed.'

Leidis sighed. Truly, the woman's indoctrination had ruined her. Nevertheless, he thought back to his lonely bouts of incarceration in the Tower of Purgatory on Eden, and the time it had given him to arrive at his views, and had to concede that she had a point.

'Perhaps you are right in that too. There was no single moment of revelation that I remember. No epiphany. There are times I wish there had been, if only so that I could better explain it now. If I could return in time to Eden, to suffer another sermon on the Graces of Restraint or Mercy, then I would do so, if only so that I might bludgeon Chaplain Dreo with the *Book of Sanguinius* and flee with it into the night. On Coroline IV, when the Black Rage almost took me and my brothers held me down and dragged me screaming from the field, I wish I could say that I slaughtered them all and never once looked back afterwards.'

He glanced speculatively at Ginevah, eyes narrowed, as if hungry for the slip into revulsion that never came. This was the first time he had spoken aloud of the Flaw. To do so with one not of the blood, even a trusted serf, would have been a crime punishable by exsanguination and death for the both of them on Eden.

Here, it was an interesting diversion.

'They were so close-minded,' he went on, 'wearing their hypocrisy as though it were armour. They slaughtered millions for an Emperor who no longer watched over them, and then punished themselves for what they saw as the sin of doing so. They deny their Thirst even as it flows to them from Him, even though it is the one source of strength that, like the Nails, might allow them to prevail over their foes. That is why I left, Ginevah. I left because they are wrong. Blood is sacred, Ginevah. It is beautiful. The way it looks and smells and tastes. Even the sounds that it makes as it leaves a body. And I have been blessed to see it. I am not broken. I have been *elevated* above my brothers on Eden. This is what I came to realise after all those years spent killing in His name, begging Dreo for the absolution of the whip or the slow excruciation of solitude, none of which ever placated my Thirst. I came to realise that there was a truth in the universe greater than that which the Reclusiam would freely share. Every day, I expected to be exposed for the apostasy growing in my heart and every day that that did not happen I grew surer in my beliefs. The Chapter possessed none of the answers they claimed to be the gatekeepers to. And when I met Arkhor on Gremulid, I...'

He hesitated, licking his dry lips.

'When I met Arkhor, he taught me what I had always known. That I *had* been right. That is what the Butcher's Nails are to me, Ginevah. They are the truth that I have been searching for all this time. They are the meaning that I need. The strength I deserve.'

'But–'

Leidis shook his head, cutting her off with a warning growl. She was tired, but that was no excuse for doubt. He almost smiled, however, as it occurred to him that she was only, tentatively, beginning to do the one thing he had always dismissed her as incapable of – thinking for herself.

Perhaps she was simply mortal.

She could do no right.

'No more questions,' he said, tightening his grip over Arkhor's shoulder as the warleader groggily began to struggle once more. 'Go and rest. You are no more use to me here.'

She shook her head. 'There is too much to do.'

Leidis got the sense that she was lying.

He wondered if her dreams suffered the tumult in the warp as Arkhor's did, and what ghosts plagued her there if they did. Leidis' heresies had surely lent grievances to many.

'Sleep,' he said. 'I command it.'

She rubbed her eyes, as though she had not realised how tired she was until Leidis had mentioned it. 'When Corvo returns to replace you, lord. I will rest when you do.'

'I am not sure that Corvo will be coming back this time.'

'Lord?'

Leidis sighed in annoyance. Ordinarily there was no bribe great enough, or threat dire enough, to make Verroth keep his forked tongue behind his lips. Until there was information that actually *needed* to be shared that was. 'We intercepted a ship-wide transmission from the command deck that Lord Kossolax seeks the services of a Warpsmith to replace one slain at Kalkin's Tribune. I was here with you at the time, but he told Verroth that he meant to put himself forward.' Leidis doubted they would see him again, and not because he would be serving as Warpsmith to Lord Kossolax.

'What is a Warpsmith?' Ginevah asked.

'It is how the World Eaters refer to their Techmarines.'

'Left...'

Ginevah turned her head towards the small circular viewing portal on the other side of the engine block. It looked out over the hangar from underneath the shuttle's tailplane. She looked thoughtful, as though the idea of leaving this warband was a foreign one that she would never have considered had it not been introduced to her.

The sound of gunfire rattling off the exterior armour startled her from her reverie. Leidis' first instinct was to simply ignore it. It would hardly have been the first time the hangar's warring bands had taken shots at one another, nor caught the shuttle in the crossfire.

'*Leidis.*' Verroth spoke through the vox, proving Leidis' belief that the renegade was incapable of spending ten minutes in solitude. '*I am at the cargo ramp with Strykid. You need to get down here, now.*'

Leidis gave a long sigh before activating his vox. 'Do not be a fool, Verroth. I cannot leave Ginevah alone with–'

'*Bring the human too.*'

Leidis frowned. The strains of bolter fire crackled through the vox, coming split seconds before the sounds of their banging against the shuttle's bodywork. He heard what sounded like war cries, garbled by interference, but coming decidedly closer.

'*But do it quickly.*'

Aside from the singularly hazardous manoeuvres involved in transitioning to and from the medium of warp space, there was no more perilous activity for a warp-capable vessel than plunging headlong through the empyrean. More ships were lost in the warp, destined to end their voyages agglomerated into the mass of a drifting space hulk, than would ever be destroyed in battle. For a ship as fundamentally corrupted as the *Conqueror* those dangers were lessened, but no vessel travelled the Sea of Souls entirely without risk.

Lesser daemons, mindless things of raw instinct and half-formed intention, screamed as they burnt up on the Geller fields, while greater entities, those dangerous enough to emulate genuine intelligence, followed in the ship's burning wake, waiting for that picosecond dip in the field that would permit them aboard.

Even with the viewing portals shuttered and live feeds severed, the Geller field projecting a shining soap bubble of corporeal reality around the monstrous vessel, a ship at warp was a realm of nightmares. Epidemics of insanity swept the decks, rashes of murder, suicide and attempted sabotage, all instigated by the most insistent of voices in the receptive mortal's head. What was true of any Imperial ship of the line became exponentially truer to one packed to the bilges with World Eaters and their thralls.

The Mistress had been bound to the *Conqueror* for a long, long time and she knew her business.

The majority of the newcomers had chosen to remain with their own landing craft, and had been securely locked down in the hangar for the duration of the transit. Others, those with larger warbands to accommodate and greater ambitions, had spilled out onto adjacent decks before the ship could contain them, claiming further territories there and fighting one another for the right to control them. Left to their own devices they would absorb or be absorbed by the warbands already resident in the *Conqueror*'s halls, then new blood would arrive and the cycle would repeat anew. The Mistress had seen it happen, over and over. The *Conqueror* had been pressed to flying the banner of a dozen warlords since Angron's fall on Terra.

They all overreached in the end. Only the *Conqueror* itself was forever.

In an attempt to safeguard her ship from its passengers, she had sealed the warring champions off from one another with bulkheads, force fields, void spaces and heavy gun emplacements.

In spite of her best precautions, she could feel the madness seeping into her ship from without and from within.

There was no more perilous activity for a warp-capable vessel than plunging headlong through the empyrean – except doing so with Angron of Nuceria aboard.

There were more lethal measures she might have taken to quell the violence breaking out aboard her ship, if her attention had not been drawn to something impossible.

The *Conqueror* was being followed.

Physical distance in the empyrean was subjective. Time was not linear. Everywhere was part of an infinite *anywhere*. Every time was now. Angron's armada followed him in only the loosest sense, drawn by the *Conqueror*'s warp wake and guided by the Malakbael beacon so there was at least the outside chance of his ships arriving in the right place at a broadly similar time. But to actively seek and shadow another vessel was nigh on impossible without powerful daemonic assistance or the direct will of the gods. The Mistress did not believe she could have done it herself.

And yet the *Conqueror* was being followed.

The second ship was about an eighth of the *Conqueror*'s mass, and with a sharper profile, lacking the Gloriana-class battle-ship's heavy gunnery and armour plating. A realspace contest between the two vessels would have been as one-sided as it was short, but their pursuer ploughed through the maelstrom of false colour and torment like a perfectly adapted predator, its prow contoured for speed through a sea lacking in all the dimensional realities for such a concept to be calculated. The conflagration of daemons on its shields was a corposant defining its hull, and in the great bonfire of Neverborn, the Mistress marked the outline of dorsal tower, prow batteries and keel guns, but nothing to disclose its identity.

The anthropocentric notion of distance between them closed as the mysterious vessel drew abeam, near enough for the ever-flickering shoal of soul-fire to leap between their shields.

The Mistress had seen a ship like it once before.

Six hundred years ago, before Angron's defeat on Armageddon.

It was silver.

The void craft had not been built that could outrun a warship of the Grey Knights at warp. Webs of hexagrammic shielding repelled the hostility of the medium before it could come into contact with consecrated silver armour. To employ a terrestrial metaphor she was an icebreaker, employing lore unbeknownst to the wider Imperium to force passages that other ships simply could not dare.

On departing the Red Angel's Gate and scrying the warp for the source of Angron's galactic summons, Graucis Telomane and his Brotherhood of Thirteen had found themselves thousands of light years from where they needed to be and on the wrong side of the Cicatrix Maledictum.

For any other vessel of the Adeptus Astartes or Navis Imperialis, that would have propositioned a journey of several months via one of the stable warp corridors across the Rift.

But not even the Cicatrix Maledictum could present the *Sword of Dione* with an insurmountable challenge.

The enraged warp burnt its fingers in battering at her defences, screaming uselessly in every language ever known to man, alien and god with every conceptualised light year it conceded. The shrieks of the Neverborn hurled onto the silver pyre of her hull scratched through concatenated layers of shielding, finding their way into a mortal mind every time a crew serf listened to the static in an augmitter handset or allowed their eyes to follow the start-up screed on a workstation monitor.

Out of a crew of forty thousand, barely a dozen had ended their own lives since the departure from Armageddon, or required euthanising by vigilant crewmates. A conventional Astartes vessel would have anticipated an attrition rate a hundred times as great.

Standing alone in the ship's solar, beneath a gold-beamed skylight in which the tempestuous warp thrashed and raged, Graucis stared into the immaterium, feeling it recoil from his regard even as it fled before the prow of the *Dione*, searching for fleeting glimpses of prophecy amidst its Chaotic patterns.

Wherever Angron was bound, he had an insurmountable head start over the *Sword of Dione*, but this was the warp. With sufficient will, or favour, physical distance could become merely the first option in an infinite array of possibilities.

The ancient flagship of the XII Legion was a monster of a vessel. Its armour had thickened over the long ages, calcified like a gnarled shell, while its guns appeared to have lengthened and multiplied. Its prow was smeared crimson, as though it had glutted itself only recently on the flesh of some other vessel. The scars on its bronzed plating spoke of the great battles of Terra, Isstvan and Armaturia, of wars with which Graucis was familiar and others that had been lost even to the lore of the Grey Knights, unremembered anywhere but in the vanity of this behemoth's bones.

Eyes locked on the World Eaters battleship, Graucis raised his aged voice in a chant. The splinter of corrupted bronze buried in his leg shifted inside the muscle, turning like a compass needle towards magnetic north as it responded to the same psychic pull that had called every World Eater in Imperium Nihilus to Angron's side.

Graucis focused through the pain and continued to chant.

He could have followed the primarch anywhere.

Angron had not commandeered his former flagship without cause. The powers that resided within the warp were often inscrutable, but they did not act without reasons of their own. Angron was set on a real, tangible course, for reasons Graucis had yet to divine. And if he was to have any hope of doing so before the primarch reached his destination, then Graucis needed to slow him down.

He needed to get there first.

Fortunately, there was more than one power within the warp, and no two that held universally common cause.

Approaching his incantation's crescendo, he raised his Nemesis staff high, ignoring the spasm of pain in his injured leg, and brought it crashing down onto the tiled floor. Power rippled out across the solar, causing the bulkheads to flex and rattling the armaglass skylight in its heavy frame. The warp beyond writhed and began to discolour.

Any Imperial citizen party to such a rite as Graucis had just performed would have decried it all as rank sorcery, but the warp was contextual.

The Emperor's Gift rendered all that it touched divine. He had to believe that wherever a Grey Knight acted in the defence of mankind, it was pure by definition.

If he did not then there would be no refuge from his doubts.

He looked up and watched, unsmiling, breathing heavily, as the light falling through the viewing portal shifted from a bloody red to a garish, nightmarish pink.

Leidis was firing as he descended the cargo ramp from the shuttle's side. A World Eater in riveted Mark II armour charged out from under the wing of a Storm Eagle gunship and into the volley of high-explosive shot. The torrent of bolter fire splintered the warrior's breastplate, tearing off one arm, but still he staggered on, like a Dreadnought against a burst river, before a headshot finally put him down.

Leidis grunted his appreciation of the splatter pattern that the kill left across the body of the Storm Eagle, already switching targets.

They were everywhere. He took his pick.

A warrior with diagonal black stripes painted across his armour, spiked pauldrons festooned with severed heads and mummified hands, ducked around the shuttle's snub nose, looking around as though for something to kill. Leidis' first volley pinned him to the fuselage, the second drilled him through and painted him across thirty square feet of the hull.

They were not making it difficult for Leidis to shoot them, but Space Marines of any kind took a phenomenal amount of killing.

Leidis lowered his bolter, just enough so as to gawp over the brushed-metal finish of the ring sight and upper receiver. Armoured bodies lay strewn around the shuttle's open hatch in various states of dismemberment, laid out in tree-ring patterns roughly delineating sight lines and the range of Verroth's bolt pistol.

And there were thousands more penned together in this hangar.

'Why are they attacking us?' Leidis yelled.

'They are attacking everything,' Verroth snapped back.

He had one boot on the foot of the ramp and one on the *Conqueror*'s deck, upper body weaving like a charmed snake as it somehow evaded a howling World Eaters berzerker and the chainaxe in his fist. Ducking around a spectacularly wild lunge, he stabbed the warrior eight times through the softseals that covered the throat between gorget and helmet before he had a chance to adjust.

'I do not know why and frankly I do not care.'

The World Eater crashed to Verroth's feet and rolled down the ramp to the deck. Verroth licked the blood off his knife.

'We cannot hold them here in the open,' said Leidis.

'Really, brother? Do you think?'

'You were the one who called me out here.'

As if to demonstrate his point, another World Eater came storming out from behind the Storm Eagle parked directly across from the shuttle's side ramp.

Firing on the hoof with a bolt pistol, he clipped Verroth's pauldron, forcing the warrior onto the back foot and leaving Strykid blinking dumbly at the bottom of the ramp. Confused, he swung his fully loaded bolter like a club. Leidis heard the meaty *thwack* of it impacting with the side of the World Eater's head, but the warrior barely slowed, tackling Strykid and the wrong-footed Verroth and bearing them both to the ground. The ramp bowed under the weight of three falling Space Marines, wobbling dangerously as they rolled towards the hangar floor. Leidis corrected his stance as the ground lurched underfoot, Ginevah unloading with a shrill but ferocious *pap-pap-pap* sound less than half a yard from his ear.

'Get back inside,' Leidis yelled at her, then turned to Verroth, who was aggressively disentangling himself from the World Eaters berzerker. 'We should just close the hatch and let them slaughter each other out here.'

'Believe it… or… not… brother… I am not a… fool.'

Strykid hauled the raging World Eater off of Verroth, holding the berzerker from behind while Verroth raised his bolt pistol, took an inordinate amount of care over his aim, and blasted the warrior's face off from a yard away.

Blood sprayed over them all.

Leidis lapped it off his face and hands. He felt strength tingle through his muscles, a flame lit under his soul. Forcing himself to raise his bolter rather than simply charge down and indulge himself in the melee at the foot of the ramp, he gunned down another World Eater just before his chainaxe bit into Strykid's back.

Verroth straightened with a curse. 'They do not stop long enough for us to close the doors.'

Two more World Eaters rushed them. One of them was in the white-diamond-pattern wargear of the Bloodless, although the design had clearly been recently applied over a pre-existing heraldry.

Leidis made sure to drop that warrior first.

They kept coming.

Two more tumbled out of an Arvus lighter berthed next to the Storm Eagle, tearing at one another like animals even as they ostensibly ran at the shuttle. At the same time, seven warriors in the colours of four different bands were spilling into Leidis' firing arc from three different directions.

Verroth hastened to extricate himself from the close combat at the foot of the ramp and drag Strykid back to safety.

If there was ever a time for Omid Corvo and his damnable heavy bolter, then it was now. If the Foresworn failed to do it for him, then Leidis would murder the Techmarine himself.

'Have you had a good enough look at them?' Verroth snarled over his shoulder. 'You can start shooting them now.'

Squeezing down the trigger, Leidis strafed fire in a wide arc over his retreating brothers' heads. It did not slow the World Eaters at all.

A World Eater of truly gargantuan proportions, his armour bedecked with brass plaques and skulls mounted on spikes, broke ahead of the pack and charged up the ramp with a roar.

Leidis shot him in the face.

The impact dented his visor and snapped his head back, but failed to penetrate the ceramite to trigger its mass-reactive core and so the warrior blundered on, shouldering into Strykid and sending them both tumbling over the edge.

Suddenly exposed and halfway from cover, Verroth took two shots to the groin softseals and went down with a hiss like a vanquished snake.

'Verroth!'

'Do not excite yourself, brother. I will not die in the cold.'

Lying on his back on the slope of the ramp, Verroth held his bolt pistol in a firm, arm's-length fist and blazed back.

Bolt-rounds *slanged* across the neighbouring Storm Eagle, and his shooter ducked back behind the fuselage. Not all World Eaters were created equally insane.

Suddenly, the shuttle's tail autocannon roared to life.

A torrent of sustained, high-calibre abuse gouged into the Storm Eagle's landing stage where Verroth's shooter had been sheltering, carving straight through one leg and pitching it forwards to rest with one wing as an impromptu strut and a resounding *clang*. Leidis grinned as the World Eaters stumbled out of its way and scattered.

Bless Ginevah and her witless loyalty.

They might just weather this after all.

Allowing his aim to drop, Leidis beckoned for Verroth to get up and fall back. Strykid was gone, fallen somewhere in the heap of bodies under the ramp, and would have to look out for himself. It would be no great loss if he could not.

'In,' Leidis barked. 'Now.'

Verroth gave a sour grunt and pushed himself up onto his wounded leg.

He never quite made it.

All of a sudden, there was no Verroth. There was no ramp.

Leidis tasted acid in the back of his mouth and felt an ache on the base of his brain where a mortal human would have experienced existential terror. For one fraction of a second the universe ceased to exist, and then it came back, shunted two yards to the left. Leidis felt the *crunch* of ceramite and the pain of broken bones, realising that at some point between causality's stall and its abrupt resumption, he had been thrown into the side of the shuttle and dumped ten feet to the hangar floor.

He lay face up on the deck, dazed, trying to work out where he was and what had happened. Strangely coloured spots floated across his eyes. He blinked in an attempt to clear them, but they persisted, and so he ignored them instead, staring through them towards the high ceiling. Strobing alarum beacons carved the girded metal into lurid shades of pink, klaxons droning out warnings that sounded urgent but which Leidis felt too divorced from to heed.

Smoke hazed the air. He heard moans.

Something was screaming.

And… laughing?

He heard a creak on the metal beside him. Footsteps. Slipper-soft. Leidis fumbled for his bolter, but it was not there. He had lost it in his fall. A sickly, cloying perfume worked its way into his nose, and he looked up.

Leidis had never glimpsed a creature like it. The thing was tall and thin, simultaneously monstrous and horrifyingly elegant. Its androgynous curves were clad in scalloped plates of black leather. The eyes that stared down at him were wide ovals of black onyx, infinite wells of sensation but utterly void of compassion. *Geller collapse,* his logical mind howled at him, as though that meant something important to him. *Geller collapse!*

He half-heartedly continued to root around him for his bolter, eyes still locked on the long, thin face of the creature now squatting down beside him. He gave up, sighing openly. The thing snapped a pincer claw the size of his entire torso, and smiled.

CHAPTER TWELVE

The daemonette pressed itself seductively into the curve of the corridor, beckoning Kossolax with a *snickt* of its pincer claw while several identical siblings giggled, and hissed, and pouted, and bared their glass-needle teeth in inviting smiles.

With a disgusted growl Kossolax punched the powered spike at the top of his axe through the beckoning daemonette's chest.

The warp creature mewled ecstatically, its fingers going up in smoke as it clawed ineffectually at the crimson power field around the axe's bloody edge, even as Kossolax hoisted it off the ground like a soft, squirming, lavender-oiled fish he had plucked from a red stream.

He felt… something.

They were beautiful, he conceded, these reflections of Slaanesh, but not nearly so beautiful as the blood drizzling from their sucking chest wound, spattering his bone-white armour with all the colours of the warp's infinite rainbow.

He gave a harsh sigh.

If ever he was in need of a sign that he had become one of Khorne's creatures, then it was here.

The rest of the daemonette pack cried out in outrage and delight at their sibling's demise, swiftly concluding the game they had made of slaughtering mortals to come capering down the corridor to meet him.

The corridors between Kossolax's chambers and the command deck were largely uninhabited by mortal serfs, a consequence of the World Eaters' appetite for slaughtering them whenever they found them, and so he had brought few with him as a consequence. There was his muscular armsman, Grarn, who had himself brought with him a handful of nearer-to-baseline subordinates toting autorifles, lascarbines and combat shotguns fitted with rusty bayonets.

He had also, by chance, stumbled upon a single World Eater butchering a daemonette pack in the corridor outside his chambers.

He had the appearance of a Warpsmith. His armour was a scrap-metal collage of bizarre and byzantine modifications, studded with load-bearing suspensor ports for the carrying of heavy equipment and, most likely, weaponry. His power pack had been heavily retrofitted with bronze spikes, glowing icons and enough additional plug-in ports to single-handedly operate a small outpost.

Kossolax had not yet stopped for long enough to ask him his name.

The Warpsmith's unhelmed, stitched-together face fractured into a hundred different lines, none of which came anywhere near to being a smile, as he brought up a hand flamer.

Shrieks of pain and laughter filled the corridor as the Warpsmith soaked it in flame. Kossolax saw one daemonette go up in smoke. Another thrashed its slender arms about it, apparently dancing, as it was devoured by the flames. Grarn growled something in a dialect descended from a degraded form of Nagrakali, the language of dead Nuceria, and the front rank of mortal peons dropped to their knees.

Red las-beams and auto-fire thicketed the daemon-perfumed corridor, obliging the daemonettes to gaily bend, twist and vault their way through the mortals' gunfire. Every so often one paused to perform a solo dance, pulling solid rounds from the air with dainty nips of their gigantic claws or evincing whole-body shivers as roasting beams cut circular burns into their perfect skin.

Lesser daemons were simple creatures, dead skin sloughed off the bodies of greater powers, but they were never easy to kill.

Kossolax shook the disintegrating corpse off his axe, spun the weapon in his grip and then out, braining a capering daemonette with the butt. The complex and ever-changing set of runes along its haft and energy-sheathed blade flared into a new configuration and the stunned daemonette staggered into the Warpsmith, where it met an ecstatic end under the teeth of a chainsword.

Another sharp twirl of the axe, a heavily armoured step forward, and Kossolax eviscerated another. Even as the daemonette bled back into the empyrean, the axe's top spike appeared to lengthen, running the creature through with such ferocity that the point went on to impale the daemonette behind it, and then the one behind *it*, the third and final creature practically throwing itself onto the blade as though desperate to share in the sensation of death.

Kossolax wondered if the weapon had a bloodlust that was independent of his, drawing the favour of daemons of its own that imbued its base metals and mundane energy fields with some small measure of sentience and hate.

There were times when he liked to think so.

All he knew for certain was that it excelled in the killing of Neverborn.

Ripping the axe free of the skewered bodies, Kossolax swung up his bolter and put the roar of the half a dozen autoguns ranked either side of him to shame.

The Warpsmith howled with bloodlust, augmitters stitched directly into his vocal cords crackling, and gave the corridor another thorough dousing. Daemonettes squealed and writhed, one last ecstatic dance for the pleasure of their butchers as they were pulled apart by bolter fire and cremated.

Kossolax stomped through the bubbling, still-attractive effluent that the daemonettes had left on the deck until he was in sight of the monstrously thick blast doors to the command deck. Reaper autocannon turrets, ripped out of their cupolas by huge claws, hung from the ceiling by their wires. The doors themselves had been savaged as though by a genetically upscaled crab.

Knowing the *Conqueror's* belligerence towards him, Kossolax had been expecting to have to cut his way through the doors himself and was both relieved and somewhat concerned when they opened for him of their own accord. Machine senses recorded his approach and triggered the door mechanisms, grinding the solid adamantine slabs back on heavy gears with a gust of daemonic incense and a trilling of delicate laughter.

Grinding his teeth against the irritation of the Butcher's Nails, Kossolax strode inside.

That a rival power should be so bold as to strike at the XII Legion flagship, and with Angron himself aboard... It was an insult on the World Eaters themselves, and whoever or whatever lay behind it, Kossolax would ensure they spent the next thousand years paying for it in blood. Could Angron's return have stirred a rival to bring forward some scheme of their own? The gods knew that the primarchs nursed petty vengeances the way a sole surviving battle-brother nursed his last bolter rounds. Had Fulgrim, or one of his immortal lackeys from what was left of the old III Legion, stirred himself to wreak havoc on the primarch's ship?

He peered into the strobing lights and scented smoke.

Autoguns barked from roughly welded forts, the Bronze Age silhouettes of mortals and daemons warring over the occasional ramparts drawn by muzzle flashes in smoke. Silks rustled at the edge of hearing. Laughter rang from the beams. The forces of Slaanesh were in full, if temporary, ascendency and the brazen touch of Khorne in rout.

It was fortunate that Angron's return and the daemonic menace he had brought with him had forced the deck crews to fortify their stations and discipline themselves. If they had not done so, then the daemonettes would surely have overrun the command deck and slaughtered its entire crew already.

And that would have angered Kossolax greatly.

The Warpsmith appeared at his side. He panted wetly as he sniffed at the sweet corruption, giving the occasional jerk of thinly restrained violence as he fumbled the simple task of plugging a fresh canister of liquid fuel into the base of his hand flamer.

There was, Kossolax had long ago concluded, no such thing as chance. The galaxy was too broken to allow it. That a Warpsmith should happen to fall in his lap, just at the time that he required one, was because the gods saw his efforts and rewarded, or punished, them as they saw fit.

'What is your name?' he said.

'Omid Corvo, lord regent.' The Warpsmith finally forced the fuel canister to slot home and growled in satisfaction. 'Techmarine to Arkhor the Redbound.'

Kossolax smiled. He liked that. It had been a long time since he had found a warrior who could refer to themselves as *Tech-marine* without mockery, never mind one who had apparently received genuine tutelage on Mars. 'No longer, Corvo. From here on you belong to the Foresworn.'

The Warpsmith dipped his head. 'Yes, lord regent.'

Kossolax turned to Grarn, who drew his heavy slouch, a natural consequence of his overmuscled physique, into a stance of attention. 'Send half your warriors to assist at astrogation. I want to know where we are and where we were heading. Lead the rest yourself and claim auspectoria for me. I want to know what happened.'

The armsman touched thick fingers to his temple in salute. 'Yes, lord regent.'

Kossolax turned towards the command throne, its central keep surrounded by subsidiary fortifications, his axe squirming like a worm in his grip as though eager to be thrown.

The Mistress descended the steps from the dais.

Even without a face to betray it, she looked war-weary, as though she had somehow been engaged against this daemonic insurgency alongside her corporeal crew. Strands of what looked like grey hair, come astray from a transparent ponytail, brushed her hollow cheek. Several rips marred her dull, white uniform. There was even, and Kossolax found himself wondering at this most of all, a few spots of what looked like blood on her sleeve.

'*Lord Kossolax,*' she said, and Kossolax was sufficiently startled to lower his axe, rather than give it one more daemon to kill.

The Butcher's Nails scratched at his brain in protest at the act of self-control, making his eyelid twitch and his jaw tremble, but he ground his teeth and bettered it. The spirit had never acknowledged him directly, not without first being threatened or challenged in some way.

He was curious.

'I'm glad to see you made it,' she said. *'I need your help.'*

The smiling horror cracked into ceramite as though breaking open a crustacean shell, tearing gleefully into the leathery transhuman flesh inside.

Leidis watched, rapt, as it reeled out entrails and scattered them, making of them an artwork of breath-taking vision that transcended the limited materials of flesh, blood and offal from which it had been made.

There was truth here.

Leidis saw that, even as blood drizzled across his face and armour.

Meaning.

If he could only look at it hard enough, *for long enough*, experience it deeply enough, wire his brain in just the right way to interpret it in the way it was meant to be seen. Then, maybe, he would perceive the great truth he had always suspected lay beneath the civilised veneer of what fools called reality.

In his earliest memory, a screaming child pulled from the arms of harsh but more-or-less loving parents to be remade into yet another weapon for the unliving Emperor, he had felt its nature.

Now, made a party to this creature's art, he could literally taste it on his genhanced sensory organs.

'Yes,' the daemonette whispered. Its voice was sultry and hard-edged, gently coaxing and subtly cruel. *'You have always appreciated artistry, haven't you, Leidis.'*

Leidis nodded, his eyes lost in the allure of its form. 'How... how do you know my name?'

The creature gave him a bewitching smile of fish-comb teeth. *'It was not for the crime of slaughter that your ignorant brothers cast you from their home. No. It was for the joy you took in it.'*

Leidis stared dumbly. His rapture deepened.

It was so obvious, when it was put to him in such dazzling simplicity, he could not believe he had never considered himself in that light before.

'You are a child,' it said sympathetically, mockingly. *'It is no fault of yours that you did not seek us out of your own desire. It is only unhappy chance that led you into the company of Arkhor the Redbound and his crude worship of blood. It is he, not you, who set your path. It might easily have been another, and it is not yet too late to find the true delight of slaughter.'* It extended a pale lilac claw smeared in transhuman offal.

Leidis pulled his gaze from the daemonette's. He looked at the outstretched hand.

Beyond it lay a disembowelled corpse, so thoroughly remade by the needs of the creature's art that Leidis did not immediately recognise it. He blinked to clear his eyes and to reset his still-glitching lenses, working his mouth to revive his horribly parched tongue.

'S-Strykid?'

The warrior, unsurprisingly, did not answer.

Leidis had never seen a Space Marine more dead. The lavender-skinned siren crouching between them was wearing a good proportion of his insides, as a mortal might don a robe.

'You would be welcomed into the carnivals of excess, Ortan Leidis, celebrated as a prodigal son returned and a shining example to all such wayward souls. You would be embraced as a brother. Please,' it said, though Leidis did not feel it was truly asking for his permission. *'Allow us to show you the delights of the paths not taken. The Dark Prince knows better than to deny his servants the sensation they crave.'*

Leidis' mouth opened and closed without forming a sound. The sight of Strykid lying there, defiled and profaned in the name of art, unsettled something deep in him. Strykid had been the least of Leidis' brothers, but he had been a brother.

He tried to find the words to deny it.

Any words.

He looked inside himself for the familiar anger, the rage with which to throw the creature's temptations back in its hideously perfect face, but it was not there.

What if the creature was right?

If only Arkhor had been able to offer him the Butcher's Nails.

What if he–

There was a loud *bang* followed by the bursting of something vacuously ripe as his temptress' head exploded.

Even that, Leidis noted, it did balletically. Too absorbed by the inherent beauty of its death to be startled by the unexpected suddenness of it, he watched as blood and brain and bone fanned out into an abstract art form that made a part of him yearn to put a bolter in his mouth and emulate it.

The thick red spray settled out into a fine pink mist.

Still, Leidis watched it.

He heard a wet growl from above him. Leidis turned his head to look up.

Arkhor the Redbound was on the ramp, a couple of yards to his right. He was unhelmed, as Leidis had left him, scabbed wounds arranged like constellations up the neck and around the temples where he must have ripped free of the neural restraints on his chair. He was breathing hard, shoulders hunched, as though fighting against some greater impulse bidding him to shift the smoking main barrel of his plasma pistol half an inch down and to the left to where Leidis lay and fire again. His chainaxe purred in the opposite fist, his thumb tweaking the activation rune on and off, on and off, *on and off*.

A violent seizure brought a jerk of the head, wiping out the uncertain smile of recognition that had come Leidis' way, the pulsing of the Butcher's Nails visible in the throbbing of the skin above his temple. With a savage howl, the warleader turned and leapt from the cargo ramp, red cloak fluttering out behind him as he hit the deck with a heavy *clang*, chainaxe already shrieking into a perfumed monster's back.

Leidis did not know what he was supposed to feel any more.

To his horror, he found he felt nothing but ennui about any of it.

He brought his hands to the sides of his head as though to drown out the rampant stimulation, and screamed.

The Mistress brought Kossolax and Corvo to the strategium.

A low palisade of sharpened wooden stakes surrounded the large central station, a couple of mutant serfs clutching autorifles over a drawbridge that they had welded into place from looted armaglass panes. It would have been the work of a moment for Kossolax to tear it apart, but at a faint gesture from the Mistress, the guards came upon the unexplained notion to lower their weapons to winch it down.

Beyond the gate was a tiered bailey comprising a rough cross-section of the command deck's pits, platforms and staircases, all roughly enclosed by the station's basic walls. Injured fighters lay everywhere he looked. There were mutants with pin-heads, with vestigial eyes, with elongated fingertips that ended in nostrils and suckers, or with toothless mouths gasping from their throats; creatures from the farthest extremities of the human spectrum wearing armour sewn together from bleached squares of stolen flak. The one common feature they could agree to share was the colour they bled.

On their walls, the fighting continued.

Kossolax could hear the *clang* of metal. The clatter of light gunfire. The delighted androgyn laughter of daemons and the screams of their occasionally willing victims. All funnelled in and downwards by the curvature of the walls.

There, the huge brass font of the sanguilith sat empty, the basin smeared red inside. Crusty meat hooks, hanging from the ceiling, clinked at the end of long, rusted chains, swaying with the disturbances of the ongoing battle. The *Conqueror* would need to find more witches to hang. Kossolax wondered, and not for the first time, if the sanguilith was by any measure an improvement over the auspectoria originally installed by the shipwrights of Terra.

Perhaps it was not better, but then nor was it exactly worse. It was *changed*, and would not be changed back. That was all that mattered.

He put the question from his mind. It was one better suited to the already insane.

The Mistress turned, beckoning Kossolax to follow her up a plasteel staircase and then halted before a terminal. Its cogitation core buzzed inside its corroded steel housing, light flickering from behind the optical interface. It appeared to have been abandoned in favour of an autogun or a spear by whatever thrall had been tasked with minding it. She spread her thin hands across the cream-coloured bone keys of the control board and suddenly hesitated, an air of confusion crossing her expressionless face.

Chuckling unkindly, Kossolax stepped through her empty form and took her place at the controls.

'What do I wish to see?'

'*Internal augurs,*' the ghost murmured after a time, as though remaining focused was becoming an effort for her.

With the forced delicacy of a giant threading a needle, he clacked his gauntleted fingers on the control-board keys. The cogitator rattled, kicking like a gestating infant inside its metal womb as it processed the command, mysterious brass cogs turning like spiked wheels through mud. While its arcane processes ground along, he glanced to the ghost over his shoulder and asked the question he had been unable to have answered since his claiming of the *Conqueror*.

'Who are you?'

The Mistress appeared unsettled by the question but, after a moment or two, seemed to visibly accept it. '*I am the* Conqueror. *I am its will amongst its mortal crew.*'

'They do not even hear you.'

'*Oh, they hear me.*'

'They do not see you.'

'*Only because there's no need. They know I'm here.*'

'But this woman...' Kossolax indicated the small, frail form beside him with a curt up-and-down movement of his chin. 'This uniform. Obviously, you were human once.'

'*Yes...*' The Mistress appeared to look down at her own insubstantial hands, as though remembering something too far in the past to be truly unpleasant, but which disturbed her nonetheless. '*I had a... separate existence then. I...*' She shook her head, a shimmer passing through her, and said nothing more.

'Why am I the only one who sees you?'

'*Are you?*'

Kossolax gave her a quizzical look, but before he could follow up with another question the cogitator emitted a grinding stall and a stinging waft of coppery smoke.

The optical screen slowly brightened, cathode ray tubes projecting an unsteady internal augur of the *Conqueror*. The two-dimensional deck schematic it was based on was hopelessly out of date. The bleeding icons denoting World Eaters units were smeared across walls that were now corridors, mustering in agriponics silos and machine decks that had not existed since a ship named the *Adamant Resolve* had departed Terran dry dock.

No one had been able to properly map the changes to the ship's layout since, and not for want of lives and effort.

'I'm glad we've had this opportunity to get to know one another better,' the Mistress murmured as she turned from him to examine the screen. *'It's possible our first impression of you was mistaken. Perhaps we can... perhaps we... perhaps...'* The featureless shape of her face flickered and wavered, then looked down again as though peering at the flickering screen, uncertain what she was doing.

'Mistress?'

'We were attacked,' she said, whatever she had been attempting to say before evaporating before the ship she represented's greater need. *'By another ship.'*

'While still in the warp? Impossible.'

'Extraordinarily difficult. Dangerous. But not impossible.'

'Whose ship?'

'Its profile appeared to be that of a Space Marine strike cruiser.'

Kossolax grunted. 'Which Legion?'

'It was Imperial.'

'Impossible,' he said again. 'They do not have the warpcraft, and would not use it if they did.'

'It was Imperial, though not in the livery of any Chapter I recognise. They were able to track us, close with us, then hit us with some kind of psychic attack that pierced our Geller field for a split second. I immediately attempted to pull us out of the warp, but was only able to make a partial translation.'

'Did you say partial?'

The Mistress nodded silently. *'We have failed to break cleanly back into realspace. Something holds us back, allowing daemons to flood the ship on all decks, but particularly here, here and here.'* With a finger that never quite touched the violently rattling glass of the cogitation display, she indicated the enginarium, primary hangar deck and command deck. *'Everywhere the mortal thralls are most populous. Or were. Enginarium has been wiped out as far as I can tell. The crew here are holding them off, as you can see for yourself, and your World Eaters in the main hangar are still fighting hard. But the attacks won't stop until I can restore power to the warp drives, break whatever force is holding us, and pull myself the rest of the way into realspace.'*

Kossolax studied the screen. One look was enough to take it in.

'I will head here.' Kossolax rapped a finger on the glass over the hangar deck. The display fuzzed under the impact before restoring itself. 'There are thousands of World Eaters there, but they are leaderless renegades. I will rally them to crush the incursion there and then lead them victorious on to the enginarium.' He nodded towards Corvo, who was standing patiently to one side, failing to remark on the apparent fact that his new lord was speaking with himself. But then, he was a World Eater. The Warpsmith would have seen stranger behaviour from his leaders than this. 'We will reawaken the warp drives and push ourselves clear of this trap.'

For a moment, the Mistress appeared to smile. *'Reinforcements are already bound for the hangar from elsewhere. Those warriors will be properly led, but trust me, you won't want to be in the way.'*

Kossolax gestured towards the augur screen. It showed a large clump of red icons closing on the hangar. 'Are these your reinforcements?'

The Mistress spent several long seconds over the flickering display.

'This is what I need you to deal with.'

* * *

Shâhka Bloodless had no idea where he was or what was going on, and he had never been closer to contentment, pink phlegm foaming up through his lips as the Nails whipped his brain numb. The void spaces inside of his skull had swelled, thoughts thinning out like gases possessed of some idiot need to fill the room they were given. There were patterns in them, if boredom gave him the time to look. Random shapes. Hints of purpose in the apparent disorder. But rage kept it all in motion. No sooner would he alight on the tail streamers of a thought than it would be swept away. He didn't know why he was angry. Only that it was good.

He swung his heavy power maul with a roar. Something soft-bodied and slender splatted against the metal wall and died. He pulled the weapon free, swept it back the other way, lifting something with far greater heft from the deck and crunching it into the opposite wall. It fell to the ground in a clatter of mangled plate and weeping sparks. Shâhka ignored it and ploughed ahead.

He wanted more.

An elfin thing of trailing ponytails and snipping claws pirouetted around a hail of bolter fire, and struck for him with an open claw. Shâhka didn't bother blocking it. The thought of blocking it never occurred. The daemon's pincer clamped across his wrist and squeezed hard enough to shatter diamond.

He heard the vambrace bend, heard it buckle, heard it snap. He felt dry, empty pain and with a roar, headbutted the lissom thing, sending it skidding down the corridor with its delicately monstrous head caved in.

Lengthening his grip on the maul, he slid the off-hand down the haft.

There was some tingling in the fingers where the daemonette had sought to sever his wrist. It felt good.

Two-handed, his uppercut mashed another delighted monster into the ceiling. The metal plating fell apart under the blow, sending half a dozen jets of pressurised, daemon-tainted water shooting across the corridor.

Dozens of the daemonettes gambolled towards him. Scores. Singing, screaming, sprinting at ninety-degree angles along the walls and vaulting double-jointedly over one another's backs in their glorious need to rip him apart.

They were strangely attractive creatures.

In a killable sort of way.

Shâhka threw his head back and howled with the raw ecstasy of the Nails.

A búlkier thing, of flesh and bone this one instead of daemonic ectoplasm, tried to push around from behind to get at them first. It was clad in red adorned with white squares, symbolic of their champion's barren veins, a shrieking chainaxe in one hand and a spitting bolter in the other. Shâhka backhanded the axe from its grip with force enough to shatter the arm and slam it into the wall. The thing's armour cracked on impact and it slid to the ground with limbs askew.

Shâhka stomped down on it, crushing the warrior's groin underfoot. Not maliciously. The warrior simply lay between Shâhka and the blood he needed to spend to buy himself another few moments of peace.

'Captain Shâhka.'

A grey woman frowned up at him, unperturbed by the anarchy around them and ignored by it in turn. Something about her triggered the Nails to bite so hard into Shâhka's brain that his knees trembled and he almost cried out for the pain.

He knew this woman.

No!

He shook his head fiercely.

There was a reason that when the Despoiler had summoned all foes of the God-Emperor to the Eye of Terror, Shâhka had carved his red path as far from Cadia as he could go. There was a reason he had aligned himself with infantile wretches like Drak, Goreth and Tōrn to fight over a worthless rock in the depths of Imperium Nihilus.

There was a reason…

What was the reason?

Would he even know it if he remembered?

'Returning home was the hardest challenge I ever faced,' said his Angel. *'But in the vengeance I took on it there was satisfaction of a sort.'*

Vengeance?

Yes. Perhaps. He thought that he might like vengeance. All he had to do was find another warrior to crush. Then another. And another.

And another.

Shâhka could forget again, smear his eyes in enough blood that he could no longer see what was in front of him and be at peace of a sort.

Until he ran out of warriors.

'The curse of the killer who cannot die,' growled his Angel. *'The one victory that counts, the chance to spit in your abuser's eyes, is denied by the very one who made you what you are.'*

The grey woman was still with him. However hard he pushed, she wouldn't disappear like his other ghosts. *'Where are you going, captain?'*

'H-h-hangar,' he panted, voice slurred by the brain damage caused by the Nails. His gifts would repair it, eventually, but it would be painful. 'More killing there.'

'I need you down in the enginarium.'

Shâhka shook his head. 'N-n-n-no.'

There was nothing there. His Angel had told him so.

'The real Angron is mightier than the ghost who haunts you now.'

He snarled and swatted at her.

'Stop this.'

The Nails sent pain slicing through his brain, jagging from left hemisphere to right and turning his vision red. His nostrils flared like those of a bull, the Nails so deeply interconnected with his speech centres that they were able to punish him simply for hearing the word 'stop' and understanding what it meant. He howled, scratching at his skull, almost blinded by the sudden agony, and swung for her with his maul. There was nothing there but another World Eater of the Bloodless. His power maul hit the side of the warrior's helmet so hard it crushed his head instantly.

The warrior's dying reaction was to squeeze on his bolt pistol's trigger, loose fire blazing down the corridor and arcing upwards into the ceiling as his body dropped.

Debris rattled across Shâhka's armour like hailstones.

'Ignore her.'

Shâhka looked up at his Angel, feeling his two hearts clench with hate.

The figure had flown ahead of him and was standing now at the far end of the corridor before a set of sturdy doors, a butcher clad in bronze plate, leather skirts and iron rings, wild-eyed with the madness of a hard day devoted to the business of death. Dreadlocks of blackened steel snaked down gigantic shoulders. One strand twitched while Shâhka was looking. It constricted like a mechanical viper, pulsing its electrical venom directly into the Angel's skull, causing one eyelid to twitch, his lips to pull up into a snarl, and shifting his expression from outrage to fury to blind hate from one moment to the next.

This was what enraged Shâhka found most hateful of all – after everything he had given up, everything he had shed, his father was still in pain.

Angron beckoned him closer.

The screaming horde of lavender-skinned daemonettes between him and his Angel had become suddenly incidental.

'I'm waiting for you, my most broken son.' His Angel gave him a smile that was a murder described in rusted iron pegs. *'Haven't you always wished to fight with me? Or do you simply want to fight me?'*

With a howl of blind rage, Shâhka lowered his head and charged.

At the primarch.

And at the doors behind him.

A thunderous *boom* rolled across the hangar deck.

Leidis could no longer tell what was real, what was a dream, and what was just the latest symptom of his descent to madness. Quite clearly, he was insane. If it was not him, then it was the universe, and Leidis was unsure which of those two binary conditions appealed to him least.

The hangar had devolved into a slaughterhouse floor, thousands of World Eaters penned into a steel corridor bookended by two immense Titan-scale doors. The deck heaved with them. Still more were clambering up onto the roofs of gunships. The heavy craft rocked like wooden dinghies in a storm swell, spitting bolter fire and curses at the winged harpies that swept overhead and swooped, lances lowered, to snatch them up in turn. Other gunships were attempting to take off, fans raging hot, spraying firepower in every direction, only to be drawn back to the deck by creatures with elastic limbs and squirming tentacles, eager for one final embrace.

Beautiful monstrosities of the kind Leidis had already seen

up close careened through the frenzied mobs of Space Marines on the backs of perverse steeds with long, sinuous necks and lolling tongues, snapping heads from necks with delicate nips of pincer claws.

The coherence field, disengaged prior to translation in favour of huge adamantine doors, now fizzled a pinkish colour as though delighting in the simple joy of being contrary. Faces came and went through the field. Smiling. Laughing. Mocking. Sneering. A hellish aristocracy of beast and man and anthropo-morphised feeling pressed to a flickering pane to watch mortal gladiators spill blood for their amusement.

He was insane. Or the universe was.

Another heavy blow struck the aft deployment doors.

That *did* sound almost real.

Still sitting under the shuttle's wing amidst the ruin of Stry-kid's desecrated corpse, Leidis turned his head towards the rear of the hall.

A dent the size of a Dreadnought's power fist had appeared in the door there. Flames licked around the edges of the frame and up the central seam. The buckled metal bubbled and began to run. A terrific bellow from the other side rattled the deck beneath him.

Leidis would have expected a spike of clarity, combat hormones sharpening his thoughts, ceding muscle control to indoctrinated memory, but what he felt instead was a swelling of his hearts, a kind of painfully, deeply confused pride. His fingers twitched reflexively in and out of fists, as though uncertain whether to clasp this newcomer's hand in welcome or to strike it from his wrist.

A low growl escaped his lips. It was all he was able to say.

'Leidis!'

Verroth kicked him, and not gently, in the back of the head.

Leidis rocked forward under the blow and turned, shocked by the existence of something so real as his hated brother. The renegade stood over him, the shuttle high at his back, the moondust and dirt caking his armour freshly scratched to reveal the bright green and yellow paint underneath. His dead eyes were fixed ahead, face impassive as he issued snap-shots to any nightmare that grew sufficiently bored of the melee to attempt a run at the shuttle's ramp.

'Where is Arkhor?'

Leidis shook his head. The task of speaking felt epic. 'Gone,' he managed, pointing into the anarchy.

'Strykid?'

Leidis looked down at the mess he was sitting in.

Verroth swore. 'Can you stand?'

Leidis could only blink at him.

'We need to fall back to the shuttle. We will hold out longer inside. Leidis!' Verroth kicked him again, this time in the small of the back. He sprawled into Strykid's entrails, scattering shell casings and armour components across the deck. 'Daemons can bewilder the weak of mind, particularly those unaccustomed to their forms. I saw it first-hand when the armada of the Emerald Snakes perished in the cold. I thought you better. After all, you had enough wit to abandon your brothers and find your way here.'

Another savage blow struck the aft doors, the vibrations kindling something in Leidis' chest.

He had not simply found his way here.

He had *led* them here.

The fingers of his right hand curled inwards, scraping through the fast-congealed gunge of Strykid's innards and locating the haft of one of his axes. It was a simple implement, a heavy alloy blade with a moderately sharp edge and bonded to a plastek composite shaft.

Killing was simple work, but infinitely variable. It was the execution that made it beautiful.

Gripping it tightly, Leidis sucked back a deep breath of daemonic musk and Space Marine blood and pushed himself up. The sense of his swelling hearts grew ever more intense, until it felt as though they were pushing against the sides of his chest and into his throat, bursting out of him as a mad howl.

Leidis knew what he was. He knew where he belonged.

Sweeping up his axe, he gave a furious yell, rising from a crouch into a suit-powered sprint to join his brothers.

Throughout his many years in command, Kossolax had never once submitted himself to the *Conqueror*'s teleporters. The ship had tried to kill him so many times, and in so many callously creative ways, he had seen no reason to make it easy for it.

Somehow managing to sweat despite the monstrously thick armour bonded to his skin, he backed into the teleportarium slot. The alcove enclosed him like the walls of an upright tomb. Knots and veins of insulated copper cabling traversed the walls. Harmonic silver plates and spools of brass wire hummed as the phenomenal sums of power required to force an individual through the pores of realspace ran through them. Sprinkler nozzles squirted out sticky scarlet fluids on a regular repeating cycle, reanointing the profane machinery, and Kossolax's corrupted wargear, every thirty seconds or so with copper-scented mineral sprays and daemonic oils.

While he muttered his own prayers, a scowling priest of the Dark Mechanicum trundled along the companionway in a chariot made of brass.

The priest exhaled a thick, red smoke from the chimney stacks built into the rear of his chassis. A hunchbacked daemon, about the size of a mortal human's hand and covered in soot, rode with him; bound by a collar and chain, the creature worked tirelessly to shovel fresh offal directly into the furnace of the priest's belly. Brandishing an icon of the spike-wheeled Cog Mechanicus at the leering faces that swam through the machinery in the walls, he growled at them in aggressively sequenced binharic. A prehensile pink tongue extruded from one of the interface panels, licking lasciviously at the air before recoiling from the taste of the priest's incense and shrivelling back into the activeglass with a mocking slurp.

Kossolax leant from his alcove to watch the priest's clattering procession down the companionway.

The veil separating the warp from realspace was thin here. Something about the mysteries of teleportation technology made the barrier that much easier to breach. Hence the thickly drawn wards on the bulkheads, the constant blood sacrifice and vigilance of the Dark Mechanicum and their acolytes and, failing all that, the monstrously heavy bolts on the doors.

The *Conqueror* was already deeply corrupt. It would not yield to another power easily, or readily, but the challenge was what made it such a prize to any with the gall to succeed.

He leant back into the alcove, drawing his large axe in close so that it sat fully within its bounds. The last thing he wanted was to arrive at his destination with half of his weapon left behind in the teleportarium. He smiled briefly, forgetting his anxiety, and quickly checked that the package the Mistress' servants had entrusted to him was fastened securely. It was in a skin bag, which had in turn been hammered into his thigh with a nail. His armour was still weakly magnetic, but it came and went and Kossolax could no longer rely on mag-lock as he once had. However, its self-healing properties served almost as well if not better, fixing the embedded nail in place with an osseous glue stronger than ceramite sealant.

Kossolax could not have pulled it out himself.

'I am ready.' His voice echoed amidst the growling machines. 'And I.'

Corvo stood rigid in the alcove opposite, knee-deep in swirling crimson vapours. In spite of his spiked pauldrons and the extensive modification the Techmarine had applied to his backpack and armour, a slot designed for Terminator-clad warriors and Dreadnoughts conspired to render him small. Teleportation was a rare, arcane and power-hungry technology, liable to instantly molecularise anyone not protected by Terminator armour, but the Techmarine's armour was far from Codex Astartes standard, and the *Conqueror* did not hold to the same laws of conservation of energy and physical logic as its Imperial counterparts.

Kossolax reasoned that his new Warpsmith had at least an even chance of surviving the experiment.

He might have liked to draw on Grarn and his warrior-thralls once more, but if Corvo had an equal chance of surviving as not then the mortals would certainly not. They were much better employed securing the command deck against daemonic incursion in his absence.

And so, instead of leading six thousand World Eaters on a blood-soaked rampage through the bowels of the *Conqueror*, as he had intended, he found himself making do with one. He smiled horribly at the thought.

Perhaps the *Conqueror* was still trying to kill him yet.

He took a deep breath to carry with him through the teleportation sequence, an old habit that had endured since his upbringing on Terra, and banged the butt of his axe's haft on the alcove floor to summon the adept. What was an eternity of war without the occasional thrill? As bitterly as he had always fought against the downward path laid out for him by his father's genetics, he was still a World Eater.

The priest struck a brass gong, and then pulled on an enormous lever that projected from the wall.

Power pulsed through the copper wires in answer to the dark adept's prayers, sympathetic warp energies vibrating from the resonance dishes built into the alcove's walls. Kossolax felt himself disintegrating, his body and spirit submerging into the polluted waters of the warp. The experience lasted somewhere between a moment and an eternity, until the Dark Age arcana of the teleportarium pulled him gasping into the physical universe, just as he had been at the initiation of the cycle, but *baptised* in the corrupting energies of the gods.

He found himself in a corridor, teleportation's sticky afterbirth clinging to his armour and sizzling in the scant reality that still existed in the *Conqueror*'s lower decks. Corvo had appeared behind him and was already firing, dousing the passageway with lit promethium and turning daemonettes into screeching pyres.

The corridor was a clogged artery, graceful daemonettes and frenzied World Eaters berzerkers slaughtering one another with joyous abandon as they each sought to force a way through the single channel. Clearing the area around himself and Corvo with great sweeps of his axe, he looked around for the warrior he had been sent here to stall.

His breath caught as he spotted him down the length of the corridor, the shock of recognition somehow made even fiercer by the extent to which the warrior had changed.

A hideous chill went through Kossolax, emerging from him on a bitter laugh.

Shâhka.

The champion they called the Bloodless was *Shâhka.*

So, it seemed his former captain had not, as he had for millennia assumed, been butchered like a mad dog by some long-dead pawn of the Corpse-Emperor after all.

First Angron. Now Shâhka the Bloodless. A lesser man might think the gods were taunting him, offering up these monsters from the past one by one, but he wondered if they might not be presenting him with a gift.

No one would have loathed the misbegotten, half-metallic horror that was now dragging its bloody wings across the bulkhead towards him more than Shâhka. It brought Kossolax a sense of pleasure he had not known in centuries.

The Bloodless turned from the reinforced doors he was halfway to smashing through, entirely heedless of the daemonettes swarming around his waist. His deep-set eyes showed no recognition when they alighted on Kossolax, but boiled with such fury it was impossible to believe there was not a small part of the Shâhka he knew inside.

Good, he thought.

The Butcher's Nails burned inside his skull as he strode on his former captain, barging daemonettes into the bulkheads as he built up momentum.

For ten thousand years he had risen, gathered strength, won favour, the thought of planting his boot on Shâhka's sneering face and *showing* his old captain how far he had climbed never far from his ambitions. After the passage of so many centuries he had assumed that death had cheated him of that dream, but the gods, as always, knew well the hearts of those they claimed.

Holding his weapon two-handed, he hacked it across Shâhka's belly, but Shâhka was suddenly no longer there to receive it.

His axe slammed into the doors, shrieking through the metal as though in protest at being fed such cold, soulless fare with a veritable feast of daemon flesh all around it. Kossolax blinked in surprise, but before he could adjust, Shâhka's maul crashed across his jaw.

Lights exploded across his eyes as he slammed sideways into the bulkhead. Sparks drizzled across him as he shrugged his Terminator-armoured bulk out of the wall. Shâhka flew at him with a berserk howl. Kossolax brought up his axe between them and held it there, not to strike back with or even to parry so much as to fend the monster off. His former captain attacked the way a beast would, all flailing paws, gnashing teeth and acidic spittle, the maul in his fist as good as forgotten.

Kossolax's armour shuddered, giving off painful *clicks* of bone as it struggled to counter Shâhka's strength with its own. He bared his teeth and snarled, refusing to accept that, even after all this time, he might still be lesser.

How had Shâhka spent the millennia since Terra?

He had fled, disappeared into the galaxy, while Kossolax had rebuilt the Legion. He would not be Shâhka's subordinate. He would not be anyone's subordinate.

Never.

Again.

'Angron.' Shâhka sprayed his face with spit. 'I want Angron.'

'Angron does not want you,' Kossolax returned through gritted teeth. 'Why do you think he made you into *this* instead?'

Shâhka howled, slamming Kossolax to the bulkhead and pinning him there with one hand while pawing distractedly at his own head with the other.

It was more than distraction enough for Kossolax to shrug off his grip, swing up the butt of his axe, and crack Shâhka a fierce blow across the jaw.

The blow tore flesh and sent Shâhka staggering back down the corridor, but in spite of the open wound, it failed to yield a single drop of blood.

Kossolax stared at the bloodless injury, appalled, even as Shâhka bulged with fury, his face turning an even deeper shade of pink. 'Angron!' he bellowed, running past Kossolax and charging again at the doors.

With a thunderous peal, the deployment doors gave way. Fire gouted through the torn opening as adamantine slabs, each the height, breadth and weight of a Warlord Titan, crashed inwards, crushing Space Marines, daemons and bullet-riddled gunships alike.

Leidis wrenched his axe from the back of a writhing daemonette and rose, turning to stare across the acres of melee as blood, fire and fury itself strode through the ruined doors.

It was more massive than a Dreadnought, more terrible than any daemon. It bore a sword of nicked, hate-blackened bronze in one raw-meat fist and a howling chainaxe in the other, and those daemonettes that had not been crushed under the falling doors shrieked and scattered before this incarnation of rage. Leidis stared in awe as a dread to which he had supposedly been rendered immune froze his limbs in place.

Even the gene-wrights of the omniscient God-Emperor had not, it seemed, foreseen the needs of this moment.

He felt as though he should be lowering his weapon. Was that not what death-fearing mortals did? All his hand would do though was grip it tighter, until the axe shook and his whole body was trembling.

For the first time since the daemons had manifested over the deck, Leidis heard the daemonette before him issue a shriek that conveyed nothing at all of pleasure.

He silenced it with a blow to the head that cracked its delicate skull and spewed its brains across his boots.

He grinned wildly.

'Angron!' he yelled, pumping his axe above his head as the roar went on and on and on inside his head long after the breath in his lungs was spent.

He charged forwards, one small part of a wild surge several thousand strong, all desperate to shed blood at the primarch's side.

Kossolax caught Shâhka's wrist and hauled him back from the doors.

The Bloodless whirled, blindingly fast, and threw an elbow that rolled across the haft of Kossolax's hastily upraised axe and cracked his chin. Kossolax grunted, shaking his head, ignoring the pain as he had spent a hundred lifetimes ignoring worse, and dragged Shâhka back by the arm until the warrior was hopelessly overbalanced and fell to the deck with a *clang*.

Kossolax hauled him away from the doors along the floor.

He was aware of a molten force of aggression building up on the other side of those doors like a storm surge behind a dam, leaking out through the joins in the metal and into the corridor beyond. Even the trickle was enough to make daemonettes scream in dismay and World Eaters throw themselves onto them with renewed savagery.

'You are mine now,' Kossolax snarled, far from immune himself. 'The World Eaters will answer to me and me alone. Just because Angron will not kneel, it does not mean he does not serve.' But fighting Shâhka was like wrestling an anvil.

The World Eater turned his wrist in Kossolax's grip, taking a grip of his own and pulling on him with such strength that Kossolax fell on top of his armoured form. They were on the ground together just long enough for Kossolax to spit a curse before Shâhka surged back to his feet with a roar.

One hand pinned Kossolax's wrist to the deck. The other was a crushing vice around his throat. Then, Shâhka hoisted him off the ground and above his head, both of them so massive that together they blocked the corridor, and slammed Kossolax's back into the ceiling.

With his one free hand, Kossolax smashed at the wrist of the hand that was crushing his gorget ring into his windpipe.

It did nothing.

Dark spots blotting his vision, he gave up the effort of breaking free, reaching instead for the package that the Mistress had prepared. Tearing the skin bag from his thigh plate, leaving the nail stuck fast in the bone, he held the concealed object like a knife and stabbed it deep into the side of Shâhka's head.

His former captain grunted, but did not otherwise register the blow.

Kossolax's lip curled with contempt, even as it slowly turned blue. Shâhka may have grown stronger, but he had become stupid. He was as much a slave to the Butcher's Nails as Angron before him.

'I. Want. Angron,' Shâhka slobbered, in spite of the bagged device sticking out from his cranium.

'Angron will take the sons he is given. Like always.'

Shâhka roared, his insanity bottomless, and Kossolax croaked as the warrior crushed the thick cartilage of his neck. 'Mistress,' he managed, hoping the phenomenal pressure being brought to bear on his gorget had not disabled the vox-pickups buried there. His hand fell away from Shâhka, pulling the bag free from the furiously blinking teleport homer sunk by its attachment spike into the dense bone of Shâhka's skull. 'Teleport.'

The creature was already bending out of the way as Leidis charged in, willowing around the wild sweeps of his axe with a mocking smirk on its beguiling face. Leading with the shoulder, Leidis ran on through, bearing the daemon down and trampling its slender body under his greater mass with a sound like chitin being smashed to pieces with a hammer. Killing these creatures was no longer what mattered most to him. All that mattered now was fighting his way closer to Angron.

The primarch bellowed, the rampant embodiment of divine rage, causing metal to curl and blood to quicken, and daemons of rival alignment to spontaneously combust in pillars of oily purple flame. With a roar he kicked over a Stormraven gunship. The stocky multipurpose aircraft rolled onto its side, snapping off the wing and crushing daemons and Space Marines alike. The World Eaters in the hangar exulted equally.

Leidis howled as though he had never before felt such clarity in rage and feared he never would again.

Lissom daemons swarmed around Angron's thighs, snipping at the clattering bronzes of his armour, but failing to pierce the corrupted metals. Angron in turn crushed them underfoot by the score. Every swipe of his shrieking chainaxe sprayed the deck with kaleidoscopic ichor that hissed where it landed on ceramite and drove warriors into berserk raptures where it struck flesh.

Leidis yelled at the top of his lungs, no longer able to find the words for the fury he felt inside. The only means he had of expressing it fully was with volume.

Gripping his axe as though meaning it harm, he smashed it dementedly into the leering face of a daemon, still screaming, a perverse smile on the creature's face even as it came apart under his blows. A pair of World Eaters berzerkers in hatched war plate took advantage of his brief pause to overtake him, powering on towards a dozen or so beckoning monsters. Chainaxes shrieked, bolters roared, and suddenly glittering blood and supple limbs were flying everywhere. Leidis felt his mastery of the battlefield, gene-crafted and deeply indoctrinated, struggling to compete against the giddying rapture of combat. He picked out the signature pitch of Verroth's voice from amongst the horde behind him. The usually cold-blooded warrior was bellowing as though there were a toxin in his lungs that needed to be expelled, clicking the action of an already emptied bolter before mashing the stock into the back of a daemon's skull.

The daemons remained numerous, occupying ground over large swathes of the hangar, reinforcements continuing to pour in through some entry point that Leidis had been unable to discern, but the fight had turned decisively with Angron's arrival. He had provided the World Eaters with a point of focus, a champion around whom to rally, and an excuse, for a time at least, to be Space Marines, united in savage brotherhood and the implicit worship of their hated father.

And Angron himself was unstoppable.

He was the singularity around which everything ended.

Leidis raised his gore-slicked axe in salute of his rampaging primarch as a group of daemons of a type he had not yet witnessed charged the World Eaters' centre. They were centaur-like fiends with voluptuous torsos stacked atop the galloping frames of sinuous reptiles, and with the horned, multi-eyed heads of warrior insects.

A single swipe of Angron's off-hand blade split the lead creature messily in half, its humanoid torso and head sailing away from him as he stamped his brazen hoof on the body of a second with a ship-breaking *thud*. The World Eaters around him responded with a calamitous roar as they surged, fighting to be first in amongst the broken charge, only to be trampled in turn as the frenzied primarch strove to tear into the routed daemons himself.

'*L-L-L–*'

Leidis tore his eyes from the slaughter as one of the trampled bodies before him twitched. The broken warrior looked up at him, raising a limb that should not have bent as it did as though to beckon him closer, the focusing rings around its bionic right eye clicking and whirring. It took Leidis a moment to pull enough of the red mist from his eyes to recognise the warrior's face.

It was Arkhor the Redbound.

His breastplate had been crushed under Angron's hoof, but not before he had been scalped by a daemon's pincer claw. The roof of his head was missing. Blood crusted the jagged bowl of skull and flesh, his brains slowly spreading out across the deck plates behind him.

'L-L-L–' he said again, as though desperate to impress upon Leidis some parting words of spite.

Leidis felt no pity or grief for his crippled mentor.

Only rage.

He made to move on, to rejoin the primarch and leave his warleader to bleed, when he caught sight of something blinking from inside Arkhor's shattered brainpan. With a frown, lip curled with suppressed bloodlust, he crouched down and pushed his finger into soft brain matter, exposing a barbed metal rod and an array of glitching electronics. He attempted a smile, but the rage to which even those non-violent muscles were currently beholden turned it into something bestial.

The Butcher's Nails.

The devices had external processes that Leidis had seen before, fine cabling that ran through the roof of the skull and down the neck, heavy staples holding it all in place, but half the warleader's body being so thoroughly augmetised he had never been certain where one component ended and another began.

But here they were at last. What he had been looking for since Eden.

It was enough to penetrate the fury.

Arkhor made a long, drawn-out 'L–' as Leidis pincered the exposed tip of the implants and pulled them free.

They did not come cleanly, spider-thin threads of neural wire and electrodes embedded into the white matter with hooks that relinquished their hold on their host brain only at the cost of wrinkled chunks of meat.

'L–!' Arkhor slurred, jerking once with a final seizure before falling still.

Leidis curled his fingers around the warleader's bloody Nails, as the electrodes blinked out, one by one.

Shâhka had been fighting in a corridor. Now he wasn't.

He looked around. The chamber he found himself in looked like the chancel of a cathedral, but filled with an unholy octad of heaving pistons and bellows to a machine that took its sacrifices live. Blood-splattered slave pens and ritual gallows surrounded a central furnace. A monolithic chimney rose like a brazen godhead through endless miles of echoing companionways towards the plasma exhausts above the ship's spine.

He was in the ship's enginarium, but the furnace was cold and the pens empty. Blood splattered the cage floors, the spray patterns across the surrounding deck mimicking the placement of the bars, flesh and scraps of clothing swinging from their ceilings. Every surface glowed with a residual charge. The air felt heavy on the tongue.

It tasted like–

'Hnnng!'

He bent over his thighs and threw up. Acidic bile flecked with traces of blood splashed the metal, hissing as it began to dissolve the lighter elements of the alloy.

Shâhka was no stranger to finding gaps where memory should be.

How many times had he been up to his elbows in slaughter on some nameless planet, only to wake screaming in his pod as if from a nightmare, then to be wading through an entirely different foe on an entirely different world? The Nails spared him the drudgery of an interminable existence. They gave him meaning, if not glory. Equilibrium, if not peace.

But this felt different.

There had been a transition, a sense of being captured, like a fish in a net, and deposited in a new bowl as though he would not notice.

Shâhka tossed his head and snarled. His muscles fizzed with leftover aggression. His mouth was dry. His hearts fought like rabid birds in his chest.

He tried to remember where he had been, but could not. For some reason, he felt as though it had been important.

Who am I…?

'How delightful. A playmate.'

Shâhka turned.

A huge, many-limbed godling, a hybrid of man and woman, human and beast, disgust and desire, reclined in the blood-stained metal of the furnace mouth as though the mangled metal of the grille were the softest of beds. With a rustling of silks, a creaking of leathers, a sharpening of blades, all pleasant sounds in one, it stretched its many arms and gave a sigh of staggering boredom and ebullient delight.

'If I had known this ship would be as dull within as it appeared from without then I would have gladly left its sacking to another.' The Keeper of Secrets, for such it was, held a perfectly sculpted hand before its multifaceted eyes, as though examining the sharpness of one lethally curved claw. *'Where is the challenge? Why, even the mighty Angron pursues lesser pleasures when he might be battling me to release my hold upon his precious ship.'*

Shâhka had no concept of beauty. If any part of him ever had, then that warrior was no longer the Shâhka who stood in

the enginarium here and now. In that regard, the daemon held
no power over him.

But he had desires.

He had *a* desire.

Drip. Drip. Drip. That was the sound of the daemon's voice
in his head. *Drip. Drip. Drip.* Not a sound but a sensation, his
wrists cut, his throat, his thighs, blood leaking out of him and
onto the decking around his boots. Pooling there. *Drip. Drip.
Drip.* Tears welled up in his eyes.

It felt–

'Hnnng-nnng-nnng!'

The sudden, spectacularly violent seizure forced Shâhka down
onto his knees.

The Keeper of Secrets was the warp-borne distillation of
pleasure, and the Nails fought back against it as they always
did, crippling pain darkening every cluster of brain cells even
remotely connected to the processing of such sensations.

The greater daemon stirred, drawing itself idly from its bed
of gore. *'You resist. How fun. Could it be that this boorish vessel
has amusements for me after all?'*

Shâhka screamed until his breath seared his throat walls white
and expelled everything in his chest that was not rage. With
shaking hands he ground a fiercer grip out of his gigantic maul,
and charged.

The Keeper of Secrets sighed as it struck him an idle backhand
that sent him crashing through the gantry circling the furnace
dais. Shâhka shook with fury as he fell, roaring as, with a wrench
of ceramite and a splitting of flesh, a pair of vast, bronze-scaled
wings erupted from his shoulders. His pinions ballooned out
behind him, catching him even as he plummeted into the
churning machine pits that made up the bulk of the enginarium's substrata, and swept him back towards the main furnace.

The Keeper of Secrets clapped with magnificent boredom, drawing swords into two of its long-fingered hands and clacking an elegant pincer. *'Entertaining. Very entertaining. Show me your limits, my delicious savage.'*

He angled his body as he swooped around the dais, screaming wordless sounds until the acid in his spit was burning the enamel from his teeth, and swung his maul for the greater daemon's bejewelled crown. It swayed lithely out of the way, smiling encouragingly all the while, its infinitely reflective black eyes catching the maul's spasming energies as it swept across the crown.

The greater daemon bent until its back was parallel to the deck, swords *snicking* across his path like the blades of a corpse mill.

There was no way to avoid them and so Shâhka did not even try, taking one blade to the hip and another through the back. Both strikes carved open his muscular ceramite as though it were sodden clay and sent him crashing to the deck.

'Wonderful,' the Keeper of Secrets declared with a pirouette, coming about so swiftly that the hands with blades, the hands with claws and the hands with none all blurred and switched.

Shâhka made himself dizzy trying to track them, then grunted and shook himself off. He got back up with a pendulum-like swing of his maul.

'Hnnng!' Bubbles blew from his nose. *'Hnnn-nnn-nnng!'*

'Eloquent,' said the Keeper of Secrets. *'Your father must be very proud.'*

Blinded by fury, Shâhka charged again, damaged plates grinding aggressively as he threw a pulverising blow that the daemon evaded with contemptuous ease. It whirled into a counter-attack, claws and blades weaving a dance about him, only too eager to forgive a willing but blundering partner his reckless flailing and climaxing each perfect movement with a blade through his chest. Shâhka shivered, something in him dying with ecstasy each time a daemon sword slid through his organs, and then again, in something like madness, as it was withdrawn to begin again. The Keeper of Secrets was too fast. Shâhka had not yet managed to graze it even once, but every mocking blow it landed on him was a moment in which it put itself in his reach.

With matching swords criss-crossing through his torso, the daemon close enough to his squashed nostrils to smell its perfume, Shâhka slammed his forehead into the creature's chin. It moaned in ecstasy as its jaw snapped under the blow. It was inhumanly strong and shadow-fast, but it was unarmoured and, for a daemon, surprisingly delicate. Shâhka's head, on the other hand, was as much warped ceramite as transhuman flesh. The Keeper of Secrets reeled from him, multicoloured and sweet-smelling bloods trickling down its chin, driving Shâhka into a jealous fury as he spun his maul through a sequence of expanding figure of eights. Swing after massive swing forced the wounded daemon onto its heels until its back was to the central furnace. Sharply reversing his grip, Shâhka thumped the head of his maul into the greater daemon's chest. The blow shattered its ribcage, the unleashed disruption charge sending it crashing back from him and through the furnace gates.

Shâhka barged the buckled gates aside, following the stricken daemon into the furnace with a squeal of terrified brass.

His nose wrinkled.

The furnace was as cavernous inside as the mustering deck on an Astartes strike cruiser. The walls were black, the floor underfoot brittle with the remains of fissile starter briquettes and human fuel. The air was ash. His armour shuddered and squealed. As if in rage. Perhaps in pain. The almost sentient musculature of his corrupted body swelled against the harness from within, straining to push through it and fuse the damaged plates into their own bulging mass.

The Keeper of Secrets looked up at him from its reclined position amidst the charred bones. *'Yes,'* it sighed, taking in his brutalised physique, the dozen unbleeding punctures, the curse that even a daemon weapon could not break, and finally appeared satisfied. *'What ambitious torture, so far in excess of anything I could inflict or devise. I see there is nothing more for me to do here.'*

With a roar, Shâhka obliterated the greater daemon's head between his maul and the floor, its lifeless body dissolving into a toxic effervescent slurry that seeped into the soot as its spirit recoiled to the warp.

A jolt passed through the ship, the walls of the furnace tremoring like a reluctant bell. Shâhka felt a sudden release of tension and a sense of motion, as though an immense and inviolable force had held them static and now they were free. The pressure he had felt pressing against his skull from the outside slowly began to abate.

Shâhka was damaged, but he was no fool.

If it was the Keeper of Secrets who had been holding the *Conqueror* bound, then Shâhka's unexplained appearance in its lair was surely no coincidence. He shrugged the revelation off.

All men started life as tools to be used. Some were made to be weapons.

And Shâhka knew what he was.

CHAPTER THIRTEEN

+Help–+
  +Please–+
  +Stop–+
  +This way–+
  +The Emperor pro–+

The warp on this side of the Rift clamoured with voices. Opening one's mind to it was like opening a door onto millions of screaming petitioners, all of them begging, all of them shouting, all of them desperate to communicate but in a language of riddles in which Graucis Telomane had not been tutored. The ability to pluck a single voice from the tumult of a battlefield, to hear one cry for help from a billion, was of no advantage when the voices were unspoken and their messages unclear.

With both hands braced to the marble door frame that his mind had constructed to give this realm order, he bent his head to the clamour as if to a howling gale, and strained to listen.

+A witch sings on Phoenix wings… The prince of spiders spins a *web for the priest of ravens… The worms crawl beneath my skin, my skin is dying but it flourishes with new life… Help us, help us, help us…+*

Astrotelepathy employed a common lexicon of dream imagery and allegory that allowed a trained psyker anywhere in the vastness of the Imperium to send their thoughts into the warp in the reasonable hope, via one or more astropathic relays, of having their cry received by another receptive mind and understood. It was akin to writing a short riddle, sealing it in a bottle, and tossing it into an infinite ocean, hoping for it one day to be read.

Graucis' was a potent mind, but untutored in the nuances of astrotelepathy.

There were too many voices. If he were to live another six hundred years and devote every moment he had left to the task, he could not have hoped to heed them all.

With an effort of will, Graucis leant the metaphysical door to the empyrean closed, and drew his mind back into his own head.

He came to in the meditation chamber aboard the *Sword of Dione*. He was kneeling on the smooth marble flooring, breathing hard from the attempt at scrying the warp through such a tumult. His eyes were closed, colours swirling across the backs of the lids to the flicker of candlelight. The warp engines thrummed, the agonies of the Sea of Souls as it burned against the *Dione*'s silvered hull a tremor through his armour-plated knees.

The passage was less turbulent than it had been before his strike against Angron and the *Conqueror*, but he could still feel the warp's turmoil. It agitated the old burns from Armageddon and the unhealed wound in his thigh. The latter manifested itself on this occasion as an icy burn that extended a crippling sense of fatigue as far down as his toes.

Graucis took a risk, he knew, sending his mind into the warp while the immaterium remained in a state of such agitation, but he did not expect the seethe to lessen anywhere on this side of the Cicatrix Maledictum. He would find no better conditions anywhere else in Imperium Nihilus. His strike on the *Conqueror* had bought the *Sword of Dione* a small lead. Now he needed to use it, to discover where Angron was bound with such determination that he had lured World Eaters from across the galaxy to join him.

Wherever it was, Graucis would find it first.

'You push yourself to self-destruction, brother,' said Geromidas, turning from his vigil by the viewing portals. The Chaplain was still in his armour. Barring a brief ablution in the wake of their return from the Red Angel's Gate, to ensure no hint of that realm's taint remained, Graucis had insisted the Grey Knights remain battle-ready. Nihilus was the very definition of hostile territory. Battle could come upon them at any time. Geromidas observed Graucis with concern bordering on suspicion, as the cyber-cherub Young Pious MMXIV buzzed around him, concluding its fraught auto-hymnal before folding itself back into the reliquary casket by the chamber's entrance and returning its functions to somnolence. 'And worse, I fear you do it for no good cause. There has been too much suffering here, with too little hope of surcease. All of Imperium Nihilus has been poisoned by it, and even with the Rift now behind us the power of the warp is too great.'

Graucis rubbed absently at his thigh, feeling the splinter of tainted bronze shifting under his palm.

'I can defeat it.'

'Your mind is capable. Of that I have no doubt. It is the strain you place on your body that concerns me.' The Chaplain smiled, but there was a degree of judgement behind it. 'With the injuries you took on Armageddon, you could have taken a role in the Sanctum Sanctorum, or in the Dead Fields, but you made yourself go on…' He shook his head, but did not say more.

Geromidas understood Graucis' obsession. It was the same for all of the Brotherhood of Thirteen. Whatever private doubts any of them might harbour towards their master, their commitment to ensuring Angron's final defeat was one they all shared. But the doubts were there, nevertheless. Graucis could see it in his brother's prolonged regard.

The wrath of Angron still burned in those who faced him that day. They did not often speak of it amongst themselves. Indeed, it was rare that the survivors of Armageddon came together at all, and that was partly by intention, for they all saw something in each other that they did not care to acknowledge in themselves. Paladin Dvorik was the only fellow survivor that Graucis had spoken with in centuries and, even with him, their reunions were fleeting by necessity, over before they became uncomfortable. The fury that had touched them as younger warriors had reshaped them in ways that were never easy to perceive, and in all cases more subtly than Graucis' obvious suffering, driving them down paths to excellence that they could not escape.

Crowe had become castellan of the Chamber of Purity and a byword for psychic fortitude. Hyperion now commanded the Augurium. Malchadiel had excelled in his studies of the Martian mysteries and had risen to become Armourium Master aboard Apex Cronus Bastion, the great star fort in orbit of Titan. Stern was now captain of the Third Brotherhood, while Mordrak was not only Grand Master of the Second but admiral of the entire Titan warfleet, serving in both roles for longer than any brother in their Chapter's long history.

Graucis rubbed absently at his leg.

'It must be done,' he said. 'Angron must be denied, whatever his purpose might be, and we are the only ones in Nihilus with enough forewarning to intercede.'

Geromidas shook his head slowly, as though teasing out his next words. 'We have already won a piece of the primarch's True Name. This, in and of itself, is a prize that would earn us all a statue in the Chamber of Champions. We should return to Titan, now, lest this lore be lost to the Chapter with our deaths.'

'I have considered that,' said Graucis. 'But how can we decide on the course before us when we do not yet know what Angron intends? How can we turn our backs and return to the safety of Titan knowing that a fallen primarch and the might of his broken Legion is at large?'

The Chaplain sighed. 'Our ritual to bind him rested on the certainty that he would return to take his vengeance on Armageddon.'

'I have accounted for that too, brother,' said Graucis, tapping the phial of soil that he now wore from his belt with the other relics he had rescued from the survivors of Armageddon. He had taken it from the polluted banks of the Styx River, where, six hundred years ago, Angron had fallen in battle to the Grey Knights, and the unusually iron-rich soil was red and moist to this day. 'But we must now divine his destination, and swiftly.'

Geromidas crossed the small round floor of the meditation chamber, boots thudding heavily on the marble tiles. He laid his gauntlet on Graucis' shoulder. 'Then at least rest, brother. Allow me to perform the sending in your place.'

Graucis reached up with his own hand, laying the gauntlet across the Chaplain's. 'You do not have the psychic ability, brother. None of you do, except perhaps Liminon, but I fear his torments in the dungeons of the Artful Sublime have cost him some of his control. I will require all of you for the ritual that will end Angron permanently, I assure you, but this step can only be mine.'

Geromidas frowned down at him. They had a bond that few others could share. They were closer than brothers, but they were not friends. Graucis had permitted himself no friends. And Geromidas, for his part, though his distrust was not of his choosing, could not help but be on his guard around him.

'There is a reason the Grey Knights do not temper their youngest brothers in battle. Do you know why?'

Justicar Aelos had asked him that question before the Grey Knights' departure from Titan. Graucis had known the answer then, but he had not understood the question until now.

He had been too inexperienced to face the Sanguinary Unholiness and perhaps that, beyond the obvious fact of his injury, was why he had suffered these past centuries while Mordrak and Crowe and Dvorik and all the others had prospered. If he had perished, as all the laws of probability must have supposed he would, then the costs would have been easier to bear, but his spirit had been unprepared for the burden of survival.

'I will have your strength with me at all times, brother,' he said.

Geromidas bowed his head in surrender and stepped back, careful to avoid disturbing the concentric rings of candles that had been set up around Graucis. 'Then I will bend every thought to your success, brother.'

Graucis looked aside, staring into the candles until the hexagrammic wards were printed onto his retinas, took a deep breath, and *sent*.

It was raining over Mount Anarch.

Raindrops of liquid ethane spotted the towering glassteel panes. In under one-fifth of standard g, the rain was not falling so much as gliding, parading from high atmosphere towards the desolate surface of Titan as though time had already surrendered to its legions.

His mind stood once again in the Saturnalium, looking out from the upper battlements of the Citadel across the peaks of lesser crags and cryo volcanos.

The ancient mechanisms of the Deimos Clock *tick-tick-ticked* to the rain's graceful march. Graucis looked up to study it.

The position of Saturn and its moons were a nonsense from which he could infer no date or time. The candles set out around the mosaic floor and stone tables presented an exact replica of the arrangement his physical body had left aboard the *Sword of Dione*, as though the imprint on his retinas had relit them here in the psychic realm.

The empyrean, as he had been taught, was a domain of the mind. Just as physical toil and the proper instruments could be used to mould the architecture of realspace, so too could the warp be reshaped by the tools of will.

This was the place that Graucis' mind knew best.

When his mind was freed to go anywhere, it was to this place that it always returned. It was the last time he could recall that there had been choices before him, some destiny other than the defeat of Angron or death at the primarch's hands.

The inexperienced young warrior that he had been the last time he physically set foot in this chamber – for even on his occasional returns to Titan he had always avoided it since – sighed.

It was not for glory that he pitted himself against the might of the Emperor's fallen son. Over the course of six centuries, he had won enough acclaim to satisfy the most vainglorious of heroes. Nor did he begrudge, or even envy, the likes of Malchadiel and Hyperion, who had made peace with the traumas of their younger selves and sought newer challenges to suit the darker age. He was a Grey Knight, incorruptible and above such mortal foibles.

He repeated the insistence, determined to make it true.

He did not begrudge his brothers for leaving this task to him.

Striding forwards, ignoring the tugging pain in his thigh, he walked to the psychic doors to the true empyrean and threw them wide.

The voices screamed into the Saturnalium the moment the doors were ajar and their silvered wards broken. The psychic force blistered the old burns on his face, the words filling his ears like cold rushing water, too loud, too numerous and too *deep* for him to catch more than fragments.

+*Hasten*–+

+*Please*–+

+*Hope*–+

+*Save*–+

+*End*–+

Graucis gritted his teeth and hardened his heart.

Thirteen Grey Knights represented strength enough to turn the tides of war on any world. But for a hundred worlds? For a hundred thousand, spread across half a galaxy that had already gone dark?

There was nothing Graucis could do but hear their pleas and then damn them with his silence.

The Grey Knights fought for the fates of trillions, not for the lives of millions.

Leaving the tranquillity of the Saturnalium behind him, he stepped out onto the rocks of Titan. To the layout of the Citadel, the jarring transition made no sense, but to the geometries of the warp it did not need to. The doors closed behind him and disappeared into the maelstrom of voices.

The freezing hydrocarbon rain scalded his peeling skin. The

immense yellow disc of Saturn loomed over the dark grey sky, glassy rings frozen in state, like the exposed workings of a delicate clock.

+I am with you to the very end, brother,+ sent Geromidas, from at once six feet and a million light years away.

+I too,+ came Dvorik's voice, from the arming chamber.

+And I,+ sent Liminon, from the enginarium.

+In the face of the Primordial Evil there can be no second thoughts,+ sent Justicar Gallead, mentally quoting from the *Spiritus Compendii* even as he trained his body alongside his brothers. +We succeed, or we consign all humanity to the fate of Nihilus with our failure.+

Graucis felt the gathering of their psychic presences as an aura about him.

With psychic hands they armoured him in silver, repelling the astrotelepathic screams that would torment him, boiling off the frigid rain before it could strike his mind's newly gleaming plate. Buoyed by the advocacy of his brothers, he lengthened his stride until he was bounding across the surface of his small world and then, with one great leap, leaving it behind him.

The Citadel fell away beneath him. Mount Anarch shrank and became a speck, swallowed by the frozen arms of Titan.

The clouds thinned.

Light pierced through.

Graucis blinked in the sudden brilliance, though it was a soothing light rather than a blinding one, unable to believe that he had not been able to see it before.

Angron's rage had cast a shadow across the entirety of realspace and the warp, obscuring everything that lay beyond. But now the *Sword of Dione* had pulled ahead at last, and the Beast's destination lay clear in sight.

A light. White and brilliant.

Graucis' first thought was that by some strange curvature of the warp, the *Sword of Dione* had been turned around and pointed back at Terra, but even Angron, with his Legion of old and all his daemonic allies beside him, could not seriously intend to conquer the Throneworld alone. The light drew him closer, as it appeared to be drawing Angron, like an ice comet towards a star, and he saw that the beacon shone from a different world to Terra.

Though it shamed him, he felt relief in that.

There would be a battle for him yet. His long centuries of preparation would not end with him watching the primarch fall against Terra's walls.

From the high vantage of a mind hurtling faster than light, he observed.

The world was fractionally smaller than Terra, but no less ruined by the exploitative presence of man. It was a world in which great mountains had been broken down to fill in the beds of long-drained oceans, forests and jungles and marshlands torn up and made level for shrine complexes, cities and massive fortresses, and deep, forested valleys. Thick clouds of pollution obscured swathes of its surface, broken only by the pinnacles of fortresses and the very greatest shrines to the God-Emperor. From the most magnificent of these bastions, the light of the Emperor shone like a beacon against the encroaching night.

Graucis did not know how it could be. With the Emperor enthroned on Terra and all of Imperium Nihilus isolated from His illumination, it should have been impossible, but there was no doubt in Graucis' mind that the light enveloping this world was His.

Embodied by astral projection as he was, the revelation still rendered Graucis light-headed.

The Astronomican was a manifestation of the Emperor's

psychic self that had endured for over ten thousand years, but this was not His light as a guide and a beacon.

This was His will as a weapon.

This was what Angron sought to destroy. In his blind rage and all-consuming hatred of his father, the daemon primarch would tear it down regardless of its purpose.

Graucis resolved that he would lay down his life, and the lives of all his brothers, to ensure that Angron did not succeed.

As he looped around the planet and out beyond its yellow sun, psychically slingshotting himself back towards the Saturnalium and his physical self aboard the *Sword of Dione*, he glimpsed the world from its opposite face. He recognised it. It was the world he had seen in his vision when the shape of the warp had first brought warning of Angron's return to realspace. From the minds of the billions hidden beneath its clouds, and ensconced within its orbiting city-plates, the name *Malakbael* fastened on to his thoughts.

And across the vastness of the Sea of Souls, the Red Angel roared.

A single word.

+*No!*+

A drizzle of caustic anti-burn gels stung him awake.

His eyes blinked open.

Young Pious MMXIV had emerged from its hibernaculum and was now hovering unsteadily above him, its arcane anti-gravitics causing the candles around him to gutter. Its mummified expression was at once deliberately sanguine and unintentionally horrific as it droned in a slow circle to apply spray to Graucis' back. Geromidas, too, had knelt to join him on the floor. He held Graucis upright with his hands on Graucis' shoulders. His armour was dazzling on tired eyes in the candlelight.

'Did you...?' Graucis began, smoke curling from his lips the moment he opened his mouth. He coughed and tried again. 'Did you see what I saw?'

'The beacon on Malakbael. The light of the Emperor in Nihilus. Yes, brother,' said Geromidas. 'Gallead is already on his way to the command deck to advise Shipmaster Oren of our new course. Forgive me my earlier doubts. There is no question that we must do all in our power to defend this wonder from the Lord of the Twelfth.'

'No, brother.'

'No?'

Graucis tried to sit, but his efforts in the psychic realm had left his body too stiff to obey. He would need to rest after all, after this, or he would be of no use at all when the time finally came to ensure the Red Angel's fall. 'Angron must not be allowed to set foot anywhere near that world. The world I saw is well defended, but it is not Terra. It is not even Armageddon. No, if the Lord of the Twelfth is allowed to continue his voyage to Malakbael unopposed then the force he will be able to gather to him will be unstoppable, regardless of our presence there.'

'Then what, brother? He is set on Malakbael.'

Graucis looked inward.

The plan that he and Dvorik had first formulated, long ago when what would become a Brotherhood of Thirteen had comprised just two, had been to confront Angron on Armageddon.

Every augury that had ever been cast had foreseen his return through the Red Angel's Gate to lay waste to the world that had denied him six centuries before. Moreover, facing him there made pragmatic sense as, for whatever resonant cause, it was where Graucis had always felt his psychic abilities to be at their strongest. He had always assumed it had to do with his own link to that world, and the primarch whose fate both he and Armageddon had been tied to ever since.

The relics he had set his brotherhood to gathering over the last six hundred years represented the one hundred and nine Grey Knights who had bested him once before. They were to provide Graucis with symbolic resonance and spiritual might while the earth of that world, already watered once with Angron's unholy essence and primed to receive his soul in perpetuity, would have been the perfect receptacle for the binding ritual.

Graucis had already made adjustments in that regard.

He set his hand once again over the phial of soil that he wore on his hip. The warp turned on the power of symbolism, but he had no certainty at all how effective it would prove. There were no easy shortcuts. Malakbael, however, presented not a means to cheat but an opportunity to alter the field of play.

Perhaps a true son of the Emperor, an inheritor of His genetic legacy with the relics of one hundred and nine of his brethren to attest to his pure intent, could harness a portion of His light as it traversed the warp between the Golden Throne and Malakbael. Another might have decried even the mere notion as heresy, but Graucis was a Grey Knight – such labels did not apply. All he needed was to find a world, one world, lying in direct conjunction with Malakbael and Terra.

'The astropathic pleas we have been ignoring since crossing into Nihilus...'

'What of them, brother?'

'Have Gallead inform the shipmaster that one of them is to receive an answer.'

With half the galaxy aflame, it was almost a certainty that one of its cries would be originating from a world in the necessary conjunction. Finding the required world was half the challenge.

Drawing Angron from his chosen course and luring him to it would be the next.

Geromidas again wore that look of concern. 'I am familiar with the rituals used to bait the Sanguinary Unholiness. But to draw an entity of Angron's independent will and potency, you would need to condemn–'

'–a world,' Graucis finished.

He absently kneaded at the ghost pain in his thigh, but strangely the pain had all but disappeared. He took it as a sign.

How else to bait a trap for the Red Angel, but with slaughter?

CHAPTER FOURTEEN

Colonel Tanika Yarrer, of the Adeptus Astra Telepathica Hyades garrison, woke to the sound of the alarms. Still half in sleep and steeped in the blood that filled her dreams of late, she pulled the loaded sidearm from underneath her headroll and rolled over.

She squinted blearily at the radioactively luminous face of her bedside chrono. It read a quarter-hour past midnight. She had been off-shift for a little less than three hours.

Running her hand up the brick wall behind her, she found the rune-switch to rouse the lumens. They came on in fits, rousing themselves as sluggishly as Yarrer herself and painting her meagre cell and its contents in jaundiced yellows.

Stiffly, her muscles aching from no exertion she could remember, she swung her legs off the hard pallet and, from there, slid her feet into the pair of black leather jackboots waiting on the bare metal floor. Stifling a yawn that was equal parts a shiver, she pulled on an armoured jacket. She was already in her fatigues. Alarms had become routine, as regular as mealtimes and prayers.

The facility's astropaths were agitated as she had not seen them since the months following the Darkening. Some doom was approaching and all the psykers could feel it.

Yarrer holstered her hellpistol, stretching her eyes open by pulling down the cheeks as if to admit more light into her exhausted brain.

It was not only the psykers who felt it. She was almost grateful for the fact that her charges so rarely allowed her more than a few hours' sleep each night.

Picking up her hotshot lasrifle from where she had left it propped against the end of the bed frame, she positioned her less-favoured left hand around the stock and her right hand under the forestock. She had been forced to retrain her grip from right to left to account for the loss of her trigger finger to a psychic incident eighteen months earlier and it still felt awkward to her. As though she'd just stepped out of a mirror and found everything backward.

Suppressing a shiver, she flipped the weapon over and checked the charge dial moulded into the black plastek receiver.

Older packs had a tendency to lose charge over the course of a night. It was becoming more and more of an issue as the Basilicarum Astropathica's limited stores from before the Darkening dried up. She knew this, but when she read the *forty per cent* numeral under the hovering needle she could shrug off the certainty that it was the violence of her own dreams that had somehow drained it. With a shake of the head, ignoring the fearful whisperings as the martial academies of the Scholastica Psykana trained its pupils to do, she went to her door, pulled the bolt, and pushed it open.

The corridor was as dark as her room had been with the lumens off, but the alarm was twice as loud without the thin metal door to block it, two-tone wails crowing from augmitter boxes roosting in the cobwebbed beams. Scrivener adepts in ink-stained robes tussled with sanctioned psykers in bulky execution collars, all of them streaming past her door. It was in the nature of psychic work that much of it had to be performed at night. Yarrer did not know why, but she suspected that the warp was somehow *closer* during those hours. Adeptus Astra Telepathica Standing Edict 10014-κ demanded the evacuation of all personnel graded epsilon and above to shielded wings in the event of a psychic incident, but such events were not supposed to be nightly occurrences.

Yarrer did not need to be telepathic herself to sense the frayed tempers, the irritation at yet another aborted sending, of experiments thrown awry and divinations ruined, the violence simmering beneath the scholarly snarls.

She wondered if any of them, whenever it was they slept, had been having the same dreams as her.

The feeble gleam of her room's lumen picked out the glossy black body armour of one of her troopers, escorting the fractious workers.

As the ranking officer on Hyades, Yarrer had command of an infantry section, three squads of ten apiece, tasked with garrisoning the Basilicarum Astropathica. Her duties required her to liaise with the planetary and municipal commanders, with the canoness of the Adepta Sororitas mission in Hyades Capitolis, but her troopers rarely fraternised outside their own ranks. Yarrer knew all thirty better than she had ever known her own family. She believed she could pick out any one of them in pitch darkness.

'Hedrod,' she called out, squinting into the gloom as she beckoned him over.

Hedrod was a large man, as some men tended towards without any effort on their part. Had he not found a duty in one of the

Emperor's many military arms, he would undoubtedly have become fat, but as it was he was muscularly solid, with a residual doughiness about his features and a thick blond beard bushing from underneath his black visor.

'Are you the sergeant on duty?' she demanded as Hedrod threw her a salute.

'Yes, colonel.'

'Is this a psychic incident or an attack?'

The Basilicarum Astropathica had yet to come under direct assault, but several raids by the rebel 'Consortia' on other capitolis targets had hit close enough to breach the wards and trigger alarms. Given that whoever controlled the Basilicarum Astropathica was, in effect, Hyades' voice to the wider Imperium, that seemed remiss on the rebels' part.

A part of her wondered if the Consortia's nebulous leadership were now somehow aware of what the lady-governor herself had to expect, even if she had never been explicitly told.

There was no Imperium out there to speak to.

The fighting for the capitolis had intensified in recent days. It was as though whatever malady was disturbing the astropaths was troubling less receptive minds across the continent too. At least, that was how it looked from the battlements, what it sounded like through the small window in her cell.

'Incident,' said Hedrod. 'I've just come from Theta Block.'

Yarrer groaned. Theta Block. Again.

'How many times now?'

'Just this week? Five.'

'Coven Master Pyrrhus should have purged the entire wing.'

Yarrer knew why he had not, though that did not make her like it. Without reliable contact with the Scholastica Psykana and the Black Ships, without access to the City of Sight and the soul-binding rituals it performed, there had been no way to replenish their choirs. Old age, the rigours of astrotelepathy and las-bolts to the head had depleted their numbers. After eight years adrift from the Imperium, they were in danger of running out of astropaths.

Not that there was anyone to speak to, but there was bureaucracy to be observed, forms to be archived, and standing edicts dictated that the attempts continue to be made.

Taking her hotshot lasrifle in its awkward, mirror-form grip, she turned in the opposite direction to the evacuating adepts and started up the corridor towards the containment blocks.

'With me, trooper,' she called back to Hedrod.

After a few hundred yards, they came to a locked door set into the left-hand wall. It was a dark, psychically impermeable hardwood, further reinforced with warding sigils and several rows of black iron studs.

Hedrod unlocked the door using a key from the heavy set hanging from a brass ring on his equipment belt and pulled it outwards.

Yarrer swept inside.

The guard cell was unfurnished except for a single alloy chair. The latter was currently empty, as Trooper Siwan was agitated enough to need to stand. 'Theta,' she said, as Hedrod entered and locked the door behind him. 'Again.' Siwan was a painfully thin-looking woman, gaunt-faced and abstemious with stubble-length black hair.

Despite the lady-governor's injunction to ration the capitolis' power, the small room was not completely dark. A barred window admitted the flickering lights of Hyades Capitolis. Yarrer could hear what sounded like tanks growling along the sandy processionals below, the barked voices of militiamen and autorifles, the rumble of low-flying aeronautica over the capitolis' airspace.

A parade perhaps.

Or a large mobilisation.

The Basilicarum Astropathica occupied its own walled quarter at the southern reach of Hyades Capitolis. From this vantage, on a clear day, one could see six hundred miles over the Dust Sea, as far across the Kotha Basin as the nearest Consortia outpost at Kwat. The skies were not clear, and nor was it day. Sand blowing in off the basin swept across the capitolis' flat roofs, obscuring all but the dimmest ghosts of the cathedrum basilica, and the Imperial governor's manse on the promontory. Rust locusts and red cicadas sawed from their hiding places amidst the potted succulents that grew along the window ledge.

The work of her predecessor, Yarrer had been told. He had, apparently, gone quite insane. Nothing grew on Hyades.

Casting the goings-on outside from her thoughts, she crossed the guard cell. An identical second door stood directly opposite the first.

'Passphrase: *verisimilitude*,' she said.

With a nod, Siwan unlocked the second door.

Only the duty guard was permitted to hold the key for the inner door, while the sergeant at watch was the one individual in the facility who could open the outer. Only a handful of people knew the correct passphrase and it was changed daily. The dangers of psychic coercion or mental domination were too real and so compartmentalisation, challenge and constant, overbearing oversight was the standard rule for even the simplest of procedures.

Yarrer opened the door.

A gust of cold, desiccated air breathed out from beyond the threshold. There was a smattering of quiet screams, muted by the imperfectly aligned baffler fields and thick stone walls, but not many. The containment blocks had been heavily depopulated over the past years, and none more so of late than Theta.

Yarrer tightened her grip on her rifle.

She took a deep breath to settle her unease and went in. Hedrod followed with his heavier tread. Siwan pulled the door closed behind them and locked it, the rattle of the iron key in the lock echoing down the cell-lined passage as though to remind Yarrer that it was still there.

The corridor cut at a right-angle to the one she had just left. There were no windows. There was nothing on the other side of these walls but several more yards of stone. The Basilicarum Astropathica was less the fortress that it appeared to be from the outside than it was a prison. Its high, black walls and elite garrison were there not to safeguard the adepts, but to deny whatever malefic force that might desire the freedom of those incarcerated within. One did not command an Adeptus Astra Telepathica garrison for two decades without hearing stories, of the things that could sometimes slip loose whenever one of the astropaths sent themselves across the veil. She had even seen such a creature once. She was sure Hedrod had too. But they all knew better than to talk about it.

Frost hung in the air. It veined the metal doors of the cells.

Yarrer's breath turned to smoke.

'Left-hand side or right?' she asked.

Hedrod shrugged. 'Do you have a coin?'

Forcing a smile onto her tired face, she waved Hedrod sideways. 'Colonel's prerogative then. You take left.'

The trooper went to the first door on the left.

Something was slowly beating against it from the inside and moaning. Hedrod rattled the latch, checked the lock, then slid back the hatch to uncover a narrow window at eye level and peered inside.

Whatever it was he saw within made him blanch, and he slammed the hatch shut. He took a moment to compose himself.

'Eight-eighty-one, secure.'

Yarrer lowered her rifle.

She had served alongside the man for over a decade, but at the slightest hint of his willpower being compromised by the inmate within she would not have hesitated to pull the trigger. She would have said a prayer for him before and afterwards, but it would have been necessary. She fully expected him to do the same for her.

Leapfrogging him down the corridor to the first cell along the right, marked *8-82*, she mirrored the exact routine, levering her shorter frame onto tiptoes to peer inside.

The wretch within was sitting upright on a bare alloy bed frame, straitjacketed and gagged, and shackled to the frame's metal legs. Long, numerological equations composed in blood and faeces ran all around the walls and up onto the ceiling. How he always managed to transcribe his minor heresies despite being sedated and bound was a mystery that successive garrison commanders had never been able to solve. If the loss of contact with Terra and the Black Ships had not made trained astropaths so valuable and rare, then Yarrer would have shot him long ago.

The air inside was far too cold for it to stink as badly as it did.

Yarrer snapped the hatch shut and gave the handle a twist to lock it.

'Eight-eighty-two, secure.'

Hedrod hunched into his rifle, a briefly reassuring smile snapping the icicles that had formed in his beard, and continued on.

'Eight-eighty-three, secure,' he announced.

'Eight-eighty-four,' said Yarrer, a moment later.

'Eight-eighty-five.'

'Eight-eighty-six...'

In spite of all the Adeptus Astra Telepathica's lore and

technology, in spite of the wards, the drugs, the baffler fields and the alarms, the silver alloy shackles and the careful routines, psychic intrusions somehow managed to occur. They had never been everyday occurrences, however, even through the worst days of the Darkening, and their regularity now worried Yarrer.

Ignore it, her training told her. *Ignore it and focus only on your duty.*

'Eight-eighty-seven, secure,' said Hedrod.

Yarrer took the next on the right.

The Gothic numerals *8-88* had been inscribed on its brass plaque. Something about that arrangement of characters left her distinctly uneasy though she did not know why.

She took hold of the latch, and screamed.

It was freezing cold.

She could feel Hedrod standing a few yards behind her, finger tensed over his hellgun's trigger. She tried to let go of the latch, but couldn't get her fingers to move. The cold had burned them to the metal. With a scream, steam hissing from under her palm as she wriggled it against the handle, she braced her boot to the door and pushed back hard against it, tearing her hand away.

She stumbled back into the corridor and bumped the opposite wall.

The skin of her hand continued to sizzle from the latch where she had left it.

Cursing through gritted teeth, she blew on her flayed palm and clenched it to her armoured chest.

Hedrod hesitated over his hellgun.

'I'm all right. It's just cold,' Yarrer told him, wincing as she subjected the hand to a tentative flex. The last thing she could afford to lose now was the use of another hand. Bionics had become scarce, and the Adeptus Astra Telepathica had other ways for invalided officers to be of service to the Imperium. *'Really* cold. I'm not possessed.' With a jerk of the head, she gestured towards door 8-88. 'Whatever triggered the alarm, I believe it came from in there.'

'Should've known,' Hedrod muttered, taking a step back and shifting his aim to cover the window hatch.

While he did so, Yarrer shrugged the sleeve of her fatigues down to make an impromptu glove over her wounded hand. Steeling herself against the pain, she nudged the clasp up before bashing the thing fully open with her rifle butt.

Hedrod covered her as she looked inside.

Yarrer swore softly. She was accustomed to the horrors of the witch, but it was impossible for any sane soul to ever become truly inured to them. And the past weeks had left her weary of horror. So very, very weary.

Astropath 88-θ, as the sanctioned witch was correctly designated, was levitating two feet above his bed frame, entangled in a spider's web of frost-encrusted chains. The stone walls shivered and creaked like glaciers while a wind from no material source gusted around the frozen cell. 'Thirteen,' he screamed, and though his head had been covered by a black bag after 88-θ's last psychic incident, Yarrer heard him clearly. It was the wind that spoke. 'Thirteen indomitable crusades did the son launch, but only one bears His son. Rejoice. Rejoice. Rejoice. Rejoice. Rejoice. Rejoice. Rejoice. Rejoice.' The speed of the psyker's breathing caused the sack to suck in and out around the hollow of his mouth. In and out, it went. In and out. As though whatever vision his warp-sight granted, it terrified him beyond reason. 'He bears the torch that has burned for ten thousand years and comes for the light that still shines. Eight times rejoice, for His son comes to Hyades and this war will soon end!' He struggled in his chains as though trying to wake himself up from his nightmare. 'Rejoice. Rejoice. Rejoice. Rejoi–'

A thump from behind startled Yarrer back from the door.

She slammed the hatch on reflex and the wind fell away, shuttered from her by the warded metal and stealing the words just as abruptly.

Shakily, she turned.

Two more troopers had arrived behind them. It took Yarrer a moment longer than it should have to recognise them. Otho and Bernesse, from Sergeant Clio's squad. Like Hedrod, they were in full battlefield dress, but supplemented with the sun visors and flowing white over-robes commonly worn by the planetary militias as protection from Hyades' two giant red suns. They had brought the sand of their perimeter duty in with them. Yarrer tasted it on the air as they threw sharp salutes.

'What are you doing away from your posts?' Yarrer asked.

'There's something going on out there, colonel,' said Bernesse. She was a local woman, drafted in from the Hyaden militias to cover for the recent rash of unexplained deaths, accidents and suicides. She had dark brown skin and darker hair dressed in ringlets of engraved bone. Her face and hands were scarred from her world's years-old civil war, in the way that all Hyadens of fighting age were scarred, her eyes and speech hollowed out by the nightmares she had been forced to endure since trading front-line duties for the Adeptus Astra Telepathica garrison. 'You need to come and see.'

Yarrer shook her head. 'Whatever it is will have to wait.'

'You've been *summoned*,' said Otho, with an admonishing look at Bernesse.

For a moment, Yarrer was almost surprised enough to forget the presence of 88-θ behind the door beside her. 'The coven master has left his chambers?'

Otho nodded. 'The lady-governor summoned *him*.'

'Ilsetza is here?' This was unprecedented.

'She was summoned too,' said Otho.

'Who could command the lady-governor?'

'That's what you need to come and see.'

Yarrer let the import of that sink in. She patted over the pockets of her carapace jacket while she thought what to do. Throne of Terra, she needed a smoke, but real chaq leaves were impossible to get hold of in the capitolis any more. Ever since the Consortia had captured the agri-domes of the temperate southern pole and tightened its grip on the Dust Sea. She blew out through her lips.

At least she could say she was awake now.

'Bernesse,' she mumbled at last. 'Stay here with Hedrod and see that Eight-eighty-eight is fully secured until an adept can be sent down to assess the astropath.'

'Yes, sir,' said Hedrod and Bernesse together.

'And you.' She turned to Otho. 'You come with me.' The trooper looked relieved as Yarrer marched past him, back the way they had come.

At the end of the corridor, she thumped her uninjured fist on the door and called for Trooper Siwan. She found herself waiting an interminably long while before she heard the rattle of the key in the lock and the door yawned open.

She stepped through, and then stopped short, Otho almost walking into her back. Her mouth hung open as she took in the reason behind Siwan's delay.

Coven Master Pyrrhus bowed his head to her in greeting. Yarrer had not seen the psyker in almost two years, but his solitude hadn't changed him. His head was bald and abnormally prominent, his pale, blueish skin threaded with conductive wires that somehow conspired to make the hollow pits of his eye sockets bulge, as though seeing more than he could have wished for or liked. His slender frame was swaddled in turquoise robes, beringed fingers clutching an ornate staff worn smooth by the fingers of countless hands just like them and embossed with the faded insignia of the Adeptus Astra Telepathica. The chrome petals of a plug-in port gleamed from his temple.

The woman beside him cut a more martial, but no less prepossessing figure. She had come in a military dress uniform, brilliant white with cascades of golden braid from the shoulders. An enamelled flak vest slotted comfortably over the top. At her hip she wore a basket-hilted rapier in a gilt scabbard, a manicured hand wearing the Imperial signet on a single heavy ring resting over the grip.

Yarrer had never seen Lady-Governor Ilsetza IV in person, although one did not serve a world for twenty years without recognising its absolute monarch. To all intents and purposes, Ilsetza was said to be both competent and fair. A citizen could ask for little more. The accepted form of deference would have been for Yarrer to bow.

Instead, she fell to one knee and looked up with wide eyes.

The two notables shrank beside the majesty of the third figure between them.

He was a god amongst them, a giant encased in slabs of granite grey. The symbols etched into his thrumming war plate reminded her of the wards etched throughout the fortress, but in the way a child's pencil-drawn attempt at depicting the Emperor might remind her of a cathedrum fresco. They shimmered as Yarrer looked at them, functioning to project an almost physical barrier of light around the giant man. One side of his face and the backs of both hands, currently clasped around an ornate silver staff, were cracked as though recently burned, but the strength they retained was undeniable.

The stranger met Yarrer's eyes.

She jerked from the intrusion of his mind into hers. The Scholastica Psykana had instructed her in several mantras by which to recognise and resist psychic incursion, but the words themselves fled her conscious brain before she could rally them, the rote exercises becoming as smoke in her thoughts. She had the uncomfortable, though not overtly threatening, sense of her personality being dissected, her doubts, fears and insecurities peeled away and pinned back layer by layer until there was nothing left for the stranger to observe but the indivisible core of who she was that lay beneath. The sense of approval welled up from within as the stranger withdrew his mind, carefully replacing all that his intrusion had disturbed, rebuilding her exactly as she had been found.

The giant looked down on her.

'I am Graucis Telomane,' he said, in an impossibly deep voice made thin by great age. 'Of the Six Hundred and Sixty-Sixth Chapter, Adeptus Astartes.'

'I am Colonel Tanika Yarrer, of the Adeptus Astra Telepathica Hyades garrison.'

The Space Marine smiled knowingly. Of course, he knew that already.

'My brothers and I heard your cry.'

Yarrer felt as though she might faint with relief. Eight years of war, surely soon to come to an end. 'Are you here to save us, lord?'

'My brothers are deploying to the surface as we speak. In the meantime, however...' The look in the Space Marine's grey eyes was profoundly sad. 'I require the use of your astropath.'

CHAPTER FIFTEEN

Hyades Capitolis was a dusty city.

Its original foundations had been laid in an ancient wadi where, in the deep geological past, seasonal rains had once emptied into what the Hyaden cartographica now referenced as the Dust Sea.

It was a city built on sand: a fact that veered only unintentionally into metaphor.

The sprawling districts of the governess' manor perched along the crest of the northern mesas overlooking the dried-out wadi. The royal dwellings were a rich golden-brown colour that blended naturally into that of the sky, shaped by the devoted toil of generations into crenellations, minarets and domes.

Hyades Capitolis was a faithful city. Even now.

The churches of the Adeptus Ministorum and the bastions of the Adepta Sororitas mission were as numerous over the old city as spines on a desert cactid, sandstone spires glittering with gold foil as they vied for the same dusky heavens as the governess' manse.

The settlement's imposing curtain wall was not even stone at all, but sand from the dunes that had been packed, raked and baked as hard as granite under the world's two red suns. The battlements had been shaped by hand, every crenel a unique piece of architecture with the initials and prayer of the artisan concealed somewhere in the design.

But the city's first defence had always been the desert.

The Dust Sea and Kotha Basin were effectively impassable. Trade caravans and Imperial missionaries had once snaked their way between the Hyaden polities without ever leaving behind anything as permanent as a road. The surest way to travel was by dirigible, of which the capitolis alone maintained a creaking fleet, but even for aircraft, sandstorms were a common and potentially lethal hazard.

Hyades had no true clouds. What little moisture the world held was aggressively harvested by the polar agriplexes and hoarded by the Consortia. Sand picked up by the vast, planet-straddling storms created cloud-like patterns in the sky, bands of yellow and cream and brown that were always changing and which, according to local variants of the Imperial creed, would present to His faithful as saints and angels in times of need.

Graucis wondered what the faithful of Hyades Capitolis had been seeing for the last eight years of war, and if they saw anything different there now.

He could not say he saw much of anything. Just random brushstrokes against an atmosphere basking in the solar radiation of two giant stars.

In projected form, his mind walked the grand processional, the ancient stream bed that formed the heart of the city, his feet leaving no prints in the sand, his presence attracting no stares. Men and women in fluttering white robes crowded the statue-lined pavimentum, loading equipment onto tarp-covered trucks and Chimera transports. There was no safe or easy way to cross the Kotha Basin and assault the closest recidivist enclave at Kwat. That was not to say it could not be done, or that men would not attempt it.

Hate alone could not move a mountain, or bridge a desert, but it could fuel a man to risk all in the attempt.

Hyades Capitolis had become a hateful city.

Graucis' mind had explored these streets several times prior to his physical arrival on Hyades two days earlier, but not as often since. He had sent his mind to spend time in the lesser polities too, those loyal to the Imperial governess as well as those aligned to the rebels of the Consortia, and only confirmed for himself what he had already felt.

This world would be perfect for his needs.

Ensnaring a god was not, as it turned out, a complicated a thing. One needed only the proper lure.

His thoughts paused to linger on the loading gangs as his weightless footsteps carried him past.

Living minds inevitably drew the psychic eye, more than the most palatial redoubt or gilded church. It was much the same for the unholy denizens of the empyrean as well. They were drawn to the animate, enticed by the emotional, repelled by the hidebound, the mechanical and the rigid. So Malcador the Sigillite had written, it was believed, in the *Liber Daemonica*. Some minds, some emotions, burned brighter than others. The human condition was one of infinite hierarchies, a feature of human nature that predated the opening of the Cicatrix Maledictum by about half a million years, but which had been greatly exacerbated by its influence. There was no objective rule for measuring the inherently indefinable, but Graucis was certain the effect in Nihilus had been doubly pronounced.

He allowed his mind to drift where his thoughts wished to take it, and–

* * *

–heaves the heavy crate onto the truck. Its contents clank as the box slides across the metal bed. According to the logisticarum stamp it is a consignment of auto-rounds, bound for the heads of the apostates at Kwat, Emperor willing. With a pious grunt, she throws her shoulder into the crate, pushing it until it is truthfully as far as it will go and not caught in sand or a rut in the weathered metal. She will not sin against the God-Emperor and His own blessed soldiers by sending a vehicle over the basin with less than its fullest load.

'Take this death to the heretic,' she says, spitting on the crate, marking it with her own precious water as a token of hatred for the machine spirits therein to imbibe.

Fahranet is too old to pick up a rifle and fight. That is her sin. Her labours under the highsuns are her offerings to Him for vengeance.

'Hamiz! Jumar!' She turns to shake arthritic knuckles at the old men, sharing a canteen of reconstituted water in the half-shadow under the statue of Saint Yasimin. 'You shame your grandsons and daughters who follow the God-Emperor's angels into battle.' Suitably chastened by her tongue, the men hurry back into the loading line, and Fahranet–

–drifted on towards the capitolis' gates.

The huge iron and adamantine structures sat across the mouth of the wadi. It was a walk of several miles, the processional meandering along the cracked trail left by the ancient river, passing dusty barricades and Militarum checkpoints, Munitorum convoys and masses of tanks struggling in the heat, but Graucis' mind travelled it in the passing of a thought. He could cast his mind across the infinite voids of the immaterium and orbit a distant world, brush against the psyches of the millions who dwelled upon it and pluck a single thought from their collective consciousnesses.

This was a simple exercise by comparison, but necessary.

It was not enough merely to offer the sacrifice.

Honour, and guilt, demanded that he *feel* it.

The walls were a hundred feet high, thirty feet thick at the base, barring the entrance to the wadi and scrambling on up the sheer slopes of the mesas that enclosed it on either side. They were wind-pitted and rugged, hazed by the sand and heat of the desert and lacking in the blessed uniformity that characterised most Imperial constructions. They were strangely beautiful for that and Graucis felt a pang of regret at what would soon become of them. They were a product of this world, sculpted from it and by it, instead of being imposed upon it in prefabricated dumps in the manner of Imperial architecture on the majority of its worlds.

At the top of the flight of gritty stairs, he–

–rubs at the stump of his leg. He'd lost the limb to a mortar attack when he'd been with the garrison at Qasfan. His fighting days are over now. Or so the commissar had told him when he'd been caught out trying to limp aboard the troop's Chimera with his old comrades. But he still has his eyes, doesn't he? He has hands. He can prop himself against a wall with an autorifle and watch for the inevitable Consortia counter-attack.

He hopes they show themselves.

He prays for it.

He rubs at his stump. It itches under the baking suns.

The Consortia owes him for the leg. They owe him tenfold more for the men of his squad who hadn't been watched over by the Emperor that day. They owe him, and he wants to wring his share from the Consortia with his own hands. It was prideful, he knew, to think he alone could make a difference. But if his hatred of the heretic was wrong, then why did the priests shout it from their pulpits?

Wiping the sweat from his hand on his robe, he takes a firmer grip on the autorifle and lowers his eye to the heat-softened plastek eyepiece of the scope.

If they come, when they come, they will find Payaz ready.

Most of the capitolis' sizeable permanent garrison had been deployed to the various front lines on the day of Graucis arrival, but further reserves continued to rumble through its gates.

Mechanised infantry columns, escorted by clattering Leman Russ battle tanks and Baneblade super-heavies, ground a slow, winding path through the Kotha Basin towards Kwat. Dirigible units, hastily resanctified and mobilised and co-ordinated by the enhanced command-and-control suites aboard the *Sword of Dione*, were even then escorting Militarum Tempestus Scions and Sisters of Battle to the more distant rebel enclaves at Qasfan and Sharaad.

The *Sword of Dione* was anchored at low orbit. The Hyades System had no standing fleet of its own. The Imperium was too vast for every planet in its realm to be defended as though it were an Armageddon or a Cadia. A desert backwater with few resources and a population too meagre even to tithe troops to the Astra Militarum was not even worth the periodic Naval patrols that stopped at other mid-grade worlds every decade or so. The principle of the Imperial war machine, when it came to the defence of low-quality worlds like Hyades, was for the imperilled populace to send for aid, and then to rely on lightly trained and poorly equipped planetary militias to hold their invaders at bay for the months, years or decades it took for their distress cry to reach the nearest astropathic relay station and be forwarded on. By the time a reprisal fleet could be mustered and regiments of the Astra Militarum made ready, the planet may well have fallen, but the Imperium worked on economies of scale.

A world could be lost, but through its stoic selflessness and its sacrifice, the surrounding systems, the subsector, might be saved.

If the Imperium could claim an inexhaustible surplus in one material, then it was manpower. Dead worlds could be resettled, the cycle begun anew.

Until Nihilus.

The Cicatrix Maledictum had broken everything. Suddenly, there were no more reprisal fleets, no more Astra Militarum on whom to call. Worlds no longer fought to buy precious time for their neighbours to reinforce themselves and one day avenge their sacrifice, but simply because there was no other hope but through bloodshed. And so they fought, and they despaired, and desensitised themselves to greater and greater acts of barbarity, billions upon billions of souls raging against the dying of the light as the gods beyond their understanding glutted themselves on the strife and grew strong.

In such an arena, the *Sword of Dione* could have obliterated the principal Consortia settlement of Banhar from orbit and ended Hyades' insurrection in a week.

But that would have been too impersonal. Too quick.

Too bloodless.

Thirteen Grey Knights, however, although intended for a higher plane of conflict than this, could conquer a single world even without orbital support. They would be enough, and then some, to tilt a stalemate decisively into one side's favour.

Graucis needed a bloodbath, a slaughter that the demigod he sought to entrap could not ignore.

He stepped off the wall, and let the wind take him.

The walls of Hyades Capitolis fell away, swept away from him as–

–anti-aircraft fire rattles off the Stormraven's thickly armoured fuselage. The salvo would have ripped through the skin of most aircraft, as the mangled frames of Hyaden dirigibles, burning like bonfires

in the desert attest, but the Consortia militias are not equipped for Adeptus Astartes armour.

Hanging from the side of the Stormraven by an overhead rail, Dvorik watches the troops on the ground. The fierce desert wind whistles through his armour on its way to being sucked into the Stormraven's howling turbofans, solid rounds from the Consortia's heavy stubbers streaming wide of the aircraft's armoured hull.

He is pleased to discover that the centuries have not tempered him in the least. He still lives for the challenge of battle, of serving humanity through the resolution of strife.

This is not the method of waging war he would have chosen, but he understands Graucis' reasoning and trusts his judgement. He too fought Angron on Armageddon. Luring him to the battlefield of their choosing and vanquishing him for all time is more important than the concerns of Dvorik's conscience.

In the battleground beneath their deployment zone, Consortia troops hastily redeploy their guns into heavier cover. The Stormraven pivots on its dorsoventral axis, its assault cannon opening up in an eruption of noise that chews one of the mobile flak batteries to a slagged frame.

He hears the loyalist drop-troops with whom he shares a compartment whoop, barely restraining themselves long enough for their dirigibles to pass over the assigned drop zone before throwing themselves overboard with archaic grav-chutes and promethium flamers.

Such eagerness is unbecoming.

Worse, it is a danger to the soul. Dvorik knows better than most where it leads.

But he trusts his brother.

Resisting the instinct to join them, to take the burden of this slaughter upon his own mighty shoulders, he turns to the front of the Stormraven and bangs his sword against the hull. He can see his brother in the cockpit, through the canopy glassteel.

'Take us into the city!'

There, two miles on and through several overlapping fields of flak, a bunker shelters a dozen Consortia mortar teams that have just begun dropping shells on the loyalist drop zone. Dvorik opens his mind to signal his veteran brother, then smiles thinly as he recognises the faint tingle issuing from a little-accessed corner of his mind.

+You are still living vicariously I see, brother.+

+It is necessary.+

+It is voyeuristic.+

+And also necessary.+

Dvorik sighs.

Of them all, Graucis carries by far the heavier burden. +I know.+ The presence does not answer.

Dvorik grunts, disappointed but unsurprised, and–

–he held on to his thoughts as the wind carried them up high.

A storm was coming. In the slow, unthinking gestalt of its sentience, the planet felt it. Hyades had been moved to the centre of events that, without Graucis' intervention, would have passed it by, and it rebelled. The earth trembled under the march of tanks. The skies darkened under flights of dirigible bombers. Electrostatic cyclones ripped across its dusty surface. Sandstorms merged into freak weather systems that blanketed the entire hemisphere, crackling with the psychic potential of a slaughter that had been, was being, and would soon be unleashed across it, forcing Graucis to–

–sprint down the rubble-strewn side street.

Every rasping breath filled the chambers of his lungs, the way a dust tsunami would slowly bury the rooms of a church. A krak missile from the ruins had blown out the Chimera's tracks and forced them to abandon their transport. He lost contact with his unit sometime after that. He cannot even say for certain how long ago that was. He has no chrono. No vox. The only equipment he was given before shipping out from the capitolis was the autogun he is hugging to his chest. His sandals are broken. His feet have been run ragged, but he doesn't know what he would do if he were to stop running.

Sharaad was his home. Or it had been, before the Consortia.

He'd arrived in Hyades Capitolis with the first wave of refugees. He'd been the first, too, to volunteer for the holy war to retake it. For the God-Emperor who rules from Terra, and for Lady-Governor Ilsetza who ruled this world by His divine right.

He doesn't recognise it any more.

Days of relentless shelling from both sides have turned the once familiar places into dunes of sand and rubble. The church he had attended for thrice-daily prayers. The bazaar where he had been employed by a southern merchant dealing in chaq. The Administratum offices where his wife had toiled as a clerk. The small hab-unit where they had lived a hard but contented life with their seven children.

All of it now gone.

Much like his wife, and their seven children.

He was the one who had turned them over to the enforcers in exchange for a flight to the capitolis, but it was the Consortia who had murdered them. It was the Consortia whose heretical egalitarianism they had confided to him over that day's meagre dinner.

He remembers it as though it were yesterday.

The Consortia will pay for it. They will all pay.

Las- and auto-fire crackles dully from the half-collapsed ruin of a municipal hall.

He stumbles to a halt, trying to get a fix on the sound amidst the echoes. He clutches the battered autogun to his chest. Is it loyalist guns, or Consortia? In his heart, he's no longer sure it even matters. His family are dead. He just wants someone to blame. Someone to pay.

Someone to bleed.

Gripping his rifle tight, he breaks into a run, and–

* * *

–Graucis struggled to–

–*scream himself hoarse as he stabs the rusty bayonet over and over into the loyalist fool's chest. 'Why?' he asks with every piercing thrust. 'Why? Why? Why? Why?'*

How is it that his own countrymen can be so blindly loyal to an Emperor they cannot see, to the extent they would reject all that the Consortia has to offer? Did they not all bleed the same colour? Did Ilsetza and her witless followers think their precious Emperor even cared from whence it–

–Enough!

Graucis had seen enough.

Hyades was more than ready.

He drew himself–

–*in through the reinforced door, tearing it from its hinges and sending it clanging and scraping into the survival bunker with a solid barge from his shoulder.*

Autoguns roar in the enclosed space, the sound of a bear with its back to a plascrete wall, sprays of bullets burning up on psychic kine-shields and banging uselessly off of thrice-blessed battleplate that deserves so much better than this.

The weapons snarl, hungry for more ammunition, as Gallead brings up his silver-plated, Deimos-made bolter.

He hears the first screams then.

He hears them through five different sets of ears, refracted through the psychic communion he shares with his brothers. He hears them enhanced, refined and triple-filtered of background noise by the spirits of his helmet auto-senses, so that every cry sounds like a clear plea to him and him alone.

Targeting reticules sweep the room, tagging the Consortia's leadership with sequential markers in order of assessed priority and threat.

This is mercy, of a sort.

'For the Sigillite and the Emperor,' he mutters. 'May they forgive us for–'

–Graucis took a gasping breath, fighting to recentre his mind within his body and focus on its actual, physical surrounds.

He was in the uppermost tower of the Basilicarum Astropathica, high above the hatred and violence spilling out across the capitolis below.

The psyker designated by the logisters of the Adeptus Astra Telepathica as Astropath 88-θ had been hardwired into a throne of copper and crystal glass at the centre of the chamber. It formed the focal point for a circular mandala of quixotic machinery, psyk-conductive cabling splaying out from the astropath like the branches of a tree. A silver refractor filled the ceiling, a moonlike dish busy with quasi-primitive etchings designed to evoke established astrotelepathic dream-ciphers in the subject's thoughts.

The psyker groaned, writhing in his chair.

Even without eyes, his face was a picture of torment.

Graucis had heard of the psychic missive this particular astropath had been reciting over the past several days.

Thirteen indomitable crusades the son did launch, but only one bears His son.

Governor Ilsetza and the Adeptus Astra Telepathica coven master were both adamant in their belief that it referred to Graucis and his brothers.

With a little reinterpretation, and knowledge that the Hyadens naturally lacked, it was possible to infer that 88-θ could have been prophesying the coming of the Indomitus Crusade fleets of Roboute Guilliman.

But Graucis suspected otherwise.

Somehow, 88-θ had become ensnared by the same psychic beacon that was luring the World Eaters to Angron's ship.

The message was not a promise of relief. It was a portent of certain doom.

In deducing that, it had not been difficult for Graucis to exploit the pre-existing connection, retuning the psyker's mind from a passive receiver into a focused transmitter. Now, with his mind focused on Angron and the *Conqueror* and his body restrained, 88-θ could soak in every bloody travesty being enacted across his world whilst simultaneously blasting it across the empyrean.

He had, in effect, become a beacon.

The storm trooper colonel, Yarrer, kept a steady watch over her charge alongside a five-man squad, hellguns covering the astropath from every angle. Liminon and Epicrane, the two most gifted psykers in the brotherhood after Graucis himself, had taken up positions around the chamber's circumference, their locations corresponding to the celestial geographies of Malakbael and Holy Terra, respectively. Astropath 88-θ and his seat, both of them products of this world, made a symbolic representation of Hyades itself.

The Grey Knights' steady chanting served to direct the psyker's increasingly incoherent moans.

Graucis closed his eyes for a moment, assuring himself of his purpose, before turning his head back towards the dark, glazed windows and looking down.

The vantage overlooked the basilicarum's impressive array of psychic and physical fortifications, and the dusty sprawl of Hyades Capitolis beyond. There was no war here. The world looked almost peaceful.

And yet the echoes of bolter fire and screaming children continued to harry at his thoughts, like sand against his spirit.

The Basilicarum Astropathica was draughty, and full of whispers.

With a grunt of pain, he put his hand to his armoured thigh and smiled in spite of himself.

'Tell me that all of this slaughter is needful, brother,' said Geromidas. He stood with Graucis by the window, his silver armour glittering in that liminal plane between the sunlight outside and the darkness within. Brothers Baris and Lokar stood guard in the corridor outside. They would be called for, along with Dvorik and Gallead and the Justicar's Terminators, once Angron was closer. 'Set my doubts to rest and I swear on the *Liber Daemonica* that you will not hear of them again.'

'It is, brother,' he croaked, expelling a waft of charred breath from his latest astral walk across Hyades, and then tried again. 'You know that it is. Once again the nature of Chaos makes a mockery of our attempts at foresight, and we have but the slenderest of windows to engage him on ground of our choosing.'

'The massacre of half a planet sits ill with me, brother, and it troubles me that you are without similar doubts. Knowing of your injury as I do, I cannot help but wonder at your judgement where he is concerned.'

Graucis felt the Chaplain's thoughts shift towards the splinter in his leg.

He drew his hand from it.

Such accusations should no longer sting. He had become well accustomed to the doubts, always veiled as the concerns, of his brothers on Titan. Could a warrior elevated by the Emperor's Gift ever succumb to the temptation of anger? Could anyone burdened with a splinter of pure rage ever hope to resist it fully?

He had come to resent the question.

It would have enraged him, had he allowed himself to suffer from that human foible. The fact that it still did not was surely demonstrable proof of his probity, beyond the doubts of even the most suspicious from the Chambers of Purity. After his maiming on Armageddon, he had actively sought out solitary duties and had pursued a position in the Librarius as a means of evading such constant, if well-meaning, scrutiny. It had been a necessary choice too, as all his choices were, to maintain his vigil against Angron's return and to prepare for it, unshackled by the duties of brotherhood.

But it had also, he would be the first to confess, been a convenient one.

Tending to the mortuaries of the Dead Fields, or cataloguing the artefacts brought to the Librarium Daemonica, had brought him all the time and solitude that he required and considerably greater access to the Citadel's resources.

It was that much easier to trust in the purity of his motives without his brothers' constant scepticism.

And what if they are right?

No.

No.

He rejected the very basis of the notion, for it rested on the conceit that a Grey Knight could fail to resist the corruption he fought. Was it mental resilience alone that blessed them with such fortitude, or did the Emperor's Gift render them infallible? That was a question of philosophy that had animated the more scholarly members of the Ordo Malleus for about as long as there had been an Inquisition, and this was not the time to consider it again.

Time.

Graucis shook his head ruefully. He had spent six hundred years preparing for this day, and now he did not have enough time.

Not for doubts.

All that he had done, he had done in defiance of Angron. Inviting planetwide genocide brought him no satisfaction, but it was a necessary act. His duty, and his nature, as a Grey Knight explicitly made it so.

'The Consortia has invited its own demise, however blindly. Ignorance of Chaos is a shield, it is not an excuse.'

'It is not the Consortia I pity, brother,' said Geromidas. 'Simply by arriving openly and announcing our mission to this world, you have condemned any that survive its war to the Inquisition.'

'My lords?'

Colonel Yarrer, who had, outwardly at least, been minding her own thoughts until then, looked sharply their way.

Graucis gave her a thin smile. 'Even if there were an Ordo Malleus at work in Imperium Nihilus, even if I were prepared to sanction such palliative measures on their behalf, everyone still alive on Hyades is doomed to perish once Angron arrives here.' With a shifting of heavy plates and a whine of delayed-responsive servos, Graucis gave Yarrer an enormous shrug. 'Shielding you from the truth of your peril seemed counter-productive and, in light of the facts, pointless.'

Yarrer's lips moved soundlessly as she dutifully processed that. The soldiers around her muttered amongst themselves but, to their own credit and hers, did not speak up.

'So… you are not here to save us.'

'Against the might of a fallen primarch and his broken Legion? No, colonel. No. From that, even we could not protect you.'

The woman blinked. Graucis felt the body blow to her soul.

The nine primarchs officially acknowledged by the Adeptus Ministorum were demigods, worshipped throughout the Imperium as the God-Emperor's perfect sons and second only in divinity to Him. As far as most citizens need ever know, there had only ever been nine. A primarch could no more fall than the Astronomican could go dark.

And yet here they all were.

'Why us?' she asked simply.

Graucis smiled, not unsympathetically. 'A fair question. You may call it simple misfortune. Had Angron made his return last year, or next, and the stars been in a slightly different alignment, then it would not have been you. Had the *Conqueror* been engaged at St Thule instead of Kalkin's Tribune then we might have been pressed to consider the cry of another astropath's distress and left you to yours. But consider it this way, colonel, if you wish for solace – your end will come swiftly now, and will have a meaning far beyond the fate of one world.'

'There… is just one thing I do not understand.'

'What do you wish to know?' he asked.

'If half the galaxy is now at war, then what is so unique to Hyades that it will lure your enemy here?'

'He will come,' said Graucis. 'He will come because his nature will not allow him to pass this slaughter by.'

With thudding steps, he crossed the floor of the focusing chamber towards Astropath 88-θ. The tortured psyker was dying.

That he was still alive was a miracle, and testament to the invigorating strength of the fury he had been bound to channel. The meat sloughed from his face, lumps falling into his lap and hissing where they touched the arms of his chair, turning his jawline into an anatomical scream of red meat and dripping bone. A sweet, crimson haze of sublimating tissue rose off him, recoiling and rebounding from the silvered refractor into mind-bending shapes that could not be unseen: men bayoneting other men, people screaming as those most precious to them were gunned down before them, daemons with ember eyes and horned faces cavorting around lakes of blood and mountains of skulls. The chamber's arcane machinery hummed as it struggled to contain the violent psychic emanations.

Blood beaded on the chamber's surfaces, hardening into rubies as they grew cold and shattering under Graucis' heavy tread.

Yarrer and her troopers lowered their hellguns and moved quickly out of the way as Graucis stomped between them. He read the fear and disquiet in their minds as plainly as the expressions on their faces. Geromidas remained by the window. He knew what was coming next.

Everything built towards this moment.

'Angron can no longer be said to think as a man thinks,' Graucis explained. 'His thoughts are not even equivalent to those of a child. He is a beast, a creature of instinct and raw emotion, closer in nature to a true Neverborn than the demigod he once was.' At the astropathic throne, he halted, actuating servos in his armour whining as they powered down. The bulky instrumentation built into the throne and packaged into its base raised 88-θ's sightless eyes to almost level with Graucis' own. 'Recall this face, Astropath 88-θ,' he said. 'Bear it with you across the warp, and with this message: thirteen of his father's true sons wait for him on Hyades.'

He raised his storm bolter.

'You ask why he will come, colonel. He will come because, like any beast, he will be unable to help himself.'

The splinter embedded in his thigh throbbed painfully, as though every nerve in his leg had been individually pierced with a needle of brass, as he called to mind the desire to kill.

It was not extraordinarily difficult to find.

The firing of a single Astartes-slaying shell in the confined space of the focusing chamber blew out the windows, sending glassteel shards cascading over the Basilicarum Astropathica's jagged ramparts. Sand whipped inside like enraged spirits set free.

Yarrer and her troopers spun away, struggling to pull down their visors and shield their eyes from the sandstorm, while 88-θ's last, bloody thought rose with a howl from his headless shell. Electricity arced between the containment paddles built into the chair's arms and back. The wards inscribed by the Adeptus Astra Telepathica, cruder than those known to the Grey Knights but effective in their limited purposes, glowed yellow and spat, showering the chamber floor with sparks.

Liminon and Epicrane raised their voices, screaming injunctions from the *Cabulous Luminar* into the psychic maelstrom and shaping it, syllable by syllable, word by word, to their will, directing it outwards into the warp.

Mind braced against the rising storm, Graucis lowered his steaming gun to his side.

'He will come because it is not Hyades, but one of his father's own that calls him.'

CHAPTER SIXTEEN

The *Conqueror* shuddered in response to its master's howling fury.

In redly lit, blood-smeared corridors, the ship's mangled voice ripped its way out of augmitter horns, showering feral crew-things in boiling blood and razor shards of broken plastek. The browned-glass bell jars enclosing the alert klaxons shattered. Cracked screens displayed line after line of alarming gibberish, fragments of old Gothic and Nagrakali bastardised with indecipherable screed in the true language of the gods before exploding over those who ventured near enough to spy their warnings.

From sections long abandoned by the sane and the living, ghosts wearing archaic heraldry smeared with blood emerged from the shadows of their past lives to rout the living crew and scream.

Enthroned upon its command deck, Kossolax the Foresworn gripped the arms of his throne of skulls as the great battleship gave another titanic shake.

Crew-serfs went flying from their battlements, hauled into air-cycler fans in explosive showers of meat or impaled on one of the many blood-and-brass stalagmites that jutted up from the deck plates like teeth. The less immediately fortunate simply broke, arms, backs, necks and skulls shattering against bulkheads, still alive as they were dragged away by pit crews or by raw-skinned bloodletters who were still creeping back into that section of the ship to reclaim their lost territories.

'What in the gods' name is happening to my ship?' Kossolax roared, the Butcher's Nails spiking his thoughts with the wild urge to rise from his throne and put a bolt shell through everyone too craven to answer. He gritted his teeth and resisted it, his fingers gouging ever-deeper furrows into the throne's arms.

The other World Eaters on deck were not so restrained.

In the wake of the daemonic incursion, and their harrying by adversaries unknown, Kossolax had demanded the presence of two full squads on the command deck at all times. The ragged barks of their bolter fire echoed over the wails of system alerts and crippled mortals alike. A part of Kossolax wanted nothing more than to share in their indulgence. Bloodlust bled from every surface. It bellowed from every vox-horn, goaded him from every augmitter panel and noisily buzzing screen. He continued to fight it back.

He was Kossolax, the Foresworn of Chaos, and he gave in to no one's will but his own.

'What...' he snarled through tightly ground teeth. 'Is. Happening?'

No one answered.

It looked as though no one could. The crew thralls were too distracted with the task of holding on, evading slaughter by their own transhuman overlords, or with the terrible burden of having no answer to give him.

'Brace!' someone roared.

'What is–'

Kossolax experienced the sudden, nauseating sensation of his soul racing on ahead of his body.

His fingers tightened on reflex, but the effect lasted only a fraction of a second before a fresh cacophony of klaxons added their notes to the din, the brutal *slam* of deceleration from indefinite velocity to a trifling light speed rippling through the deck. World Eaters were hurled forwards like iron shavings to a magnet, their crushed bodies making a mangled heap of twitching, grunting armour at the forward end of the deck. Of the mortal crew, the majority simply burst on the spot, like bags of wet meat that had been struck with a hammer or squashed. Blood in unimaginable volumes simultaneously doused every bulkhead, every console, every dazed and bleary-eyed survivor.

Wiping blood from his eyes with the finger of his gauntlet, Kossolax saw that the warp shutters were rolling back up, unveiling the star-speckled black of the material void.

He cursed.

They had translated back into realspace.

With a last, crushing squeeze, he let go of his throne and rose from the seat. There was a parallel, protesting grind of servomotors as the newest members of the Four drew up with him.

There was the Warpsmith, Corvo. The Butcher-Surgeon, Donnakha. The Champion of his Chosen, Luftos.

All three had impressed Kossolax in one way or another during the Slaaneshi incursion.

Luftos had single-handedly held the command deck's primary access corridor for the hours it had taken Kossolax and Corvo to fight their way through to the enginarium and stabilise the Geller fields. He had continued to hold it for several hours afterwards too, slaughtering anyone who tried to tell him the fighting was done. Donnakha meanwhile, even more impressively, had kept his head through the entire battle, salvaging enough gene-seed and equipment to rebuild at least some of what had been lost.

Kossolax had left the fourth position deliberately open.

It was for Shâhka.

The Bloodless could be a killer to rival Khârn himself. Kossolax would see him tamed or he would see him broken, and he would be satisfied either way.

With the three warriors in tow, he crossed the blood-slicked deck.

A disoriented World Eater stumbled across his path.

With a snarl, Kossolax lifted the warrior by the throat and tossed him across the deck. The Butcher's Nails spasmed, rewarding his damaged brain with the faintest kick of pleasure that faded almost as quickly as it was noticed, leaving his mind with only the memory of how it had felt and the craving for more. He cursed the loss of control.

This was Angron's influence.

It was becoming increasingly difficult for Kossolax to keep his head clear.

Folding both arms determinedly across his breastplate and gripping his pauldrons, he drew his increasingly belligerent entourage to the portal. It struck him as absurd, but without the ability to refill the sanguilith and locate new savant incubi to read its portents, the only way to know for certain where they were was to find a window and look.

The *Conqueror*, however, seemed to know perfectly well what its master required of it. In addition to the snap translation and the rolling back of the shutters, Kossolax could feel the tremors as the battleship ran out its guns and shunted drive power to realspace engines and reactive thrusters, readying itself to void assault bays whether the warriors inside had retreated to their assault craft or not.

He looked outside. He gazed down on a dusty yellow world. They were practically in orbit.

Quietly, he seethed. The dangers of performing a warp translation inside of a system were staggering. It was very possible that the *Conqueror* was too ancient and reckless to care much for its own wellbeing, but Kossolax had invested too much ambition into it to watch it tear itself apart in a misjudged gravity well now.

He watched as other ships, without a scintilla of the *Conqueror*'s sheer power or physical presence, tumbled out of warp space in the flagship's wake.

Gothic cruisers and their escorts slid out sideways, spinning around on dorsoventral axes, venting drive plasma or shedding armour plating from their hulls in the sudden, crippling shear of a mature solar system's gravitic field lines. An orbiting pebble or a speck of stellar dust could cripple or even kill a warship – if that ship's master was enough of a fool to risk manifesting his regulator choirs or drive blocks in a cluttered orbital space. Ugly, cactid-like blooms lit the window with ship deaths, but for every vessel that destroyed itself in orbit, whether by fluke or by a captain's favour, another winked into the materium intact. At first Kossolax counted dozens, then scores, then a fleet of hundreds and still growing – warships of every size and age and class spilling into freak orbits like the final break-up of an ancient space hulk vomiting itself back into the void.

With a growl of frustration, because there was absolutely nothing he could do to preserve his fleet, he scoured the surface of that sand-coloured world for any hint as to where they had emerged.

Was this Angron's intended destination?

Had this desert hole been his destination all along?

He saw no void assets, no orbital fortresses, no more than a handful of urban centres large enough to be glimpsed from orbit. It looked too insignificant to warrant the attentions of a primarch. Had it been Kossolax, he would have left a few hundred warriors to burn it and then passed it by.

He turned from the porthole, looking back across the deck to where the ghost of the Mistress continued to drift amongst the burst-splatter remains of the crew thralls before heading through a stack of interplexed cogitators that had been raised up off the floor as a fane and disappearing.

The Mistress had not spoken to him since his departure from the command deck to fight with Shâhka at her behest. Whatever it had cost the *Conqueror* to imbue the spirit with enough presence to engage with him directly, it clearly did not consider it a worthwhile effort now.

He would have welcomed the ghost's counsel just then, but it seemed that his rapprochement with the vessel was already over.

He rounded again on the portholes, impatient for any clue as to where they had been brought and why. 'Are we under attack?' he demanded. 'Is it the Space Marine cruiser that ambushed us in the warp?'

'I have no idea,' Corvo growled back.

While Kossolax watched, an eruption of what looked like blood burst through the *Conqueror's* hull, originating from several miles aft and a hundred decks down and spurting untidily towards the planet below.

It was daemons. Thousands of daemons.

They surged from the *Conqueror's* ruptured bowels like a horde charging through a castle's gate. They ran on foot, rode on the backs of thundering quadrupeds of sentient brass, drawn in the backs of chariots, the armaglass viewing portal rumbling as though there was no abyss beneath their cloven hooves, no vacuum in their ears, and no physical law that the gods would not seek to abuse.

Even from afar, Kossolax could not mistake the crimson avatar soaring ahead of his Legion on wings of blood, wreathed in a flame that fed off an immortal's rage as lesser lights did off oxygen.

He shivered, experiencing the same urge to pick up a weapon and follow him, the same sense of *pull* he had felt since Angron had first appeared over Kalkin's Tribune to renew his claim on his ship and his sons.

He had resisted then.

It felt twice as difficult to do so now.

Angron and his daemon army hit the atmosphere, splatting across the upper envelope and burning up, enough of its daemonic fury making it through the conflagration intact to plunge towards the planet's yellow-brown crust like a flaming sword.

'Gather the Foresworn,' he grunted, his temple pulsing to the rhythm of the Butcher's Nails, the pain in his head building for every moment he spent watching from above. He wondered if this was how his brothers felt all of the time. 'Make ready my Stormbirds.'

For the first time in many years, Kossolax the Foresworn would wage war in person.

Colonel Yarrer watched the red star fall.

It plunged through Hyades' false clouds like a meteorite, trailed on its groundward journey by a dark, unwholesome shower of what looked like bloodstained glass. The foul rain rattled against the turrets of the Basilicarum Astropathica like a portent of the apocalypse, an old world rain of blood, as the sky to the east turned red, then bleached to pink and from there bloomed into a ruddy mushroom cloud of yellow as the meteor struck the Kotha Basin.

Yarrer felt an unconscionable moment of relief that, whatever doom this falling star promised to Hyades, it would be the armies mobilised at Kwat that felt it first.

The earth gave up a sullen tremor, enough to bring congealed droplets of 88-θ drizzling from the web of ceiling cabling, and to make the carpet of glassteel chips around the broken window sing like a falsetto choir.

'The fallen primarch lands at Kwat instead of the capitolis,' she asked herself. 'Why?'

'It is the front line of your war against the Consortia,' said the skull-helmed warrior she had heard Lord Telomane call *Geromidas*, overhearing her from the far end of the chamber despite her intent to address only herself. 'As I understand it, the bulk of the secessionists' troops and armour were garrisoned there and, at my brother's insistence, it is where the majority of your forces were dispatched to besiege it. It is where the fighting has been, and remains, the heaviest.'

In all, there must have been a million men waging war there. Geromidas nodded as though reading her thoughts. She wondered if all of Telomane's brothers were as powerfully psychic as he was.

'There is a reason that my brothers were not sent there to aid your forces. They are the bait for the trap.'

'A sacrifice...'

The Space Marine dipped his head, as if in sorrow. 'Indeed. There is no force on this world that can deny Angron, nor the force he has mustered to him. Not even I and my brothers. Were he and his Neverborn host to make planetfall here and assault this compound directly then all would have been lost. Even with us here to strengthen your defences we would not have been able to hold him at bay for long. Nor could we hold your walls for you whilst also working to complete the ritual that will bind Angron's soul.'

'How will that work… exactly?'

The Chaplain smiled sadly. 'It is difficult to explain. Suffice it to say that it should not, if not for the brief conjunction of Hyades between Terra and Malakbael.'

The thought of sharing any form of cosmic connection with Holy Terra, even over such distances, added steel to Yarrer's wavering courage. For her, Terra was a distant world, but not so far away as to become a mythical one. All of her wretched charges had been processed at the Adeptus Astra Telepathica stronghold on Terra. They had all had their sight burnt out in the presence of the God-Emperor, their souls forever slaved to His. Knowing Terra to be a real world, inhabited by the real physical embodiment of the Master of Mankind, only made its sanctity more precious. She had never heard of this Malakbael, but it must have been a similarly great and holy world to hold such prominence. She felt proud that Hyades should stand in unity with them, even if only for the shortest of times.

'I understand, and my soldiers will do their part. Whatever that might be.' Yarrer turned to the centre of the room.

Telomane stood as he had for several hours since his summary execution of Astropath 88-θ. Over the course of that anxious wait, tech-priests in long, hooded robes that concealed their silver augmetics – a sub-faction of the Machine Cult which Yarrer observed with wonder – had arrived from the *Sword of Dione*. They came bearing weapons, ammunition and equipment, as well as fresh blessings for those armaments already present. More notably, however, they brought with them sub-assemblies of some manner of apparatus, so revered and so powerful that it took six priests to carry each small piece and six more to encode hymnals and to resanctify the air before them with incense from aspergillum rods and auto-aerosolisers. With the aid of the Tech-marine, Liminon, the third and last of the Space Marines who had remained in the chamber throughout, they had raised what turned out to be a bipedal fighting harness around Telomane's body. He had remained patiently unmoving throughout, even as the sounds of drilling, soldering, welding and prayer had drowned out those of battle from the outside.

It was called the *Sanctity in Trust*, Geromidas had told her, and it was a Dreadknight.

It had been designed for destroying daemons.

Looking at it, Yarrer could not imagine anything that could stand against it.

In his towering war harness, Telomane looked beautiful and terrifying in equal measure, like an ogre made of blood-splattered silver. A red haze that she could only dimly make out, but which a lifetime of indoctrination subconsciously com-pelled her to reject, was rising off the Space Marine. 'Eight times rejoice,' Telomane muttered, episodically repeating 88-θ's final missive, strung up in his gigantic armature like a blasphemer in a penitent cage, eyes rolled up into his head and staring into nothing through the whites. His mind was elsewhere, she knew, bridging the warp between Hyades and whatever it was that had just landed in Kwat as the dead astropath had formerly done. 'His son comes to Hyades and this war will soon end.'

'My mind is His mind,' Hedrod muttered beside her, the heavy-set sergeant reciting the rote phrases taught by the Scho-lastica Psykana to unclutter the mind and fortify the will against witchcraft and heresy. 'My soul is His soul, His soul is my life...'

Yarrer signed the aquila.

For a moment, the Space Marine had appeared no less horri-fying than that which he claimed was soon coming.

'Go to your walls, colonel, and await the return of my remaining brothers,' said Geromidas. 'There is no saving your world now, but every moment that Chaos is kept from this chamber is precious.'

Yarrer saluted.

It would be done.

ACT THREE

THOSE WHO PRAISE KHORNE

CHAPTER SEVENTEEN

Kossolax yelled his war cry, fist-sized blocks of foamstone and permacrete shattering under his tread as he charged down the enemy's throat. Auto-rounds sprayed from both sides of the ruined street, ricocheting from his heavy armour, las-beams striking off him at right angles like light blasted into a tank-sized prism. His bolter roared in his fist.

Warriors of the Foresworn, thousands of them strung with lengths of chain and crusted blood, fired wildly from the hip as they stormed after him. The old Legion had used to chain themselves together to fight in gladiatorial pits and training, Kossolax recalled, whole squads linked to one another like the slave-gladiators of Angron's abusive childhood to impose discipline and brotherhood on warriors who valued neither. Kossolax had resurrected the practice with his own warband with, thus far, mixed results.

But Kossolax was nothing if not determined.

Two squads of Imperial defenders outfitted for urban warfare, bulky armoured suits designed to survive stepping on a frag mine or a hail of shotgun pellets at point-blank range, emerged from a building, opening fire with heavy stubbers and flamers to cover the withdrawal of the main force from the Foresworn advance.

Kossolax gleefully mowed the mortal soldiers down, continuing to murder the wall behind them even after the last man was a red smear on the roadside. The Butcher's Nails sang their fury into his skull.

A phalanx of Predator tanks, their adaptable chassis making them a firm favourite since before the Horus Heresy, rumbled down the rubble-lined avenue. Their turret lascannons tracked, corrupted auspexes sniffing the air for the scent of armoured prey, but finding nothing worthy of their firepower, they blasted indiscriminately at the mortals' firebases amongst the ruins instead.

Off to his left and way, way ahead of the lagging World Eaters infantry, a Rhino festooned in brass plates careened headlong into a tank trap and gouted smoke. Its overeager driver, or maniac daemonic spirit, gunned its engines all the harder, shredding the vehicle's underside as it mounted the rockcrete spurs in the road. It finished up on its side, the assault ramp coming jerkily down, but not fast enough for the chainaxe-wielding berzerkers inside who were already carving their own way out.

A battery of Imperial heavy weapons, including a Leman Russ Punisher, hull-down in the rubble and camouflaged under a layer of dust, opened up from the building directly across from the tank traps.

The torrent of fire blasted chunks through the rockcrete traps and rattled across the Rhino's thickened armour. The tank squealed, its daemonic spirit pitting its supernatural vigour and rage against the overwhelming torrent of fire, mending the wounds in its shell as they appeared, only to be forced out of its dying host with a shriek of rage. The berzerkers who were still cutting their way free jerked as they were riddled in turn, pitching up against the bullet-chewed traps like corpses mounted on spikes.

At the same time as this ambush was being sprung, a second force, clearly moving in co-ordination with the first, deployed a pincer from the opposite side of the street.

A battalion-strength force of mortal infantry, a thousand men in desert camouflage and flak vests, wielding lasguns, deployed across the head of the boulevard and began unpackaging heavy weapons onto tripods. Squads of Battle Sisters in sand-pitted black power armour, escorted to the front by two-score shield-toting bullgryns and several dozen Sentinel armoured walkers, pushed hard into the leading edge of the World Eaters' assault.

The lead Predator gave out with a belch of flame as a pair of Sentinels sliced it in half with bisecting lascannon beams. A Battle Sister's heavy flamer rinsed a second with a prome-thium jet.

Then the rest of the Imperial gunline opened fire.

Thousands of scarlet beams stippled the street from left to right, leaving smoking black rings on dusty brickwork and Astartes armour alike. Chaos Space Marines jerked and fell, the sheer volume of fire coming at them through the choke point of wrecked machines and rubble culling dozens in the opening salvo alone. With their support weaponry finally set up onto tripods and loaded, heavy weapons teams belatedly opened up in turn, the barks of heavy bolter and autocannon fire raking back and forth across the street, mortars tearing great chunks out of the road and showering the charging World Eaters with rubble.

Kossolax howled to be heard above the tumult.

The death toll in those few seconds would have decimated a Chapter, and he did not care, because in the frenetic moments that followed them the first World Eaters slammed into the Battle Sisters and the Imperial counter-push dissolved into a frenzy of shrieking axe blades and inhuman screams.

This was what Kossolax's dreams of glory had denied him for so long.

He gunned down a Battle Sister with liturgical scripture streaming from the body of her slimmed-down bolter, then turned without breaking stride and punched two shells through the breastplate of a second. The unit's Sister Superior, a broad-shouldered woman with a tonsured head, called him out, condemnation on her black-and-white-chequered lips and white-hot blasts from an inferno pistol vaporising chunks of his armour at a time. Her screaming chainsword struck his vambrace, and rattled down it without causing injury. She stared up at him in hatred and in shock, as Kossolax hacked her head from her shoulders with a savage blow from his axe.

A shiver of ecstasy coursed through him.

When it was gone, he felt only emptiness in its place.

'Is this it?' he howled to no one in particular, as the bodies piled high around him. 'Is that all that Angron called us to do?'

With a frenzied howl, Corvo stepped up behind him and let rip with a heavy bolter. Detonations rippled through the air, high-explosive shells tearing into rockcrete blocks and sandbag barricades and forcing the Imperial militias embedded there to go to ground. Luftos and Donnakha surged ahead to join him, eager to add their own bolt pistols and plasma weapons to the onslaught.

Off to the right, where the Imperials' attempt at a flanking manoeuvre had stalled against the roadblock of burning

Predators, a pair of Maulerfiends bulled through the stalled vehicles. Mauler fists and magma cutters pulled the lightly armoured Sentinel walkers apart as though they were made of twigs. Return las-fire ricocheted off the gnarled and knotted brass of their hides while lasher tendrils messily dismembered any Battle Sister that rushed too close in an attempt to intervene.

Overhead, meanwhile, squads of Seraphim and Zephyrim were leaping from the rooftops and boosting towards the fray, only to find the Foresworn's Warp Talons and Raptors, their jump packs mutated into fire-breathing organs of true flight, already in the air amongst them.

'Slaughter!' Kossolax growled, and beat his chest in a bid to resuscitate his own fury. He waved his off-hand to gesture to the Imperial gunline and the street beyond. 'Follow the primarch. Kill them all!'

The Foresworn were the largest and best-equipped warband under Kossolax's control, numbering several thousand warriors, but as many again answered to the hundreds of lesser champions sworn to his cause.

While his flotilla of crimson-and-gold gunships had put down within a few hundred yards of Angron's raging assault, additional forces continued to rain out of the heavens in flaming drop pods and madly careening transports, jagged pieces of a blood-red comet breaking up in the sky. Small groups of World Eaters unattached to Kossolax's advance were fighting their own way into what was left of the municipal centre from nearby dropsites. The bulk of his extended forces, however, were still stuck in orbit, pursuing Imperial fighter craft across the burnt-yellow sky, or pockmarking the surrounding desert. Plumes of dust and sand marked dozens of fierce skirmishes, lone World Eaters squads or rampaging Helbrutes engaging their hated adversaries amongst the dunes.

Compared to the hordes that surrounded the likes of Typhus or Eidolon or even Khârn, champions that Kossolax thought of as contemporaries and peers even as they disregarded him in turn, the Foresworn were an average-size force at best.

But there were no other World Eaters in this galaxy with the discipline to pick out a landing zone and stick to it through the temptation of combat.

By virtue of that discipline, Angron himself was still no more than half a mile ahead of them and there was no other warband closer. He waded through a street that ran roughly parallel to the Foresworn until an intersection two miles ahead. The local building stock, though largely levelled now, was predominantly single-storey habs with flat sandstone roofs, and Angron's dripping wings and bulging shoulders were visible even through the haze of grit and debris. With every earth-splitting bellow and deranged howl, every pulverising swipe of Spinegrinder or the immense daemon sword, Samni'arius, vehicles and even bits of building went flying and filled the close desert air with screams.

As Kossolax paused to bask in the sheer majesty of his father unleashed, a column of Leman Russ Demolishers and Hellhound tanks painted in desert camouflage rumbled towards him. With *booms* that rattled the roofs of tanks as far away as the Foresworn, the Demolishers' stub-barrelled siege guns opened fire. Explosions tore chunks from Angron's armour, momentarily cloaking the primarch in smoke as the armoured column growled forwards and more guns piled in.

A pair of colossal Shadowsword super-heavy tanks rolled up behind the main column and pivoted their Titan-killing main guns towards the flame-wreathed primarch.

Kossolax held his breath.

He felt his hearts stop.

Raging against his foes' impotence, Angron burst through

the wall of ordnance and the Shadowsword's siege-breaking beams and stamped down on the glacis plate of the lead tank. Angron ground the Demolisher into the road, then leapt off it, small-arms fire spitting after him as his wings carried him over the armoured column. He crushed a Hellhound with his landing. The tank exploded violently. Gallons of superheated promethium flushed outwards through the lines of tanks and set the entire street ablaze. His upper body on fire, haloed as much by his own rage as the fierce heat, Angron slammed his shoulder through the side armour of a Chimera transport, denting the thick plating and forcing the vehicle off the road.

The first Shadowsword loomed over him.

Sponson- and pintle-mounted bolters decorated the primarch's breastplate with low-calibre explosions while its main gun recharged and the battle tanks around it struggled to manoeuvre. With an outrageously loud shriek from Spinegrinder, Angron sheared through the volcano cannon's long barrel.

'He is even mightier than I remember,' Kossolax muttered under his breath.

Or perhaps it had simply been too long since he had last seen his primarch in battle.

The wounded Shadowsword struggled to back up, hemmed in by masses of skirmishing troops and its own escorting vehicles. A Hellhound let out a ferocious jet of flame, engulfing several squads of desert militia that Kossolax could not see for the intervening buildings but whose screams he heard well enough even over half a mile and his own battle, and set the primarch alight again.

But Angron was in amongst them now.

It was a bloodbath.

Kossolax watched a little longer. The Butcher's Nails almost compelled him.

The surviving tanks threw themselves into reverse, crushing their own terrified infantry in the ensuing panic, glacis bolters and Demolisher cannons thundering in vain even as the tanks raced back up the street and away.

Angron roared, his wingspan doused in burning promethium, his dreadlocks writhing like living things in the pyre, and gave chase.

'It is impressive that they do not all run,' said Luftos, drool running down his chin and pooling under his gorget as he unloaded his plasma pistol into the withdrawing Battle Sisters. 'It is a rare mortal that would dare fight back at all.'

Kossolax nodded in agreement.

The local forces on this world were committed troops, he would give them that, well dug- in and evidently well organised. Even so, he would not have expected them to withstand the Foresworn for the few minutes that they already had. Kossolax wondered if the only reason they fought so hard now was because a withdrawal to the next intersection would buy them no more than an encounter with Angron instead of Kossolax and the Foresworn.

'There is another large armoured battle group inbound from the east,' said Corvo, lowering his apparently jammed heavy bolter and consulting the auspex slate that had been bolted to his vambrace. His helm-distorted voice was a sullen growl, barely audible above the tumultuous back and forth of bolter fire.

'I hear the fighting already,' said Luftos, licking his prominent upper lip. 'The other warbands will slow them down until we are done here.'

'Fighting strength?' Kossolax asked.

The Warpsmith shook his auspex unit angrily. 'The auspex dislikes all this sand.'

'Then guess,' Kossolax growled.

'Somewhere between three and five hundred vehicles. A mechanised infantry corps would be my guess. Chimera transports and mobile artillery. Griffon armoured weapons carriers and Basilisks. And at least one more Baneblade, or something of equivalent size and power.'

'I hear them,' Luftos announced again, barely getting the words through the fresh saliva filling his mouth.

Kossolax took a deep breath, the last embers of frenzy guttering in his chest, but not dying.

This was beginning to feel like a trap.

A primarch on the battlefield was force-equivalent to a Titan and, as the ancient saying went, the only way to kill a Titan was to send another Titan. If Kossolax were to attempt to murder his father – and what World Eater had not conducted that thought exercise while lost in the throes of the Butcher's Nails? – then something like this might be how he would do it. Hem him in with massed infantry, hold his attention with slaughter, and then pound him to oblivion with heavy armour and artillery. It might even work. Angron was immortal, but he was not invulnerable. With enough firepower his body could be destroyed and his soul hurled back to the immaterium where it belonged.

He looked up as Hell Blade and Hell Talon fighters screamed across the burnt-yellow sky, chasing a squadron of Imperial aircraft towards what looked like another, larger settlement beyond the dunes.

'What is *that*?' Donnakha murmured.

The Apothecary was staring in the same direction as Kossolax.

It looked as though a faint shower of stardust were falling over the distant city, making its heat-blurred skyline shimmer against the wavering dunes. A single point of light shone from a point above the city like a beacon, as though gathering those falling motes into itself to enhance its own brilliance. It was bright, and getting steadily brighter. Already, it stung Kossolax's eyes to look upon directly. He hissed and looked away. Donnakha, however, continued to stare open-mouthed, too full of his own narcotics to notice the steam bleeding from his eyes.

Kossolax cursed the death of the Dark Apostle, Khovain, for it reeked of sorcery.

This was *definitely* a trap.

'How far to that city?' he said.

'About…' Corvo stared down at his auspex. The device snarled back at him.

'*How far?*'

The Warpsmith thumped the unit's pitted case and shook it. 'Two hundred and fifty miles east, lord regent, and over challenging terrain. That is a lot of desert to cover in Land Raiders and Rhinos.'

'And with maybe five hundred tanks to get through first,' said Kossolax.

'I hear them…' Luftos mumbled.

Kossolax ignored him. Not every warrior was cut out for the Four.

'Get me an uplink to the *Conqueror*,' he said.

It was time to free up some of the warriors he had been keeping in orbit against an eventuality like this one. And he knew exactly who to send.

CHAPTER EIGHTEEN

The World Eater who had given his name as Lobaz, in one of his brief moments of lucidity, hacked at the shuttle's exit hatch with his chainaxe. The adamantine teeth had been dulled from the abuse, the belt snapped, but still every blow brought slivers of metal flying from the frame. The warrior's nerveless face was a scowl of concentration. His scabbed lip twitched between blows, the Butcher's Nails causing his muscles to burn so hot that he shone with sweat. The hatch looked as though it had been attacked by an animal, but the shuttle was still on course for re-entry.

The rest of Leidis' new squad were scattered around the passenger compartment.

Warriors hung in scraps of war plate, blood reds vividly marked with bone whites, readying themselves for battle in the best ways they knew how. They abused blades with age-dulled sharpening stones, drowned axe teeth in oils, dismantled firearms to clean them before losing patience and hurling the pieces away. Verroth sat by the small window that looked out over the tailplane, idly passing his combat knife across his knuckles and occasionally flicking it from hand to hand.

'We should have gone down with the first wave,' he said.

'Those were not our instructions.'

'Did you come all this way to follow instructions?'

'I did not come to listen to your complaining,' Leidis countered. 'We are on our descent now.'

Verroth tutted, his placid smile never wavering, and turned back to the window.

Lobaz, a snarl on his face, continued to bash dementedly at the hatch.

'This would not have happened if you had not given our shuttle to the Bloodless,' Verroth muttered.

'Arkhor is dead, brother. Strykid, Lestraad and Kraytn are dead. Corvo is gone. You and I are all that was left of the Redbound and a ship of our own is an indulgence we can no longer defend. The *Conqueror* is no place to be without a patron, and it is not as if the Bloodless took it from us.'

'No, it is worse. He made us share it.'

Leidis stood in the middle of the compartment, the unit's de facto champion by virtue of ambition and sanity, securing himself against the occasional buffeting of atmospheric re-entry by holding on to the ceiling grips. He could tolerate a little turbulence. The squad's mortal thrall, a younger male with a split lip, torn hair and a sleeveless vest with frowning stitching, occupied himself with painting white squares over the bright red of Leidis' armour.

Leidis looked down on the work with pride.

For the first time since his arrival, he felt as though he was more than just another renegade in scavenged motley, still sporting the flaking maroon and black of the Chapter he had spurned.

He was a World Eater. A sworn warrior of the Bloodless.

He belonged.

The thrall raised a dripping brush to the hip flexor where Leidis had secured Arkhor's bloody Nails from a loop of bent wire. Leidis snarled and the thrall, spilling apologies, quickly proceeded to paint elsewhere.

There had been no time to find a surgeon and have the Nails properly implanted.

He had fought alongside Angron, and the hours, days or weeks since – he was unsure now of exactly how much time had elapsed – had been a violent blur. Despite the rationale he had given to Verroth for lending their blades and their ship to Shâhka Bloodless, he actually recalled little of it. He wondered if the reason he had not yet *made* the time for the surgery was because he was having second thoughts.

No.

He dismissed the flirtation with doubt out of hand.

This was what he wanted.

Shâhka Bloodless and the Butcher's Nails were his chance to sever his last ties to the Angels of the Grail and to remake himself as he chose to become, rather than accept himself as the weapon he had been made to be, to spurn the flaws of his primogenitor and embrace the inheritance of his true father.

He was ready.

Half a century after Eden's Apothecaries had transformed him from human child to living weapon, he would soon be transformed again.

He ran his gauntlet finger down the crusted metal of the Nails.

What would it feel like?

The memories of his short, human life were already foggy to him. Aspirants to the Adeptus Astartes were at their most biologically malleable before the physiological changes induced by male puberty, and so he supposed there had not been a lot of life for him to remember. He wondered if his service with the Angels of the Grail, and his subsequent years as a renegade, were destined to fade in the same way. Would he be the same warrior that he was now, only fiercer, stronger, more driven? Would he look at a pattern of blood on a sheet of metal and be moved in the same way by its artistry?

Or would he be a monster like Shâhka? A lunatic like Lobaz?

The other World Eater snarled as he crunched his ruined chainaxe again and again into the hatch.

Would Leidis even remember these final doubts, or were they too destined to be burned away in the fury of the warrior he would become?

He closed his eyes as though to mutter a prayer, but he did not know any.

Another thing Arkhor had never taught him, and that his life on Eden had poorly prepared him for.

He drew his hand from the Nails as though stung by them, refastening his grip on the ceiling loops.

He needed to get out of here. To move. His Astartes physiology was built for action. All the embedded pathways that humankind had evolved over millions of years for the resolution of stress had been cunningly rewired to railroad his instincts towards heightened aggression and superiority in combat. It was what he had been built for. It was what he needed. There was a war going on out there, and he wanted it.

Wanted it badly.

He growled, saliva bubbling through the crooked gaps between his teeth, and the thrall recoiled, mumbling apologies for whatever he imagined he might have done.

Leidis sneered down at him.

Immune to fear, it seemed, but not to anxiety.

He refused to miss this fight.

'I see him,' Verroth hissed, excitement pulling his voice higher than usual, and with the exception of Lobaz, still set upon breaking through the hatch with his toothless axe, they all crowded around the small window.

Leidis felt the shuttle wobble as five armoured Space Marines carelessly repositioned their weight over its port-side wing, before Ginevah, in the cockpit, was able to right them.

He peered out.

The window was chipped and dirty, but Leidis could still make out the dusty streaks of wind that whipped across their wings, and the Imperial settlement that was about five hundred feet below. It was being pounded. Giant figures in dusty red pushed through its narrow streets, even as buildings collapsed under the artillery barrage and buried them in sand.

Leidis pressed his hand to the armaglass. His gums ached. Then he saw what Verroth had called their attention to.

Angron was engaged in a pitched battle amidst the dust-clogged ruins of one of the settlement's outer suburbs. A heaving throng of World Eaters berzerkers and brawny, red-skinned daemons fought against Battle Sisters of the Ebon Chalice and what could only be described as a swarm of Imperial tanks and soldiers.

Leidis felt his parched mouth begin to water.

Finally, he would get his chance to be deployed into battle as a World Eater, in *Angron's battle,* the great battle that the primarch had brought them all to this place and time to fight.

He watched as Angron lifted an Exorcist tank and hurled it. The World Eaters gathered around him bayed their approval and beat their fists against the windows, even as the shuttle adjusted its course and stole the primarch from view.

Leidis fought to push his face to the window and look back. The other World Eaters howled in protest.

Verroth sighed, shook his head, and gave his attention back to his knife.

'No!' Leidis thumped the window. 'No, take us back!'

The armaglass quivered in its sturdy frame, but it had been designed to withstand the stresses of repeated re-entries and the risk of void battle, and was never in any danger from his fist.

'*We have co-ordinates from the Foresworn, lord,*' came Ginevah's voice through the vox-rig. '*East of here.*'

With a snarl, Leidis rounded on his squad. 'You. You.' He pointed out the two warriors closest to him. He had already forgotten their names, or neglected to ask and forgotten that. 'Help Lobaz get that hatch open.'

'Are you going to jump?' Verroth asked, still seated.

'I don't know. But I didn't come all this way to fight anywhere but at the primarch's side.'

Leidis turned towards the cockpit door.

It was an internal alloy. Not nearly as sturdy as the outer hatch.

The squad's mortal thrall scrambled out of his way as he stomped through, spilling paint and scattering his brushes, and leaving huge white footprints on the floor. He drew his chain-axe. He had acquired it from a corpse after the battle on the assault deck.

'Open this door, Ginevah,' he snarled.

'*I am sorry, lord, but I cannot.*'

And so, the last bonds of fealty broke. In a way, he was proud of her. She had finally arrived at the place that he had years before.

He punched the frame. 'Put this shuttle down.'

'*I have directives from Kossolax the Foresworn.*'

'You are not pledged in service to Kossolax the Foresworn.'

'*No, lord, but Shâhka Bloodless is. My duty in this is clear.*'

With a blood-curdling howl, he lost patience, striking his

chainaxe into the door at shoulder height. The whizzing teeth ground up slivers of metal alloy and spat them back at him. It would take him several minutes to break through. Too long.

'We are passing over another settlement,' said Verroth, still sitting by the window. 'Larger than the last, I would say. I see no fighting here yet. I see little sign of anyone at all.'

'Then what in the primarch's name are we–'

He stopped, interrupted by the sound of hard slugs banging across the outer fuselage. He lowered his still-spinning axe and looked aside. A string of whistling holes had appeared in the bulkhead. This was not a gunship. It was a modified Arvus shuttle. It had no shields, no weapons. It did not even have the manoeuvring agility to evade incoming fire.

His stomach lurched, not in the unpleasant or debilitating way that it might have in a mortal, but simply to report that they were falling.

It dawned on Leidis, as it should have before but never had, that he was descending out of orbit in what amounted to a very slow and painfully fragile drop pod.

He stared at the perforated fuselage, incandescently furious, but at the same time transfixed by the perfect eightfold geometry of the string of holes perforating the wall. A second burst of quad auto-fire, from a Hydra anti-aircraft turret judging by the sound and the impact damage, peeled away the outer hull armour until Leidis was looking at sandy sky. Disassembled bolter components and painting tools left the floor and flew at the sucking wound in the shuttle's flank as though rushing to repel a foe. A moment later, the screaming thrall went after them, leaving his fingernails in the deck. The gash in the hull widened as the wind savaged at it with teeth and claws, a beast scenting blood and baying for the living flesh inside the broken armour.

The flak in front of them intensified.

Leidis felt the ground beneath pulling them down.

'Brace. Brace. Brace.'

The shuttle broke up around them, but still Ginevah flew them on. Was it loyalty, Leidis wondered, or was she doing what a loyal servant of the Great Angel should have done years ago and killed herself, and him?

He could practically feel the rooftops scraping the underside of the shuttle.

'Brace!'

Lobaz continued to hack furiously at the rear hatch, opening it up to sand and daylight just at the moment that an impact sent him hurtling towards the forward bulkhead.

Leidis let out a frustrated roar, striking his unarmoured head against the metal of the cockpit door, and embraced the crushing, tumbling, darkness of falling masonry.

Colonel Yarrer slid in behind the wall and swung her hellgun up over the parapet. Sergeant Hedrod thumped in alongside her, followed in quick succession by the rest of his squad, deploying in a clatter of stiff carapace jackets and a scuff of high-energy cabling. Clio and her squad had taken up positions to the left. Zander led his troops to one of the watchtowers, to set up an enfilade on anyone attempting a frontal assault on the gate.

The Basilicarum Astropathica was not large. It made it easier for a small force to defend, but it also offered limited options for retreat, and no secondary platform from which to mount further resistance should the wall fall. If the gates were breached then the only option was to retreat into the keep and prepare to fight corridor by corridor, until they were pushed all the way to the focusing chamber's doors if they had to.

Conscripts drawn from the ranks of the Adeptus packed the

bailey. They were her second line of defence. By the coven master's decree, the containment blocks had been emptied and the astropaths brought forth. In spite of their blindness, they had been given autoguns and orders to fight alongside their gaolers. Coven Master Pyrrhus himself was there with them. They were astropaths, not primaris battle psykers, but their abilities might still prove useful as a last resort.

Yarrer did not expect them to hold a Chaos Space Marine for long.

They would, at least, provide a shock to anyone who believed that the Adeptus Astra Telepathica were nothing more than savants and messengers.

'I'm at thirty-five per cent,' said Hedrod, shouting to be heard over the continuous roar of the five Hydra turrets studding the walls of the keep. Aggressively contoured landers made persistent efforts to deposit assault troops over the basilicarum walls, invariably ending up shredded by autocannon fire or silenced by a missile from the silver Stormraven patrolling their skies. 'You?'

Yarrer turned her hellgun over and checked the power gauge on its side. 'Sixty.'

It would have to do. This was it. There were no spares.

Leaning over the parapet, she peered through the rifle's scope.

Rhino tanks, frustrated by successive switchbacks and tank traps, had effectively barricaded the steeply sloping approach against their own advance, but warriors were continuing to push through. They looked like a barbarian rabble, their spiked raiment cloaked in Hyades' sand and dust, but that was distance taking her for a fool. These were Heretic Astartes, each one capable of tearing a squad of men apart, and they already outnumbered her troopers several times over with more forcing their way onto the approach all the time.

In their brute size and armoured profile, they did almost

resemble Telomane and his brothers, but where the Space Marines had radiated such virtues as divinity and splendour, these were corruption incarnate. Simply witnessing them, hearing their warped voices as they charged up the slope towards the gates, poisoned her spirit in a way that could never be fully redeemed.

She understood now what Geromidas had let slip to her – simply being a witness to this evil was enough to share in its death sentence.

She saw, too, why it needed to be so.

When an angel fell, it fell harder than mere mortals and it was a fate that no human should ever see.

'Power dials to maximum,' she ordered. 'I want armour penetration with every shot.'

'*Yes, sir.*'

There was a whine of power packs. A hot glow of conductive cabling.

'We could use those Space Marines,' said Hedrod.

'They are occupied with their ritual. They cannot help us here.'

'Or the Ebon Chalice?'

'Deployed to Kwat with the militia. They left only a skeleton garrison at their mission in the capitolis.'

Yarrer thought of the promise that Telomane had made her, that they would all of them die today, and in dying serve the God-Emperor as most never would in life.

No soldier could ask for more.

'We hold these walls,' she yelled, taking careful aim, ensuring that every precious shot would count. 'For the Adeptus. And for the Emperor!'

It was called a Penitent Engine and it refused to die.

The war machine lay on its back, arms and legs half-buried

in the rubbled sandstone of the bunker that Shâhka Bloodless had just thrown it through. The frontis plate was buckled, spitting out sparks and leaking fiercely alkali fluids that burnt dusty ground where they dripped. It resembled a Dreadnought, only the corpse was on the outside. A muscular woman in soiled, whip-shredded undergarments was strapped into an open sarcophagus mounted on the machine's front where she could be seen. She was strapped down and blindfolded, every taut muscle studded with drips and electrodes and clenched in such raw agony as Shâhka knew very, very well. With the sound of dust-clogged bells, choking on penance, the engine heaved itself back upright.

The Sororitas mission was at the foot of a hill, at the outskirts of a habzone where a poor road wound up towards a fortress. Most of the World Eaters that Shâhka could see were surging up that road, but he could not say why. Shâhka did not know what he was doing here. He did not know how he had got here.

But none of that mattered.

He tackled the armoured walker at shoulder height.

The refractor field that shielded the open sarcophagus buzzed like a force field stuffed with nails, obscuring the screaming penitent behind a wall of colour as he bore the engine back to the ground in a plume of pulverised rockcrete.

From the road around him, he could hear soldiers screaming. Butchers yelling. Gunfire clattering.

A bolt shell from the Sororitas mission stubbed his cheekbone and spun off without detonating, exploding instead amongst the sandbags stacked up around its ornately carved gates.

'The light,' said Kossolax, in his ear.

Shâhka tossed his head, but the voice would not go away.

Ever since his battle with the Keeper of Secrets, he had heard the Foresworn's voice in his head. The champion was not there when he turned his head, the way he could sometimes catch the other voices if he was quick enough, but his voice was always there. A buzz in his ear. A hiss of static. A voice commanding him not to fight when all he wanted to do was fight, to sit down, to be still, to not slaughter the thralls before they could nail him into his Dreadclaw assault pod and fire him towards this world. Somehow, the Foresworn had got a vox-bead into his ear, or made some manner of bargain with his armour's ancient spirit. He gave a violent twitch, triggering a misfire in the Nails that soaked his brain in static.

The thoughts went away.

The hiss remained.

'You have to destroy the light.'

The Penitent Engine raised its arm.

It was a heavy bolter built into the central housing of a chain-fist with a pair of electro-flails swinging from the barrel and smoking off burnt incense.

Shâhka pinned its wrist under his boot and raised his power maul up high. His armour bulked around him, plates tensing like living muscle, as he smashed, smashed, smashed the penitent's sarcophagus until the human underneath the wobbling refractor field was a pulpy jelly, slurping away into her own solid-waste extraction tubes and splattering out the engine's back.

The machine jerked, as if to throw him off in its death throes, and Shâhka set to work on the chassis. Decorative metals crumpled under his hammer, gold leaf and intricate vellum scrollwork coming loose and fluttering away on the wind as he smashed, and smashed, and smashed, and smashed–

A gunship roared overhead.

It disappeared into the smog and confusion. He did not know where it was going. Did not know which side it was on. Were there sides? Which was his? A pack of berzerkers, their blood-red and gold ceramite crudely adorned with white diamond patterns, chased after it, firing their pistols in the air before they disappeared too. Somewhere nearby, a heavy bolter was firing. He could hear it *crump* within the smoke, see the actinic flicker of its fire.

Astartes weaponry on Astartes armour. There was no sound in the galaxy quite like it.

'It– *hnnng-nnng!*'

He grunted as the Nails sent a pulse of shredding agony through his nervous system.

You're not killing, he heard it scream. *Why are you not killing?*

With a roar, he shoved the Penitent Engine's limp arm out from under his boot, and stumbled drunkenly back.

The war machine gave another violent jerk.

Shâhka looked down at it, narrowing his eyes suspiciously, as the supposedly slain machine picked itself up, only this time it shrugged off its broken armour like a coat of nails and stood before him unclothed. His Angel stood before him, straightening its back as though it had outgrown the suit it appeared to have stepped out from and shook its coppery wings. It glared down on Shâhka with a towering fury, eyes like cratered wounds to the molten mantle of its soul, and the Nails trembled under their regard. It bared its rusted-sword teeth and spoke.

'Follow.' And then with a stroke of its enormous wings it left its earthly wreckage behind, and took to the air.

Shâhka saw nothing here that was strange.

Kicking aside the shattered Penitent Engine and mounting the ruined bunker, shrugging off the light bolter fire that was spitting out from the firing slits in the mission's chancel, he unfurled his own scaly wings and cast off in pursuit.

The ground spiralled away beneath him, opening up an

infernal vista that he had no recollection of falling into and less interest in committing to memory now. Memories did not last. Only pain. All that mattered was his Angel.

He had always wanted to kill an Angel.

It bellowed over the battlefield, smiting it with its wings. Climbing by sheer belligerence and trailing fire from its wing tips, it banked left, narrowly avoiding a thumping volley of autocannon fire from the fortress on the clifftop. Shâhka swept through the spray of flak as though he had been born to the wing, beating hard to keep on his Angel's fiery contrail.

A black-bodied gunship bedecked in hateful white decals banked hard into his path with a throaty roar. Shâhka dived to evade it. All that mattered was his Angel. The gunship dropped in behind and adjusted its burn, staying with him and drenching his airspace with bolter shells. Shâhka scowled, fighting to shake it off whilst keeping an eye on his Angel.

There was another roar, this one considerably louder and originating from some place darker. A Heldrake, a daemon engine that was equal parts atmospheric fighter and bronze dragon, snatched the Sororitas gunship in its talons. The corrupted aircraft bit down on the gunship's nose section like a raptor with a mouse, crunching through plasteel and adamantine, and pitching both aircraft into a death roll that finished with a fiery crater in the settlement below.

Shâhka looked furiously around until – *There!* – he caught a glimpse of his Angel up high.

It was beating its wings to stay level, maintaining a belligerent hover above the black walls of a castle, ignored by the black-armoured human soldiers who battled on as though unable to see the Angel above their heads. The castle stood on top of a sandy promontory amid a cluster of other fortified buildings, black and shiny where everything around it was a dusty yellow and curiously painful to the eye. World Eaters clawed at the iron gates, las-fire spitting down on them from the battlements, but neither Shâhka nor his Angel cared about that.

'Fight!' it roared at him.

Beating his wings hard, Shâhka climbed through the smoke and the petrochemical fumes and the sand.

This time, his Angel did not flee.

'The light,' Kossolax reminded him. *'Somehow, the Imperials have laid a trap for our father. It is the light, Shâhka. You have to destroy the light.'*

'Let them try and end me,' his Angel bellowed. **'I welcome it!'**

'The light, captain,' said the shipmistress' ghost. Sarrin. That was what her name had been, he remembered. But he was not sure what she was doing there. *'I need you to put a stop to it now.'* Should she not be on the ship? Yes. He was almost certain that she should be on the ship.

'Shâhka.' Kossolax's voice snapped in his ear. *'You were a champion of the Legion once,'* it lied. *'I will make you one again if it breaks you.'*

As if he were not already broken.

'My gift to you, my son,' his Angel snarled.

Shâhka covered his ears and growled.

Too many voices. Too little head.

His vast wings beat the air, las-fire as well as solid rounds from servitor batteries and Hydra turrets bursting across his inviolable frame as he plunged towards the castle's battlements.

'Destroy the light.'

Beating his wings once more to arrest his flight, Shâhka crunched onto the parapet. Like a frenzied carnosaur, he bellowed, mortals screaming as they scattered, las-beams and bayonets flashing across his armour. He ignored it all. His two hearts were beating so hard he thought his chest was going to implode. *Please, gods, let it be so.* His Angel raised a sword of black bronze, bared teeth dribbling red iron and daring him to strike. With a roar, Shâhka hammered his maul across the Angel's guard. The daemon sword rang like a bell the size of a galaxy, but then his maul seemed to go *through* it, as though there were no sword there at all, and smash into the parapet between his feet.

The wall crumbled like stale bread under the blow.

And then the ground beneath him fell away.

Yarrer flung herself from the parapet just before the monster's sledgehammer broke through it. She rolled onto her back, lying flat across the inner bailey's shell-pitted sandstone flags, face plastered in grime, as the wall caved in. She watched helplessly as Hedrod and half his squad, along with the fallen Space Marine, were swallowed in the ensuing landslide of rubble.

Any hope she might have held on to that the abomination had buried itself in its own rampage was soon put to the axe as it shrugged its way out of the wreckage. Roughly clearing the breach, unearthing the occasional bruised hand or severed foot or a length of crushed cabling, it threw out its tatty wings and took to the air again.

It swooped towards the high oriel window of the focusing chamber.

A storm of autocannon shells from the two Hydra batteries capable of drawing a bead on it converged, exploding amidst the chunks of debris still raining off the Space Marine, and appeared to do no damage at all.

Yarrer screamed in fury.

She had known that her resistance had been doomed from the outset, but she had not expected to fail so soon. She could only pray that she had bought Telomane and his brothers enough time. They were on their own from here.

Pulling herself up so that she was sitting amidst the rubble, dust sliding off her shoulder pads, she brought her hellgun up into her lap.

Heretic Astartes were surging towards her, forcing their way through the cleared breach like a sandstorm churning with daemonic howls and faces.

She would buy as much additional time as her death was worth.

'Emperor!' she yelled, pulling down on the trigger and keeping it held.

Leidis charged through the rubble of the breached wall. He had lost contact with the rest of his squad after the crash, but he no longer cared about that. There were no units or companies any more, just warriors, every one of them a champion surging towards the same slender path to glory. His suit had been damaged. Intermittent power failures caused his left leg to drag and the arm to spasm, sparks periodically flaying off from a torn conduit on the side of his power pack where it had broken his fall.

Willpower and fury alone drove him to keep pace with the charge, and now he could practically taste the blood on his lips.

Two human troopers in scuffed, glossy carapace charged him out of the pall, hotshot laser beams shedding power as they spat through the thick dust and then splitting harmlessly across his armour plates.

A blow from Leidis' bolter stock staved in the first trooper's head. The second screamed, spraying Leidis' shuddering battle-plate with close-range fire before receiving an elbow guard to her chest. She flew back, crippled for life, such as that would be, even before she slammed into the spiked wreckage of a World Eaters bike at an unnatural angle. She lay in the rubble, moving her lips and trying desperately to breathe.

Leaving her to drown in her own blood, Leidis dragged his tongue across his gums and glowered over the inner bailey of the fortress that Kossolax the Foresworn had demanded he take.

It was mobbed with undernourished citizen levies, packed in so close they were almost begging to be shot.

Leidis swung up his bolter, the stock barely even dented for being pressed into service as a bludgeon. His first shot went wild. He never missed, and for some reason it thrilled him. Unloading the rest of the sickle magazine with a single squeeze, he threw the gun away, laying into the conscript rabble with nothing but his chainaxe and the pulverising weight of his armour.

He laughed as he killed.

This was slaughter.

This was *freedom*.

The sky above the fortress had turned into an ugly cataract of yellow, swollen and stitched together with fiery turbofan contrails and anti-aircraft tracers.

He should have known that Shâhka Bloodless had access to his own landing craft, and more warriors than those he had seen aboard the *Conqueror*, but seeing them all converging in a common action startled and excited him. Shâhka had simply never struck him as a warrior with the ability to hold a larger warband in line. Clearly, Leidis still had a great deal to learn about how the World Eaters functioned.

Howling berzerkers hurled themselves into the fray, shrugging off every injury and butchering dozens for every one of their own that could be brought down. A clanking Defiler vomited promethium fuel over the melee. A roar of deeply frustrated insanity rang from somewhere inside its metal organs as it picked up a struggling trooper and eviscerated him in its claws. An Imperial psyker in an impractically heavy robe, and with a blueish pigment to his skin, took a step towards it. Wreathed in flickering after-images of cause and effect, he threw a phantasmal blue fist that ripped the Defiler's claw-limb from its chassis and sent it crashing to the broken flagstones on its side. Leidis ducked as the loose limb sailed over his head and crunched into the ground behind him, rolling over several routed defenders and a World Eaters berzerker who never saw it coming before rolling to a stop.

Even Shâhka himself was there.

Infamous for being unkillable, feared and loathed both, the exalted champion was in the air, shaking off the attentions of two squads of hellgun-armed heavy troopers and several point defence turrets as he made for the castle's highest point. The fortifications that Leidis and the rest of the Bloodless host had broken through so far were merely the outer rings of this central gaol-keep. Its dark tower, utterly unlike any of the settlement's sand-brick native structures he had seen so far, was studded with glassteel windows that were themselves tinted black. The largest and highest of these, and the one to which Shâhka appeared to be bound, was already shattered. From what Leidis could tell from below, it had been broken from the inside, and a ferocious brilliance blazed through the jagged wound. It hurt his eyes to look at. It filled his mind with rage.

'You will... never... prevail... heretic scum,' said a woman that Leidis had taken to be dead. She was white with blood loss, fetched up against a chunk of wall, one leg at a perverse angle, her black carapace armour fractured in several places. The ground around her was strewn with gargantuan corpses, World Eaters marked with black rings between the eyes or molten scorch marks over the positions of primary and secondary hearts. 'The Emperor... is... with us,' she went on. 'He sent us... His... sons.'

She haltingly began to sing.

Leidis wanted to offer something barbed in retort, but he found that he could no longer find the words. Instead, he simply struck his chainaxe through the roof of her skull, splitting it through to the collar bone and roaring in delight as the buzzing teeth sprayed his greaves with blood, brains and chips of bone.

Panting heavily, too enraged to think any further on who the woman was or what she had been trying to say, he stomped back into the fight, and after Shâhka.

CHAPTER NINETEEN

Shâhka Bloodless crunched into the shattered glassteel that carpeted the space inside the broken window. He folded his wings, grimacing in discomfort as the bulging musculature of his armour pulled them back in, indestructible glassteel nuggets splintering and bursting under his enormous weight as he pushed his way inside. He was in a large, circular chamber decorated with arcane machinery and more broken glass. Twelve Space Marines in silver and gold moved from positions equidistant around the room's circumference in order to block him from entering further. One had the skull-helm of a Chaplain, one the bulk of a Techmarine, one the bearing of a champion. Six were clad in Terminator armour.

Who were they? Why had they come here?

What did they want from Shâhka Bloodless?

Who was Shâhka Bloodless?

'Shâhka. The light.'

A thirteenth Space Marine stood at the circular chamber's centre point.

He was armoured, as his brothers were, his battleplate encased again in the armature of a fighting harness that trebled the warrior's size. It was the source of the light. A white brilliance that would suffer no division into baser colours blazed from within it, reducing the warrior's outline to that of an atomic shadow while pure illumination struck through the bars of his cage.

Shâhka could not look at it directly.

He knew that burn. He had felt it before and some things were not allowed to be forgotten, even by the likes of him. They endured, beyond the flaws of those doomed to suffer them.

They were perpetual.

'*Father…*' his Angel growled, but the voice was distant, as though that light had forced it to the outer edges of being.

'*Stop it, Shâhka,*' said Kossolax. '*Stop it now. Before it is too late.*'

'I don't–'

The Space Marines opened fire.

The munitions burst into psychic flame mid-flight, and Shâhka writhed under the fusillade, every shot a hit and every hit a rebuke to the corruption in his flesh. He was accustomed to pain, but not from the outside.

What had he become?

'*Fatherless sons, conceived in desperation by a god who had run out of time and out of hope,*' his Angel growled through the torrent of psychic abuse. '*Is there any wonder that the species falters?*'

'*Shâhka,*' said Kossolax.

'*Captain.*' The shipmistress.

'*The light!*'

'*Kill it.*'

With the howl of a wild animal in pain, Shâhka swung

his power maul in an overhead loop. It caught one of the power-armoured Space Marines a glancing blow across the pauldron and crunched fully into a Terminator's breastplate, forcing the others to fall back or be pulverised. The hugely armoured Terminator staggered, but managed to keep on firing, while his lighter brother went spinning, faceplate cracking against the floor and taking out another warrior as he rolled through his legs, both of them crashing to the tiles.

With the amount of fire punching into his armour suddenly lessened, Shâhka lunged forwards.

He slammed shoulder first into the staggered Terminator.

The warrior beat his force sword three times into the side of Shâhka's stricken face, but was restricted to hammering with the pommel and caused little damage, before colliding headlong with the wall behind him. A grunt of pain escaped his helmet grille, though his thick armour had fully withstood the blow. He made to raise his storm bolter, only to find that his arm was firmly trapped in the chrome teeth of the machine bank he had just been driven into. He shouted a warning to his brothers as Shâhka launched himself back, body spinning, pulling the maul along with it, trailing blue-white claws of disruptive energies as it went up, then down, and crushed a power-armoured Space Marine with a blow that would have broken open a bunker. The floor beneath them shivered as shockwaves hurled the rest of the warrior's squad back, sand cascading down from the machinery in the ceiling.

The beacon in the centre of the room spasmed as the warrior perished. The sudden brightening caused Shâhka to recoil before it was wrested back under the Astartes' control with an audible moan from the figure encased within the armature's cage.

A hail of bolter shells forced his attention from the light.

The Chaplain walked steadily towards him, his storm bolter

spraying out bolt shells, psychic energy burning holes through the eye-lenses of his skull helmet.

Shâhka jinked aside and around a column of machinery, just as the weakened floor collapsed beneath him.

The warrior he had already slain slid into the hole. Another who had been attempting to reclaim the body, called out for aid, trying and failing to catch hold of a length of rebar projecting through the ruined floor and disappearing into the dusty pit. Shâhka heard the *clang-clang-clang*, growing fainter, as the Space Marine's hugely armoured body dropped through the bowels of the fortress.

'Baris!' someone yelled.

'Fall back, Anchrum,' said another. 'The binding ritual requires us all.'

'But the relics...'

'Fall back, I say!'

Shâhka swung around, but he had lost the Chaplain in the dust and confusion.

An enormous axe with spiked teeth flashed towards him.

He jerked his head back, just avoiding feeling its teeth across his neck, and watched as it scraped the gore from the front of his breastplate, exposing the base grey of virgin ceramite. Shâhka snarled with relish as a succession of armour-breaking blows from force axe, fist and whirring servo-arm forced him onto the back foot. It was the Techmarine. Shâhka's ruined face split into a savage grin. He could no longer remember what he had come to this place to do, but his brain buzzed with the chemical rush of battle with a foe that seemed genuinely able to do him harm.

'The light, Shâhka,' said Kossolax.

'The light...' he mumbled.

The room seemed decidedly brighter than it had been before. The Techmarine threw an axe-stroke overarm.

Shâhka caught it on his maul's haft, ducked his head before the snapping servo-claw could wrench it from his neck, and then used the pivot along with his enormously greater strength to spin the Techmarine around. He threw a sharp kick, a low blow intended to smash the servos behind the knee joint and leave his opponent crippled, but the Techmarine somehow managed to see the incoming blow even with his back turned and parry it. Shâhka roared with joy, his armour bulking out with fresh muscle as it responded to his psychotic need to kill or be killed.

He had not been challenged like this in an age and he found that he–

The broad, psychically shimmering edge of a force sword punched through his chest. Its halo of silvery warp fire filled his nostrils with the scent of cooked meat and soldered cera-mite and instantly cauterised the daemonic flesh around the horrendously gaping wound. Shâhka groaned, hurt in a way he had not been hurt since before his change, and sank slowly towards his knees.

'The binding,' yelled the voice behind him, the same voice from before. 'Attend to the binding.'

'*Hnnn-nnnn-nnng!*' Shâhka dribbled, the pain in his skull over-whelming that in his chest, as he wrapped his fingers around the protruding sword, and began to rise.

Graucis Telomane was only dimly aware of the fighting.

He could spare it no attention, entrusting it fully to Dvorik and Yarrer, but elements continued to intrude: splinters of vio-lent thought and impure emotion, death peppering the psychic realm like shrapnel, spiteful flashes of imagery tinted red by a murderer's eyes and the minds of dying soldiers. It seethed, the fiery mantle that lay beneath the higher plane that Graucis' mind sought to access.

He knew nothing of Malakbael. He had not heard its name before committing to this voyage, or of the technology that had somehow lain dormant there, unmolested since before the collapse of the Emperor's dream. He knew only what his mind had been able to glean from afar. The light that it emitted was not its own. It shone, instead, like the face of a moon, reflecting only that brilliance that was turned upon it by Terra. The silvery thread of cosmic ley lines stretched across the angry maelstrom of the empyrean, tethering one distant world to the other.

Unreachable. Untouchable.

Graucis reached for that psychic ley line nonetheless.

He touched it.

'You are not ready, Telomane. Not for this.' Justicar Aelos stood over him, armoured in silver, haloed in brilliance. It was him, and it was also Him. A god standing cross-armed in judgement of His creation.

'I am ready.'

'That you believe yourself to be so only proves how unready you are.'

Graucis tightened his grip on the thread and Aelos folded back into the glare.

'Chaos will always find the means to enact Chaos.' The voice was that of Supreme Grand Master Kaldor Draigo, as Graucis recalled it from the one time they had met in person. Graucis had accepted an invitation to return to Titan with the *Sword of Dione* for his investiture. It had been a timely opportunity to consult the Librarium Daemonica, and to confer with like-minded brothers in the Chamber of Purity and the Augurium. *'Even if we are to accept that we, as Grey Knights, are beyond the reach of Chaos, do our actions not carry consequences that extend far beyond ourselves?'*

Draigo too sank back into memory, and for one shining moment that would bleach all such recollections forevermore,

Graucis felt the power of the Emperor as he claimed it in his outstretched hand.

In this coincidence of time, place and opportunity, this impossible thing became possible. The collective will of His genetic sons stretched their hands across the seas of the empyrean and found Him waiting. Thirteen minds, united by common cause, that unity symbolised by the blood of Armageddon and by the tokens of the thirteen times thirteen that they carried with them, and who stood by them now in spirit.

Graucis felt none of his father's thoughts in that moment. If they were present within the ley line then they were fundamentally beyond the limits of his mind to perceive. There was only *power* and *will*, beamed across the vastness of a human Imperium in the form of light to enact such purpose as only He could ever know.

Graucis had shed no tears for the brothers lost on Armageddon. He had never once surrendered to self-pity over the pain he had been forced to endure ever since. And yet he wept freely and without shame as he closed his hand around that cosmic thread and drew it back with him to Hyades.

To his dismay, he found that he could not hold it. The light leaked through his fingers, however hard he strove to capture it and draw it from its Emperor-ordained trajectory.

Even as he tried, he felt his grip weakening further.

Something was wrong.

Turning his thoughts back to his physical body, safely enshrined in the *Sanctity in Trust* within the secure walls of the Basilicarum Astropathica, he was immediately struck by the grief of his brothers.

Baris and Lokar were dead.

He felt it now. Their minds had been torn from the ritual and the relics they had carried with them had been lost. From a distance once removed he could hear Justicar Gallead issuing telepathic orders to his Brotherhood Terminators, glimpse Dvorik and Liminon as they fought to bring down the warped fiend that had broken through the outer defences. Yarrer and her troopers were dead too. He sensed it by the utter absence of their thoughts. Hundreds of World Eaters had breached the keep and were, even then, slaughtering their way up the stairs towards the last of the Grey Knights.

Graucis shuddered, his attention torn between his mind's struggle in the warp and that of his brothers in the tempus materium.

He did not have the time. He no longer had the strength.

Even if there was a way to conclude the binding ritual now without Baris and Lokar, and he was able to find it, there would be no time to complete it before the rest of the World Eaters force fought their way in far enough to break through the door and finish what their champion had begun. If, on the other hand, he was to return fully to his body then he had the firepower in the *Sanctity in Trust* to slaughter every World Eater currently at large in the fortress and perhaps even see some of his brothers safely to the *Sword of Dione*. The Dreadknight had been intended as nothing more than a precaution. If all else were to fail, then the Lord of the XII Legion would need to be fought as he had been on Armageddon, and even with the partial True Name that Graucis had wrested from Stovrwrath the Brazen Eighth, the might of a daemon primarch would not be bested with force staff alone.

But at what cost?

He had devoted himself to this quest for six hundred years, and against even the slimmest chance of its success, his life and the lives of his brotherhood meant nothing. Hyades had already perished, but if the sacrifice of all Imperium Nihilus was the price of imprisoning the Lord of the XII Legion until the last age of mankind then Graucis would not have considered it too high. The power of the beacon represented one last opportunity that was too great to surrender.

He could still destroy Angron's physical link to the tempus materium.

With a scream that echoed across both realms, he threw his mind fully into the empyrean, took a hold of that power, and refused to let go.

Shâhka was on his feet when the war machine in the middle of the room exploded. Light in infinite shades of white shot from it, and Shâhka screamed, no longer even able to feel the sword in his back as the blast wave burnt through his eyes like an acid formulated just for him. His soul was on fire. He closed his eyes, covered them with his hands, but the brilliance found its way into him regardless, bursting immediately into flame on contact with the blackness inside.

He physically twisted his face into an expression of fury and snorted, 'Hnn… Hnnn,' trying to trigger the spasm of agony that would make the pain go away, but it did not come.

For the first time in forever, the Butcher's Nails were not the answer.

'No!' He shook his head, scratching at his eyes, unable to avoid the sight of ten thousand years of lies boiling off him as light. 'No, no, no. Shâhka can't be fixed.'

'Do you forget?' said his Angel. He sounded subdued and bitter, lost somewhere in the burning white. *'Russ believed he could fix me, fix us, and he was not the first to try.'* The voice sneered from its cage of brilliance. *'But we taught him otherwise. Didn't we, Shâhka?'*

'I… didn't… I wasn't there. Ghenna was before my time.'

The disembodied Angel chuckled cruelly. *'Tell me there is one warrior in your infantile Legion who never boasted of how Angron mauled the Wolf. You were all so proud. As though the deed were your own. It was no different after Nuceria...'*

Shâhka tore at his ears, but it was no use. The light was inside of him now. *No.* He was burning up. *No!* Every barrier the Nails had erected out of the wreckage of his personality crumbled in the inferno.

He remembered it all.

'No!'

'Yes,' his Angel laughed. *'I know you remember Nuceria, or had you forgotten that I was there too?'*

Shâhka pressed his hands to the sides of his head and screamed.

He had been there, the day that Angron had ascended to daemonhood.

And it had not been Magnus with his learning, nor Lorgar who had shown all who came after him the true way, nor even Horus, first amongst equals.

It had been Angron, the Lord of the XII, that the gods had chosen to recognise first.

Shâhka had always been prideful and quick to wrath, traits that the Nails had only brought further to the fore of his personality, but after the destruction of Nuceria he had become withdrawn, his natural pride turning too easily to bitterness and depression. The rebirth he had been a witness to on Nuceria had changed him. He had glimpsed the powers that lay beyond the veil and they, in turn, had seen him. A corruption of the spirit that had metastasised itself into one of the flesh over the long millennia of exile.

'Do you think I raised you to captain of the Third Company because you were the best of your brothers?' The hidden Angel

roared with mocking laughter. *'If I had wanted an exemplar then I would have promoted Kossolax. I did not want an exemplar. I never wanted to be reminded of the best. I appointed you so that you would drag your brothers back down to my level.'*

Shâhka wailed as his dissolution continued.

Accelerated.

He saw the fiercely competitive and literate legionary he had been before accepting the Nails.

No.

The stoic barbarian, so proud to have been lifted from the savage plains of Bodt to wear the white and blue of the Emperor's Red Angel.

No.

A boy, wrestling with a laughing giant, all thick beard and heavy furs, too small to realise that the giant was allowing him to win.

No!

He flailed with his fists, trying to tear his way back out of the light and to the chamber occupied by the Space Marines, but every direction was the same and there was no way out.

He saw every moment of his long, long life as it was plucked from his thoughts and burnt. Every order obeyed. Every massacre enacted. Every horror perpetrated. And worse, the great dream of an apotheosis for humanity that he had helped to expunge, offered up in sacrifice to the gods that Lorgar had given them, and for no better reason than that Angron had simply never cared.

This, he realised, was why he had spent the millennia since Terra furious and alone, and shunning the company of his brothers.

Because a part of him, like Angron, had always remembered what he used to be.

'We were broken!' he screamed, seeing too, too clearly now

that there was nothing in his eyes but light. 'You could have fixed us! You were given so many chances to fix us, but you chose to leave us in pain.'

There was no answer.

Even his Angel had gone.

Shâhka wondered if this was what insanity was like, but no, insanity was what he had taken comfort in over the last ten thousand years. What he was experiencing now was the feeling of absolute and irrefutable sanity after millennia spent walking in madness.

He gasped as a cut appeared across the back of his hand.

He stared at it, as though at a minor miracle, looking on in wonderment as the wound split and began to bleed. He cried out in delight, holding the hand up to the light as another wound split across the first. Then another parallel to it. His amazement turned to agony, laughter emerging from his lips as a gurgle, as ten thousand years of physical punishment caught up with his body over the course of a fraction of a second. Moving like a puppet made of broken sticks and tangled wire, he lifted his hands to his chest as though to make an aquila out of his shattered fingers.

'For. Give.'

The entreaty burbled, unfinished, from the dribbling red smile that had just appeared to cut his throat in two.

He remembered the day he had taken that wound.

It had been on the eve of the ground invasion of Terra, in a moment of lucidity that would never again be repeated until now.

He had done it himself.

Shâhka howled as the explosion of light finally passed through him, blasting his corruption ahead of it and leaving nothing but the red mist of a purified soul behind.

And the explosion grew.

* * *

The beacon pulsed once, a split-second, thousandfold surge in brightness that left every World Eater with a line of sight howling in rage and pain as they cradled the scorched ruin of their eyes. And then, like a dying star at the end of its red giant phase, it imploded into its core, throwing off its psychic mantle in a burst that annihilated the castle that had sought to contain it and driving deep into the thin, rocky crust beneath its foundations. Millennia-old desiccation cracks and long-dormant planes of tectonic weakness split open. Swathes of the capitolis simply collapsed as the underlying wadi disintegrated, as though struck by a beam that reduced them immediately to sand. The great wall crumbled. The gothic, gold-plated spire of the cathedrum basilica, the pride of Hyades, sheared from the chancel roof and demolished the adjoining Sororitas mission. The deeply superstitious people of Hyades would have seen this as a clear sign of their God-Emperor's withdrawn favour, had there been more than a handful of its elderly, juvenile and wounded left behind to see it.

Two hundred miles away, across the desert basin, Kossolax watched in slow-dawning horror, barely even aware of the sting in his eyes and the blood leaking down his cheeks. 'Shâhka.' He tapped the vox-pickup in his gorget ring, and then again when the Bloodless still failed to respond. 'Shâhka... Shâhka!'

The psychic blast was a wall of light, thin like an electrical sheet and still expanding, rippling out over the devastated capitolis settlement and onto the desert basin. It knocked out aircraft where it struck them in flight, picked up tanks, trees, chunks of rubble, hurling it all ahead of it in a rolling peal of sonic booms and a frothing tsunami wave of sand.

All around Kossolax the fighting had stalled.

World Eaters berzerkers howled in agony as corrupted armour systems seized and bare skin turned red as though flash-cooked under the radiation of a supernova. Lesser daemons evaporated from the battlefield wholesale, while even their greater kin were forced to devote all of their willpower to simply holding on to their forms. Their Imperial adversaries fared little better. A handful of the more zealous Sisters Superior took the opportunity to gun down World Eaters who were suddenly no longer fighting back and claim more defensible ground, but the majority simply stared, as slack-jawed as their foes, as the sorcerous blast rolled across the desert towards them.

And few of them more so than Kossolax himself.

There could not have been many on this battlefield, perhaps just one, who had felt this power once before. He was ancient enough to have once known the Emperor's presence. He had never come as close as this, of course. Before the betrayal at Isstvan, he had been too unimportant. After it, he had been too badly led, and had broken his company against Dorn's walls and the fury of the IX without ever coming near to His throne.

But the shiver he had felt from sharing a solar system with Him was not one he would ever forget. It was the feeling of power, beyond all other powers, the tremor one could sometimes feel through the earth and through one's bones prior to the arrival of a god-machine.

Dread overcame him. He had returned, and somehow, for some reason, He had come here to Nihilus. By the time Kossolax's logical mind was able to reject that objective impossibility, there was no time left to run.

The tsunami struck first, a wave of earth and sand and flung vehicles that crashed over the outskirts of the ruined settlement, smothering World Eaters and Battle Sisters alike, obliterating the Imperial militia fighters instantly and burying their tanks alive. The air became a brown haze. Even Kossolax's chosen three, mere yards away from where he stood, disappeared into the sudden pall.

Only the primarch remained visible.

Angron burned like an out-of-control furnace behind the rusty yellow grate of the storm.

His face was a gory slick of blood, ash and inhuman fury. Sticky lips peeled back over the rusted metal of his teeth and, without even deigning to first draw breath, he issued a roar that smote the air with the rage of one immortal's hatred for his father. Dust and sand and enough blood to water a desert swirled out of the haze as if drawn into the shape of the primarch's rage, assuming the form of a barrier that encompassed the entirety of the battlefield.

Coming a few seconds after the tsunami, the blast front itself arrived.

The impact was devastating.

The entire settlement subsided. Huge chunks of rubble and sixty-ton fighting vehicles slid towards the sinkhole that was forming at its nadir beneath the primarch's feet. The god-slaying wave raged against Angron's rubble shield, the physical manifestation of his wrath, and swept most of the township away with it. Even as it broke across the primarch's psychic barrier, the blast front flayed the armour from his back, roasting crimson flesh to black, but still the primarch was standing and the worst of the impact was already passing over the battlefield, its fury waning. Kossolax felt the storm begin to weaken, as the front rolled on and bore its devastation west.

But Angron's fury did not break.

He had felt his father's presence, as surely as Kossolax had, and then had it snatched away from him, and now the entire world would feel his rage.

The skies roiled, drawn into a nascent cyclone thousands of

yards across and with the incandescent primarch raging at the centre of its funnel. The ground beneath him cracked wide, deep fissures splitting the duricrust and causing the primarch to sink even further, vast cataracts of sand breaking over him as they gushed into the belly of the earth. Kossolax could barely see him. The earth had swallowed him. Just a raging storm-halo of light and fury that even the breakage of a world could not fully hide.

Less than a mile away, Kossolax felt the first earthquakes breaking open the ground beneath him. His escorting squads of Mutilators and Terminators broke formation as the tremors grew more strident, massively armoured limbs windmilling about them as the hard-packed sand crumbled beneath their feet.

There was anguish in Angron's fury now.

In a way, that was worse.

This planet would crack before his wrath was spent.

'We should retreat to the gunships!' Corvo screamed, struggling to be heard over the calamity that was about to befall them.

'There is no time.' Kossolax tapped the vox-pickup in his gorget ring once more, and keyed it to a new frequency. The electro-magnetic feedback whine of blanket atmospheric distortion spoke back to him through the link. It was time to trust that the *Conqueror* and its Mistress no longer sought his death.

'*Conqueror*,' he said. 'Commence emergency teleportation.'

The teleport homer he carried in his armour began to blink furiously.

'Lord?' said Corvo, rounding on Kossolax with a face that was a familiar blend of betrayal and fury.

Kossolax raised his bolt pistol and shot the warrior in the knee before he could come any closer and potentially disrupt the teleporter signal. The Warpsmith collapsed to the earth with an enraged growl as Kossolax turned away and looked up. The rest of the Foresworn were engaged with the battle. Luftos and

Donnakha were too far away, and too distracted by the awesome sight of their primarch breaking open a world through sheer rage to notice who Kossolax was speaking with or to care.

The XII Legion had been broken before Kossolax had arrived to fix it.

He could do it again.

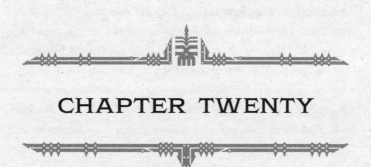

CHAPTER TWENTY

The air was a sticky mist. It filmed the face, coated the back of the throat. No sooner had the pocket of dusty atmosphere brought over by the *Sword of Dione*'s teleporters dispersed into the corridor than Graucis' body was attempting to retch it back up from his lungs. It was an automated defence that his body had not been built to accommodate. Space Marine physiology rendered him impervious to most toxins. He could not be poisoned, would not sicken or age, had never succumbed to biological infection. As a consequence, the reflex that existed in humans to protect them from foul vapours and possible toxins had been deliberately attenuated, enabling him and those like him to fight without distraction in the most malign conditions known to the early gene-wrights of man.

That knowledge had never extended to any environment so inimical to sanity as the bowels of the *Conqueror*.

His diaphragm spasmed, pectoralis muscles undergoing point-less cycles of tension and relaxation as acid burned a gorge up his throat. He bent his head forwards, as though to throw up, but his Dreadknight harness, the *Sanctity in Trust*, held him upright. Psychically wired to his mind, as opposed to the direct nervous control of his flesh, it remained inert without conscious instruction, and for that at least Graucis was grateful.

In the confines of the *Conqueror*'s innards, an unconscious twitch could have easily crippled or slain one of his brothers.

+Angron endures. We have failed.+

In the moments before the destruction of the Basilicarum Astropathica and the loss of Hyades, the *Sword of Dione* had teleported the eleven surviving Grey Knights directly over to the *Conqueror*. It was the only ship in the system sturdy enough to weather the imminent destruction of the planet.

Graucis turned towards Liminon, who had sent the thought. 'He endures, but we have not failed. Nor will we concede while there is still one amongst the Brotherhood of Thirteen who can still hold a bolter or a blade.'

As one, the Grey Knights bowed their heads, as though making silent peace with what he must inevitably ask of them now.

'If Angron is allowed to return to this ship and leave the system then he will resume his course to Malakbael. There, he will destroy that which can never be replaced, and the union of the Twelfth Legion with their primarch, however anarchic and brief, will be a blow that a wounded Imperium cannot suffer. No, brothers. If Angron will not be bound, as we had intended, then the best path still open to us is to destroy the *Conqueror*, and ensure that he never arrives at the true object of his hate.'

'Let our incorruptibility be absolute,' said Geromidas, his voice a rasp on the tainted air. 'The warp is ours to tame.'

'Though sorceries will be against us, no witchcraft will bring our doom,' Dvorik continued, taking up the verse that the Chaplain had selected from the *Cabulous Luminar*.

Gallead and his Brotherhood Terminators, meanwhile, drew themselves into an Inverted Eight, a combat formation that was most unfavourable to the essence of the Sanguinary Unholiness with two warriors facing forwards and two back, and the Justicar himself at the interstice in-between.

As soon as they were in position, Graucis felt his breaths coming more easily, congealed blood no longer sucking at his intake filters.

'Though spell or incantation blocks us, the Emperor shall see us victorious,' Gallead and his squad spoke in unison.

The strength of their collective aegis enclosed the Grey Knights like a fortress. Tainted blood boiled where it pressed against the mental force field. From the inside looking out, it appeared as though millions upon millions of frenzied insects threw themselves against the invisible barrier, enclosing Graucis and the Grey Knights in a dome of black smoke and short-lived fires beyond which he could see precious little. Everything here was inimical to human existence, more deadly than the void, more brazen in its insanity than the Red Angel's Gate or the murder fields of the Styx. Graucis felt the conscious malice that lay behind it, a mind of brass and slowly turning hatreds, thoughts pushed along uninsulated copper wires on pulses of electricity.

'There is a daemonic force at work on this ship,' he said. 'Perhaps even the mind of the *Conqueror* itself.'

'Which way, brother?' Dvorik held his force sword two-handed in a ready stance. The silver bindings of the *Liber Daemonica* rattled against his breastplate as though it, too, felt the pull of what lay ahead.

Graucis gestured forwards. 'This way.'

He could not say how he knew, only that *he knew*.

It was in the nature of beings such as Angron to bend the fates of others around them. Graucis had been pursuing the primarch for centuries, across light years and beyond the fragile bounds of his reality. In that alone, he and the *Conqueror* were much alike.

'I had Shipmaster Oren teleport us as close to the coordinates as I could perceive them from afar.'

'Everlasting shall be their duty,' Geromidas murmured.

Dvorik signed the aquila across his breastplate.

In retrieving the Grey Knights from the Basilicarum Astropathica and teleporting them on to the *Conqueror*, the *Sword of Dione* had exposed herself to the entire World Eaters armada. Even if she had had the speed to outrun Hyades' death, she would not be able to escape the Heretic Astartes' guns. Most of the World Eaters would likely relish the prospect of a battle with another warship, even with Hyades promising the doom of their own ships as well.

The Sanguinary Unholiness did not reward those souls that went quietly to its stronghold of blood and brass.

So it had been written in the *Liber Daemonica*, and so it was.

'*Et Imperator invocato diabolus daemonica exorcism,*' Graucis intoned.

Servos whined as Gallead's Terminators tightened their grips on their storm bolters. Liminon took a step ahead, open hand outstretched towards the struggling envelope between the purity within and the overwhelming hatred of Angron and the *Conqueror* without, sending forth his mind to scout the way ahead.

'What does your mind's eye see, brother?' Graucis asked.

+Our incursion has been noted at last.+

A howl of outrage trembled up from somewhere deep within the corrupted ship. Without any discernible change in the shape or size of the passage ahead, Graucis *felt* the twist around him, like a rope of intestine wrangled by a butcher to squeeze out something foul. Anchored fast to the metal deck plates by their boots' mag-locks, the eleven Grey Knights held firm, the aegis flaring up in such visceral bursts that Graucis' mind turned the sub-hypnotic patterns into words.

+Foes,+ Liminon cried, still firmly mag-locked to the deck as his off-hand dropped to his force axe's haft, sliding back half a pace to stand between the two Terminators as though braced for a charge.

The corridor in both directions erupted with screams. Fire in the humanoid shape of a horned Neverborn bloomed across the aegis.

'Bolters down,' Gallead barked, as blow after furious blow shuddered against the barrier. Every impact was the fiery death throes of one of the *Conqueror*'s legion of lesser Neverborn. No lesser choir, however infinite their numbers, would breach their aegis, and when one's ammunition was hand-crafted from silver and consecrated in the forges of Deimos then wastefulness was a sin.

+With me, my brothers,+ Graucis sent, speaking simultaneously into each of his brothers' minds as he awakened the *Sanctity in Trust* with a thought. Servos whirred in a cascading sequence, powerful hydraulic pistons lengthening the Dreadknight's limbs and propelling it forwards into a walk that thudded the deck beneath its clawed feet. +This is our course now. Our only course. As it has been for me since before many of you were first taken by the Gatherers from your birthworlds. As thirteen Grey Knights survived the slaughter on Armageddon, so will thirteen now return to complete their task. In the name of Malcador the Sigillite and the Master of Mankind, not one amongst us here today will stray from this path before its end. By the power of the one hundred and one True Names recorded in the *Conclave Diabolus*, this ends only when Angron is no more and the last of our brotherhood is finally at rest.+

'For Baris and Lokar,' Dvorik cried.

'For the Sigillite and the Emperor!' Geromidas yelled and, one by one, the warriors still with him took up the oath.

+*For the Sigillite and the Emperor!*+

With Gallead's Terminators presenting the front and rear of their formation, the *Sanctity in Trust* anchoring their centre, the Grey Knights advanced down the corridor, a rolling aegis that burned the corruption from the walls and drove impotent Neverborn from their path. Those filling the corridor behind them hissed in growing fury, repelled as much by the psychic aegis as the Grey Knights' invocation of Him they knew as the Anathema.

With a thought, Graucis spooled up his psycannons with sacred munitions. They were not moving fast enough. The aegis was an inviolate barrier against the lesser choirs of the Neverborn, but the *Conqueror* had other servants upon which to call.

A World Eater carrying an enormous shield studded with spikes and a rusted mace bulled his way through the Grey Knights' quivering force field. Smoke billowed from the foul alloys of his armour, cancerous mutations erupting into mists of bloody lymph, but his lobotomised frenzy allowed for neither hesitation nor pain.

A torrent of null-rounds from the Eighth Brotherhood Terminators ended him, proving no less efficacious against meat and metal than against the Neverborn. More of the Heretic Astartes came howling at the aegis and Graucis was compelled to add his heavier fire to that of the Terminators. A psychic impulse raised one of the Dreadknight's power fists, the underslung heavy psycannon clunking as it was fed from the attached box magazine. The weapon spoke as a torrential roar, mowing through World Eaters Space Marines and lesser Neverborn alike. Those that made it through the hail of explosive, psyk-reactive fire and the ensuing showers of meat tottered into the precise arcs of Dvorik's force sword and the perfect, humming sweeps of Liminon's Omnissian axe.

The Techmarine was the first of them to perish.

A blaze of autocannon fire from a ceiling hard point somewhere beyond their roiling aegis, and thus beyond Graucis' ability to make out, punched through Liminon's visor plate and exploded from the back of his head in a welter of blood and ceramite. Geromidas screamed, his grief so palpable a psychic force that it caused the emotive metals of the corridor to recoil and the *Conqueror* to retaliate with a fresh surge of Neverborn that annihilated themselves in a pyrotechnic frenzy against the aegis barrier.

+*For the Sigillite and the Emperor*...+ came the whisper of a thought that Graucis would have sworn belonged to Liminon.

He had to stop himself from turning to look down at the Techmarine's body.

'We are purity amongst the impure,' Graucis roared, his old voice hoarsened by the psychic endeavours of the past hours and by his grief. 'We cede not to the unliving or the Neverborn.'

Dvorik's sword dissected a World Eater with a buzzing chainfist welded to each arm, and ducked back from the decapitating axe blow of another. A pulverising swipe of Graucis' Nemesis power fist obliterated a third. Anchrum and Epicrane blazed wildly through the aegis, but with psychically guided accuracy as they avenged their fallen Techmarine.

Graucis doubted whether these decks of the *Conqueror* had heard a purer sound in ten thousand years, assuming they ever had. Even before Angron's corruption by Chaos, the *Conqueror* had been a ship waiting for the opportunity to fall.

Graucis advanced into the storm of withering silver, crushing a twitching, half-slain heretic underfoot, and then hurled three more that had been charging rabidly at Dvorik back the way they had come with a telekinetic blast.

It felt... *good.*

He had spent too long in warded libraria in pursuit of forgotten daemon-lore. But his moment was coming. He could feel it. When the psychic echo of this deed made it across the warp to the Prognosticars of Titan, all that he had done to bring about Angron's demise would be seen. His memorial in the Dead Fields, below Titan's frozen crust and beneath the Citadel's foundations, would finally get to rest alongside all of those lost on Armageddon.

His long quest would be vindicated in death.

Graucis caught a suggestion of movement from beyond the aegis. He turned towards it.

There was a *whoosh* of flame. A promethium jet burst through the ephemeral barrier and devoured Epicrane whole, incinerating the power-armoured Strike Brother to the bone in the split second it took Gallead to throw out a hand and bellow the command that had the flame breaking from him in all directions and rippling across the walls, ceiling and floor like shallow water. The Justicar's command of pyromancy rivalled Graucis' mastery of fulmination, and Graucis did not even feel the flames' heat as they rushed across his armature's adamantine feet.

But they were already reduced to nine.

And the reprieve was temporary.

A squad of Chaos Space Marines encased in oily Terminator armour stamped through the aegis as though it were not there at all. The receding sheets of flame shimmered across the brass embellishments and glistening scabs of their armour, even as the champion at the fore seemed to reabsorb the heavy flamer into its arm and replace it with the half a dozen venous talons of a lightning claw. Gallead opened fire on the other members of the squad, his Terminators joining in a moment later, but the champion's endlessly mutating armour shrugged it off as though he were walking through rain. The warrior gurgled, furious with glee as he proceeded to parry Gallead's force sword, and then punch his lightning claw through the Justicar's breastplate.

Ignoring the still-kicking Justicar even as he peeled his mag-locked boots from the deck and hoisted him overhead, the raging Chaos Space Marine raised his left hand towards the other Grey Knights.

Each of his knuckles had become the barrel of a bolter.

Graucis demolished the fallen Terminator's skull with a single blow from the Dreadknight's Nemesis power fist, slamming both him and Gallead into the bulkhead behind them.

Neither got back up.

The Grey Knights' aegis guttered as Gallead's brothers struggled to absorb the shock of their Justicar's demise. But, just as Graucis feared that it might falter and allow the hatred of the *Conqueror*'s daemonic legions to defeat it, he felt Gallead's strength surging back from somewhere within them all to reinforce it anew.

'Not one amongst us strays from this path,' Graucis cried. 'This ends when Angron is no more and the last of our brotherhood is finally at rest.'

So he had spoken and, by the strength of their dying oaths and by the last lingering photons of the Emperor's brilliance, he had made it true.

His fallen brothers walked beside him still.

The rest of the mutated Terminators traded fire with the surviving Grey Knights as a second hulking champion and his warriors blundered through the aegis. This one wore no helmet, but an expression of permanently scowling brass. With lightning claws sprouting from each powered fist, he disembowelled the nearest of Gallead's vanguard. The Grey Knight Terminator fought on without so much as a grunt of discomfort, sending three more howling warriors to their ends before being dragged down under their weight of numbers. The champion then accounted for the second of Gallead's vanguard, beheading the last of the Strike Brothers, Anchrum, in the same blow before Dvorik was able to claim his head in turn. The aegis faltered. A brass-bodied juggernaut, the size of a large equine but with the mass of a Baneblade, stampeded through the weakening barrier. The slavering Neverborn on its back burst into flames almost immediately, but the steed itself was so massive that it had trampled another of Gallead's Terminators under its hooves before it too crumbled under the might of the aegis. A horde of lesser Neverborn surged into the temporary breach in the psychic barrier, black swords rising and falling as they descended on the fallen Terminator like a flock of crows.

Graucis, Dvorik, Geromidas and a single Eighth Brotherhood Terminator, Orpheo, were all who remained.

'The *Conqueror* sends its master's mortal legions to deny us,' Graucis called out to them. 'It cannot be far now, my brothers.'

Further packs of bloodletters ripped into the buckling aegis from ahead and from behind. A baying daemon hound with a spiked collar made of brass managed to fling itself through the barrier and bite down on Orpheo's ankle. The Terminator bellowed, null-rounds from his storm bolter ripping the hound to shreds. Already unbalanced, however, he fell a moment later with a heavy *clang*, and the hordes of Neverborn shrieked as they surged.

Geromidas turned towards them, unburdening his soul of his grief over Liminon in preparation for death, and threw his fury back down the corridor as a ball of psychic flame. 'For the Sigillite… and the Emperor,' he breathed, sagging spent to the deck, where he disappeared alongside Orpheo under an unspeakable tide of bronze teeth, hacking blades and frenzied claws.

'Brother!' Graucis yelled.

Only he and Dvorik remained.

But their efforts had not been in vain.

A sturdy set of adamantine doors barred the final step of their path. There was evidence of recent melta damage to the locking mechanism, but Graucis had the sense that these doors presented more than a mere physical barrier. As Dvorik and his force sword held the hordes behind them at bay, he took a moment to study it. The unsteady impression of a daemonic presence, female in appearance with a red smudge filling the suggested outline of her chest, stood across it with arms spread as though it intended to physically bar his passage.

You intrude upon the lair of Angron of Nuceria, came the voice in his head, at once feminine and monstrous. *Don't say you weren't warned.*

Graucis did not reply, and the daemonic apparition soon dissipated before his will.

'Guard my back, brother,' said Graucis.

'Always,' Dvorik returned, as Graucis raised his Nemesis fist, and summoned his power.

CHAPTER TWENTY-ONE

The doors crashed inwards, torn from their rails by a lightning-wreathed telekinetic fist. The two crumpled halves struck the deck and screeched inwards, too heavy to bounce, all efforts at striking a spark off the metal floor smothered under the dense, crimson pall that settled over the deadened terminals like a mist. Graucis strode through, electrical tendrils crawling over the Dreadknight's powered frame, its stamping footfalls announcing his arrival like the last tolling of the Bell of Lost Souls.

He was on what appeared to have once been a command deck, albeit one that had fallen deeply into the eightfold corruptions of the Sanguinary Unholiness and since been abandoned.

The conventional theatres of command were all present and accountable, recognisable enough in their new forms to turn a mortal's stomach. The workstations had become butchers' tables, smeared with blood and encrusted with brass spikes from which the severed heads and dismembered torsos of Heretic Astartes in a variety of World Eaters heraldry slowly dripped like trophies. A throne dais rose above the centre of the deck. A carrion figure of greying flesh and tufted hair lay slumped there, mummified by the passing millennia and clothed in the tattered remnants of a white shipmaster's uniform. Lesser choirs of the Neverborn, their molten yellow eyes burning thin holes through the lingering red fog, scratched at the deck with brass claws and whined from their places of hiding, scavengers lured to the lair of a god-predator and unwilling to flee now even as it bared its power.

With a sound that resembled that of a fist unclenching from around a piece of gristle, Angron straightened from the foot of the dais and turned towards the blown door. It was like watching the statue of a primitive war god, smeared red with millennia of blood sacrifice, coming slowly to life.

Graucis resisted the urge to take a backward step.

The daemon primarch did not appear to have been engaged in any obvious activity prior to Graucis' interruption. His brush with annihilation on Hyades had left his skin black and peeling, wreathed in red smoke as his corrupted body healed. Every thought, every visceral expenditure of energy in that unholy frame, seemed bent solely towards the awesome magnitude of his rage.

Angron had been wounded, he had been *chastened*, but that was when a beast was at its most dangerous.

Graucis had experienced visions of Angron almost every day over the past six hundred years. The forbidden texts he had collected and pored over in that time were of Angron of Nuceria, Angron the daemon primarch of the XII, and of Angron the Great Beast of Armageddon, and it was Angron, unsurprisingly, who emerged from his memories to stalk his dreams when he was forced to stop and sleep. When he had meditated, it was on the means to destroy a demigod of battle, and when he would rouse himself again to resume that great work it was Angron's voice that lingered in his thoughts to mock the hubris of the Emperor's loyal sons.

For all that, he felt underprepared for the vision of him now.

The daemon primarch felt somehow larger than the monster who had dominated the battlefields of his nightmares. A greater mass of bleeding musculature hunched his broad shoulders under their weight. The corrupted bronze of his piecemeal armour had grown thicker, and darker, as though stained by six centuries of spite, while his flesh had become the furious red of his choler, coloured by every drop of blood spilled in his name since. His crest of cybernetic dreadlocks, though blackened by the fires of Hyades, framed a spitting halo in the chamber's darkness. When he blinked, a film of blood smeared pupilless yellow eyes. And when he grinned it was with apparent recognition of the one who had given everything in their failure to destroy him, burnt lips peeling back over a sticky, rust-coloured snarl.

A fist the size of a Chaos Space Marine's entire torso tightened around the grip of the bronze sword Samni'arius. At least the destruction of the Black Sword on Armageddon had proven more permanent than that of its master. With the other hand, he bent to pick up the immense chainaxe Spinegrinder, which had been left to lie carelessly on the deck.

Graucis hissed, seizing against the restraint bars of the Dreadknight's command harness as the pain in his thigh suddenly became greater than he had ever known it. A trickle of weakly acidic saliva dribbled down his chin as he fought to wrest his body back under his mind's control.

Angron gave a wet gurgle of seeming amusement. He spoke no words. Was the primarch's mind clear enough to exercise that human power?

Graucis did not know, only that it did not matter.

The fallen primarch expressed his intent more eloquently than any Chaplain. Fury enough to burn every word in every librarium in all the citadels of man raged behind his eyes. The heat of it beaded his ridged, bestially elongated brow in bloody sweat. Every out-breath was the snort of an enraged ambull preparing a charge, droplets of blood and sizzling embers of manifest hatred spraying from his flattened snout.

Graucis felt his hearts quicken as the pain in his thigh turned to the clean heat of anger, and then to an unexpected, but not at all unwelcome, sense of joy.

He felt the same fire as he saw in Angron kindling in him and there was a part of himself that liked it.

Angron was an abomination, the very worst aspects of human nature united in wrathful flesh and encased together in bronze, leather and bone. The thing he had sunk to would tear the Imperium asunder if left free to do so. He would burn whatever was left of humanity's ruins to the ground, ushering in a new era of darkness from which nothing would flow but blood, and the tortured howls of a daemon lord with nothing but half a billion lifeless stars and the bones of his former species to unmake.

All the comforting excuses of honour and purpose failed Graucis then. He grasped for the protestations of genetic divinity that excused all sins, but under the yellow, almost familial, glare of those Stygian eyes, he could no longer find them in him. With the startling clarity of eyes drenched in red, he saw more clearly than he had ever desired to see. He *hated* Angron, and he was right to do so. To feel any other emotion or, worse, no emotion at all would have been unthinkable. It would have been sinful. The father that he and Angron both shared had never intended for abominations such as this to exist and, in His omniscience, had forged the Grey Knights as the holy instrument by which His error might one day be undone.

That day would be soon.

Emperor willing, it would be *now*.

It was His rage that Graucis could feel coursing through his veins, he was sure of it, as sure as he was of the perfect genetics coding every vibrating cell in his body. In that time, and in that place, there could have been no purer feeling.

Graucis breathed lightning into his fists.

Power thrummed through the Dreadknight's warlike armature as it sensed its pilot's aggression, converting it into useable kinetic energy for its force shielding and psychic weaponry.

'We are the masters of our minds,' Dvorik called to him in warning, still holding true to his word to deny the entrance to the *Conqueror*'s Neverborn. 'Our emotions are naught but the winds that disturb the sanctity of our thoughts. Pay them no heed, but that of being ignored. You will not defeat the Lord of the Twelfth Legion with rage.'

'For the Sigillite!' Graucis roared, leaving his brother to ward the entrance behind him. 'And for the Emperor!' His words leapt from his lips on *snaps* of lightning as he pushed the *Sanctity in Trust* into a charge. 'For the souls of the one hundred and nine!' His war machine ploughed headlong into Angron, its bull-rush driving the daemon primarch ahead of him as he beat at him with knees and fists.

The Dreadknight chassis had been specifically designed to channel a Grey Knight's formidable psychic prowess into direct physical fighting strength. Clad in a Dreadknight frame, a Grey Knight could fight toe to toe against the Neverborn of the greater choirs, nightmares such as those named in the *Liber Daemonica* against whom a full squad of Brotherhood Paladins would struggle to prevail. But Angron was a test beyond even the mightiest of the Neverborn. The tortured scrap of his humanity was not a flaw. It was a force multiplier. It kept his soul in pain, and his torment only served to pour fuel onto his rage.

With a roar, the daemon primarch picked up Graucis by the bars of his harness and hurled him through a nearby vox-terminal.

The Dreadknight crashed through the instrument stand, but Graucis was able to slow its journey with a flex of will. Psychically thickening the air above him to a greater degree than that below, he pivoted the Dreadknight to ensure it landed on its feet, crushing the vox-station's cogitation array under its splayed toes in an explosion of browned glass and ancient steel.

Angron took no time at all to recover.

The daemon primarch flew at him in a rage, wings unfurled and with bloody ropes of saliva swinging from his chin.

Graucis threw up a hand on instinct, the Dreadknight's Nemesis fist slamming across Angron's face like a sledgehammer. The daemon primarch's jaw crunched. Spit flew from his mouth. With a grimace of concentration, Graucis willed the opposite fist to rise, lensing through it a telekinetic blast that struck Angron in the shoulder. The kine-blast snapped the daemon primarch's bone as though it were dried wood, and Angron bellowed in pain as the bronze pauldron imploded. The expanding cone of psy-waves radiated off from the buckled plate and crumpled a swathe of ceiling. Gaseous chemicals that had stewed in their brittle pipes for thousands of years erupted from the broken ceiling, setting off a firestorm as they crossed shorn electrical cables and raising screeches from the scores of lesser Neverborn who found further reason to flee towards the command deck's shadowed corners.

In the roar of the flames, Graucis heard what sounded to him like a woman's voice, raised in anger, but he had not the time to give it attention.

Angron strode unharmed through the flames.

Blade, fire and witchcraft – these were supposed to be the

instruments that the Neverborn feared, but Angron appeared to have grown mightier in his exile.

Graucis desperately batted aside a lunge from Samni'arius on the back of his power fist. The daemon sword went wide, but with the colossal strength of Angron behind it, the near miss was enough to stagger him. He crushed another piece of bridge infrastructure underfoot, barely able to get another fist in place to block the wild swing of Spinegrinder. Bleeding musculature swollen to epic proportions, the daemon primarch scythed down with both weapons at the same time. The *Sanctity in Trust* whined as Graucis crossed both its wrists above his head, pushing the armature to the very limits of its capabilities to block the blow. Samni'arius rebounded from Graucis' reinforced aegis, but Spinegrinder sheared the psycannon from its wrist hard point, the weapon nosily bouncing down the consecrated silver plating of the Dreadknight's forearm, breaking ward after ward before sparking off its force shield.

Graucis snarled in relief, and rage, and slammed the still-intact Nemesis fist into Angron's ribs. The primarch bellowed in return as armour cracked and bones snapped.

Angron had battled one hundred and nine of Graucis' mightiest brothers on Armageddon, slaying all but thirteen, but he had not done so alone. He had marched at the head of the Cruor Praetoria, the oldest and most blood-soaked of the greater Neverborn, who had in turn commanded the Eight Legions of the Sanguinary Unholiness.

This time, he was alone. His own fury on Hyades had made sure of it.

Graucis laid into the primarch with an intensity that Angron blindly returned in kind, his strength appearing to swell in direct proportion to Graucis' growing anger. Their combat carried them the length of the command deck and then back again, demolishing every instrument and workstation that fell under their path, regardless of its apparent solidity or size. Dreadknight harness or no, those frenzied minutes should rightly have seen Graucis slain a dozen times over. He could not spare the mental energy to explain how they did not, only noting that every time the primarch's chainaxe broke his guard and threatened to pierce his harness' force shields, it was as though Liminon's axe or Geromidas' crozius arcanum was there to turn the blow aside. Whenever the Dreadknight's footing stumbled in debris, the roar of Gallead's bolters would ring like a strident echo in his ears and Angron would be falling back, flailing at the thick red fog that surrounded them both instead of administering the killing blow as he might.

Graucis' brothers were with him.

Their souls went in search of the Emperor, but He held them here yet, the power of their oaths to Him commanding them to remain while the task was unfinished and one of their brotherhood still fought.

'Everlasting shall be their duty,' Graucis murmured, recalling Geromidas' earlier refrain before concluding the verse with a shout. '*Et Imperator invocato diabolus daemonica exorcism!*'

While Angron reeled under half-imagined fire, Graucis levelled his remaining psycannon and blew the daemon primarch's breastplate apart. The beating that the Dreadknight had endured until then caused its aim to slip before the massive recoil, half of the volley blasting red pulp from the primarch's chest while the rest ended up as explosions in the walls.

He charged at Graucis with a roar, head down, soaking up the psycannon's warp-deadening output with sheer bulk, and smashed the Dreadknight to the ground.

The fighting suit crashed to the deck on its back.

With a whir of servomotors Graucis psychically bade it to

rise, but Angron's boot forced it back down. Graucis swung the psycannon around. Angron kicked it aside, so hard it dislocated the armature's shoulder and severed the psyk-conducting interface to the rest of the suit. The arm thudded to the deck, dead.

The Lord of the XII bellowed in triumph.

Graucis, despite his pristine genetics and all his conditioning, could not help but roar right back.

'Desist, abomination,' came Dvorik's yell from somewhere close behind.

Graucis turned his head to look over the Dreadknight's shoulder.

Angron's rampage, and his own firing spree, had scattered the lesser Neverborn from the entrance, and driven even the handful of World Eaters supporting them back into the corridor. The occasional servitor, compelled by its programming towards absolute adherence to their defensive protocols, struggled on through debris and fire before expiring. It was a short respite, but enough for the Paladin Ancient to lower his sword and, for a moment at least, turn to address Angron.

'*In nomine veritas*, I command you.'

There was a resounding *crack* as Dvorik's heavy jawbone dislocated from its skull to admit the torrent of inhuman word-sounds and verbal profanity that flowed thence from his mouth. With the spoken element came psychic pulses. The raging disdain of a son for his father's works. The fury of a damaged angel. The shame of being pushed, once again, into the bondage of another's designs. With word and with thought, the Paladin screamed the True Name of the Beast. He channelled the impotence and the rage. He embodied it.

Dvorik lacked Graucis' psychic mastery, and the name they had obtained from Armageddon was but a fragment of the whole, but its effect upon the fallen primarch was immediate, and dramatic.

Angron threw back his head.

Smoke poured from his mouth as the veins bulging from his over-muscled frame burst simultaneously into flame.

A physical impact that was both sound and psychically manifested fury struck Dvorik like a backhand fist, lifting the Paladin off his feet and hurling him clear across the deck.

The daemon primarch's outpouring of rage continued.

Graucis felt it pummelling the *Sanctity in Trust*'s force bubble, bringing it out in a squall of angry reds as the sheer power of it pinned the harness down as forcefully as Angron's boot had a moment before.

Setting his mind against the primarch's outrage, Graucis groaned and struggled to rise, pushing all his willpower into the Dreadknight's one functioning arm and hauling the Nemesis fist an inch off the deck.

He screamed, and managed to lift it another.

The fury unleashed by the speaking of Angron's True Name spiralled ever further out of control. It was a hurricane. The Dreadknight's arm trembled as Graucis fought to raise it far enough to make a fist, to finish what Dvorik had begun while Angron was debilitated. Meanwhile, rage beyond mortal limits continued to rip free of the daemon primarch's throat and ravage the deck.

It tore plates from the floor and hurled them in fits of centrifugal violence towards the far bulkheads. Heretic icons toppled before its wrath. The jets of flame, still geysering from the ceiling, bent around the eye of Angron's storm like coronal mass ejections falling into the ever-hungering maw of a black hole. Terminals exploded in showers of sparks as they were ripped from their pedestals, pulled to shreds in the accelerating and increasingly furious vortex.

Only the throne dais at the centre of the deck, the mummified corpse of some mutant hunched in its seat, seemed immune. For a moment, Graucis felt the impression of a grey-haired woman in a starched white uniform over his shoulder, her neat appearance entirely at odds with the swirling maelstrom she had chosen to manifest within.

Graucis felt a chill of unease go through him. He had devoted all his efforts to Angron's caging or destruction. He had neglected to consider that the *Conqueror* had a will of its own.

Before he could conjure a response, the bulkhead directly behind him blew out.

There was no explosive signature that Graucis' auto-senses were able to pick up, just a sudden and inexplicable decompression as though the dormant electrochemical circulatory system running through the wall had chosen *exactly* that moment to blow. As improbable as that was on its own, sequential bulkheads proceeded to fail in similarly explosive fashion until the *Conqueror* simply ran out of walls.

Hermetically locked inside his consecrated war plate, itself buttressed by the *Sanctity in Trust*, it took Graucis half a second longer than it should have to register the abrupt cessation of gravity, or the whistling escape of the command deck's atmosphere. The flame jets from the ceiling bent towards the hull breach and then snuffed themselves out. The glittering metal debris that Angron had ripped into a vortex around himself began to fan outwards as the venting atmosphere pulled against the attractive force of the daemon primarch's rage.

Graucis turned.

Stars twinkled at the end of a long, long corridor of mangled bulkhead frames.

'Throne,' he cursed, as the decompression dragged his damaged Dreadknight along its back towards empty space.

With a pulse of thought, he mag-locked the entire armature to the deck plates.

It held him in place for a moment, until the deck plates themselves came away from the flooring, man and machine flipping over and tumbling towards the open void. Bulkhead after bulkhead flashed by him, his one responsive arm flailing instinctively for a purchase it could not quite reach until he was falling out into space.

He cleared the outer skin of the *Conqueror* and went on falling. The deck-load of loose debris that evacuated alongside him dispersed into a twinkling shower that glittered like stellar dust in the incident light of Hyades' two red suns. Angular momentum rotated him slowly about his axis until he was facing back towards the *Conqueror*'s sunward side. Seeing the great battleship from the outside, and without the benefit of a ship of his own, or the astronomical distances that ordinarily inoculated a warrior from his own insignificant scale, Graucis could not help but appreciate its immensity. At over twelve miles in length, it was a literal mountain of brass, adamantine and scarred muscle, far outweighing and outgunning any natural peak still standing proud over Terra.

It was truly monstrous. The original eater of worlds.

Continuing around his slow rotation, he caught a glimpse of Dvorik.

The Paladin had cleared the hull breach several seconds after Graucis, tumbling free on an entirely different trajectory.

Drawing deep on his armour's supply of air, Graucis centred his thoughts and threw his mind like a line towards his brother. He felt the clench in the back of his skull as Dvorik caught the psychic lifeline and then, slowly, the effort of mind bringing a swell of pressure behind his eyes and a slow bleed from the back of his nose, he reeled his brother in. The angle of their relative trajectories began to narrow and then to close. It was a small thing, under the circumstances of being adrift in the void, but once they were closer together, it was possible that they could–

With a roar that startled even the airlessness of space, reverberating inside of Graucis' skull long after it had passed, Angron surged through the now-distant breach in the *Conqueror*'s belly. The daemon primarch's metaphysical nature was entirely untroubled by the voiding of the deck or the loss of atmosphere, and he swept into the open void on bleeding wings. Ignoring Dvorik for now, Angron turned towards the greater psychic threat that Graucis represented, growing larger with every impossibly leathery creak of his wings.

Graucis braced, sequestering a portion of psychic power to holding tight to Dvorik's line. He had sacrificed a planet and his entire brotherhood to this quest. He would not surrender another brother to the void.

As Angron roared across the inconceivable distances of space and into arm's reach, Graucis threw a punch towards the daemon primarch's red jaw. Absent the sensory feedback of air resistance, the buzz of air molecules splitting into their constituent atoms against the Nemesis fist's disruption field, the blow felt laboriously slow. Angron parried with contemptuous ease.

The counterforce, without friction or gravity to overcome, cannoned Graucis onto an entirely new trajectory.

He tumbled through space, spinning head over heels and fifty times faster than his sedate pace of rotation before. His field of view changed faster than even a transhuman visual cortex could process, bringing on a vertigo-like sensation that he struggled to contain.

He saw the *Conqueror*.

Blackness.

Conqueror.

Blackness.

Conqueror.

Deeper blackness.

Planet.

In the split second it was with him he saw the damage scrawled across its dusty surface. Cracks split its crust like the shell of a broken egg, six-hundred-mile-long clefts straddling its hemisphere. The mantle-deep crater that Graucis' accidental destruction of the Basilicarum Astropathica had left was visible from space. Gases jetted up through the sundered crust, reaching towards the upper limits of the atmosphere and ejecting Hyades' mineral content into orbit. Were the planet to survive then, in addition to its crater, Hyades would one day inherit a dully siliceous ring system to memorialise the day that Graucis Telomane had failed to slay a demigod.

But it was not going to survive.

Hyades was already dying.

It was impossible to be certain of that from the single glance he was given, but somehow he could feel it. The wild spiking of its geomagnetic field threw field lines deep out into space, fumbling through his psychic processes like a mortis cry. Graucis gave his head a shake, even that motion sufficient to warp his course and spin, and quickly threw a wall around his emotions.

So much death, and for so little.

The destruction of Hyades would decimate Angron's fleet, that was true. The primarch had brought no other vessel to this system with the mass and endurance of the *Conqueror*, and the deaths of a thousand Heretic Astartes or more was no insignificant triumph, even at the cost of his own brothers' lives. But Graucis should have known... Had he been nearly as prepared as he had believed himself to be, then he would have understood that the Sanguinary Unholiness did not care from whence the blood came.

All bloodshed nourished it equally.

Had Dvorik not tried to warn him? Had Geromidas not sought to advise him on his plan from the outset? Had he not himself sensed how Angron's power had swelled since Armageddon?

'You cannot defeat the Lord of the Twelfth Legion with rage,' Dvorik had told him.

Graucis cursed his own blindness.

He had done this. With his own determination, bordering on rage, he had fed the primarch's spirit. With the sacrifice of Hyades and all who fought upon it, he had made him strong. But, it occurred to him that he could still *undo* it. He could revoke the gift of blood and anger that he had unwittingly made and deny the primarch a total victory, even if it must cost him the slim chance that remained of claiming one of his own.

That would have to be victory enough.

With his own hand, psychically disconnecting it from that of the *Sanctity in Trust*, he touched his gauntlet fingers to his thigh plate and winced. The old wound was bleeding again, under the armour. A single tear of pain and the threat of despair moistened his eyelids, but he smiled grimly in spite of it.

With a flash of crimson, Angron banked across the void, angling his wings as though catching the empyreal thermals rising from the dying world, and flew at him a second time.

+Let me go, brother.+ The reddish speck of Dvorik's armour, the consecrated silver stained by the light of Hyades' two suns, had grown distant, but his voice in Graucis' head was as strong as ever. +Angron's defeat is all that matters.+

+No, brother,+ Graucis sent back. +It is not. Not if it should come at the cost of our own souls. Not if the very attempt turns us into that which we seek to destroy.+

He saw that now.

Angron had been defeated long ago.

He had fallen on Nuceria, when Lorgar Aurelian had invited

the warp to inhabit his flesh and possess his soul and he had failed to resist. The shell that remained of him now was the worst of the human spirit, its perfectly engineered form reshaped and reimagined to better encapsulate the hideous ideal it had been reborn to represent. He was the embodiment of a universal truth, and truths could not be fought.

They could only be denied with will.

Graucis could not kill what was already slain, but perhaps the most injurious act one could do upon a god of battle was to do nothing at all.

With the last of his mental strength he propelled Dvorik away from him, guiding him back towards the *Conqueror*, where he might yet find sanctuary from the death of Hyades, and turned his head towards the raging primarch. 'I deny you, daemon,' he murmured to himself, and lowered the Dreadknight's Nemesis fist to its side.

The empyrean, as he had been taught, was a domain of the mind.

Just as physical toil and the proper instruments could be used to mould the architecture of realspace, so too could the warp be reshaped by the tools of will.

Closing his eyes, he sent his mind away, far away from this place of pain and blood and fury, and let it fly to that place it always went to, when freed to go anywhere at all. From that far-away place, he felt Samni'arius pierce his abandoned flesh, the daemonic metal greedily reclaiming the splinter of its former sibling that had been left lodged in his leg so many years ago and perhaps, just perhaps, trapping itself with a piece of Graucis Telomane's immortal spirit in exchange.

Graucis' younger psychic-self smiled, finding a victory of sorts in Angron's entirely unheralded howl of rage.

The universe began to darken.

But it was still raining over Mount Anarch.

Yes, he thought. *Here.*

EPILOGUE

Ortan Leidis drifted in and out of consciousness. He had only broken recollections of his escape from the planet. He remembered light, a flash so brilliant it had cut the world in half and cast no shadows. He remembered lying in rubble, his body mangled, his black soul charred, and waiting for death. He remembered the voice of a woman in his ear, small mortal hands shaking at his battered shoulder.

'Wake up, Leidis. Wake up. Wake up, wake up, wake up.'

His eyelids un-gummed and fluttered open.

He was in a small cubicle, a place of polished finishes and serrated edges. Bloody streaks decorated the mirrored doors of surgical cabinets. They smeared the enamelled surfaces, and everywhere but for the glinting sharpness of the various knives and saws magnetically taped to the walls.

His eyes fluttered closed.

They felt hot inside his skull.

Consciousness retreated from him, and he slept.

Faces came and went through his narcotic sleep. Some familiar. Some monstrous. Most were nightmare fusions of both. He saw Ginevah. The armswoman was seated on a folding stool, her head bowed over the much-read copy of the *Angel's Verses* in her lap. The poem she was reading aloud angered him but, worse, it brought him a kind of pain he had not felt since their flight from Eden, and he could not sustain his rage.

He sank again.

He stirred some time later, from a dream in which the Angel Sanguinius had been standing over him in judgement while Ginevah read to him from his verses.

Half asleep, he sniffed at the air.

He was in an apothecarion.

They all shared a common scent, Imperial technology favouring standardisation in the counterseptics, salves and unguents it could employ. The air was rank with blood and bile, vomit and faeces, air scrubbers buried in the rusted panelling slurping on it as though on a cold soup. Leidis did not believe they had ever been cleansed. He felt his nostrils flaring, his breaths coming in faster, faster, as they pulled in that sweet-scented air. He recalled the incense that the Angels of the Grail had used to burn in their apothecarion to obscure the scents of blood and found that he missed it.

Opening his eyes slowly, he looked down the length of his body.

He had not been wholly dreaming.

A vastly muscled World Eater in a sleeveless tunic that had been white once, but which was now brown with blood, stood hunched and grunting over the ruin of Leidis' right leg. There was nothing left of him but minced meat and chips of bone below the knee. There was a wet *thump*, then a rattle, as the stump tipped off the table and fell into a bucket.

The Butcher-Surgeon moved on to the other leg.

Leidis felt nothing.

He mumbled a question and drifted back into sleep.

The high-pitched shriek of a bone drill brought him back around.

The Apothecary was gone.

So were his legs.

Rudimentary metal prongs stuck out like forks from the cauterised stumps, ready to receive whatever bionic replacements a ship as half-feral as the *Conqueror* was equipped to provide. He could feel a dull vibration through the bones of his skull and neck, a terrible pressure building up inside his head until, after a minute or two of drilling, it stopped. The bit withdrew from his skull. The vibration ceased.

A sudden stab of pain brought him fully alert.

He had never experienced pain like it. It was a migraine ache that even Astartes physiology could not fully numb or ignore, frustrated spasms running through anaesthetised muscles to jerk his arms and legs against the surgical table to which he had been bound. Foam bubbled up from his mouth as he struggled to get free, to scratch the pain from his skull, to rip out his own eyes and dig his fingers into his brain if that was what it took. He jerked in place, seizing the way Arkhor had used to, rattling the entire table beneath him as tears of white-hot agony streamed down his face.

Ginevah was on the stool where he had seen her last, the *Angel's Verses* still open in her lap. She did not appear to have moved at all.

'My lord,' she said, softly, tentatively reaching out for the back of his hand, only to draw it back when he visibly recoiled from her touch.

He bared his teeth in a snarl.

'Y-Y-Y–'

Leidis tried to frame the words, but there seemed to be something shorting the circuits between mouth and brain and the pain in his head was only getting worse. It felt as though his skull would have to crack. Spit trickled down his chin, as though to relieve some of the pressure inside his head.

A sudden thought, appalling in its scope, came to him then.

He looked down.

Arkhor's Nails, kept on a loop of wire from his hip flexor, were gone.

'It is all right now, my lord,' said Ginevah, whispering as though to spare his thumping head. 'You are back aboard the *Conqueror*, and once the Foresworn's Apothecaries had you stabilised I made sure that they performed your surgery.' She leant forward, eyes glistening, cutting him open with her loyalty. 'You are a World Eater, lord. You have all you ever wanted. And with the Bloodless' fall on the planet, you–'

Leidis would forever wonder what the armswoman had expected Shâhka's death to do for his status.

Ginevah choked.

The *Angel's Verses* spilled from her lap, her metal stool clattering to the floor, as a hand Leidis only distantly recognised as his own raised her up off the ground.

Somehow, it had broken out of the wrist restraint, overcoming the effects of the anaesthetics that were still preventing him from experiencing the sensation first-hand.

'N–' he said, and closed his eyes, clenching them shut in frustration. With all the conscious effort his aching mind could still muster towards one task, he made his lips the centre of its attention, forcing them to make the words he wanted them to say. 'N-N-N–' He shook the woman in annoyance, as though Ginevah were at fault for deliberately failing to comprehend.

'N-N-*No,*' he managed, his agony too great to feel pride in the miniscule achievement of uttering a word.

He glared at his armswoman expectantly.

She stared glassily back, her head hanging limply over the finger of his hand by her thin, broken human neck.

She was dead.

In that moment of realisation, he experienced such a rush of pain relief that his sense of guilt was swept before it, leaving him gasping for breath on his surgical table and fighting back laughter.

It lasted for an entire second.

And somehow he knew that he would never again know such a prolonged state of bliss.

Already, he craved more.

'*Hnnng!*' he grunted, throwing away the body of his last and most loyal companion, already forgotten as he turned his attention to breaking out of his remaining restraints.

He was a World Eater now.

ABOUT THE AUTHOR

David Guymer's work for Black Library includes the Warhammer Age of Sigmar novels *Kragnos: Avatar of Destruction, Hamilcar: Champion of the Gods* and *The Court of the Blind King,* the novella *Bonereapers,* and several audio dramas including *Realmslayer* and *Realmslayer: Blood of the Old World.* He is also the author of the Gotrek & Felix novels *Slayer, Kinslayer* and *City of the Damned.* For The Horus Heresy he has written the novella *Dreadwing,* and the Primarchs novels *Ferrus Manus: Gorgon of Medusa* and *Lion El'Jonson: Lord of the First.* For Warhammer 40,000 he has written *The Eye of Medusa, The Voice of Mars* and the two Beast Arises novels *Echoes of the Long War* and *The Last Son of Dorn.* He is a freelance writer and occasional scientist based in the East Riding, and was a finalist in the 2014 David Gemmell Awards for his novel *Headtaker.*

An extract from
Renegades: Harrowmaster
by Mike Brooks

Jonn Brezik clutched his lasgun, muttered prayers under his breath, and hunkered further into the ditch in which he and seven others were crouching as the world shook around them. The weapon in his slightly trembling hands was an M35 M-Galaxy Short: solid, reliable and well maintained, with a fully charged clip, and a scrimshaw he had carved himself hanging off the barrel. He had another four ammo clips on his belt, along with the long, single-edged combat knife that had been his father's. He was not wearing the old man's flak vest – not a lot of point, given the state it had ended up in – and as enemy fire streaked overhead again, Jonn began to do the mental arithmetic of whether, right now, he would prefer to be in possession of a gun or functional body armour. The gun could kill the people shooting at him, that was for sure, but he would have to be accurate for that to work, and there didn't seem to be any shortage of the bastards. On the other hand, even the best armour would give out eventually, if he lacked any way of dissuading the other side from shooting at him–

'Brezik, you with us?'

Jonn jerked and blinked, then focused on the woman who

had spoken. Suran Teeler, sixty years old at least, with a face that looked like a particularly hard rock had been hit repeatedly with another rock. She was staring at him with eyes like dark flint, and he forced himself to nod.

'Yeah. Yeah, I'm here.'

'You sure? Because you seem a bit distracted right now,' Teeler said. 'Which, given we're in the middle of a bastard *warzone*, is something of a feat.'

'I'll be fine, sarge,' Jonn replied. He closed his eyes for a moment, and sighed. 'It's just the dreams again. Feels like I haven't slept properly for a month.'

'You've been having them too?' Kanzad asked. He was a big man with a beard like a bush. 'The sky ripping open?'

Jonn looked over at him. He and Kanzad did not really get on – there was no enmity as such, no blood feud; they just rubbed each other the wrong way – but there was no mockery on the hairy face turned in his direction.

'Yeah,' he said slowly. 'The sky ripping open. Well, not just our sky. All the skies. What does that mean, if we're both having the same dream?'

'It means absolute jack-dung until we get out of here alive,' Teeler snapped. 'You want to compare dream notes after we're done, that's fine. Right now, I want your attention on the matter in hand! And Brezik?'

'Yes, sarge?' Jonn replied, clutching his lasgun a little tighter.

'Stop calling me "sarge".'

'Sorry, s– Sorry. Force of habit.'

A throaty drone grew in the air behind them, and Jonn looked up to see lights in the night sky, closing the distance at a tremendous speed. The drone grew into a whine, and then into a roar as the aircraft shot overhead: two Lightnings flanking an Avenger, all three heading further into the combat zone.

'That's the signal!' Teeler yelled, scrambling to her feet with a swiftness that belied her years. 'Go, go, go!'

Jonn leaped up and followed her, clambering out of the ditch and charging across the chewed-up ground beyond. He desperately tried to keep up some sort of speed without twisting an ankle in the great ruts and gouts torn into the earth by bombardments, and the repeated traversing of wheeled and tracked vehicles. He could see other groups just like his on either side, screaming their battle cries as they advanced on the enemy that were being savaged by aerial gunfire from their fighters. Jonn raised his voice to join in, adrenaline and fear squeezing his words until they came out as little more than a feral scream:

'FOR THE EMPEROR!'

Streams of fire began spewing skywards as the enemy finally got their anti-aircraft batteries online. Jonn heard the *thump-thump-thump* of Hydra quad autocannons, and one of the fighters – a Lightning, he thought, although it was hard to tell at this distance, and in the dark – came apart in a flower of flame, and scattered itself over the defenders below.

'Keep moving!' Teeler yelled as one or two in their group slowed slightly. 'We've got one shot at this!'

Jonn pressed on, despite the temptation to hang back and let others take the brunt of the enemy gunfire. Presenting the defenders with targets one at a time would only ensure they all died: this massed rush, so there were simply too many of them to kill in time, was the only way to close the distance and get into the enemy lines. Once there, the odds became far more even.

They passed through a line of metal posts, some no more than girders driven upright into the mud, and the fortifications ahead began to sparkle with ruby-red bolts of super-focused light. They had entered the kill-zone, the functional range of a lasgun, and the defenders now knew that their shots would not be wasted.

Kanzad jerked, then jerked again, then fell on his face. Jonn did not stop for him. He would not have stopped for anyone. Stopping meant dying. He charged onwards, his face contorted into a rictus of fear and hatred, daring the galaxy to come and take him.

The galaxy obliged.

The first las-bolt struck him in the right shoulder and burned straight through. It was a sharp pain, but a clean pain, and he staggered but kept moving. It was his trigger arm, and his lasgun was supported by a strap. So long as his left arm could aim the barrel and his right could pull the trigger, he was still in this fight.

The next shot hit him in the gut, puncturing the muscle wall of his stomach and doubling him over. He managed to retain his feet, just, but his momentum was gone. He began to curl up around the pain, and the stench of his own flash-cooked flesh. Eyes screwed up, face towards the ground, Jonn Brezik did not even see the last shot. It struck the top of his head, and killed him instantly.

'Die, heretic!' Stevaz Tai yelled, as his third las-bolt finally put the man down. He whooped, partly in excitement and partly in relief, but anxiety was still scrabbling at the back of his throat. Throne, there were just so *many* of them! Even as he shifted his aim and fired again, he thought he saw something off to the left, closing in fast on the Pendata Fourth's defensive line. He blinked and squinted in that direction, but some of the great floodlights had been taken out by that accursed aerial attack, and the shapes refused to resolve for him.

'Eyes front, trooper, and keep firing!' Sergeant Cade ordered, suiting actions to words with his laspistol. It was more for show than anything else, Stevaz assumed, since the heretics were probably still out of pistol range, but it would only be a matter of seconds until that was no longer the case. And those seconds could be important.

'Something to the left, sarge!' he shouted, although he snapped off another shot as he spoke. 'I didn't get a good look, but whatever it was, it was moving fast!'

'Was it in our sector?' Cade demanded.

'No, sarge!'

'Then it's Fifth Squad's responsibility, or Seventh's – not ours! We've got enemies enough in front of us,' Cade snapped, and Stevaz could not argue with that. He jerked backwards as an enemy las-bolt struck the dirt in front of him, and wiped his eyes to clear them of the mud that had spattered across his face.

'Full-auto!' Cade bellowed. 'Let 'em have it!'

Stevaz obediently flicked the selector on his lasgun and joined its voice to the whining chorus that sprang up along the trench. It would drain their power packs rapidly, but the sheer volume of fire should put paid to this latest assault before they needed to reload–

Something exploded off to his left, and it was all he could do not to whip around, lasrifle still blazing. It was immediately followed by screaming: high, desperate screams born not just of pain, but of utter terror.

'Sarge?!'

'Eyes front, trooper, or you'll be the one screaming!' Cade yelled, but there was a note of uncertainty in the sergeant's voice as he fired at the onrushing cultists. 'One problem at a time, or–'

Something large and dark flew into their midst from their left, and landed heavily on the trench floor. It clipped the back of Kanner's leg and she tripped backwards, and her cycle of full-auto shots tracked along Dannick's head and blew his skull to smithereens, then took Jusker in the shoulder. They both fell, and Cade roared in anger and frustration, and not a little fear, as his squad's output reduced drastically. Someone moved to help Jusker. Someone else fell backwards as a lucky shot from the onrushing enemy found the gap between helmet and trench top. Stevaz could not help himself: he turned and looked down at what had caused all this commotion.

It was a headless body, bearing the insignia of Fifth Squad.

Fear paralysed him. What had broken into their lines? What had decapitated this trooper, and hurled their body so easily into Fourth Squad's ranks? It couldn't have been the explosion he heard: what explosion would take someone's head off so neatly, but hurl their body this far?

Cade was shouting at him.

'Tai, get your arse back on the–'

The sergeant never got the chance to finish his sentence, because something came screaming over the top of the trench, and landed on him. The buzzing whine of a chainsword filled the air, along with a mist of blood, and then Sergeant Cade was bisected. His murderer turned towards Stevaz as the rest of the heretics' assault piled into the trench, rapidly overwhelming Fourth Squad.

Stevaz saw a snarl of fury on the face of a woman probably old enough to be his grandmother, and the light of bloodlust in her eyes. He raised his lasrifle, but her howling weapon batted it aside, and the rotating teeth tore it from his grip. He turned and ran, fumbling at his belt for the laspistol and combat knife that rested there, hoping he could at least outpace her until he had his secondary weapons drawn.

Too late, he realised he was running towards where Fifth Squad had been stationed.

He rounded a corner of the trench before he could stop himself, and collided with something enormous and very, very hard.

He fell backwards into the mud, and looked up to see what he had run into.

Two glowing red eyes stared balefully down at him, and Stevaz nearly lost control of his bladder until he recognised them for what they were. The eye-lenses of a Space Marine helmet! The promised help had arrived! The lords of war were here on Pendata!

Then, despite the darkness, he took in the colour of the armour plate. It was not silver, but blue-green, and the pauldron did not display a black blade flanked by lightning strikes on a yellow background, but a three-headed serpent. His heart shrivelled inside his chest, because he suddenly realised what he must have seen, moving so fast towards Fifth Squad's lines.

'You're not Silver Templars,' he managed shakily.

The helmet tilted slightly, as though curious.

'No.'

A weapon with a muzzle as large as Stevaz's head was raised, and the bolt-shell it discharged detonated so forcefully that his entire upper body disintegrated.

Derqan Tel turned away from the dead Pendata trooper, and followed the rest of his team into the culvert that ran back from the front lines. No more defenders were coming from that direction: the Legion's human allies had breached the trench-lines now, and could be relied upon to make a mess of this first line of resistance.

'What is a Silver Templar?' he asked the legionnaire in front of him.

'No idea,' Sakran Morv replied. 'Why?' Morv was big even for an Astartes, and carried the squad's ancient autocannon.

'That mortal seemed to think I should be one,' Tel said. He searched his memory, but drew a blank. 'I cannot think of a loyalist Chapter called the Silver Templars. You?'

'Perhaps he meant Black Templars,' Morv suggested. 'Although I think Va'kai would have recognised their insignia.'

Something wasn't sitting right in Tel's gut. Three loyalist strike cruisers had emerged from the warp since the Legion had made planetfall, and were now engaged in void combat overhead with the *Whisper*, the flagship of the Serpent's Teeth. Morv was correct: Krozier Va'kai, the *Whisper*'s captain, would know a Black Templars ship if he was shooting at it.

He activated his vox. 'Trayvar, have you heard of Silver Templars?'

'Is this really the time, Tel?' came the voice of Trayvar Thrice-Burned in reply. He was at the head of the advance, farther down the trench. He had also been the first into the defensive lines when Eighth Fang made their assault rush across the ground left dark by the destroyed floodlights; it was that sort of full-throated aggressiveness that had won him the renown he enjoyed, and also seen him doused in burning promethium no less than three times in one particularly brutal assault against a position held by the Salamanders Chapter.

'The mortal I just killed appeared to be expecting them,' Tel informed him. 'It could be a new Chapter. Or, as Morv pointed out,' he continued, 'a misremembering of the Black Templars.'

'Silver Templars, Black Templars,' the Thrice-Burned muttered. *'You'd think they would have some imagination, wouldn't you?'*

'The Imperium, endlessly repeating minor variations of the same tired routines?' Morv laughed. 'Surely not.'

'I'll vox it in,' Trayvar said. *'The Harrowmaster might know something.'*

'Acknowledged,' Tel replied. Harrowmaster Drazus Jate led the Serpent's Teeth, and it was his tactical genius that had led to Pendata's fall. Once they broke this last loyalist bastion then the resistance would be shattered, and the raw materials the

Serpent's Teeth so desperately needed – promethium, metal, plasteel, perhaps even ceramite – would be theirs for the taking. There would be no sharing of the spoils with other Legions, either: the Teeth were not part of the Warmaster's 13th Black Crusade, and there was no one here but them to claim the winnings. Abaddon would surely fail, as he always did, for all that he was closing on Terra and had ripped the very fabric of reality asunder across the galaxy. If there was one thing the Black Legion could be relied upon to do, it was to fail, and Drazus Jate knew better than to get caught up in *that*.

Trayvar's bolter opened up with a roar, and Tel heard screams as the defenders realised that not only had their lines been breached, but also heavily armoured transhuman killers were now amongst them. The desperate stabs of las-fire cast shadows, but in the narrow confines of the trench Pendata's mortal troops could only bring a couple of weapons to bear at once: nowhere near enough to stop Trayvar. Tel broke into a run as Eighth Fang accelerated ahead of him, stealth abandoned in favour of shock.

'Over the top, and east!' Trayvar barked over the vox, and Tel sprang upwards without thinking about it. The trench through which they were running was still deep enough here that a mortal would think twice before jumping down into it, let alone trying to climb out, but Tel's superhuman muscles were boosted by the servos and mechanical sinews of his power armour, and he cleared the lip with little effort.

A scene of chaos met his eyes.

What had at one point presumably been a highly ordered Imperial camp was now in turmoil. Blazing fires showed where the aerial assault had hit vehicles or fuel dumps, and the burning wreckage of a Lightning had landed on a prefabricated building which, to Tel's eyes, bore the hallmarks of a command centre. Imperial troops – a mix of Astra Militarum forces and the Pendata Bluecoats, the local militia – swarmed like colonial insects attempting to defend their mound, but unlike those minuscule creatures, they had little unity of purpose.

'Let's make some noise,' Trayvar declared, and Eighth Fang opened up.